"I want to get you closure. I really want to find Lexi and her killer."

"...old you—"

He pressed his fingers over her lips. Then his eyes—those eerie pale brown eyes—darkened as his pupils dilated. His fingers slid across her mouth. . .caressingly.

He jerked his hand away from her mouth. "I know who you think killed your sister. I know."

And she waited for him to refute her belief as he always had. But he stayed silent again.

"You're not telling me I'm wrong this time," she said.

He emitted a weary-sounding sigh. "I'm not as cocky as I was six years ago."

He was different. No less serious or determined or driven, but perhaps a little less confident. Lexi's case had shaken his confidence.

Or maybe it had him second-guessing himself.

Because now he uttered the question she'd been waiting for him to ask since she'd overheard his confrontation with the reporters.

"Is h...............................?"

THE AGENT'S REDEMPTION

BY
LISA CHILDS

Published in Great Britain 2015
by Mills & Boon, an imprint of Harlequin (UK) Limited,
Eton House, 18-24 Paradise Road, Richmond, Surrey, TW9 1SR

© 2015 Lisa Childs

ISBN: 978-0-263-25321-4

46-1015

Harlequin (UK) Limited's policy is to use papers that are natural, renewable and recyclable products and made from wood grown in sustainable forests. The logging and manufacturing processes conform to the legal environmental regulations of the country of origin.

Printed and bound in Spain
by CPI, Barcelona

Lisa Childs writes paranormal and contemporary romance for Mills & Boon. She lives on thirty acres in Michigan with her two daughters, a talkative Siamese and a long-haired Chihuahua who thinks she's a rottweiler. Lisa loves hearing from readers, who can contact her through her website, www.lisachilds.com, or snail-mail address, PO Box 139, Marne, MI 49435, USA.

With great appreciation for my sisters, Jackie
Lewakowski, Phyllis Elsbrie & Helen Glover

Chapter One

Bulbs flashed, and Jared Bell flinched with each bright light as he ran the gauntlet of reporters with their microphones and cameras. "Special Agent Bell!" they called out to him as he walked past where they had lined up along the residential street. "Special Agent Bell!"

He ignored them or at least he tried to ignore them as he ducked under the crime scene tape across the end of a driveway.

"Have you found her body yet?" a reporter hurled the question at him. Even though Jared wasn't looking at the guy, he recognized the artificially deep voice of Kyle Smith, and he wasn't surprised Smith had showed up. This narcissist didn't just report the news; he tried to make himself part of the story—at least of this story, this case. He was as relentless as he was insensitive.

Jared flinched at the question, hating how it would hurt whatever member of the missing girl's family might have heard the question or would hear it on a later news broadcast.

They were anxiously awaiting news—any news—of their missing loved one. They didn't need to hear it like this—on the news. They needed to hear it from him directly—as soon as he learned something.

"Have you ever found Lexi Drummond's body?" another reporter yelled out the question. "It's been five years."

Six. Lexi had been the serial killer's first victim. And no, her body had never been found. Her family still waited for closure. But he had nothing to offer them. No body. No suspect. No clues...

If his head hadn't already been pounding from the concussion he'd sustained a few days ago, it would have started hurting then. Pain throbbed inside his skull where he could feel his heart beating—fast and frantically. As an FBI profiler, he had caught a lot of killers over the years—but not this one. Lexi Drummond's killer had eluded him and killed again and again and again.

Now the killer had taken another girl. Another victim...

Jared would find her, though. She would not become another Lexi Drummond. Not in any way. He had gotten way too involved in Lexi's case and way too involved with Lexi's family. He'd failed them and himself.

For the first time in his career, his professionalism had slipped. But that had happened only that one time; he wouldn't let it happen again.

Jared ignored the reporters and flashed his shield to the officer posted outside the duplex. Then he slipped through the open front door. The girl hadn't been abducted from her home, but the police were searching it for any clues to who might have taken her.

Jared had to study all the aspects of the case in order to construct a profile of the killer. He studied the crime scenes, the evidence—if any—left behind, the manner in which the victim was killed, and he profiled the victim, too. He didn't believe this killer randomly chose his victims. So getting to know them better would help lead Jared back to their killer.

But hopefully Amy Wilcox was only missing. Hopefully she wasn't dead yet—like all the other victims. Even though Lexi Drummond's body hadn't been found, too much of her blood had been discovered at the crime scene for her to have survived whatever wounds she had suffered. Six years had passed, but he could still see all that blood. So much blood...

He blinked away the memory of that horrific crime scene and focused on his current surroundings. Amy Wilcox's duplex was painted in fun colors—bright greens and yellows, like a highlighter that outlined the many picture frames hanging on the walls.

To get to know her better, Jared studied those pictures. There were photos of her water-skiing and rock climbing and running races. As athletic as she was, she wouldn't have been easy to abduct—which explained the signs of a struggle at the primary crime scene: the ransacked and blood-spattered dressing room from which she'd been abducted.

She had almost gotten away from her assailant there. Maybe she would get away from him again. Jared moved on to the next picture and froze, his whole body tensing.

She wasn't alone in this picture. She had her arm around another girl who was laughing into the camera with her. Unlike Amy who had dark hair and eyes, this woman was blond with sparkling blue eyes and a dimple in her right cheek when she smiled.

Lexi Drummond...

HER HAND SHAKING, Rebecca Drummond pushed hard on the off button of the remote. The TV screen flickered before going black but not before she saw *his* face again. Special Agent Jared Bell. With his reddish-brown hair and light brown eyes, he was still handsome—maybe even more handsome than he'd been six years ago because his features were more defined, more rugged. Dark circles rimmed his eyes and faint bruises darkened one side of his face.

The reporter's words rang in her ears: "FBI profiler Jared Bell checked himself out of the hospital against doctor's orders in order to take over the investigation into the disappearance of Amy Wilcox, which confirms speculation that she is the latest victim of the Bride Butcher serial killer."

Horror gripped Rebecca, paralyzing her. She wanted to run, but she couldn't move from the couch where she was sitting. She could only think of… Jared.

He had been in the hospital.

Why?

How badly had he been hurt that he had checked himself out *against* doctor's orders?

He was obviously still obsessed with the case. Obsessed with finding a killer that he already would have found had he listened to Rebecca.

But he had refused to listen to Rebecca about anything. Seeing him again should have brought back anger or pain or resentment. Instead, other feelings—so many other feelings—rushed over her, overwhelming her.

She grabbed a pillow from the couch and wrapped her arms around it, but she wanted to wrap them around herself—to hold herself together. The doorbell dinged, startling her into jumping and letting out a short cry of surprise.

The door shook as a fist pounded on it now. And a deep and familiar voice called out, "Are you all right?"

He'd heard her. She couldn't hide now, like she wanted to hide. She'd promised him that he would never see her again. She hadn't *fixated* on him because he was investigating her sister's disappearance. Her face heated as even now, all these years later, the embarrassment rushed back.

She had been a fool to think herself in love with Jared

Bell. And she would be an even bigger fool to open the door and let him back into her life.

The door rattled harder. "I'm coming in!"

He would break it down; she had no doubt that he would, just like he'd broken down the walls of her grief and pain and opened her heart to him.

She had rebuilt those walls since she'd seen him last. She wouldn't let him back into her heart. But she had no choice about letting him into her life. She opened the door just as he was putting his shoulder to the wood, and he stumbled inside the living room.

He spared her a quick glance before visually searching the room for any threats. Even battered from whatever had sent him to the hospital, he was still in full protective FBI mode. He turned back to her and asked, "Are you all right?"

No. She hadn't been all right with seeing him on her television—even though she had seen him on the news occasionally over the past six years. She certainly wasn't all right with him being in her house.

What if...

She shuddered to think of it—of *them* meeting. But that wouldn't happen. She would get rid of Jared quickly. She would make certain he was long gone before Alex came home.

She nodded and assured him, "I'm fine. The doorbell startled me because I wasn't expecting anyone." Not for an hour yet. "Especially not you."

His handsome face moved with a slight wince at her jab. But she knew that she hadn't really hurt him. He would have had to care for her to be able to hurt him.

"Why are you here, Jared?" she asked, and then reminded him, "You were the one who thought it best we didn't see each other anymore."

"I'm sorry," he said. "I didn't handle anything very well concerning your sister's case."

"My sister's case…" That was all Rebecca had been to him—just part of a case. She was the one who had foolishly thought they were more.

"Why are you here?" she asked again. "You didn't come here to apologize."

"I should have," he said, as if just realizing it himself.

The man was a genius. A real one. He had graduated high school at thirteen, college with a doctorate in criminal psychology at nineteen and then had been recruited into the FBI. He had worked many cases—solving them all—before he'd come up against her sister's killer. And lost…

Jared was a genius when it came to other people but he was completely oblivious when it came to himself.

She shrugged. "That was a long time ago." She wanted him to think she had moved on, but it felt like yesterday that she had lost him—so soon after tragically losing Lexi.

"I'm sorry," he said again, and the sincerity was there in the gruffness of his deep voice.

She didn't doubt that he was sorry, but she didn't care. She just wanted him gone.

"Why are you here?" she asked, impatience fraying her voice into sharpness. This was the tone that always—finally—got Alex's attention.

"Have you seen the news?" he asked. "Do you know about…?"

She grimly nodded as concern tightly gripped her heart. "There's another girl missing. She was abducted from the last fitting for her bridal gown."

It could only be one killer. Her sister's.

"I need your help," he said.

But he hadn't come to her when those other women

had been abducted. He hadn't needed her help then. Why was he asking for it now—when he hadn't listened to her six years ago?

"I already told you who killed Lexi."

He sighed—that long-suffering sigh that irritated her. Then he pulled a photo from a file he had clasped under his arm and held it out to her. "I need you to look at this."

She grimaced and backed away from him. The last thing she wanted to see was another crime scene. She already had one that she could not get out of her mind. "No."

"Please, Becca—"

"Don't call me that," she snapped at him. To Lexi, she'd been Becca. And to him…when she'd thought he actually cared about her.

But all Jared Bell cared about was his career—and how this one unsolved case could damage it.

"What should I call you?" he asked. "Ms. Drummond, or Mrs.…?"

"Rebecca," she said, refusing to reveal her marital status. It wouldn't matter to him anyway since it had nothing to do with the case.

"Rebecca," he repeated. "Please look at the picture."

She closed her eyes, and that old crime scene flashed through her mind: the wedding dress soaked with blood spilling out of the trunk of Lexi's car.

Her body hadn't been in the trunk. But it didn't matter. The coroner had confirmed she couldn't have lost that much blood and lived.

Lexi was forever gone.

"I need your help," he said again. "Please…"

She forced herself to open her eyes—to look. It wasn't a crime scene. But it might have been worse to see Lexi like she was in that old photo—alive with happiness—because it reminded Rebecca of how much she'd lost.

Just like seeing Jared again reminded her of how much she'd lost...

Panic pressed on her lungs, stealing her breath. "You need to leave," she said.

"Rebecca—"

She planted her palm against his chest. Even through his suit and shirt, she could feel the warmth of his skin and the hardness of his muscles. But she pushed him toward the door. "I can't help you—because you won't listen to me."

"Rebecca, I want to talk to you about Lexi—about how she knew this girl."

She shook her head. She couldn't look at the picture again—of her and the missing girl. "Ask Amy Wilcox's family."

His amber-colored eyes darkened with emotion. "I asked them." And from his grim expression, it hadn't gone well. "They had no idea that Amy had known Lexi."

She shook her head. "I had no idea, either."

"We need to compare their pasts," he said, "and find out where their paths might have crossed." Mercifully, he turned the photo over to the white back. But then he pointed to the date on it. "This was taken the month Lexi disappeared. That's too great a coincidence. We need to figure out their connection."

She shook her head again.

"Bec—Rebecca, I need your help," he implored her.

Heat arced between them as he stared at her. She avoided his intense gaze, averting hers. Then she noticed the clock on the wall behind his head, and her panic returned with even more intensity. She had no time to answer his questions. "You need to leave now!"

Before Alex came home—because if Jared saw him he would have more questions.

More questions she couldn't answer...

Chapter Two

Jared's heart pounded hard and fast beneath the warmth of her hand on his chest. He'd worried that she might slam the door in his face. After the mess he had made of everything, he wouldn't have blamed her if she had. But she'd let him in. Although after hearing her soft cry, he hadn't given her much choice. He would have kicked in the door to get to her—to make sure she was all right.

She was beautiful—even more so than she had been six years ago. Her blond hair was longer and lighter and her skin tanned as if she spent more time in the sun now. Of course six years ago she had been so focused on school—her first year of med school—that she'd no time for the sun or relaxation or her friends and family.

Until her sister had disappeared.

"You have to leave," she said as she shoved on his chest again.

Already light-headed from the concussion, he stumbled back a step. To steady himself, he reached out and clasped her shoulders. Her blue eyes widened as she stared up at him. The urge to pull her closer overwhelmed him. It had been so long since he had held her that he ached to hold her again.

But that wasn't why he had risked getting the door slammed in his face—or getting shoved out of her house.

"There's a girl missing," he reminded her. "Her family is going crazy with fear."

They had gone even crazier when he'd asked them about Lexi Drummond. Amy's mother had gotten hysterical, hyperventilating so badly that they'd had to call for an ambulance. Her dad had been trying hard to hold his wife together even as he began to fall apart himself, shaking uncontrollably. Amy's fiancé was the only one who'd managed to voice their fears aloud. "He has her then—that sick bastard who kills brides. She's probably already dead!" And then the man, a big burly former college linebacker, had dropped to his knees and dissolved into broken sobs.

Jared released a ragged breath and repeated, "They're going crazy with fear." More so because of him, because he had taken away some of the hope they'd desperately been clinging to.

"Just like I went crazy," she murmured.

She hadn't gone crazy, but she'd certainly been upset and vulnerable. And he would never forgive himself for taking advantage of that vulnerability—of her.

"You know what they're going through," he said.

"I can empathize," she said.

"You can help."

She shook her head. "I tried to help six years ago. I told you who killed Lexi, but you wouldn't listen to me."

"It's not him, Bec—Rebecca," he said. He wished it had been. But the guy had had an ironclad alibi.

She sighed. "You wasted your time coming here," she said, "if you're still not going to listen to me."

"All I want is for you to look at the picture and tell me how Lexi knew Amy Wilcox." That was a lie. He wanted more—much more from Becca than that. But he had no right to expect or ask for anything from her—not even information.

She had barely looked at the picture. So he held it out to her again. But she had barely looked at him, either. Instead, she kept glancing over his head.

He was surprised to find her here—in Wisconsin and so close to where her sister's car had been found. He'd thought for sure she would have wound up in another state—maybe even in another country—for her medical residency. Instead, she lived just down the road from the wooded area that law enforcement and search teams had torn apart looking for Lexi.

To no avail…

He glanced behind him, where she kept looking, and noticed the clock on the wall. Large metal hands moved across the surface of a barn picture, like a weather vane moving in the wind. Her house was cute—a sunshine-filled ranch with bright colors—like something that would've been featured in a country living magazine. He hadn't pictured Becca winding up living in the country.

She'd wanted to do her residency in a big city. A bigger life than the small town where she'd grown up—just like Lexi had wanted.

She tore her gaze from the clock to focus on the photo. But not him.

Couldn't she even stand to look at him? Had he hurt her that badly? Guilt clutched his heart, like her palm still clutched his chest. Instead of pushing him away, her hand held on to his coat and shirt—as if she needed some sort of support to look at the photo again.

"I've seen her face on the news," she said. "But that's the only place I remember seeing Amy Wilcox before."

"We can look into their pasts—see how they're connected. You can help me," he urged her.

She shook her head. "I don't know how she knew Lexi. But then again I was gone so much—for college and med school—that I didn't know all of her friends.

And Lexi was always making friends." She smiled wistfully—sadly. "Everybody wanted to be her friend."

Six years had passed, but it didn't appear that Becca's pain had lessened any. Her loss seemed as fresh and painful as it had when Lexi had first disappeared. She had loved her sister so much.

Regret clenched Jared's heart—regret that he had hurt her. And regret that his being here was hurting her again. He shouldn't have come. She wasn't the only one he could have asked about Lexi.

"Do your parents still have your sister's things?" he asked. He could talk to them instead. Maybe they would have something of Lexi's—her journals or photos—that would explain her connection to Amy Wilcox and maybe lead him to a suspect that they had both known.

Or at least the suspect had known both of them. Maybe they'd been unaware of him. Jared had apprehended many suspects whose victims had never officially met them. They hadn't even been aware that they were being followed.

"No," Becca replied shortly, dashing his hopes.

He cursed. But he wasn't surprised.

While some people kept shrines to their lost loved ones, leaving their things exactly as that person had left them, others removed every trace of them—as if that could make them forget their loss and pain. Her parents had been so broken and devastated that they hadn't been able to talk to him or any of the other authorities. That was how he'd gotten so close to Becca—she had spoken for all of them, for her parents and for her missing sister.

"They couldn't handle any reminders of her," she said with a trace of resentment.

Had Becca been a reminder of her sister, too? Had they removed her from their lives, too? It might explain why she had settled in Wisconsin instead of the farm town where she'd grown up in Ohio—where her parents probably still lived unless that reminded them too much of Lexi, too.

"So I have her things," Becca said matter-of-factly. She wouldn't have wanted to forget her sister—no matter how much pain that loss caused her. She was incredibly strong; she had been strong six years ago—except for when she'd turned to him for comfort and support.

And oblivion. She'd told him she'd needed to think about something other than Lexi. Or actually that she'd needed to not think at all for a while. That was why she'd made love with him. He hadn't had any excuse—except that he had been weak—too weak to fight his overwhelming attraction to her.

The attraction he still felt for her. But he couldn't think about that. He couldn't think about how she'd felt in his arms, how sweet her lips had tasted. He had to focus instead on the case.

So he breathed a sigh of relief that all leads weren't lost. "That's great. We need to look through her stuff and find out how she knew Amy."

She stopped clutching his shirt and shoved at him again. Her voice cracking with panic, she said, "Not now. I don't have time. You have to leave. Now!"

Behind him, the door rattled and then flew open and a little blond-haired boy ran into the house. He stopped short when he saw Jared and stared up at him—his blue eyes wide with surprise. He asked, "Who are you?"

YOUR FATHER. THE WORDS stuck in Rebecca's throat along with the scream of protest she had wanted to utter when the door had opened. Of course Tommy's mother would drop Alex off early today. The horn of the minivan tooted as Beverly backed out of the driveway.

"My name is Jared Bell," the FBI agent answered his son. "What's yours?"

"Alex…" Suddenly shy, the little boy ducked behind her legs and peered around her at Jared.

"Nice to meet you, Alex," Jared replied. Then he raised his gaze from the little boy and met hers.

She expected accusation or at least suspicion. But pain and regret flickered through his amber-colored eyes instead. "I understand," he said.

And her stomach clenched. Could he understand why she hadn't told him? She wasn't entirely sure that she understood herself. Of course his rejection had hurt her, and he'd told her that it would be better if they had no further contact. But he hadn't known that she was pregnant. She hadn't yet known she was pregnant when they'd broken up. But to break up, they would have actually had to be together. And all she had been to him was a slip in his professionalism. A mistake.

And she hadn't wanted her child to be a mistake to him, as well. So she'd chosen not to tell Jared. But occasionally guilt overwhelmed her—like whenever Alex had asked her about his father. And now, when father and son finally came face-to-face.

Jared continued, "I understand why you didn't want to talk about this *case*—with your son coming home."

Her sister had never been just a case to Rebecca. "Alex knows about his aunt Lexi," she said.

"I got my name from her," the little boy interjected as he peeked around her legs again.

Jared smiled at the boy. "It's a very good name, too."

And Rebecca's heart lurched at the deep grooves in his cheeks and at the warmth in his eyes. He was so handsome. But that wasn't the only reason for her reaction. She hadn't thought the no-nonsense FBI profiler would pay any attention to a child. He had never expressed any interest in them before. But he was being so sweet...

So Jared.

That was why she had fallen for him before—because he had been so sympathetic for her loss and so concerned for her well-being. She had thought he was falling for her, too. But he'd only been doing his job.

That was all he was doing now. She hadn't seen him in nearly six years. He had moved on to the next case—the next murder and the next killer. But he was back now—because there was another case.

Another missing woman...

Another family going through what she and her parents had gone through—what they were still going through. "I want to help you," she said.

He arched a brow as if surprised. "I thought you wanted to get rid of me."

She had—when she'd been worried that he would realize Alex was his son. But he didn't appear to have made the connection. Alex was small for his age, though. Perhaps Jared hadn't realized how old the little boy was.

She really didn't want to leave them alone while she retrieved the container of Lexi's pictures and journals. "Alex needs a bath before bedtime," she said. "He just got back from a playdate. Do you mind waiting?"

His body tensed with urgency. He probably hated waiting. Amy Wilcox had already been missing for days.

But Rebecca doubted that there was anything in Lexi's personal effects that could lead him to the young woman. If the same man who'd taken Lexi had taken Amy, then Rebecca already knew who he was.

But Jared refused to believe her. He believed an alibi instead. But the alibi could have been faked. Or a killer could have been hired.

"I'll wait," he said. And he was already pulling out his cell phone.

Of course he had calls to make. When she'd known him before, he had constantly been on his phone—following up leads, checking in with other agents. The man lived and breathed his job. When he had worked her sister's case, she had mistakenly believed his intensity had been personal.

But it was just who he was…

Intense.

Driven.

Determined.

But despite all those characteristics, he had been unable to find Lexi's body. Or Lexi's killer.

She left Jared to his calls and tugged Alex toward the bathroom. Usually after a playdate with Tommy, he was exhausted. When she hosted a playdate with the hyperactive Tommy, she was always exhausted afterward, too.

But now Alex was too curious to be tired. "Who is Jared Bell?" he asked as he pulled off his clothes and stepped into the bathtub.

Your father. The words popped into her head again but stuck in her throat. She couldn't tell either of them the truth. Not now.

But guilt settled heavily on her heart. She should tell the truth. She probably would have—had she not been devastated by Jared's rejection. But he hadn't just rejected her; he'd rejected what she'd felt for him.

He'd told her that she didn't really have any feelings for him. She was only fixated on him because he was investigating her sister's disappearance—that he had become a surrogate of Lexi to her.

For such a brilliant man, he'd been incredibly dense and insensitive.

"Mr. Bell is…" She had no idea what to tell her son.

Jared had never really been a friend. And she couldn't tell Alex that he was an FBI agent. Her little boy would never go to sleep because he would have a million questions for Jared.

Alex was such a bright and inquisitive boy. His teachers had already moved him up a grade because they couldn't challenge him. With his blond hair and blue eyes, he looked like her, but he had his father's brilliance.

She'd had to work hard for her grades. That was why she'd been so consumed with studying that she'd lost touch with her sister. Then she'd lost her entirely.

"He has a gun, Mommy," the little boy said.

How had he noticed the weapon holstered beneath Jared's jacket?

"Was that why you hid behind my legs?" she asked. "Are you scared of him?"

Alex shook his head and sent droplets of water flying across the sand-colored tile walls and floor and her T-shirt. "No. He has a badge, too."

Jared had always worn his badge clipped to his belt, but his jacket covered it. Of course her observant little boy would have somehow noticed it. He missed nothing. But a father...

"Mr. Bell is an FBI agent," she reluctantly admitted.

As she'd expected, Alex sprang out of the bath, dripping water everywhere. "Can I talk to him? Can I?"

Before he could head to the door, she caught him up in a towel and dried him off and stalled.

"Do you think he'll let me touch his gun?" Alex asked. "Do you think he ever shot somebody with it?"

She was pretty certain that he had, but not the person she'd wanted him to shoot—the person she was certain had killed her sister.

"It's your bedtime," she reminded her son.

"Oh, Mom, I can go to bed anytime," Alex protested. "He's an FBI agent!"

"And he's here to talk to me about Aunt Lexi," she said. "But you'll be able to talk to him another time." After she gathered her courage and told them both the truth.

It was time. It was actually past time that Jared and Alex learned they were father and son.

"If I see him again," Alex muttered.

"You will," she promised. But would he? Even after she told Jared the truth, would he want anything to do with his son? Would he want to be a father?

Or was he still all about his career?

The little boy dragged his feet getting ready for bed. He took forever to get into his pajamas and brush his teeth. And when she finally settled him into his bed, he sprang right back up.

"Mommy, there's a man looking in the window!"

A creative child, he always came up with inventive excuses for not going to bed. So she was only humoring him when she turned toward the window. But then she saw the man, too, staring into her son's bedroom.

And she screamed.

Chapter Three

Her earlier soft cry had struck Jared like a blow. This one—loud and full of fear—pierced his soul. He ran down the hall she'd gone through and nearly collided with her as she rushed out of a room, the child clutched in her arms.

"Someone's creeping around outside," she said, "looking in the windows."

He drew his weapon from beneath his jacket and headed toward the door. "Lock it behind me," he directed her. "And don't unlock it for anyone but me."

He stepped outside and lights flashed and voices shouted. "Special Agent Bell! Special Agent Bell!"

He flinched at the lights and the noise and the fact that he hated reporters. He wanted to step back inside and slam the door shut on all of them. But he'd had Becca lock it behind him. If he knocked and had her open it, they would see her and take pictures and bombard her with intrusive, insensitive questions like they had when Lexi had disappeared.

Six years ago Becca had hated the reporters as much as he had. Actually more. He hadn't begun to hate them until they'd turned on him—highlighting his one failure instead of all his success in apprehending serial killers.

"You're all trespassing," he informed them. "If you

don't get off this property, I will have the local authorities arrest you."

While some of the reporters knew him well enough to know that his threat wasn't empty and they began to walk away, another stepped forward—probably the one Becca had seen through her son's bedroom window since the man stepped around the side of the house.

"Your being here confirms that this place belongs to Lexi Drummond's sister," the reporter brazenly said.

"My presence confirms nothing," Jared replied. He holstered his gun, but then pulled out his cell phone. His threat wasn't idle; he intended to have them all arrested—especially this man.

This reporter was tall and thin with a thick head of mostly artificial-looking blond hair and a big, snide grin. He wasn't just doing his job; he enjoyed annoying the hell out of people, especially Jared.

The man—Kyle Smith—shrugged shoulders that Jared suspected were as fake as his hair—since they moved strangely beneath his suit jacket, like they were more padding than muscle and bone. "County tax records confirm this property belongs to Rebecca Drummond."

Jared breathed a silent sigh of relief. He had been pretty sure that the press hadn't followed him here. But with the concussion, he wasn't quite himself yet. Maybe he hadn't noticed someone—like Kyle Smith—tailing him.

But apparently they had just done the same research he'd done to find Rebecca Drummond. Or at least Kyle Smith had. Had he brought the others with him, like a pack of dogs, to attack?

Then Kyle attacked as he shoved the microphone in Jared's face and had his cameraman zoom in on him. "So is Rebecca Drummond's young son yours?"

It was probably a good thing that he'd holstered his

gun, or he might have threatened the man with it. Instead, he punched in the number for the local authorities, identified himself and gave the address where he needed backup to disperse trespassers.

"No comment, Agent Bell?" Kyle said with a sneer.

He had no comment that he could make publicly without his supervisor reprimanding him. And there was no point to answering any of Kyle's questions. The man twisted Jared's replies to suit his own purposes.

Apparently, he wanted to expose all of Jared's mistakes. Getting involved with a victim's family member had definitely been a mistake. But that had been six years ago, and the boy had to be younger than that. Alex hadn't looked much older than the toddler Jared had recently been helping protect. His head pounded, reminding him of the concussion that had rewarded his efforts. According to the doctor, he was lucky to be alive and have his memory intact.

Not that he could have forgotten Becca. He doubted he would ever be able to forget her. During the past six years, she had never left his mind. He'd seen her beautiful face in his dreams and in his waking moments. He'd thought of her often, wondering how she was doing— hoping she'd been able to move on after the loss of her sister.

"You're not here to see your son?" Kyle prodded him with the question and that infuriatingly snide grin.

Jared fought the urge to glare at the man, too. Then, against his better judgment, he replied, "I'm investigating the disappearance of Amy Wilcox."

"And how can Rebecca Drummond help you with that?" Smith asked. "She's convinced her sister's fiancé killed Lexi despite his rock-solid alibi."

Jared wished she'd been right. But the alibi was indisputable and Becca's judgment seriously biased where her almost-brother-in-law was concerned.

Sirens wailed in the distance as Jared's backup approached. "Whoever is still on this property when the local authorities arrive will be arrested."

"You've let a serial killer run free for six years, Special Agent Bell," Kyle taunted him, "but you would arrest some reporters just doing their job?"

"You're not just doing your job." Jared had gotten that impression from the reporter before—that this was personal. Had Jared put away someone he'd known and cared about? Did the guy have some kind of vendetta against him? Why else would the reporter go after him like he did?

To suggest that Becca's son was his...

It was preposterous. To think that he was a father, that he had been a father for six years and had never known...

His heart lurched in his chest as he considered the possibility that he had son.

No. It wasn't a possibility.

HER NERVES FRAYED, Rebecca waited for Jared to ask. She'd heard the reporter's speculation—the one who'd been looking through Alex's bedroom window. That man had wondered if Alex was Jared's son.

Why hadn't Jared?

Fortunately Alex hadn't heard any of the reporter's questions or comments. She had tucked him back into his bed and drawn the blinds. And, despite the excitement, he had fallen asleep. She probably needed to thank Tommy for that. If his playdate friend hadn't worn him out, there was no way Alex would have fallen asleep after catching a man looking in his window. Or with an FBI agent in the house.

Or maybe it was because of the FBI agent that he

fell asleep—because he felt safe. Was that because Jared was FBI or because Alex instinctively felt a connection with him?

It didn't matter that Alex hadn't heard the reporter's questions. He already had questions of his own. He'd already asked her who his father was.

He deserved an answer. He deserved a father. But Jared hadn't even wanted to be a boyfriend all those years ago. She couldn't imagine how he would have reacted if she'd told him she was pregnant. He probably would have thought she was trying to trap him because she was so fixated on him.

He was now focused on the contents of the plastic container in which Rebecca had preserved all of her sister's pictures, journals and letters. He kept flipping through the photos, flinching when he came across the ones of a bruised and battered Lexi.

"He did that to her," Rebecca said. But she hadn't known that until she'd found the pictures in Lexi's journal. Why hadn't her sister told her that her fiancé was abusing her? Because Rebecca had been too busy? Had Lexi thought she wouldn't care?

Lexi was only two years older than Rebecca, so they'd always been close growing up. When she'd graduated Lexi had stayed home and attended community college for a medical assistant program. Rebecca was the one who'd left home—for college and med school.

Guilt gripped Rebecca, squeezing her heart. Maybe if she had been more available to her sister, Lexi would have told her what was going on, and she could have helped her. She could have saved her...

Anger joined her guilt as she glanced at the photos, too. The man was a monster to have done that to sweet, beautiful Lexi.

"She took those photos as evidence against him," Re-

becca said, "in case something ever happened to her."
That was what Lexi had written on the journal pages between which those photos had been tucked. "She wanted
you to know who her killer would be."

Rebecca waited for Jared to bring up that damn ironclad alibi again. But the FBI profiler remained curiously
silent and focused on those photographs.

Her pulse quickened. Was he beginning to believe her?
To believe the evidence Lexi had left for him?

Of course Lexi hadn't known who would be investigating her case. But she'd known that she would die
and that there would be someone investigating her death.

Poor Lexi...

If only she'd told Rebecca what was going on.

But Rebecca had been too busy studying. She'd been
too busy for much more than a short texted reply to her
sister's usual text, You still alive?

Yes, I'm still alive.

When she hadn't heard from Lexi in a while, she had
texted her the question: You still alive?

Lexi had never answered that text.

Rebecca closed her eyes as the pain overwhelmed
her, and tears threatened. It didn't feel like six years had
passed since she'd lost her sister. It felt like yesterday.

"I'm sorry," Jared said.

"Why?" He had already apologized for how he'd
handled the situation with her—the line he regretted
crossing into her bed.

Images flashed through her mind—of the two of them
in bed, of naked skin sliding over naked skin. Of his lips
on hers as he kissed her with all his intensity focused
solely on her. He had made love to her so thoroughly, so

passionately that it was as if she could still feel his hands on her body, his lips on her…

Desire rushed through her, heating her. She didn't regret that he had crossed that line with her. She only regretted how it had ended. That he had ended it.

But she didn't want any more apologies from him. Not when she owed him one. She was the one who'd been keeping a secret from him for too many years.

"I'm sorry I came here," he explained, "and opened up all this pain for you again."

She chuckled at how he didn't understand her feelings any better than he had six years ago. "You think you just reopened it?"

He shrugged. "Maybe it wasn't me, but Amy Wilcox's disappearance had to have brought everything up again—all those feelings."

"She isn't the only victim since Lexi."

But Rebecca didn't need to remind him of that. She could see his frustration in the slight lines around his eyes and mouth. She could feel the tension in his body. He blamed himself, as much as the serial killer, for the loss of those other victims.

"No, she's not," he acknowledged, and the guilt was in the gruffness of his deep voice.

"But you never came here when those other victims first went missing," she said.

He held up the photo he'd brought with him—the photo of Amy Wilcox with Lexi. "I didn't find any connection between them and your sister."

"But their killer…"

"We don't have enough evidence to make that conclusion," he replied—uttering one of those patented FBI press release statements.

She nearly smiled. Maybe it was because he had been recruited so young into the Bureau that he was such a *company* man. Or maybe it was what she had concluded six years ago—all he cared about was his job.

"The media hasn't had any problem leaping to conclusions," she said. And not just about the murders but about her son's paternity.

But they weren't wrong about that. Had they been wrong about all the murders being the work of one killer?

"I didn't lead those reporters here," Jared assured her.

"I know."

While his specialty was profiling killers, he had made certain that he had all the skills of a field agent. He was an expert shot and defensive driver. That was why she'd been so excited when he had been assigned her sister's case—because she'd heard all the media praise about him.

But the media didn't praise him anymore—because he'd never found Lexi's killer. Or Lexi's body.

"The pain wasn't just *reopened*," she said. "It never *closed*."

He flinched again, like he had looking at the pictures of a brutalized Lexi. "I'm sorry you never got closure."

Everyone talked about needing closure. Needing a body to bury. Or a killer to curse.

"I'm not sure *closure* would make it hurt any less," she admitted. Lexi would still be dead.

He stepped closer to her, and his voice was low and gruff when he said, "I want to get you closure. I really want to find Lexi and her killer."

"I told you—"

He pressed his fingers over her lips. Then his eyes—those eerie, pale brown eyes—darkened as his pupils dilated. His fingers slid across her mouth...caressingly.

Her breath caught in her lungs, and her pulse quickened with awareness and desire. How could she want him again? She wasn't hurting over Lexi's loss alone. She was hurting over losing Jared, too.

He jerked his hand away from her mouth. "I know who you think killed your sister. I know."

And she waited for him to refute her belief like he always had. But he stayed silent again.

"You're not telling me I'm wrong this time," she said.

He emitted a weary-sounding sigh. "I'm not as cocky as I was six years ago."

He was different. No less serious or determined or driven but perhaps a little less confident. Lexi's case had shaken his confidence.

And maybe it had him second-guessing himself.

Because now he uttered the question she'd been waiting for him to ask since she'd overheard his confrontation with the reporters.

"Is he my son, Becca?" he asked. "Is Alex mine?"

Chapter Four

Jared's heart pounded fast and furiously as he waited for her answer. Or maybe because he'd touched her. He shouldn't have touched her. Because now he wanted to touch her again.

But if her son was his and she had never told him...

Could he ever forgive her? She had stolen almost six years of her son's life from him—years he couldn't get back. But her son couldn't be almost six years old. He was too small.

Like Jared had been for his age...

No. He shook his head in silent denial of his own thoughts and suspicions.

"I'm sorry," he said. "I have no business asking you that. I must've let Kyle Smith get inside my head." And of course the reporter had just been trying to get a reaction out of him—some scandalous footage to run over and over on his broadcast.

She blinked as her blue eyes widened with confusion. "Kyle Smith?"

"The reporter." Jared chuckled. "That egomaniac would hate that you don't know his name."

She glanced toward the black screen of her TV. "I try not to pay much attention to the news."

But since she'd known about Amy Wilcox's disappearance, he doubted that she was any more successful at ignoring the media than he was.

"I've been working on that myself." In his job, he had to know how to handle the media or he could tip off a suspect or undermine his own investigation. He lifted a hand toward his throbbing head. "Maybe I only let him get to me because of the concussion."

He wished he could blame the head injury. But he suspected that maybe it was wishful thinking instead... that Becca's son was his. He wanted a connection to her—something more than Lexi's unsolved murder to bind them together.

"How did you get the concussion?" she asked, her voice soft with concern.

After the way he'd treated her, how could she care about him at all? But that was just her nature, the reason she'd wanted to become a doctor, because she cared about people. All people. It was nothing personal. She'd had six years to realize that, although he hadn't been sensitive about her feelings, he'd been right. She hadn't really been in love with him.

"How did you get hurt?" she asked again, and now the concern was in her beautiful eyes as she studied his face, maybe trying to medically determine if he'd checked himself out too soon.

He shrugged off her concern and his own stupidity. "I didn't stick to just profiling."

"Do you ever?" she asked, and a twinkle flashed briefly in her blue eyes as if she was teasing him. Maybe she'd forgiven him for how he'd treated her.

"As a profiler, I do have to spend a lot of time out in the field," he said, "analyzing the crime scenes, the evidence, interviewing suspects, hopefully following leads to more suspects..."

"I know what you do," she reminded him.

Six years ago he'd kept her apprised of his investigation—probably too apprised. He'd told her when he'd interviewed her sister's fiancé. But she hadn't agreed with his findings. Even if the guy hadn't had an alibi, Jared truly hadn't felt like the man had killed his fiancée. Harris Mowery's shock and anger over Lexi's disappearance had seemed very genuine. But maybe Jared had been so cocky and overconfident back then that he hadn't read Harris as well as he'd thought he had.

"So what were you doing this time?" she asked. "That wasn't just profiling?"

"Protection duty."

She laughed. "You were playing bodyguard?"

He should have been offended. After all he wasn't the too-small-for-his-age child that he had once been. He was tall and muscular now, but he was no bodyguard. He'd learned all the skills of being a field agent, but protecting someone wasn't something he had done often enough to get good at it. Usually he came on the scene when it was too late for protection—when the victim had already gone missing or been found dead.

He rubbed his head where he'd taken the blow from the butt of a gun. He was lucky he hadn't been shot instead, but the killer hadn't wanted to forewarn his victim and have her get away again.

"I'm not a very good bodyguard," he admitted.

Her eyes widened with alarm. "Did whoever you were protecting get hurt?"

He breathed a sigh of relief. "No, but that was thanks to better agents."

She tilted her head, and a lock of blond hair fell across her cheek. He wanted to brush it back; he wanted to touch her again. He was close enough. He only had to lift his hand again, like he had touched her lips. His skin tingled yet from that too-brief contact.

Then she mused aloud, "You are different than you used to be."

A self-deprecating grin tugged at his mouth. "Less cocky than I used to be?"

She smiled, too. "Yes."

He didn't have to tell her why; she knew—because he'd failed to find Lexi's killer. He had failed all the subsequent victims of Lexi's killer, too. And most of all, he'd failed Becca.

He hadn't given her the closure she needed. She didn't seem to think it would help, but he'd seen it help others—when he'd found their loved ones' killers. He'd had a lot of success in his profiling career with the Bureau. He'd actually had mostly success and just this one failure when it mattered most.

Because Becca mattered most.

"I'm sorry," he said again. He couldn't apologize enough to her—for so many reasons.

"I wish you'd stop saying that," she murmured as she stepped back from him and lowered her gaze, as if she couldn't look at him.

He stepped closer, not wanting any distance between them. And he touched her, just his fingers on her chin, tipping her face up so that she met his gaze again. So that she would see his sincerity when he told her, "But I am...sorry. I'm sorry for how I treated you. And I'm sorry for not catching your sister's killer yet. And I'm sorry for letting Kyle Smith get to me so that I accused you of keeping my son from me."

She pulled away from his touch and lowered her gaze again. Maybe she wasn't willing to forgive his unfounded suspicion.

He groaned. "Right now I'm the most sorry about asking you if Alex is mine. I know you better than that. You would never do something—"

She lifted her hand and pressed her fingers to his lips, stilling them. "Jared…"

It was still there. The attraction. It had overwhelmed him six years ago, so that he'd acted on that attraction instead of his better judgment. If anything the attraction was even stronger now.

He lifted his hands to cup her shoulders, to pull her into his arms. But then his damn phone rang. He silently cursed the timing. But he couldn't *not* take the call. A young woman was missing.

He stepped back from Becca, so that her hand fell from his face. And he pulled out his cell phone. He recognized the number as belonging to another agent—an agent who had recently become a good friend. So it could have been a personal call. He could have ignored it and reached for Becca again.

But dread clenched his stomach into knots. And he knew…

Even before he clicked the talk button, he knew what special agent Dalton Reyes would tell him. A body had been found. He was no longer working a disappearance; he was working a murder.

"AGENT BELL HERE," he answered his cell.

But he wasn't there. Even though he stood only a couple of steps from Rebecca, he was already gone—already off to handle whatever had come up with this call.

Fear gripped Rebecca. She glanced down at the photo of Lexi and Amy Wilcox, smiling, with their arms around each other. She wished she'd known how they knew each other—what had connected them in the past. Because she had a horrible feeling they had another connection—that they were both dead—murdered by the same man.

But why would Harris have murdered Amy? Rebecca needed to go through her sister's things again and try to figure out how Lexi had known Amy and if Harris would have known her, too.

"I'll be there as soon as I can," Jared told whoever was on the phone. Then he clicked off the cell and slid it back into his pocket.

"Did they find her body?" she asked. Tears stung her eyes with sympathy for what the young woman's family would go through—for the loss and pain.

He lifted his shoulders, but it wasn't a shrug. "There's been no confirmation yet. I have to leave, though."

He was the one who would make the confirmation— the one who knew the case better than everyone else no matter how short a time he had been working it. He would have immersed himself in it. He had even risked seeing her again, although he'd had no idea how she might react, in order to investigate the connection between Amy Wilcox and Lexi.

Despite saying he had to leave, he stood in front of her yet—as if there was something he wanted to say or do before he left her. He lifted his hand to her face and skimmed his fingers across her cheek, brushing back a stray lock of hair.

Her breath caught in her throat, choking her— choking back the words she needed to say. The truth.

He leaned down a little—as if he intended to cover her mouth with his. To kiss her...

She wanted his kiss. Her pulse quickened in anticipation of his lips sliding over hers. And she closed her eyes.

But his mouth never touched hers. She opened her eyes to find that he'd moved. His head was no longer bowed toward hers. And he'd taken a step back.

He took another step. "I—I need to leave."

She nodded. "I understand."

Unfortunately, he probably had a body to identify. And then he would be caught up in the investigation. He might come back—to follow up on the connection with Lexi. Or he might be too busy to come back, so he would send another agent instead.

He took another step back, nearing the door. Then he turned and reached for the knob.

Maybe it was because his back was turned. Maybe it was because she wasn't sure if she would ever see him again, but she blurted out, "Alex is your son."

His hand tightened into a fist around the doorknob. She thought he was going to open the door and just walk out. But then he turned around and strode back to her, and his gaze pierced her heart with its intensity.

Her chest ached as her heart hammered with fear and guilt. She expected an outburst. Angry words. Accusations. At least questions.

He had to have so many questions.

Answers jumbled together in her mind.

You said we shouldn't see each other again.

I didn't know if you would think I got pregnant to trap you.

I didn't know if you even wanted to be a father.

His mouth opened, but no words came out. Maybe his questions were as jumbled in his mind as her answers were in hers. Then he shook his head. In denial of her claim? Didn't he believe Alex was his son?

Maybe he thought she was trying to trap him even now. She had obviously wanted his kiss moments ago— moments before he'd walked away.

But a muscle twitched in his cheek. And those usually pale brown eyes had darkened with emotion. Then he turned away from her and walked back to the door. He didn't hesitate this time. He turned the knob and stepped out.

She tensed, bracing herself for the door to slam behind him. It closed with a soft click, but that click echoed throughout the living room with a finality that left her shaking.

Would he come back to ask any questions? Or did he not care that he had a son? Didn't he want to see Alex? To form a relationship—a bond—with his boy?

Nervous that her legs might give out, she dropped onto the sofa. What the hell had she just done?

He was on his way to identify a body—the body of a woman whose family was probably still holding out hope for her safe return. And then once Jared confirmed the identity, he would have to notify that family of their loss.

She couldn't have picked a worse moment to tell him the truth. He was in the middle of an investigation. And she knew how investigations consumed him.

"I'm sorry," she murmured. Not only had she not been fair to Jared but she hadn't been fair to Alex, either.

She should have told them both years ago. She shouldn't have denied them the relationship they deserved to have. Why had she been so selfish?

Regret and guilt had tears stinging her eyes. But giving in to the tears would be selfish, too, and would accomplish nothing.

She would make it up to Alex. Somehow.

But she wasn't sure that Jared would ever give her the chance. She wasn't sure that he would ever forgive her.

The phone rang, shattering the silence of her living room. She grabbed up the cordless from the table next to the couch, so that the ringing wouldn't awaken Alex. She wouldn't even be able to look at her son now—not without guilt overwhelming her.

The number was blocked on the caller ID, so she hoped it wasn't a reporter. Maybe she should have just hit the off button. But she found herself saying, "Hello?"

And hoping it was Jared. Maybe he'd found his words. His questions. She would even welcome his accusations now.

She just wanted him to give her a chance to explain. But there was only silence.

Maybe he hadn't found his words yet.

"Hello?" she said again.

A reporter would have talked, would have fired a million questions at her. It had to be him. He was probably just too mad to speak to her.

"Jared?"

"No, Becca," a male voice finally spoke. It was low and raspy, and she wasn't certain that she'd ever heard it before. But how did he know the nickname that only Lexi and Jared had ever called her?

"Who is this?" she asked.

The silence fell again, but there was no dial tone. He hadn't hung up. He was still there.

"Who is this?" she asked again, and goose bumps raised her skin as unease sent a chill running through her. She shouldn't entertain some crank caller. She began to lift the phone away from her ear to hang up.

Then he spoke again in that raspy, nearly unintelligible whisper. "You need to be careful…"

"Careful?" She didn't live a life of adventure. She lived a quiet life—focused on her son and her job.

"You need to be careful," the person spoke again—this time with more urgency.

"Why?" she asked.

"You're being watched."

She peered out the window. The sun was beginning to set, setting the window aglow with a yellow glare. She couldn't see anything but the yellow shimmer in the trees and across the grass. If someone was out there, she couldn't see them. Were the reporters staked out there somewhere? Waiting to ambush her when she left for work in the morning?

"I know," she murmured. Those damn reporters.

They'd been relentless during the investigation into Lexi's case. They had followed her everywhere. And even after the case had gone cold, they'd checked in with her from time to time—wanting to interview her. Wanting to dredge up the tragedy and her pain...

"You don't know," the person said. "You don't know..."

She shivered at the ominous tone. "What don't I know?"

"That you're in danger."

The line clicked with the same finality with which the door had closed behind Jared. Then the dial tone peeled out.

Her hand trembling, she turned off the cordless and put it back down on the table beside the couch.

Why would she be in danger?

The serial killer only went after brides-to-be. She was not engaged. She wasn't even seeing anyone.

She was safe. Wasn't she?

Chapter Five

The silver car. The blood-soaked lace spilling out of the open trunk. Jared flashed back six years ago to finding Lexi's car. Unfortunately, Becca had been with him when they'd come across the abandoned silver Chevrolet.

There had been no body but so much blood...

Now there was a body...

No matter how many victims he had seen over the years, horror and dread still clutched at his heart. How could a human do this to another human? How could they act so viciously and subject another person to so much pain and cruelty?

He shuddered. And he wasn't the only one.

Special Agent Dalton Reyes's usually tanned complexion had gone ashen, and he shook slightly as he stepped back from the trunk. "That could have been Elizabeth..."

Dalton had recently found a woman in the trunk of a stolen car he'd run off the road. Fortunately, that woman hadn't been dead—just so injured that she had lost her memory.

"It wasn't," Jared said. "She's alive." And she had recovered her memory, as well.

Dalton expelled a ragged breath of relief. "She's alive, and she's amazing. I can't believe she agreed to marry me."

Jared glanced back over his shoulder and groaned.

He'd taken a Bureau helicopter from the closest police post to Becca's house; that was how he'd made such good time—arriving while the sun was still up. How the hell had the media already gotten wind of their finding a crime scene?

News station vans rolled into the middle of the Indiana wheat field, kicking up dust that shimmered in the setting sun. Jared gestured at the local police officers. "Keep them back. I don't want any pictures of this scene leaking out."

Before he'd had time to notify the family. He turned back to the trunk. The victim's face was swollen and bruised but identifiable. It was Amy Wilcox. She stared up at him through open, glazed brown eyes; he only imagined the accusation in her gaze. The blame for not catching this killer before he'd killed again—before he'd killed her.

I'm sorry, Amy...

He'd kept apologizing to Becca, too. But now he knew why she'd been so reluctant to accept his apologies— because she owed him a bigger one.

Alex was his son.

His head began to pound, and he flinched. But he pushed the thoughts back. He couldn't afford to be distracted now. He'd deal later with the shock and anger that was rolling through him like those vans through the wheat field.

Now he had to get to Amy Wilcox's family—before the media did. But he wouldn't do that until he'd made certain that the coroner removed her body from the scene without the media getting any photos of her.

Where the hell was the coroner?

Was he or she lost? The media had no trouble finding the field.

"Did you hear me?" Dalton asked.

If the other agent had been talking, Jared hadn't heard him. Despite his best intentions, he was distracted—too damn distracted.

Becca had always distracted him but never more so than now—when he'd learned they had made a child together. He had a son...

"I'm sorry," he murmured. He'd been doing a lot of apologizing tonight. "What did you say?"

"Elizabeth agreed to marry me!" He slapped Jared's back. "I'm getting married—thanks to you!"

"Me?" He was shocked—not shocked like he'd been when Becca had told him he was Alex's dad. But he was surprised that Dalton would give him any gratitude for getting hit over the head.

Dalton grinned. His color was back now. And if a guy could glow, Dalton was glowing. "Elizabeth and I feel like you're part of the reason we're getting married. If you'd been the jerk I thought you were going to be and took the case from me, I wouldn't have fallen for Elizabeth. That's why I want you to be my best man."

"So you want me to be your best man because I'm not a jerk?" Jared shook his head. "I'm not so sure you're right about that. If I'd really thought that the Butcher was after Elizabeth, I would have taken the case." But he'd never really believed that the serial killer had grabbed Elizabeth—because she'd lived.

"You would have been right to take the case, then," Dalton agreed with a quick, regretful glance in the trunk. "So will you do it? Will you be my best man?"

"How can you think about that now?" Jared wondered.

Dalton glanced in the trunk again and shuddered. "I know my timing stinks, but I don't want to wait to marry Elizabeth."

"Do you see this?" Jared asked.

"Of course I see it."

"It's a message," Jared said. "He's mad that someone tried to blame the attempts on Elizabeth's life on him. He's making it clear what is his work and that women don't survive when he abducts them."

"He's a sick SOB," Dalton agreed. "But you know that."

"I know that he might try to get Elizabeth now—to prove that she wouldn't have survived if he'd actually grabbed her. You shouldn't get married now."

Dalton sighed. "You've never been in love, have you?"

Jared sucked in a sharp breath as if his friend had slugged him.

And Dalton apologized. "I'm sorry. I almost forgot about that first victim's sister…"

Jared had never been able to forget her. And now he never would. But he didn't want to talk about Becca. "I know you love Elizabeth, so you should want to keep her safe."

Dalton said, "I will keep her safe. And so will you. You're going to stop him."

"I've been trying for six years," he reminded his friend. "I haven't been successful yet." He hadn't even been able to establish a profile of the killer until the second victim. Since Lexi's body hadn't been found, he hadn't known exactly how this killer killed until then.

"You will be," Dalton said with absolute confidence.

The arrival of the coroner's van saved Jared from a reply. Six years ago he'd been confident he would stop this killer—like he'd stopped so many others before and after him. Now he wasn't so sure. But still, when he notified Amy's parents and fiancé, he found himself making them the same promise that he'd made Becca.

He would get this guy. For them. For Amy. For all those other victims. For Lexi. And, even though she had denied him six years of his son's life, for Becca. Maybe most of all for Becca.

He would stop this killer if it was the last thing he ever did.

REBECCA HADN'T MEANT to turn the television back on after Jared left. She really didn't want to see the news—not when she was sure that Jared had rushed out because a body had been found. Amy Wilcox's body.

The camera zoomed in on the open trunk of a silver car—and the blood-stained wedding gown spilling out of it. The scene in that fallow cornfield, so much like the one she and Jared had come upon, knocked her back six years. There had been so much blood...

But on the television screen, it wasn't just a dress that had been found, like it had been with Lexi. Moments later another camera followed a gurney on which lay a black plastic bag—a body zipped inside it—to the coroner's van.

The young woman had known Lexi—had been her friend. And now both women were dead. Gone. Forever.

Was Jared forever gone? Or would he be back? He'd only been gone a few hours.

But he had been so shocked when he left. So betrayed.

He'd apologized for thinking that Alex could have been his, for thinking that she could have kept a secret like that. He had given her too much credit, and now she was the one who owed him the apology. So many apologies for all the years she'd kept him from their son.

She couldn't call him, though—even if she hadn't thrown away his phone number all those years ago. He was in the middle of what was now another murder investigation. He had a family to notify.

A killer to find...

Would he find him now? Would he look where she had been pointing him? Where Lexi had pointed her?

Had Harris known Amy Wilcox, too?

She turned off the television, shutting off the blond-haired man she realized now was Kyle Smith. Over the years he had hounded her more relentlessly than the others—wanting that follow-up interview, wanting to open up all her pain again. But he hadn't been interested in just Lexi. He'd wanted Rebecca to talk about FBI profiler Special Agent Bell, too. Like Jared, he hadn't wanted to talk about the real killer, either. Harris Mowery hadn't been newsworthy to him.

Maybe she could find what the FBI profiler and investigative reporter had failed to find—evidence leading to the real killer. She reached for the plastic tub of Lexi's photos and letters and journals and dragged it across the floor to the couch where she sat.

Rebecca had been so busy taking notes during class and studying that she'd had no time for journaling. But Lexi had written every night—sometimes just a short paragraph or sometimes pages. Remembering the date on the photo Jared had showed her, Rebecca reached for that year—the year that Lexi had disappeared. The journal cover was neon green with yellow and orange stripes. It was bright and happy like Lexi had always seemed. But inside those pages was another story—a dark story. This was the journal in which Rebecca had found those photos—of the battered and bruised Lexi.

Jared had been right: it was too great a coincidence that the women had been photographed together the month that Lexi had disappeared—especially when that woman later disappeared like Lexi had.

She had looked through this journal earlier when Jared had been there—after he had looked at it and determined that there was no mention of Amy Wilcox. The photos had distracted and angered her then. Now she focused on what Lexi had written. While there was no mention of Amy, Lexi had written several references to meeting someone she had nicknamed Root Beer. Amy's initials were the name brand of a popular root beer.

Could it be?

It was something Lexi would have done—something cute and funny. But they hadn't met that way. Lexi had met Root Beer at a support group for battered women.

Harris had been battering Lexi. Who had been battering Amy? From the news reports, Rebecca knew Amy's age; she was younger than Lexi. She must have only been in high school when she'd gone to those meetings.

So whoever had abused her was probably no longer in her life. From Lexi's comments, it was clear that Root Beer had impressed her with strength and wisdom beyond her years. Amy had actually been supportive to Lexi.

Could Harris have known?

Her pulse quickened as she skimmed over a passage. Then she read it again, aloud.

"Ran into Root Beer when I was out with Harris at the mall. She told him that she'd heard a lot of wonderful things about Harry. She said it, though, in such a way that he knew she had heard nothing wonderful about him. And he hates being called Harry. He got so mad at her sassiness that I thought he was going to hit her. But he controlled his temper until we got home and hit me instead. Root Beer saw the bruises at the next meeting and cried. It's not her fault, though. It's not even Harris's fault anymore. It's my fault for staying. But I'm even more afraid of what he'll do if I leave…"

That must have been why Harris had killed her—because she'd found the courage to leave him. Had he decided to kill Amy because he thought Lexi might have gotten some of that courage from the younger girl? But, in keeping with the other killings, he'd had to wait until Amy had gotten engaged—until she was ready to begin a happy new adventure.

Tears stung Rebecca's eyes. She blinked and wrinkled her nose, trying to hold back her tears. She had cried so many tears over the past six years. For Lexi. For herself. And for all the other victims.

Despite her efforts, she couldn't hold back her tears. Amy deserved them. But was she crying them for Amy? Or was she crying them for herself—out of guilt over not telling Jared he had a son?

She had spent the past six years trying to justify her action, or inaction, to herself. But there was no justification. Jared had deserved to know the truth and so had Alex. She had been so selfish, keeping her son—her amazing, intelligent, sweet son—all to herself.

Jared might never forgive her. Would Alex? Earlier she'd been confident that she could make it up to him. But she had spent the past six years trying to be both his mother and his father. And she'd failed.

She wasn't the male role model her son craved. She'd dated over the past six years, but she hadn't brought many of the dates around Alex. She hadn't wanted her son to get attached to any of them—because she hadn't been able to get attached herself.

None of them had been Jared, who was too smart. Too cocky. Too oblivious to her feelings…

Why hadn't she been able to get completely over him? She doubted he had thought that often of her over the past six years. But then she'd had Alex—precocious, brilliant Alex—to constantly remind her of Jared.

Heat flushed her face, and she quickly brushed away her tears—as if embarrassed that she'd been caught crying. She glanced to the hallway leading to the bedrooms and bath, but Alex wasn't standing there. He hadn't awakened.

She was alone.

Wasn't she?

Her skin prickled with awareness—of someone's gaze on her.

You're being watched...

After that ominous call, she had closed the curtains. But with the lights on in the living room, someone could probably see through the thin fabric. Someone could be out there—watching her.

Goose bumps rose along her arms, and she shivered. Not *could* be. Someone was definitely out there—watching her through the curtains. Why?

You're in danger...

And if she was in danger, so was Alex. After that call earlier, maybe she should have done more than close the curtains. Maybe she should have called the police.

And tell them what? That she got an ominous phone call? They couldn't investigate every prank call. And there had been no obvious threat made.

It had been more of a warning.

You're in danger...

Maybe she had let that call get to her—like Jared had thought he'd let the reporter get to him. Maybe that call had put her on edge, and she was only imagining that someone was watching her.

Gathering her courage, she turned toward the window and pulled back the curtain to peer out into the darkness. The light from the living room spilled out—and glinted off the eyes staring in the window at her.

She clasped her hand over her mouth to hold in the scream of sheer terror.

You're being watched...

It was no prank. Someone was out there.

You're in danger...

And whoever was out there meant her harm.

Chapter Six

Her beautiful face had paled to a deathly white, and her eyes had gone dark and wide with fear. Jared was furious with her for not telling him about his son, but he didn't want to see her like this—afraid of him.

"I didn't mean to scare you," he said. He also hadn't meant to come back to her house—especially after making the emotionally draining notification to Amy Wilcox's family. But something had drawn him back here—to her and their son. "I wasn't going to knock unless you were still up."

She stood in the doorway, trembling as she held open the door for him. The night air was cool, but he suspected she trembled over the fright he'd given her instead. He was tempted to take her into his arms, but she had her arms wrapped around herself, defensively—or protectively.

"That's why I looked in the window to see if you were awake," he explained, "but I should have realized that after you caught Kyle Smith looking in…"

His son's bedroom window. The man was doing more than covering a story; he had crossed the line.

Becca shook her head even as her body continued to tremble. "That's not why I was so afraid."

"I didn't scare you?" Then what had frightened her?

He peered around her and into the living room, but he saw no threat—nobody lurking inside with her.

"You surprised me," she said. And finally she stepped back, so that he could step inside the house with her. But she shivered again as she closed the door, shutting out the darkness.

Or maybe, despite the brightness of her living room, the darkness was already inside with her, spilling out of Lexi's open plastic tote of mementoes. Becca had been looking through her sister's things again. That was probably what had unsettled her so much.

"I'm surprised you came back," she said.

"You didn't think I would?" Was that why she hadn't told him about his son? She'd thought he wouldn't care—that he would want nothing to do with the boy. Maybe that was fair—since he'd once acted as though he'd wanted nothing to do with her—even though pushing her away was the hardest thing he'd ever done. Selfishly, he'd wanted to hold on to her.

But then she wouldn't have dealt with her grief and her loss. He hadn't thought she would heal if she continued to cling to him—to try to fill her emptiness with feelings for him. Feelings he had refused to believe were real.

He must have been right—or she would have told him when she'd learned she was pregnant. She would have let him be part of his son's life.

"I know you're busy," she said. "It was her?"

He nodded. Then he gestured at the open box. "Looks like you've been busy, too."

She expelled a shaky little breath that sounded as if she'd been crying. "It's too late to help Amy now, though. I shouldn't have tried to get rid of you when you first showed up at my door."

He knew now why she had. But he held back the words

and his resentment because he could see from her slightly swollen and red eyes that she had been crying.

"I should have helped you right away," she said, and her voice cracked with emotion—with regret.

"Amy was already dead," he said. "She was probably dead before I even checked myself out of the hospital." Guilt twisted his stomach into a tight knot. "If I'd checked myself out sooner…"

But the coroner's preliminary exam had estimated that time of death had been around the time she'd been abducted. She had probably died in the struggle. Amy had fought for her life and lost.

Yet if Jared had caught the killer the first time he'd killed, Amy would be alive and so would all the other victims. But Lexi would still be gone.

Becca shook her head and admonished him. "You shouldn't have checked yourself out against doctor's orders."

"You would say that," he said, "because you're a doctor."

"No." She shook her head. "No, I'm not."

"But you were in med school…" When Lexi disappeared.

"I dropped out," she said.

"Because you were pregnant?" Had she given up her dream so she could carry his baby—to have his baby? Alone. She'd had no one to help her—if he was right that her parents had little to do with her because she was a painful reminder of Lexi.

She shrugged. "It would have taken me too many years of med school and residency and crazy hours to become the surgeon I thought I wanted to be."

"So what do you do?" How did she take care of their son? If she'd told him she was pregnant, he would have helped her. At least financially. He wasn't sure what he could offer her otherwise. He had always been so focused on his career that he'd never considered getting married and having kids. He'd never planned on being a father, so he wasn't sure he could actually be one.

"I condensed my crazy hours into a shorter time span by switching to a physician assistant program," she said. "I'm a PA at the local hospital."

"But you wanted to be a surgeon."

She shook her head. "Not after...not after seeing all that blood in the trunk of Lexi's car. I still see blood at the hospital. But I'm not the one cutting them open."

Like the Butcher cut open his victims...

She hadn't wanted to be anything like him—even if she would have been saving lives, instead of taking them like he did.

"I'm the one stitching them back up," she said with obvious pride and satisfaction.

The pressure in his chest eased slightly. She'd stayed in medicine. She hadn't completely discarded her dream. "That's good," he said.

She smiled. "I enjoy it. And I didn't have to go through all the crazy hours of a resident. I had more time for Alex." Her face flushed and she looked away from him.

So she probably missed his flinch of pain and regret. He'd had no time with Alex.

"Why did you come back?" she asked him. "It's too late to wake Alex up now—if that's what you wanted to do."

He wasn't sure what he wanted. Or why he had come back. He'd been so angry with her—until he'd seen the fear on her face. Then he'd just wanted to hold her—to protect and comfort her. She still hadn't told him what had frightened her.

"It is late," he agreed as weariness overwhelmed him. Maybe he had checked himself out of the hospital too early, because he wasn't completely recovered. His head pounded from the concussion, and he didn't have his usual strength and energy. "Why are you up still?" He glanced down again at the open plastic tub. "What are you doing?"

Had she found something that had scared her?

"I read through Lexi's journal for the year that the picture of her and Amy was taken—"

"The year she disappeared," he interjected. It couldn't just be a coincidence. "I looked through that journal earlier and saw no mention of Amy's name."

"Neither did I," she said. "But Lexi liked to give nicknames to people she cared about. I think she gave Amy a nickname based on her initials."

She held out the journal to him, and he read the section she indicated. "Root Beer," he murmured.

Becca nodded.

"Her family didn't call her that."

"My parents didn't call me Becca—only Lexi did."

He had used it, too. He still thought of her as Becca. And he thought of her always.

"Lexi liked special nicknames," she said with a smile. But then her smile faded and she added, "She didn't have a nickname for Harris, though." She pointed to the section of the journal again, and her finger trembled. "He killed Amy, too."

If only it was that easy to find a killer.

He pointed out, "This isn't evidence of that."

"But it proves that he met her."

"It proves he met someone Lexi called Root Beer," he said. "We don't know that it was really Amy Wilcox."

She shook her head as if disgusted. "I should have known better than to think you would listen to me."

"I will investigate," he promised. "I will talk to Harris." He hadn't been able to find any connection between

Harris and the other women who had disappeared. But he had a connection now—however tenuous—between him and Amy Wilcox. He could bring him in for questioning again.

But was he doing it to solve the case? Or just to make Becca happy? Since Harris hadn't killed Lexi, why would he have killed any of the other women—even Amy?

Becca breathed a sigh of relief. "Thank you." But the tension didn't ease from her body. She was still trembling slightly.

"If I didn't scare you earlier," he said, "what did?" And what still had her so on edge?

"I got a phone call shortly after you left—"

"One of those damn reporters?" They had all been staked out at the crime scene and the Wilcoxes' house. But one of them—probably Kyle Smith—could have called her from there.

She shook her head. "Not a reporter. I don't know who it was, but he called me Becca. And he warned me that someone's watching me—that I'm in danger."

Fear clutched his heart. "Why would someone tell you that? Why would someone want to scare you like that?" Unless it was true...

And if it was true, he couldn't take any chances. "I'm staying here," he said. "I'm staying with you until I can get protection duty on you and Alex."

"Isn't protection duty how you got your concussion?" she asked. But she didn't argue with him about staying. She opened a closet and pulled down a pillow and a blanket.

"I won't need that," he said. Because he wouldn't be sleeping. He'd nearly been killed the last time he'd done protection duty. But that wouldn't happen this time. He wouldn't drop his guard for a second—now that he was protecting his family.

THE RUMBLE OF a deep voice jerked Rebecca awake, her pulse racing. She wasn't afraid because she didn't recognize the voice but because she did. She'd heard that voice in her dreams before. How had she fallen asleep with Jared in her house?

But then she probably wouldn't have slept at all if he hadn't stayed. *You're being watched...you need to be careful...*

That ominous warning echoed in her mind. But with Jared watching over her and Alex, she'd felt safe. Until now.

Now she had that eerie feeling that she was being watched again. She glanced toward the door. She'd thought she had shut it, but it was cracked open now—wide enough that two pairs of eyes peered through at her. One gaze was the same blue as her own. The other gaze was the amber brown that haunted her dreams along with his deep voice.

"See," Alex said as he shoved open the door the rest of the way and ran into her room. "I told you she would be up. Mom never sleeps late."

"That's because you always wake me up." She reached out and caught her little boy, pulling him into bed with her. He squirmed and giggled as she tickled him.

Jared stared at their son now, his gaze full of longing. Then he looked at her, and resentment flashed in those amber eyes.

Guilt churned her empty stomach. She'd been so unfair to keep him from his son. But she hadn't known that he would want him. He hadn't wanted her; why would he want a child they had made together?

"Mom! Mom! Stop!" Alex protested. And his face reddened as if embarrassed for giggling in front of the FBI agent.

She let him wriggle free. "Why did you want me to wake up?"

"Agent Bell said you have something you need to tell me."

Her stomach lurched now. Jared was going to force her to tell their son right away? Before she'd even had coffee? She could smell the rich aroma of it; the scent had her mouth watering. Then she realized why the scent was so strong when Jared held out a mug to her.

He'd made coffee? He'd brought it to her?

He should be furious with her. He had every right. She'd only seen that brief flash of resentment. Where was his anger? She searched his face but could find no trace of it. His eyes weren't hard at all; they looked almost haunted.

Like he was afraid.

She was afraid, too. And not of a voice on the phone or a face in the window. She was afraid of the reaction her son might have when he learned the truth. She suspected Jared shared that fear.

"Alex wanted to know why I was sleeping on the couch," he said.

"You weren't sleeping," Alex said. "You were just lying there with your hand on your gun." Her precocious little boy missed nothing.

Jared had been protecting them. Her and his son.

She could see from the dark circles beneath his eyes that he hadn't slept at all. And he was so tense that a muscle twitched along his heavily shadowed jaw.

"I didn't know what I should tell him," Jared said. He wouldn't want to tell a child about a threat. "He didn't believe that's the way all FBI agents sleep."

Alex snorted. "They would be too tired to catch bad guys if they never closed their eyes."

He was definitely his father's son—too smart.

The corners of Jared's mouth turned up into a slight

smile of amusement and pride. "He didn't buy that I had too much coffee, either…"

"He wasn't jumpy," Alex said, "like you get when you have too much coffee."

She nearly sputtered on the sip of coffee she'd just taken. Given that Jared had had his hand on his gun, she was glad that he hadn't been jumpy. He might have shot their son if Alex had exploded out of his bedroom like he usually did. "FBI agents can't be jumpy," she said.

Alex nodded as if she'd just made a good point. With his intelligence, she always wondered what he would become. A doctor. A lawyer. An FBI agent…

The possibilities were endless for him…as long as whoever was watching her caused him no harm. She was glad that Jared knew now that Alex was his son. She should have told him so much sooner.

And she could wait no longer to tell their son. "Jared stayed last night because we need to tell you something."

Jared sucked in a quick breath as if bracing himself for what she was going to reveal. But he already knew. He just didn't know how Alex would react.

Neither did she.

"What?" Alex asked. "Are bad guys after us? Is that why he stayed?"

"No," she assured her son. "Nobody's after us—" She hoped. *You're being watched…*

"But the man looking in my window—"

"Was just a reporter," Jared said.

"They were here about Aunt Lexi," Rebecca explained.

Her little boy nodded. He had seen Aunt Lexi's face on the news before—had overheard her story before Rebecca had been able to find the remote and shut off the nightmare.

But the remote couldn't shut it off. Only Jared catching the killer could stop the nightmare.

"Then what did you want to tell me?" he asked.

Panic had her pulse quickening, and she glanced at Jared. Should she tell? Did Jared even want to be a father?

That muscle twitched again in his cheek, but he nodded in response to the question she hadn't even had to ask him aloud. They'd once been that connected—that in sync that they'd spoken to each other's thoughts. And when they'd made love, they had instinctively known where to kiss, where to touch each other.

She shivered with another kind of awareness. But then Alex tugged on her arm, and his voice went all soft and shy as he fearfully murmured, "Mommy..."

She shrugged off her thoughts of Jared and focused on her child instead. Like his father, he also deserved the truth. "I want to tell you the answer," she said, "to that question you keep asking me."

His brow puckered with confusion. "I ask a lot of questions."

She almost smiled. He certainly did. All his teachers exclaimed over how inquisitive he was—that was how he had skipped first grade and was already in second. But she was too nervous to be amused as she clarified, "The one question I haven't answered yet."

He sucked in a quick breath. "Who's my daddy?" Then he glanced at Jared as the answer dawned on him. "Are you my daddy?"

Jared's throat moved as if he was swallowing hard. Choking on emotion? Then he gruffly replied, "Yes."

The little boy stared at him, his blue eyes narrowed in speculation. "We don't look alike."

"No," Jared agreed. "You look like your mother."

"And your aunt Lexi," Rebecca added. She clung to the fact that a part of her sister lived on in her son. It made Lexi's death seem less final to her.

But Alex was focused on Jared now. His voice quavered as he asked him, "Why haven't you ever come to see me before?"

Jared glanced at her, leaving the explanations for her to make. The explanation or the excuses. But there was no excuse for what she'd done.

She had to swallow hard, choking on guilt, before she answered, "Jared didn't know that you were his son—until last night, until after you were already in bed."

"You should have woke me up," Alex said. "You should have told me." He must not have wanted to miss another minute with the father she'd denied him for six years.

"I should have told you both a long time ago," Rebecca admitted. And she hoped that they could both forgive her someday.

"Why didn't you?" Alex asked.

She couldn't answer that honestly. It was too complicated for even a child as bright as Alex to understand. She wasn't sure she understood herself why she'd never told them. "I didn't know how…"

"To get ahold of me," Jared finished for her. "I've been really busy."

"Catching bad guys?" Alex asked him.

Jared nodded. "Trying to." As if on cue, his cell phone rang. He hesitated, letting it ring a few times before pulling it from his pocket.

He may have just found out he was a father, but he was also in the middle of a murder investigation. "I have to…"

But he clicked off the phone without answering it. Then he continued, "I have to leave."

"You got a bad guy to catch now?" Alex asked. Now the longing was in his gaze as he stared up at his father. He wanted to get to know him—wanted to be with him.

Jared nodded. "I'll be back, though," he said. And he

crouched down to Alex's level. "I'll spend time with you, getting to know you."

Alex nodded but tears shimmered in his eyes. Then he threw his arms around his father's neck and clung to him.

And Rebecca suspected there were tears in Jared's eyes, too, as his arms closed around Alex's small body. But she couldn't see clearly through her own tears.

Chapter Seven

Jared's head had finally stopped hurting. Now the pain was in his chest—his heart specifically. It ached with loss. With fear.

He shouldn't have left Becca and Alex. Not after the threat. And not after Alex had learned Jared was his father. Had he already let down his son?

"What's the 9-1-1?" he asked as he walked into the office of the chief of the Chicago Bureau of Federal Investigations. If anyone else had sent him the text, he would have ignored it. But if he ignored Chief Special Agent Lynch, he would have been taken off the case, at the least, and out of a job at the most.

Lynch stood over his desk instead of sitting in the chair behind it. He could have been impatiently waiting for Jared—since he'd had to drive to the police post and take a helicopter to Chicago. Or he could have been just standing because the man rarely sat. Despite his position, Lynch was no bureaucratic paper pusher.

"The Butcher has claimed another victim," the chief said. From the dark circles beneath his eyes, he didn't appear to have had much more sleep than Jared had. Like Jared becoming a profiler at a young age, Lynch had become a Bureau chief at a young age. But in the past six years, he'd aged—getting more lines on his face and gray in his hair. The serial killer eluding them had affected him, too. "That's a 9-1-1—one I thought you would have called yourself, Bell, after you identified those remains as Amy Wilcox's. Where have you been since you made the death notification?"

"Following up on a lead." But the photo of Lexi and Amy Wilcox wasn't why he had gone back to Becca's so late the night before.

The chief arched a dark brow over skeptically narrowed eyes. "Lexi Drummond's sister?"

"She's been threatened," he said.

"Why?" Lynch asked. "Is she engaged?"

"No." At least Jared didn't think she was. He hadn't asked her about a possible fiancé or even a boyfriend. He'd been too consumed first with his case and then with her revelation that he was a father. "But she received a strange call late yesterday afternoon—someone warning her that she's being watched and that she's in danger."

"So you put a protection detail on her?" Lynch asked.

"I don't want to take any chances," Jared said. And he wouldn't with Becca and his son. At least not with their safety. Dare he take a chance to try to act like a father to his son? Would it hurt the boy more if he tried and failed or if he didn't try at all?

Lynch uttered a weary-sounding sigh. "You're right. With the Butcher, we can't take any chances. We have to catch this bastard. *Now.*"

"Nobody wants him caught more than I do, sir," he replied.

Lynch sighed again. "That's not true. Someone else wants him caught more—the victims' families. That's why I called you here. Amy Wilcox's fiancé is in the conference room. He has questions."

"When I made the notification, I promised I would keep them apprised of the investigation," he said, "that

I would let them know when we discovered any new information. It hasn't been that long—I have no new information."

"He has questions," Lynch repeated. "Even if you don't have any answers yet, he needs to ask those questions. Go. Talk to him. Maybe ask some questions of your own…"

Jared had been keeping the chief apprised of his investigation, too, so he reminded him, "I already interviewed Troy Kotlarz as a possible suspect. He doesn't fit the profile." The profile he'd begun after the second victim was found and that he'd added to with each new victim. White male, thirties, single, charming but with few friends, professionally successful, personally unsuccessful—either jilted at the altar or broken engagement. Narcissist with a sadistic streak.

Lynch shrugged. "He may be worth another look."

The chief had become the chief because he'd earned the position by being a damn good agent. So Jared nodded in agreement. "I'll talk to him."

But he hesitated outside the conference room. The man had experienced a loss that Jared couldn't imagine. Becca wasn't even his fiancée but the thought of her just being in danger…

His heart pounded fast and furiously in his chest. She had protection. She and Alex would be safe. He had to believe that so that he could focus on his job. He opened the door and stepped inside. "Sorry to keep you waiting, Troy."

Kotlarz was a big man with prematurely thinning hair. His reactions and movements were slow. He seemed the exact opposite of the young and vivacious Amy Wilcox who'd been so athletic and adventurous. "I have no place else to be," Troy replied. "Your coroner hasn't released her body yet, so her parents can't plan her funeral."

Jared nodded. "We want to be thorough. We will catch him." And there he went—making that promise he had no business making.

Troy jerked his head up, his eyes wide as he met Jared's gaze. "You have new information?"

"Not yet," Jared admitted. "Or I would have called you. Why did you come down here?"

"I know you can't release her body yet," the other man replied. "But when can you release her things?"

"Things?" And why was it so easy for the man to talk of his fiancée's body? He was lucky to have a body to bury; Becca hadn't had one. Maybe the chief's instincts were still as sharp as ever.

"The engagement ring I gave her," Troy said. "That was my grandmother's. I really need to get that back."

Jared bit the inside of his lip and nodded. But he pulled out his phone and checked the list he'd made of everything recovered from the crime scene. "However, I don't see any record of a ring among her personal effects."

Troy gasped. "Do you think someone stole it from the scene?"

Why would he think first of a cop or a crime scene tech? Why wouldn't he blame the killer? Unless he was the killer? But if he was the killer, wouldn't he have taken the ring when he killed her?

And why would he have killed the other women?

That was why Jared had ruled out the man as a suspect. He had no motive for killing the others. There was no connection between him and any of the other women…except maybe Lexi Drummond.

"We'll search for the ring," he assured the other man. "Do you remember anyone ever calling Amy 'Root Beer'?"

Kotlarz shook his head. "No. She never even drank soda."

"Her initials…"

"Oh…" The man didn't just react and move slowly; he thought slowly.

Maybe it was Jared's pride that didn't want this man to be a viable suspect—since he couldn't conceive how Troy would have eluded him for six years.

"Did Amy ever mention going to a support group for women who suffered from domestic abuse?"

The man's face reddened and finally he moved quickly, jumping up from his chair. "I never hurt her!"

"She was in this group—" or so Becca thought "—six years ago."

"I met Amy six months ago."

And they were already engaged? That would have seemed odd to Jared if a couple other agents had recently married women they hadn't known long. Even Reyes was talking marriage.

"Did she ever talk about an abusive ex?"

Troy's eyes widened with sudden understanding. "You think he could have done this to her? There was some guy in high school who gave her a rough time. I don't remember his name. And her parents didn't know about him."

"I'll find out," Jared assured him.

"And you'll find the ring?" the man asked him hopefully.

He seemed to want the ring more than he wanted his fiancée's killer found. Jared offered him a vague nod before showing him out.

"What do you think?" Dalton Reyes asked as he followed Jared into his office.

Files, with a thin sheen of dust, covered his desk. Because of the prior case and his concussion, Jared hadn't spent much time in his office. And he didn't want to be here now, either. He wanted to be with Becca and Alex.

"I think Troy Kotlarz is a jerk," he replied, "but I don't

know if he's a killer." He would find and interview Amy's high school boyfriend, though. He had another suspect to find, too—the one he'd promised Becca he would interview again. Lexi's former fiancé.

Reyes said, "Well, I've got good news."

"The crime lab found something? DNA?" Jared needed some evidence—any evidence—to lead him to the real killer. And convict him.

Reyes shook his head. "That must've been some concussion if you think they got results back in less than a day. This isn't a damn TV show, you know."

Jared sighed. "If only it could be that fast…"

Reyes sighed, too. "Unfortunately this is the real world. But the real world can be fast, too. Penny Payne called."

"Is she a witness?" Jared asked. For six years he'd been looking for a witness. "Someone from the bridal shop?"

"She owns a wedding chapel in River City, Michigan," Reyes said.

"River City?" No victim had been abducted from there, but he knew the place. "That's where Special Agent Nick Rus has been working a case—for a year now."

"Yeah, investigating the police and district attorney's office," Dalton replied. "The corruption runs deeper than he realized. Guess he reconnected with some family, too."

"Rus has family?" Jared was surprised. He'd known the other agent a long time. Hell, they even shared an apartment in Chicago—when either of them was actually home. Nick hadn't been for the past year. But when he'd been there, he'd never mentioned having any family. Jared had identified with that because he'd been an only child, too. Like Alex…

With no one else to play with, he'd focused on school and excelled. Would Alex? His son looked nothing like Jared—except for being small for his age. Did he have any other of his characteristics? Or, because they'd never been around each other, were they nothing alike?

"You sure you should have checked yourself out?" Dalton asked. "You just zoned out. Are you feeling all right? Should I take you back to the hospital?"

"I'm fine," Jared insisted. "Just wondering if you got hit in the head, too. I don't know why you're talking about some wedding chapel in River City."

"Nick recommended Elizabeth and I get married there. Penny Payne is the woman who runs it. Her family is all bodyguards, so she can provide protection, too. She handles everything. She called me because she had a cancellation. Elizabeth and I are getting married next weekend!"

"Next weekend?" It was crazy to consider a marriage now. "That's too soon." It didn't give him enough time to find the killer and prevent him from trying to kill Elizabeth. When she'd first been found, the media had dubbed her the one who'd gotten away from The Bride Butcher. The killer would no doubt want to prove that she wouldn't have gotten away from him.

"Feels like forever to me," Dalton said.

Jared snorted in derision. "You must've gotten hit in the head. I know you love Elizabeth, but you're putting her in danger."

"It'll be fine," Dalton insisted. "This killer isn't going to get past professional bodyguards and FBI agents. So are you in?"

Jared had to be in—he had to make sure nothing happened to Dalton's bride. "Of course."

"So you'll be my best man? I asked you last night, but you never answered me."

He'd been distracted the night before. "You were serious about me being your best man?"

He hadn't thought he was. Dalton Reyes had many

friends—many more friends than Jared had made in the Bureau or outside of it. He was still the loner he'd grown up as—whereas Reyes had never met a stranger.

"I told you that Elizabeth and I feel like you helped bring us together. And you nearly died trying to protect her and little Lizzie."

"So this is a pity request?" Jared teased.

Reyes snorted. "What's your deal, Bell? Why is it so hard for you to accept that I actually want you to stand up with me?"

Had that been his problem with Becca? That he hadn't been able to believe that she could have actually cared about him? He hadn't just been an only child; he'd been an only child of parents who'd given him little time or attention.

His doctorate was in criminal psychology; while he was no criminal, he knew his childhood had affected him—had made it difficult for him to form or accept attachments. But he had a son now. He needed to change. And maybe this was a way to start. He was honored that Dalton would want him to stand up with him. They hadn't known each other long, but then they'd been through a lot recently. "Sure."

"Bring a date, too," Dalton advised.

"Date? What are you talking about?" He shouldn't even be thinking about attending a wedding—not with a murderer on the loose. But this killer had been on the loose a long time, and Jared had already given up too much in his pursuit of him. He'd given up Becca.

He'd thought he was acting in her best interests. That he needed to let her go so that she could move on—go back to med school, go back to her life. Instead, she had created a life—their son.

"I saw on the news that you went to visit Lexi Drummond's sister," Dalton said. "Bring *her*."

If her anonymous caller was to be believed, she was already being watched; she was already in danger. The last place he should bring her would be a wedding.

REBECCA HAD REFUSED to stay locked inside her house in protective custody. She wasn't even certain she was in danger. For a threat, it had been vague. So, with a sheriff's deputy following her, she had brought Alex to school and she'd gone to work.

Maybe it wasn't just that she hadn't wanted to be confined inside her house like a prisoner but that she hadn't wanted to be in her house now that Jared had been in it. She'd kept replaying that morning—him and their son waking her up with coffee.

And questions...

Maybe that was another reason she'd brought Alex to school and gone on to work. She hadn't wanted to keep answering his questions about Jared—or not answering them. His questions had made her realize how little she really knew about a man she'd thought she'd loved.

Had Jared been right six years ago? Had she only imagined herself in love with him so she wouldn't have to deal with the terrible loss of her sister?

Six years had passed now. She'd dealt with that loss—because she'd had no choice and because Jared had given her a wonderful gift. Alex had filled most of the hole that Lexi had left. But nobody had filled the hole Jared had left. She'd tried; she'd dated. But she'd felt about no other man the way she'd felt about Jared.

That she still felt about him. She'd wanted his kiss the night before. And this morning she'd wanted him to crawl into the bed with her—like their son had. She wanted to be close to him—as close as they'd once been.

She expelled a shaky breath and grasped the handle of the exam room door. She had to focus on her job—had to focus on the people she could help since Jared refused to accept her help. Sure, he'd said he would interview Harris again. But she suspected he was only humoring her. He didn't believe that Lexi's fiancé had killed her, so why would he believe that the man had killed her friend?

"Good afternoon," she greeted her next patient as she stepped inside the room.

"Good afternoon, Ms. Drummond," the man greeted her before she'd even given him her name.

And the clinic was so informal that the badge on her coat had only her first name. She lifted her gaze from the laptop in her hands to the man perched on the exam table. And her breath shuddered out in revulsion.

She had seen this man just the day before—staring in her son's bedroom window. "What are you doing here?" she asked Kyle Smith.

According to the clinic laptop, he'd checked in at the desk with the complaint of stomach cramps. He wasn't doubled over or flinching, though. He looked perfectly healthy to her and perfectly evil, wearing a wide, self-satisfied grin.

"I didn't get the chance to talk to you yesterday," he said, "what with Special Agent Bell calling the local authorities to report us for trespassing."

Unfortunately, he hadn't spent the night in jail since he'd been on the news later that evening—at the scene where Amy Wilcox's body had been discovered.

"You were trespassing," she said. "And you're trespassing now."

He shook his head but not a blond hair moved on his head, as if lacquered down or as artificial as his orange-looking tan. "The clinic is open to the public."

"To patients," she said. "Not reporters. You need to leave."

"I came here for treatment," he said. "You can't turn me away. Haven't you taken an oath to do no harm?"

She wanted to harm the man for the scare he'd given her son and her. "I'm a physician's assistant," she said. "Not a doctor. I've taken no such oath." She opened the door and called out, "Security."

The clinic had none, but she suspected that the sheriff's deputy was still hovering around on Jared's orders.

Kyle Smith jumped down from the exam table, but instead of walking out, he came closer and shoved a mike in her face. "So FBI special agent Jared Bell spent the night at your house," he said. "Are the two of you back together?"

She gasped at his audacity and his knowledge. He must have been the reporter who had discovered their relationship six years ago. The press had given Jared a real hard time about being unprofessional. She had wondered then if Jared had broken off their relationship to save face and his career. Her heart beating fast with fear, she backed away from Kyle Smith—into the hall. How had he known that Jared had spent last night at her house? Was he the one watching her? Was he the danger to her?

"Your son is his," the reporter continued. "Alex Drummond's birth certificate confirms it. You listed his father as Jared Bell." His snide grin widened. "Does Special Agent Bell know yet that he's a father?"

"A woman is dead," she reminded him. "Why does my personal life hold any interest for you?"

"You're the story," he said. "It started with your sister and you and Agent Bell."

The murders had started with Lexi. But Rebecca had nothing to do with them. "Leave me alone!"

Finally, the deputy rushed down the hall, his hand on his gun. "Ms. Drummond, are you okay?"

She shook her head. "No, please show Mr. Smith off the premises."

"I'll be back," he told her—again with that wide grin—as the deputy escorted him out.

She was still shaking as she headed toward the front desk. Hadn't the intake nurse recognized the reporter? Why had she let him back?

Before she could ask, Sylvia called out to her. "You have a call, Rebecca, on line three."

Jared. Maybe the deputy had already called him about the reporter. She stepped into a private office off the reception area and picked up the phone. "Hello?"

Her breath, still coming fast from her confrontation with the reporter, echoed in the phone. But no one spoke to her. "Hello?" she said again. Maybe Sylvia had told her the wrong line. She was reaching for another button when that raspy whisper spoke to her.

"Becca…"

She shivered. "What do you want?"

"For you to be careful," the voice ominously replied. "You're in danger."

Chapter Eight

After a sleepless night, Jared should have been exhausted—so exhausted that he should have been back at his apartment in Chicago, in his bed. But determination kept him going. He'd made promises. And this was one promise he wouldn't break. Unlike his promise to find a killer.

He'd promised his son he would return. And he stood outside Becca's house again, waiting for her to open the door. He'd already rung the bell twice. He was reaching for the button again when she finally opened the door. But she blocked the entrance—as much as she could with her slender frame.

She wore some kind of long T-shirt-looking dress that clung to every curve. And her hair was long and loose around her shoulders. The setting sun caught in the blond tresses, making them shine and shimmer.

His breath caught and his pulse quickened at her beauty. And his attraction to her. He should be angry with her. He should be resentful. He had a right to know that she was pregnant with his baby—that she'd had his child. But she'd kept that secret for six years.

"You shouldn't be here," she told him, her voice terse with irritation and frustration.

She was angry with him? Was she mad that he'd left her and Alex that morning? He'd thought she understood that he was working a case—that he was trying to find Amy Wilcox's and her sister's killer. And all those other women...

"Why not?" he asked. Maybe she wanted him working the case instead of spending time with her.

Or maybe Alex didn't want to see him. Heat flushed Jared's face with embarrassment over the present he held under his arm. He'd been a fool to think that any toy could make up for the six years he'd missed of the little boy's life.

Her face reddened as she replied, "Kyle Smith knows you spent last night here. He showed up at the clinic today and wanted to interview me about it. Then I got that call after he left..."

The sheriff's deputy had already told him about the reporter showing up and about the call she'd received. It had already been traced back to a burner cell. He hadn't known, though, why Smith had showed up to harass her.

Jared cursed, then flinched as the little blond-haired boy squeezed between his mother and the doorjamb. "I—I shouldn't have said that," he told Alex. Some father he would make, teaching his son words no child should hear.

The little boy shrugged off the incident. "Mom swears sometimes, too."

Becca's face flushed a brighter shade of red. "Alex, I do not."

He jerked his head in a nod. "You do," he insisted. "Especially when you're driving."

"I—I..." she sputtered and then laughed. "Okay, maybe I do. Sometimes..."

"She does," Alex said. Then he reached out.

Jared thought he was reaching for the present and held it out. But the little boy grabbed his hand instead and tugged him over the threshold.

Becca still stood in the doorway, so Jared collided with her soft frame. His body pressed against hers. They were so close but not close enough. His skin heated and muscles tensed as desire overwhelmed him. Did she feel it, too?

He stared down into her beautiful face. Her bright blue eyes widened, and her breath escaped in a gasp. But then Alex tugged harder on his hand and pulled him through the door and into the living room.

Becca remained in the open doorway. Maybe looking for Kyle Smith...to see if he lurked outside as he must have the night before. How else had the man known Jared had spent the night? And why hadn't Jared, during his vigil, noticed the reporter lurking around?

He needed to improve his protection duty skills—especially with Becca being in danger.

"Did you catch the bad guy?" Alex asked.

A pang of regret struck his heart—for so many reasons. He shook his head. "Not yet."

Alex's little hand squeezed his. "You will," the little boy assured him.

And another pang struck Jared's heart. How could his son have more confidence in him than Jared had in himself? Of course he'd vowed to others and to himself that he would catch the killer—even if it took the rest of his life. But he heartily hoped that it didn't take that long—that he would find him soon—before the man had the chance to abduct and murder another bride. So he vowed again, "I will."

Becca made a noise that drew his attention. He expected it to have been a snort of derision but she sniffled instead, as if fighting back tears.

Even though he didn't understand why she was so emotional, he wanted to comfort her. But when he had tried to comfort her six years ago, he hadn't been able to stop at just comfort. He'd taken advantage of her vulnerability and given in to that overwhelming desire he had for her. While he hadn't given her real comfort, he'd given her a child.

An amazing child…

"I told my friends at school that my daddy is an FBI agent," Alex said.

"You did?" Becca asked the question.

Jared was too stunned to speak. His son had been bragging about him? He didn't even know him. Becca had obviously never talked about him to their son.

Alex nodded, but his mouth pulled down into a little frown. "But they didn't believe me. They think I made it up—that I made you up."

Jared squeezed the little boy's hand and offered assurance now. "I'm real."

Alex shook his head. "They said that I don't have a dad 'cause I never talked about him before and 'cause he's never been around."

And that ache returned to Jared's heart—that hollow feeling he'd had all day since he'd had to leave his son and stay away from him. From them.

Becca sniffled again before speaking in a voice heavy with guilt and emotion. "That wasn't your fault. That wasn't your father's fault, either."

"I told them that," Alex said. "I told them he was busy catching bad guys."

Becca released a breath that sounded like relief. Her son wasn't blaming her. But then she turned to Jared, and her gaze searched his face. Over the years he'd gotten good at hiding his emotions. So she might not see his resentment, but it was there—simmering inside him.

He wasn't as forgiving as the little boy. She should have let him know when she'd found out she was pregnant. She should have let him be a part of his son's life. He wasn't sure she was going to let him be a part of it even now that he knew Alex was his.

They hadn't discussed that. They hadn't discussed anything. And maybe she'd only said that about Kyle Smith knowing he'd spent the night in order to get rid of him before they could have the discussion they needed to have.

The little boy shrugged off his friends' reactions to his news and turned his attention to the brightly wrapped package Jared was holding. "Who did you bring the present for?" he asked. "Me or Mommy?"

"You, of course," Becca answered for him.

She expected no presents from Jared. After he'd failed to find her sister's killer or even her body, she probably expected nothing from him—especially after how he'd rejected her feelings for him.

"It is for you," Jared said as he handed the box over to the boy.

"But it's not my birthday," Alex said.

Jared had no idea when his son's birthday was. How far along had Becca been when he'd told her it was better that they have no further contact? After the way he'd treated her, he had no right to his resentment.

"And Christmas is a couple months away," Alex said.

"I owe you some presents," Jared said—for all those birthdays and Christmases he'd missed. "Go ahead and open it."

Instead of tearing off the paper, as Jared suspected most kids his age would have, Alex studied the package. He narrowed his eyes and tilted his head as if he could see inside the box. Then he weighed it in his hands. "I don't think you brought me a gun…"

"Alex!" Becca exclaimed with a gasp. Then she glanced at Jared as if worried that he actually might have bought the child a gun.

He knew very little about kids, but he knew better than to arm one. "It's not a gun," he told them both.

"A car?" Alex asked.

He should have bought him a toy car. Didn't all little boys love cars? He hadn't been all that interested in cars at that age, though. Of course he'd always been a little odd. So he had no idea if he'd bought his son something he would like.

"Just open it," Becca encouraged the boy.

Alex sighed but settled onto the floor with the present. Then he proceeded to remove each piece of tape—slowly and methodically.

"He does this with every present at Christmas," Becca said. "It takes two days for him to finally open them all."

And the resentment fired back up, making Jared remark, "I wouldn't know."

But he should have known. He should have been there every Christmas, watching his son take days to open all his presents. He should have been there for birthdays and T-ball games. Did Alex play T-ball? Or soccer? Or was he as unathletic as his father had been?

"I'm sorry," she murmured, her voice low and soft and close to his ear since she'd leaned toward him.

He felt her breath and her warmth and inhaled her sweet, summery scent. She smelled like flowers and sunshine. And her closeness heated him.

Jared leaned toward her—tempted to kiss her and not to comfort her. Or to punish her. He wanted to kiss her, simply because he wanted her.

But Alex uttered a soft gasp.

Jared turned his attention to his son. The little boy

stared down at the box he'd finally unwrapped. He should have brought him a car. What had he been thinking?

"I can take it back," he offered. "And get you something else, something you'd like…"

"Like?" Alex looked up at him and blinked his long lashes quickly as if fighting back tears.

Oh, God, he'd really screwed up.

Then Alex stood up and launched himself at Jared, wrapping his arms around his waist to squeeze him tight. "I love it!"

And Jared's heart shifted in his chest as emotion—as love—overwhelmed him. A day ago he hadn't known the child existed; now he couldn't imagine a world without him in it. He patted the little boy's back and head. "I'm so glad."

And not just that he'd bought the right thing. But he was so glad he had a son. He'd never thought about being a father before. But now that he was one…

He was glad.

"What is it?" Becca asked curiously.

Alex pulled back from Jared's embrace. His voice shaking with excitement, he replied, "A lie detector test! Want to try it out, Mommy?"

Her mouth fell open in such surprise that Jared laughed.

"Or do you want to go first, Daddy?"

And his mouth fell open in shock and delight. But before he could answer his son, his phone rang—work dragging him away once again from a special moment. Now, instead of resenting Becca, he resented the career he'd once loved so much.

"Mommy will have to go first," he told Alex. "I have to take this."

Hopefully it would be good news—that the lab had

finished processing the evidence from the crime scene. Hopefully it wouldn't be news that another woman had been abducted...

REBECCA STARED AFTER Jared as he stepped outside. Her first thought was that his call was work related. Then another thought quickly chased that from her mind. What if it was personal? What if Jared had a girlfriend? Or fiancée? Or wife?

She'd never asked him. But if he'd been wearing a ring, she would have noticed. Not that all married men wore rings nowadays.

And it would be naive of her to think that he hadn't dated in the past six years. Even she'd gone on dates—hoping to find someone with whom she could share the life she'd built for her and Alex.

But none of those men had held her interest—because none of those men had been Jared. He was Alex's father; he was the man who should be part of the boy's life.

She'd been selfish to keep them apart. It had broken her heart to learn that Alex's friends hadn't believed he really had a father. She blinked hard, fighting back tears of regret and guilt.

"Mommy, can I hook you up to the lie detector?"

She was afraid of what he might ask her, so she stalled. "You have to take it out of the box first. And you should have Ja—your father—help you with that."

"He's probably gotta go chase a bad guy," Alex said. But instead of being resentful that his father might have to leave again so soon, he beamed with pride.

"He'll come back inside and let us know." If it was work calling him, she could find out another way. She picked up the remote and turned on the TV.

And Kyle Smith, with his glib grin, appeared on the

screen. If something had broken in the case, or the killer had abducted another girl, this reporter would know about it. So, albeit reluctantly, she turned up the volume. If whatever Smith was saying was too graphic for little ears, she would click the mute button.

The door creaked open as Jared stepped back inside, but she barely registered his return. Her attention was riveted on what Kyle Smith considered a news report.

"I have confirmation—" the man held up a birth certificate "—that Lexi Drummond's nephew is FBI profiler special agent Jared Bell's son. Agent Bell spent last night at the home of Rebecca Drummond and his son, Alex. Maybe if the profiler had focused more on his job than the first victim's sister, he would have caught the killer before now."

Her hand shaking as fury and embarrassment overwhelmed her, Rebecca struggled with the remote trying to shut it off. Jared's hand covered hers and his finger pushed hers down onto the button that mercifully shut off the *news* report. "I'm sorry," she murmured. "I didn't think just anyone could pull a birth certificate."

But she hadn't been able to bring herself to list her son's father as *unknown*. Because she'd known. Jared should have known, too.

She lowered her voice to a whisper. "I shouldn't have presumed to put your name down—"

He squeezed her hand. "I'm glad that you did. I would have been more upset if my name wasn't on it."

His hand was warm and strong, wrapped around hers. Her skin heated and tingled from his touch. It had been like that when they'd made love—his touch made her tingle. Made her hot...

Even after all these years, she still wanted him. And she found herself leaning closer.

Then Alex laughed.

She jerked back and turned toward her son. "What's so funny?"

"They're going to feel stupid tomorrow that they didn't believe me."

Jared chuckled.

Rebecca was not amused about her life being made so public. She glanced at the windows, wondering if Smith or other reporters lurked out there. A shadow passed in front of the glass. "You need to leave," she told Jared.

He shook his head. "After that I think it's more important I stay."

"You don't have to chase a bad guy?" Alex asked.

"Not tonight," Jared said. "My call was from another agent—letting me know about this *news* report." A muscle twitched along his jaw.

"Are you sure you shouldn't go chase bad guys tonight?" Rebecca asked with a meaningful stare, so that Jared would get the hint. She wanted him to leave.

But Jared was looking at the window, too, and reaching beneath his jacket.

She gasped. "Someone is out there?" She turned toward Alex. It wasn't just her life made so public; his had been, too. And that put her son in whatever danger she was in.

Somebody is watching you...

She shivered. "Alex, you need to go to your room."

He glanced up from his new toy. "Why—"

"Go." Jared said just the one word. He didn't shout it or say it with any particular emphasis. But Alex jumped up and rushed down the hall.

"You, too," he told Rebecca as he withdrew his gun.

But she didn't obey him like their son had. "This is my house..."

Jared ignored her as he moved quickly toward the door and jerked it open.

A scream caught in her throat as fear overwhelmed her. Jared hadn't had to chase down the bad guy. He had found them. Her sister's killer stood at her door.

Chapter Nine

"What the hell are you doing here?" Jared asked as he tightened his grip on his weapon.

Six years ago he'd thought Becca was wrong about this man. Jared hadn't believed Harris Mowery had murdered her sister. But he still hadn't liked the guy.

"You contacted me, Agent Bell," Mowery replied. He wore the same smug grin that Kyle Smith always wore. Both men were narcissists—concerned only with themselves and incapable of empathy. Both of these men fit the profile for the Bride Butcher. "You want to talk to me."

"At the Bureau office," Jared said. "Or I would have come to you." If he could have tracked down the man.

"Instead, I came to you." Harris's dark grin widened. He was all white teeth and shiny bald head. Even six years ago, his head had been shaved; he'd probably done it the moment his hair had begun to thin. He was the kind of man who would not tolerate imperfection—in himself or in others.

"How did you find me?" Jared asked. But he was more concerned that he'd found Becca and Alex.

"You're news, Agent Bell." He peered around Jared to where Becca was probably standing.

She should have left the room like their son had. Jared

blocked the doorway with his body, refusing to let the uninvited guest past him.

"You're both news, Rebecca," her almost-brother-in-law addressed her. "Congratulations."

She said nothing in return. She was probably either too angry or too scared to speak. She fully believed this man was a killer. Jared was definitely more suspicious of him than he'd previously been—especially after he'd worked up a more complete profile of the killer.

"That news report just ran," Jared pointed out. "You wouldn't have been able to get here so quickly unless…" Unless he'd been close. Unless he was the one watching Becca, as she'd been warned. But why would he have alerted her to his presence?

Just to toy with her? To scare her more?

"Kyle Smith called me," Harris admitted, "gave me a little advance report."

"You answered his call," Jared remarked. "You two must be close."

Harris sneered. "I'm not a fan of reporters. But Mr. Smith has proven to be most informative."

Jared had already been angry with Kyle Smith for invading Becca's privacy. Now he was furious and a curse slipped through his lips.

Harris chuckled. "He's not a fan of yours, either. He suggested I sue you for slander."

"I've never named you as a suspect," Jared said.

Harris tilted his head, and despite the grin on his face, his dark eyes were hard with resentment. "But you've questioned me and made the media aware that you have."

"Lexi was your fiancée."

Harris nodded. "Yes, she was."

But just like six years ago, the man wasn't exactly mourning her loss. Not like Becca had mourned her and continued to mourn her.

Jared blamed himself for that—because he hadn't given her closure.

"Have you reopened Alexandra's case again?" Harris asked.

"Lexi," Becca corrected him. Her voice was low but hard with hatred.

He ignored her, his focus on Jared now. "Is that why you left me a message that we needed to speak again?"

"I've never closed Lexi's case," Jared said.

Harris shrugged. "But you can't have any new leads in a case that old. You don't even have a body." He snorted disdainfully.

And Jared's fury built. He'd always understood why Becca hated this glib guy. He'd abused her sister. And instead of being upset or concerned when she'd gone missing, he'd been angry.

That anger was why Jared hadn't suspected him, though. If the man had killed her himself—or even hired someone to do it—he wouldn't have been furious that she was gone. He would have been happy.

Like he seemed now.

"I actually called to find out where you were the day Amy Wilcox went missing." He gave the exact date and time that Amy had been taken, kicking and screaming, from that bridal boutique dressing room.

And Harris's grin widened. "I was with Priscilla Stehouwer. We spent that weekend at a bed-and-breakfast in the country. I can give you her number." He glanced down at the gun Jared still held. "If you have a free hand…"

Jared was reluctant to reholster his gun. He couldn't risk Becca's and Alex's safety. Not if she was right about this man. "You can leave it on my voice mail," he said. "I already left you my number to call me back."

"Did you buy this alibi, too?" Becca asked him.

Now the man spared her a glance—one so hard and

hateful that Jared tightened his grasp on his weapon. "Of course not. Priscilla is my fiancée," he said.

Then maybe this alibi wouldn't be as ironclad as his had been for Lexi's disappearance. Jared definitely intended to question Priscilla Stehouwer. And maybe he would let it slip about those pictures they'd found in Lexi's journal.

"But I shouldn't need an alibi," Harris said. "I didn't even know Amy Wilcox."

"Lexi says differently," Becca said.

Harris looked at her again—with pity and disgust— as if he thought she was claiming to have had an actual conversation with her sister. "Alexandra is dead."

Her body had never been found, but Harris seemed awfully damn certain of that. Because he knew where her body was buried? Or just because he'd heard all the reports—that she couldn't have survived that much blood loss?

"She wrote it in her journal," Becca explained. "She said that you met Amy Wilcox and you didn't like her."

Harris shrugged. "She wrote a lot of stuff in that journal that wasn't true."

And if Jared told the fiancée about those photos, Harris would undoubtedly take Kyle Smith's advice and sue him for slander.

"It was the truth," Becca said. "But I wouldn't expect you to admit that—"

"Becca," Jared cautioned her. He didn't want her getting sued, either. Or worse...

He didn't like Harris Mowery showing up at her door. He didn't like it at all. "You need to leave," he told the man, and he stepped forward to usher him out.

But Mowery didn't step back. "So will you two be getting married now?"

Becca gasped, and Jared pushed, forcing the man

backward. But still Harris persisted, "Since you have a son together, you should."

Jared shoved him completely out the door.

But Harris yelled out, "And soon!"

Jared followed him out and pulled the door shut behind himself, so that Mowery couldn't talk to Becca anymore. "What the hell are you up to?" he demanded to know.

Harris shrugged. "I don't know what you mean, Agent Bell. Can't I just want Alexandra's sister to be happy?"

"If that were true, you wouldn't have showed up at her house, knowing the way she feels about you." Jared narrowed his eyes in a hard stare. "It's you, isn't it?"

Harris finally stepped back voluntarily from the front door and the illuminating glow of the porch light. He walked down the driveway toward his car and the darkness. "You already ruled me out as a suspect, Agent Bell," he reminded him. "You said so yourself."

Jared followed him and clarified. "That was in Lexi's murder." And maybe he'd done that too quickly. He intended to recheck that first alibi and definitely the one for Amy Wilcox's murder.

"One serial killer murdered all those women," Harris said. "That's something else you've always stated—at least according to Kyle Smith."

Damn Kyle Smith. That was someone else Jared intended to interrogate. Why the hell had the reporter given this man Becca and Alex's address?

"You're the one," Jared repeated and then continued, "who's been threatening Becca."

"Someone's been threatening Rebecca?" Harris sounded surprised, or maybe he was just a better actor than Jared had realized. "Why would someone do that? Unless…"

Jared waited—as the man wanted him to—in the dark as night began to fall.

Harris clicked the lock on his rental car and opened the driver's door, spilling light onto the driveway. "Maybe you two are already engaged...?"

Jared shook his head. "I haven't seen Becca in years."

"She never told you she had your son?" Harris shook his head. "Maybe she's more like her sister than I realized. Alexandra had her secrets, too."

"Yes, she did," Jared agreed. She should have told her family that Harris was abusing her. "Remember to text me your fiancée's phone number." He didn't give a damn if the guy sued; he was going to warn the woman.

And the minute Harris drove away, Jared called back the protection duty he'd released when he'd arrived. He needed protection on Becca and Alex 24/7—even when he was around them. And still he worried that it might not be enough to keep them safe.

HER HANDS SHAKING, Rebecca pulled the blankets over her sleeping son. He'd fallen asleep in his bed even though there'd been a killer in their house. He obviously felt so safe that he slept peacefully.

Rebecca would never feel safe again. She shivered and considered crawling into bed with her son—to hold him. But he didn't need comfort. She needed comfort.

And a gun. The front door creaked open again, unsettling her. But instead of hiding in her son's room, she hurried down the hall to the living room. Jared stood inside. Alone.

"Is he gone?" she asked.

"Yes."

"But you can't guarantee that he won't come back," she said. She couldn't stay here. "Alex and I will have to leave."

"I called back the protection detail," he said. "You'll be safe."

She would feel safer if he stayed, too. But she'd already told him he couldn't spend the night. "Alex fell asleep," she told him.

He glanced down at the game their son had left on the floor. "He seemed so excited about his present."

"He was. He is," she assured him. "But he's had a lot of excitement today. It must have exhausted him." She glanced down at the gift Jared had chosen for their son. "Is that really a toy?"

"I didn't steal it from the Bureau," he said, his lips curving into a slight smile.

"Too bad," she said. "If it was real, we could have hooked Harris up to it." Just saying the man's name brought back all her fear and anger and frustration. And as the emotions overwhelmed her, tears stung her eyes, and she began to tremble.

Instead of offering her the comfort he once had, Jared walked back toward the door. He was leaving?

Of course she'd told him he couldn't stay, but that had been before her sister's killer had paid her a visit— taunting her to get engaged. So he could kill her like he had Lexi, like he had all those other women.

Instead of opening the door, Jared turned the dead bolt. "The protection detail is out there," he said. "But I'm still not leaving."

She uttered a sigh—of relief. Then she was in his arms. She wasn't sure which one of them had moved— him or her. But she clung to him.

One of his hands was on her back, holding her to him. The other was in her hair. He tipped her head back, and then his mouth covered hers. This was no tentative kiss. But even their first kiss hadn't been tentative. It had been like this one—explosive: making her heart beat fast and erratically. Making her head light and her body heat and tingle.

Nobody had ever kissed her like Jared did—passionately, thoroughly. And nobody had ever made her feel like Jared did—passionate and desperate.

Desperate for his kisses. Desperate for his love. But she'd never had his love. And now she didn't even have his kisses as he pulled back.

"I'm sorry," he said between pants for breath. "I—I didn't mean to do that…"

She was glad that he had. She'd been longing for his kiss since he'd first showed up at her house.

"I only meant to hold you," he said, "to comfort you. But every time I touch you, I lose control."

"That comforts me," she said. To know she wasn't the only one feeling that overwhelming attraction and desire. Especially now. After knowing what she'd kept from him—their son—he should have been disgusted with her.

Instead, his fingers stroked along her cheek, and he stared deeply into her eyes. "You are so beautiful…"

Lexi had been the beautiful one. The vivacious one. Rebecca had been the smart one. The hardworking one. But Jared made her feel beautiful; he had always made her feel beautiful—even when grief had ravaged her. He'd helped her find the beauty in life. Then he'd given her the most beautiful gift of all: Alex.

"You should hate me," she said, "for keeping our son a secret from you."

"I should," he agreed, but his fingers continued to stroke along her cheek. Then his thumb moved across her lower lip—back and forth. "But I can't."

"I'm sorry," she murmured.

"Me, too." Then he replaced his thumb with his lips and kissed her again.

And again—until her knees weakened. Before her legs could buckle beneath her, he swung her up in his arms and carried her down the hall to her bedroom. He laid her on her bed and stood over her, passion glinting in his eyes. "Do you still want me to leave?"

She shook her head. Then she reached out for him—for the buckle of his belt and unclasped it. His hands covered hers, stopping her before she could reach for the zipper of his pants. "Are you sure?" he asked.

His erection pressed against the zipper. He wanted her. Even though he should be furious with her, he wanted her. And Rebecca had never stopped wanting him. Six years. It had been too long.

"Very sure," she replied.

And then he joined her in the bed, his hard body pressing hers into the mattress. His mouth covered hers, kissing her deeply.

She wanted more than kisses, though. She tugged his shirt free of his loosened pants. Then she reached for the buttons running down his chest and abdomen. As she undid each one, she revealed an inch of skin and muscle. When his shirt was open, she pressed kisses to his chest.

He groaned. And she smiled, pleased that she affected him as much as he affected her. But her kisses must have snapped his control because he moved quickly then, removing clothes from both their bodies until they were naked—their skin flushed with desire.

He pushed her back against the pillows, and he kissed her everywhere. Her neck, her shoulder, her elbow...and each fingertip.

She sighed with pleasure. But then he kissed other places. Her breasts, her abdomen and lower...

Her breath caught as pressure wound tightly inside her. She wanted more. Needed more.

And he gave her more. She pressed her hand over her mouth, muffling a cry as pleasure overwhelmed her. Then she reached for him, wanting to please him with her mouth. He groaned again as if he were in pain. And he rolled, pinning her playfully beneath him. He teased her some more—with his lips and his fingers.

She squirmed and shifted against the mattress. "Jared, please…"

"I am going to please you," he promised.

She arched and rubbed her hips against his. And tangled her legs with his. Then she kissed his shoulder and the bulging muscle in his arm. And his chest again.

"Becca…"

She didn't correct him. She would rather be Becca than Rebecca.

Then he parted her legs and joined their bodies. She was ready for him, but still she had to shift, had to arch, to take him deeper. But he moved, too, pulling out before thrusting deep again.

She bit her lip to hold in a cry of pleasure. It felt so perfect. So right. She clung to him, meeting his thrusts, moving with him until the pressure that had built inside her, that unbearable pressure, burst. She pressed her lips against his shoulder to hold in a scream of ecstasy.

Then he tensed before his body shuddered, as he joined her in release. His skin damp against hers, he clutched her closely in his arms. "That was…"

As wonderful as it had always been between them. But she waited for him to call it something else. A mistake. That was what he'd thought the last time they'd become lovers, that he'd made a mistake.

But he said nothing more. He just held her tightly, so tightly that she felt safe enough to fall asleep. But she wasn't surprised when, hours later, she awoke alone. Her sheets tangled, but empty.

Then she heard the rumble of a deep voice. He wasn't gone. He hadn't deserted and rejected her as he had six years ago. At least not yet…

Then she heard the high-pitched squeal of Alex's laughter. And she knew why Jared had stayed. For their son.

She dressed quickly and joined them in the living room. Father tickled son as they sat on the carpet, the lie detector hooked to the little boy. It looked like a blood pressure cuff hooked to an Etch A Sketch with a bunch of squiggled lines on it.

"You are lying," Jared said. "You're definitely ticklish."

"Did the test say I'm lying?" Alex asked between giggles.

"I don't think he needed the test to determine that," Rebecca said. "You're definitely ticklish."

"Mommy's up," Alex said. "It's her turn now."

Even if the test was just a toy, she didn't want to be hooked up to it. But she couldn't tell her son no. So she let him strap the cuff to her arm.

"So, Mommy," Alex said, "do you ever swear?"

She groaned. "Yes…"

He giggled again. "Are you the tooth fairy?"

"Alex!"

"Santa Claus?"

She reached out and began to tickle him. He squirmed and protested. "No, you have to answer the questions yes or no."

"No, no," she said and hoped the machine wasn't real.

Alex squinted at the screen and shrugged. "I don't know. Daddy, you ask her a question."

She sucked in a breath—afraid of what he might ask her. Afraid of even looking at him. But he moved closer, so that he could see the screen her son studied. And she breathed in the scent of him—some intoxicating combination of soap and coffee and musk. He must have used her shower and made coffee again. She looked up and lost herself in his amber-eyed gaze.

"What do you want to ask her, Daddy?"

He stared at her a moment, as if considering. And she saw that he had many questions. But she never guessed what he would ask her. "Will you go to a wedding with me?"

Chapter Ten

Why had he asked Becca to Dalton Reyes's wedding? And why, in the days since he'd asked, hadn't he rescinded the invitation? It was too dangerous. But then even staying in her own home was too dangerous—with Kyle Smith broadcasting her address to suspects. So he'd convinced her and Alex to stay with him—at his condo in Chicago—instead of in their home. Surprisingly, Becca had readily agreed. But then he doubted she would ever feel safe in her house again now that Harris Mowery knew where she lived.

"Why?" he asked the reporter.

"Isn't that what I should be asking you?" Kyle replied as he settled onto a chair across the conference table from Jared. "Why did you ask me to come to the Bureau office? You finally realized you will need my help solving your case, Special Agent Bell?"

Jared patted the folder that lay on the table between them. "It seems you wanted to be an FBI agent yourself."

Kyle's snide grin slid away, and he stared at the folder as if wanting to grab for it. "You had me investigated?"

Jared plastered on his own smug grin and replied, "It only seemed fair since you've been investigating me."

"Ouch," Kyle said and pressed a hand to his chest as if Jared had stabbed him. "So instead of focusing on finding the serial killer who's eluded you for six years, you've wasted time going after the reporter who revealed your dirty little secret."

Alex was not a dirty little secret. He was an amazing kid. A wonderful gift. Jared curled the hand on the folder into a fist that he wanted to swing hard into the reporter's face.

Smith's superior grin had returned. "Sounds like I have my next exposé…"

"And instead of covering the real story—about the murders—you're creating a story about me," Jared said. "Is that because you're jealous that I have the job you really wanted?"

Kyle snorted. "I'm sure I make more money than you do, Agent Bell. And I'm definitely better known."

"Seems like your career really didn't take off until you covered Lexi Drummond's disappearance."

"Murder," Kyle corrected him with the same certainty as when Harris Mowery had said it.

Sure, there had been too much blood found for her to have survived her wounds. But that information hadn't been released to the media—until Kyle had reported it. At the time Jared had thought that the reporter must have bought the information off someone in the crime lab or maybe even within the Bureau.

Now he considered that there was another way that Kyle Smith could have known Lexi was dead—because he'd murdered her. As a profiler, Jared knew that killers liked to make themselves part of the investigation—by helping search for the victims or providing false witness. No one had made himself more a part of the investigation than Kyle Smith.

Like men who failed to make the fire department became arsonists, maybe men that failed to make the Bureau became serial killers. Trying to prove themselves better than the men they hadn't been able to become…

"You're awfully certain Lexi Drummond is dead."

Kyle snorted. "So are you—even though you failed to find a body. No wonder Rebecca Drummond never told you she had your son." The man laughed. "And it wasn't like you would ever figure it out for yourself…"

Jared could have pointed out all the killers he'd caught over his career. So many, many killers who were behind bars or dead because of him. But Kyle Smith wanted him to be defensive, so then he'd know that his barbs had struck their target. Jared wouldn't give the petty man that satisfaction.

"You're a great investigator," he falsely flattered the man. Anybody could order a copy of a birth certificate nowadays—thanks to the internet. "So why haven't you found Lexi's body?"

Kyle tensed. "What do you mean?"

"You've been working this case as long as I have," Jared pointed out. "But you don't seem to care about the victims…" Only one other person didn't care—the killer. The Butcher was a sociopath with no capacity for empathy for the victim or the families he devastated when he took away their loved ones. And he was beginning to think Kyle Smith was a sociopath, too. Was he the killer? He certainly fit most of the profile Jared had formed.

"You don't even seem to care about the killer," Jared remarked. "But then I guess that you really don't want him caught."

Kyle's Adam's apple bobbed as he swallowed convulsively. "Why would you say that?"

Jared shrugged. "A couple of reasons…" One was that he was the killer. "*He* made your career. Without him—"

"I would still have a career," Kyle said as he jumped up from the table.

Jared tilted his head, then shook it. "I'm not so sure about that…"

When he caught the killer, Kyle Smith might be behind bars. He grinned at the thought of slamming the cell door shut on the slimy reporter.

"I'm leaving," Kyle announced but he hesitated, as if not sure he was really free to go.

"I'm not done with you yet," Jared said. "I have many more questions for you. I want to know if you knew any of the victims and if you had an alibi for each of the abductions."

Kyle dropped heavily back onto the chair. "You're treating me like a suspect?"

"Yes."

"Why? Is this because I told the world you took advantage of a victim's grieving sister?" the reporter fired the questions at him. "Is this your form of revenge?"

Jared gave him a pitying grin. "You really wouldn't have made it as an agent."

"You—"

Jared held up a hand to stop the insults. "If you've taken any criminal psychology courses, you would know that the perp often makes himself part of the investigation."

"I've just been doing my job," Kyle protested.

"Giving Rebecca Drummond's address to Harris Mowery? That was part of your job?"

The man's face flushed an even darker shade than his artificial tan. "I didn't do that."

Jared didn't believe him.

"He probably found it the same way I did—checking property tax records."

Maybe he could have—maybe he'd already been watching her, like the caller had warned Rebecca.

"So that's what this is about," Kyle mused. "Because

you think I gave out her address to the man she swears killed her sister."

"Why would you do something like that?" Jared asked. "Why would you report about *her* life—about *my* life?"

Kyle offered that snide grin again. "It's not personal, Agent Bell."

But it felt very personal. Was there some reason that Kyle didn't like him or Becca? Or was his animosity only because Jared had the job Kyle had wanted? The man was petty. But was he that petty?

Or was he a killer?

Jared slid a legal pad and a pen across the table. "Start recounting your whereabouts during the time of every abduction," he ordered. "And tell me if you have any personal connection to any of the victims."

Then he patted the folder he'd already compiled. "And then we'll see if your answers match mine."

Kyle picked up the pen with a shaking hand. Either he was nervous because he had something to hide, or he was angry over becoming a suspect. Resentment hardened his eyes. The man was going to hate Jared more than he already did.

So he would probably retaliate again. What form would that retaliation take? More public humiliation for him and Becca? Or something even more personal?

BECCA HAD TAKEN Alex out of school and had taken a leave from work. Hell, what she'd really taken was a leave of her senses.

Moving in with Jared in Chicago? That was more frightening than Harris Mowery knowing where she lived—because she was afraid she was falling for Jared again. Or maybe she'd never stopped…

But at least he would keep their son safe. Jared had even enrolled Alex in a new school—the one where he'd gone, for gifted children. Alex loved it; he was actually challenged. Becca wasn't sure, even if Harris was finally arrested, that she would go back to Wisconsin.

Maybe she needed to look for a job in the city—like she'd always wanted. But first, she had to find a dress for the wedding to which Jared had invited her.

"This is my wife's favorite store," Agent Blaine Campbell said as he held open the door to a little dress boutique squeezed in between a bank and bakery.

"You really didn't need to come with me," Rebecca said. "I could have found it on my own." And she felt a little awkward shopping with the burly blond lawman. She'd never even gone shopping with Jared.

"Jared doesn't want you going anywhere alone," Blaine told her. Needlessly.

She was already aware that Jared didn't want her having a minute alone—in case someone might threaten her again.

"He's wasting Bureau resources protecting me," she said. When those resources would be better used trying to find Amy Wilcox's killer.

"You've been threatened," Blaine said. "And he's not really using Bureau resources. I'm not on the clock right now."

"Then why...?"

"I'm a friend of Jared's."

"Like Dalton Reyes?" That was whose wedding Jared had invited her to.

Blaine chuckled. "Not that close. I'm new to the Bureau, but I got to know Jared when he was helping protect the bride-to-be for Dalton."

"That's who he got hurt protecting?"

Blaine nodded. "Probably why Dalton asked Jared to be his best man."

"Jared is best man at this wedding?"

Blaine chuckled again. "Yes, he is."

That put more pressure on her finding a nice dress. Her wardrobe consisted of only casual clothes, business casual and play clothes. Nothing suitable for a wedding at all. That was why she'd had to go shopping. But now she would be attending this wedding on the arm of the best man.

So she focused on the racks of dresses, trying to find the perfect dress—the dress that would make Jared proud to call her his date.

But she was more than a date. She was the mother of his child. And the woman who'd been sharing his bed since he'd shared hers the night that Harris Mowery had showed up at her door.

What were they doing? What the hell was she doing—risking her heart on a man who'd already broken it once?

"I'm actually surprised Jared agreed to be his best man," Blaine continued, "since he thinks the wedding is such a bad idea."

"He does?" she asked. "Doesn't he like the bride?"

"He likes Elizabeth," Blaine said. "We all do. She's an incredibly strong woman. But Jared's worried that the Butcher is going to go after her."

Rebecca shuddered. "Isn't her fiancé worried, too?"

"Dalton is too impatient to wait to make Elizabeth his bride," he said. "And he's found a very safe place for them to get married. With all the bodyguards and FBI agents in attendance, it'll be safe. Jared must have changed his mind about it, too."

"Because he agreed to be best man?"

"Because he invited you."

Jared wanted to keep her safe. She knew that, but why? Just because it was his job? Because she was the mother of his son? Or because he had feelings for her, too?

She pulled a blue dress from the rack and a peach-colored one. But the peach would wash out her complexion, so she moved to put it back.

"Wait," Blaine said. "That would look good on Maggie."

Rebecca smiled over the man's obvious love for his wife. Then her smile slid away as a pang of jealousy struck her heart. She wished Jared felt that way about her.

"You should take a picture of it and send it to her," Rebecca suggested. "And I'll try this one on." She glanced at her watch. Alex's school wouldn't be done for a while. She'd rather be working than shopping. She would definitely need to check with the local hospitals for any openings for a physician's assistant. But in the meantime, she grabbed a couple more dresses from the rack to try on; shopping would kill some time today.

Blaine followed her to the dressing room. But one of the retail clerks hurried over to stop him. "Sir, you can't go into the dressing rooms!"

The woman was in her fifties with frosted hair and a frosted glare. She studied Blaine's hand and then glanced at Rebecca's bare one. Rebecca's face heated with embarrassment over what the disapproving clerk obviously thought. Blaine wore a wedding ring, and she didn't.

He flashed his badge. "I need to check out the dressing room and make sure no one's back there."

"There is no one back there," the woman haughtily told him.

"I need to check it out myself," he insisted and added beneath his breath, "or Jared will kill me.

"I'll look and leave," he promised her.

She sniffed with disdain but allowed him to look. "It's safe," he told Rebecca.

"Of course it is," the woman said. She took the dresses

from Rebecca and led her back to one of the rooms. "Do you need any help?"

"No," Rebecca replied. What she really needed was to be alone. If Jared wasn't with her, someone else was—watching and protecting her. She needed a moment to breathe without anyone worrying about her safety.

So she took her time trying on the dresses. The ones she'd grabbed at the last minute weren't flattering. The A-frame waistline of the first made her look like she was expecting again. She tensed for a moment. But then shook her head. She couldn't be. And if she was, she wouldn't be showing yet.

She unzipped that one and shimmied into another. It was a pale cream. Too close to white to wear to a wedding. She was reaching for the zipper when she heard something.

Hadn't Blaine assured her that the dressing rooms were empty? Had he let someone else into them? Maybe the judgmental clerk had insisted on checking on her.

She drew in a breath, bracing herself for no longer being alone. She'd only wanted a few minutes to herself. But then the lights blinked off, plunging the dressing room into total darkness. With no windows in the back of the store, the blackness was all-enveloping.

Was this how Lexi had been grabbed from the bridal boutique? Had someone shut off the lights and attacked her in the dark?

She parted her lips to utter a scream for Blaine, but a hand clamped over her mouth. And a familiar low and raspy voice whispered in her ear, "Look how easily I got to you."

Oh, God. This wasn't just another of those eerie warnings. This was it—her abduction. But she wouldn't go anywhere without one hell of a fight. So she kicked her legs and swung her fists as she fought for her life. For her son who needed his mother.

For Jared…

She couldn't leave them like Lexi had left her. Forever.

Chapter Eleven

The interview with Kyle Smith had been an exercise in frustration and probably futility. The man hadn't been able to readily supply alibis—which probably meant he had no reason for any. Most people didn't remember exactly where they were and who they were with a week ago, let alone years before. Kyle had remembered only his alibi for Amy Wilcox's abduction. But he hadn't remembered any for the others. He hadn't even remembered the other victims' names but for Lexi.

Natalie Gilsen, Madison Kincaid, Heather Foster, Tasha Taylor and Eden LeValley had been forgotten as far as Kyle Smith was concerned. Jared hadn't forgotten them—hadn't forgotten how he'd failed them. If he'd caught Lexi's killer—like he'd promised Becca—all those other women would have lived. They would have married their grooms and probably been raising kids by now.

But just because Kyle Smith hadn't remembered the other women's names didn't mean he hadn't killed them. Jared passed the folder over to another agent. "I've started compiling information on Kyle Smith. I need you to delve more thoroughly into his past and any connection he might have to the victims. Also check to see if he was ever jilted—left at the altar or broken engagement."

The younger agent widened her eyes. "You think *Kyle Smith* could be the Butcher?"

Jared nearly laughed. The young woman obviously had a crush on the obnoxious reporter. "It wouldn't break my heart if he was."

"Oh," she said with a nod. "I saw that report he did about you."

"But Agent Bell would never be unprofessional enough to use the Bureau for revenge," a deep voice said.

Jared turned toward his boss. Despite it being several years since he'd done any fieldwork, Chief Special Agent Lynch still moved with surprising silence. He'd easily snuck up behind Jared in the hall. But maybe he wouldn't have snuck up so easily if Jared hadn't been so tired. His nights weren't sleepless because of protection duty, though, but because Becca shared his bed. Fortunately, his apartment was in a high-security building. Harris Mowery or whoever the Butcher really was wouldn't get to her and Alex there.

But Jared didn't want her with him just for her and Alex's protection. He wanted Becca in every way...

With only a meaningful glance, Chief Lynch sent the young agent running for her desk. That was why he was in charge. Jared braced himself. Not that the chief hadn't already reprimanded him for crossing the line with a victim's family member. He'd even threatened to take him off the case. That was why Jared had had to take the call outside Becca's house the night his boss had phoned—the same night Harris Mowery had showed up at her door.

The same night Jared had spent crossing the line again—in Becca's bed.

"I'm not," Jared said, "using the Bureau for revenge."

Lynch nodded and agreed. "Smith is a viable suspect. A national network didn't pick him up until he covered Lexi Drummond's murder."

So he'd used Becca's sister's murder to further his career. "I'm going to try to find a link between them." Or between Smith and Harris Mowery. Why had he given the man Becca's address? He'd claimed he hadn't, but Jared had learned to believe nothing a suspect said.

His cell phone vibrated in his pocket. "Excuse me, sir…" He needed to at least check and see who was calling. He pulled out the phone. After recognizing the number on the caller ID, he fumbled to answer it. "It's Alex's school. Hello, this is Jared Bell."

"Mr. Bell, this is Julie VanManen from Saint Agnes School for Gifted Children."

Why was the principal calling? He couldn't imagine Alex getting into trouble. Maybe out of boredom in a regular classroom. But he loved his new school. "Is everything okay, Ms. VanManen?"

"I hope so," she replied. "No one has arrived to pick up your son yet."

Jared's blood chilled. Becca had never been late to pick up Alex during the week in which they'd been staying with him. "I—I'll come right away."

Alex was probably nervous that no one had picked him up. And Jared was scared to death that no one had. His hand shaking, he punched in the number for Blaine Campbell. Even though Special Agent Campbell worked the bank robbery division, his true specialty was protecting women. He had that white knight gene—the one that made him the protector of every damsel in distress.

Not that Jared had considered Becca a damsel in distress. He'd had to insist on the protection detail. She'd thought he was overreacting—until Harris Mowery had showed up at her door.

Blaine's phone went directly to voice mail. He tried Becca's even though he suspected she had shut it off to avoid any more ominous calls. It went straight to voice mail, too. Jared cursed.

"I'll pick up your son," Chief Lynch offered. "You find Agent Campbell."

Jared hesitated a moment.

"I will protect your son," Lynch vowed.

Jared wasn't worried about him protecting Alex. He was worried about him scaring the crap out of him. The guy was intimidating to special agents who'd faced down death and endured torture.

Lynch chuckled, and suddenly he looked twenty years younger. "I am a father, too, you know."

Jared had had no idea.

"I know how to handle kids."

Jared nodded acceptance as he started walking toward the elevator. "I'll call the school and let them know you have my permission to get Alex." He pounded the down button for the elevators, impatient for the car to arrive. If he wasn't on the tenth floor, he would have taken the stairs. Maybe he still should...

But he could hear the car coming, rattling in the shaft as it rose. He punched in Blaine's phone number again. Where the hell was he? Where the hell was Becca?

His guts tightened with dread and fear. She couldn't be like those other women—she couldn't be missing. Why would the killer have abducted her? She wasn't engaged.

But he'd thought about it—had thought about how nice it was having Becca and Alex living with him. He'd thought about how amazing it was sleeping next to her, his arms wrapped tightly around her warm, soft body.

Had just thinking it endangered her?

"ARE YOU SURE you're okay?" Blaine asked, his voice deep with concern and guilt.

Rebecca shook her head and winced as pain radiated throughout her skull.

"I should have taken you to the hospital," Blaine said. He had brought her back to Jared's apartment instead. He led her over to one of the leather couches in the living room.

She was still shaking from the close call she'd had, so she dropped onto the closest couch. The leather shifted beneath her. Alex always giggled when the leather creaked and squeaked beneath him.

"Alex!" she said. "We forgot to pick up Alex!"

Blaine's face paled. But she didn't know if it was because he'd forgotten the boy, too. Or if it was because the apartment door rattled as someone turned the knob.

Blaine drew his weapon and pointed the barrel toward the door. "Who's there?"

"It's me," Jared said as he thrust open the door and hurried inside the apartment.

"Did you pick up Alex?" The school would have called him when she hadn't showed. Wouldn't they? He'd given his name and his cell phone number.

"The chief is picking him up," Jared replied as he dropped onto his knees in front of her. "Are you okay?"

"Are you?" Blaine asked. "You just said the chief is playing nanny."

Rebecca's stomach lurched. Alex was usually shy around strangers, especially men. And from Blaine's tone, she discerned the chief wasn't exactly warm and fuzzy. "We should go get him."

"Chief Lynch will bring Alex here," Jared said. "Why didn't you two pick him up? What happened?" He turned toward Blaine and glared at his friend. "Why didn't you pick up your damn phone?"

Blaine patted his pocket. "I may have dropped my phone back at the boutique."

"What the hell happened?" Jared asked again. He turned back to her. "And what the hell were you doing at a boutique?"

"I needed a dress for Dalton Reyes's wedding," Rebecca explained. "It was a dress boutique." She knew what he was thinking—what he was worrying about. "Not a bridal boutique."

But still, someone had attacked her in the dressing room. Or had she attacked him? She touched the back of her head and winced again.

"You're hurt," he said. And his fingers replaced hers, rubbing over the bump beneath her hair.

Despite her fear and shock, she reacted to his touch—to his fingers in her hair. And his closeness...

He was so close that she could feel his breath on her face. She could see the muscle twitch in his cheek from his tightly clenched jaw. He was so handsome.

Would this attraction ever lessen? Would her skin ever stop tingling when he touched her?

"It's just a bump," she assured him.

"You could have a concussion," he said.

She shook her head. "I never blacked out." Although she had seen stars for a moment. "And I'm not nauseous. It's not a concussion."

"I tried to take her to the hospital," Blaine said. "But she refused."

"Because I know it's not a concussion." She'd treated enough head injuries in the ER that she would have recognized had it been a concussion.

Jared turned toward his friend again and studied him through narrowed eyes. "You were supposed to protect her. How did she get hurt?"

Blaine shook his head. "I don't know how it happened. I checked the dressing room before I let her go back. There was nobody back there."

Jared cursed, but then he turned back to her. "Somebody tried grabbing you in the dressing room?"

"Somebody grabbed me," Rebecca replied.

Jared's neck swiveled toward Blaine again. "How? Where were you?"

"He couldn't go into the dressing room with me," she said. "And he checked it before I went inside."

"Nobody was back there," Blaine reiterated.

"So what happened?"

"I heard something," she said. "I thought it was just the clerk coming back. Then the lights went out." Her voice cracked as, in her mind, she returned to the dressing room and that moment of sheer terror when she'd thought the Butcher was going to abduct her. "And someone grabbed me, pressing a hand over my mouth so I couldn't scream."

She hadn't been able to call out for help.

"The power had gone off in the whole store," Blaine said. "But just in the store. There were lights on across the street."

"So you knew something was up and got to her in time?"

Blaine regretfully shook his head. "No, she fought off the attacker herself. I never even got a look at him. That's why I better get back down to the store. I'll get the security footage from all the cameras in the area." He patted his empty pocket. "I also have to find my phone."

The minute the door closed behind Agent Campbell, Jared focused on Rebecca again. His hand gently cupped her face. Were his hands shaking slightly? Was he that upset?

"Are you really all right?" he asked. And he stared intently into her eyes—as if he could see what she had seen—what she had endured.

She wasn't all right. She was shaking—scared and mad. But she nodded and lied. "I'm fine."

"Did you see anything?" Jared asked. "Anything that might help us identify him?"

"It was too dark," she said. "So dark that I couldn't see anything at all." And that was the reason for most of her frustration. She had been so close...but she had learned nothing.

"Did you notice anything else at all?" he asked. "A smell? His height? His build?"

She furrowed her brow as she realized something. "I don't think he was that tall. I head-butted him to get away. That's how I got the bump on the back of my head."

"And if he was that much taller than you, you wouldn't have hit his head," Jared said.

But then she shrugged. "I don't know, though. He was leaning down and whispering..."

"Did you recognize his voice?" he asked.

"I think it was the person who's been calling me," she said. That must have been why the voice had seemed familiar.

"It didn't sound like anyone else you've heard?" Jared persisted.

He obviously had a suspect in mind. For the Butcher...

She shook her head then, flinched as the throbbing intensified to pain.

"We can't risk your safety again," Jared said. "We're going to have to move you to a safe house—somewhere nobody can get to you—until the killer is caught."

"No," she protested as panic pressed on her lungs, stealing away her breath. She'd already given up her home—her job, her routine. "I can't be locked up for six years."

Jared flinched now.

"I'm sorry," she said. He already blamed himself for all the murders since Lexi's; she shouldn't have added to his guilt. "I'm sorry. I know you're only trying to protect me."

She just wished she knew why. Because he was a lawman? Because of Alex? Or because he loved her?

"You're in danger," he said.

"That's what he said," she shared. "When he grabbed me, he said, 'Look how easily I got to you.'"

Jared cursed.

"Then he said, 'You're in danger. You have to be more careful.'" And then she realized why she'd gotten away from him so easily. "It's not him…"

Jared uttered a ragged sigh of relief. "You wouldn't have gotten away if it was him," he agreed. "It wasn't the Butcher."

"Then who is it?" she wondered. "Who keeps calling me and warning me to be careful?"

Jared tensed again. "I hope it's not him. But it has to be. And he let you get away because he's just toying with you—scaring you for his entertainment."

Like Harris Mowery showing up at her house. She was right about him; she had to be right about him killing Lexi.

"Then why did he let me go?" She wasn't that strong. She wouldn't have broken away from him if he'd really intended to abduct her.

"Because you're not getting married…"

Apparently, Jared hadn't been tempted to ask her. He hadn't loved her six years ago. And he didn't love her now. Maybe that was a good thing—because until the killer was caught, she would never be able to get engaged. Because the minute she had a ring on her finger, she would be dead.

Chapter Twelve

Jared's hands shook as he straightened his bow tie, and sweat beaded on his upper lip. He couldn't breathe—in the windowless groom's dressing room. And worse yet, he couldn't see. He couldn't see outside the room to make sure that Becca and Alex were safe.

He wasn't the only nervous man in the groom's dressing room. Dalton Reyes's usual cocky nonchalance was gone. His hands shaking, he fumbled with his bow tie and cursed.

"Should've got a damn clip-on," he grumbled.

Jared smacked his hands away and tied the bow. "And that's why you picked me for best man."

"Actually, I had no idea if you knew how to tie a bow tie," Dalton said.

"So why'd you pick him?" Nicholas Rus asked as he joined them in the groom's room. "I didn't even know you two knew each other."

"He got his brains scrambled protecting my fiancée—" Dalton's voice cracked with emotion "—my bride—and her daughter. So I figured I owed him."

Jared snorted in amusement. That was why he hadn't been able to say no to Reyes. He'd never had a friend like him. Usually, his friends were as serious and no-nonsense as he was—like Nicholas Rus.

While Reyes made Jared feel like he'd finally gotten invited to eat at the cool kids' table, he appreciated Nicholas's seriousness. Especially now.

"Are you sure this chapel is safe?" Jared asked him.

Nick grinned. "Absolutely safe. All of the guests are FBI agents."

Not all of the guests. Becca was out there—along with Alex. Fortunately, Alex had insisted on sitting with his new best friend—Chief Lynch. While Lynch hadn't been in the field for a while, Jared had no doubt the man could still handle himself—and an inquisitive little boy.

"And bodyguards are protecting the perimeter," Rus added.

Jared and Reyes shared a glance; apparently they'd both noticed the same thing about those guards.

"How come they all look like you?" Reyes asked. "Did River City have you cloned?"

A muscle twitched along Rus's jaw. "I reconnected with some family."

"I didn't know you had siblings," Jared said. And they'd lived together for a few years in Chicago.

"Neither did I," Rus replied.

Knuckles rapped against the door of the groom's dressing room. "Is Reyes ready?" a deep voice called through the door. Special Agent Ash Stryker probably should have been Reyes's best man because Reyes had been his. "Or did he go out the window?"

"There is no window," Jared called back.

"As I understand it, a groom has disappeared from this room before," Rus said.

"I'm here." Dalton chuckled and opened the door to Ash. "I was more nervous at your wedding. I have no doubts about marrying my bride."

He was nervous, though. Moments later, Jared, standing next to him at the front of the church, noticed the tension in the other man. He stood stiffly, barely breathing, until a vision in white appeared at the back of the church. Then he released the breath he'd been holding.

And Jared released the breath he hadn't realized he'd been holding, too. He'd been so worried that the Butcher would try for Elizabeth—just to prove that she wouldn't have been able to get away from him.

But the fitting for her wedding dress—at this very chapel—had passed without incident. Maybe the bodyguards and agents had proved too daunting for the Butcher. He hadn't dared try for Elizabeth because the risk of getting caught had been too great. Or he was focused on another target...

Becca.

Despite all the guests, Jared easily found her in the church. She, Alex and the chief sat a few rows back on the groom's side of the aisle. Sunlight shone through the stained-glass windows, making her blond hair shimmer like crystals. Even after being attacked in the dressing room at the boutique, she had bought a dress for the wedding.

She'd wanted to attend. But he never should have asked her. He should have locked her away in some safe house just as he'd threatened. But she was right; she couldn't hide until he caught the killer.

He had no new leads. No evidence tied Kyle Smith or Harris Mowery to any of the murders. That didn't mean that it didn't exist, just that he hadn't found it yet. He needed to find it. He needed to put this killer away.

Or he could never ask Becca to be his bride. He imagined her standing in front of him—a vision in white—her hands in his as they said their vows. But until the Butcher was caught, marrying her was just a daydream.

If he even asked her to marry him, she would definitely be attacked, and the killer wouldn't let her get away from him again. The Butcher would make certain she died before she could ever marry him.

REBECCA HAD NEVER felt so safe—with all the federal agents and bodyguards in and around the Little White Wedding Chapel. She'd also never felt as envious. As she waited in the receiving line in the foyer, she watched the bride and groom. While they hugged or shook hands with guests, they leaned against each other—constantly touching, always aware of each other. And so in love that it radiated from them like the sun shining through the stained-glass windows.

She probably looked at Jared the way the bride was looking at her groom; her gaze full of adoration. From the moment Jared had stepped out of the groom's dressing room, looking so damn handsome and debonair in that black tuxedo, Becca had been staring at him with love and attraction and adulation. But she doubted Jared had ever looked at her the way Dalton Reyes looked at his bride. His mouth curved into a wide grin, he stared at her as if unable to look away.

She was beautiful—with her vibrant red hair and creamy skin. She lifted the flower girl, who wore a lacy white dress, into her arms. With curly dark hair, the little girl looked nothing like her mother. But she was definitely hers—even though, as Jared had shared, Elizabeth hadn't given birth to the child. And Dalton looked at the little girl with as much love as he looked at her mother. They were a very happy family.

The family Rebecca wished she could give Alex. While she studied the bride and groom, she felt someone studying her. She shivered with apprehension as that warning ran through her mind again. *Someone is watching you...*

But when she glanced around, the person whose gaze

she found on her was Jared. He peered around the guest
shaking his hand, as if unable to take his gaze off her.
She doubted it was because he loved her—like Dalton
Reyes loved his bride. She suspected it was just because
he wanted to keep her safe.

But still her skin tingled and heated from just the touch
of his gaze. Would she ever not react to him? To his closeness? To his handsomeness? To his intelligence?

The line moved forward, probably because Alex had
grown impatient with standing still and pushed ahead.
His hand on Chief Lynch's, he dragged the older man
along with him. The poor chief was filling the grandfa-
ther void Rebecca's father had left in the little boy's life.

Alex was as much a reminder of Lexi as Rebecca—
maybe more—so her parents wanted nothing to do with
him. That was their loss more than his, though. Alex had
eased that unbearable ache she'd had after losing Lexi.

Jared hadn't ever talked much about his parents.
Would they like being grandparents? Would they love the
little boy? Had Jared even told them yet that he had a son?

She moved forward in the line, too, close enough that
she heard what the man standing by Jared asked him. But
that man and the chief were such tall, broad men that
Jared wouldn't be able to see her anymore. There was
no one else behind them; they were the end of the line.

"So are you next?"

"Next?" Jared asked.

"First it was Blaine, then me, now Reyes," the dark-
haired man said. She'd met him earlier; he was another
FBI special agent—Ash Stryker. "So you're next, right?"

Reyes took his attention from his bride for a moment
to smack Jared's shoulder. "Ash is right. And it seems
like whoever's stood up as best man at the last wedding
becomes the next groom. So you're definitely next."

Jared shook his head. "No way."

And pain stabbed Rebecca's heart at how adamant he sounded. She'd already suspected he didn't return her feelings, but she'd thought he cared about her at least a little. How else had he forgiven her for keeping his son from him? Or hadn't he forgiven her?

"Was Kyle Smith wrong?" Agent Stryker asked. "Isn't that little boy yours?"

Maybe Jared didn't believe Alex was his son. He'd never had a DNA test to prove it. He only had her word for it and his name on the little boy's birth certificate.

"He's mine," Jared said with a glance toward where Alex hung from the chief's arm.

"I figured you for an old-fashioned guy," Agent Stryker said. "After I saw that broadcast, I thought you would beat Reyes to the altar."

"Not a chance," Reyes said. "Nobody was going to beat me to the altar." He leaned back toward his bride and dropped a kiss on the top of her head.

She smiled up at him, her gray eyes shining with love.

And Rebecca's envy returned.

Stryker grinned at the newly married couple. Then he turned back to Jared. "Well, you can still get married next."

Jared shook his head again. "No. I can't."

She sucked in a breath that burned in her lungs. He had no intention of ever marrying her. While they'd been sharing his bed since she and Alex had moved in with him, it was all he intended to share with her. Not his heart...

But then he continued, "I can't put her in that kind of danger."

"You think marriage to you would be that rough?" Reyes teased.

"I think the Butcher wouldn't care how many FBI agents and bodyguards were around," Jared said. "He would go after Becca for certain. He already has, and we're not even engaged."

The chief, thankfully, covered her little boy's ears, as the two of them moved along the line until they now stood in front of Jared. "I didn't think you believed the incident at the boutique was the work of the Butcher."

Rebecca didn't believe it. She wasn't engaged. But maybe that news broadcast had made the Butcher think that she soon would be. When he'd showed up at her house, Harris Mowery had been taunting Jared about proposing to her. He wanted her engaged, so that he could go after her—like he'd gone after Lexi and all those other poor women.

"We couldn't find anything on all the security footage Blaine turned up from the stores in the area," Jared said. "The guy that went after Becca was good at staying off camera—just like the Butcher always has."

Unless the Butcher was Kyle Smith. Jared had told her that he'd questioned the reporter. She considered it a waste of time. She knew who the Butcher was. She'd even begun to believe that Jared now suspected the same.

But he hadn't been able to break that damn alibi for Lexi's disappearance. And the man had provided another for Amy Wilcox's abduction. Maybe he would never be caught; maybe he would just keep killing more and more innocent young women.

"But you think he would risk getting caught—even with federal agents and bodyguards around—in order to grab Ms. Drummond?" the chief asked.

Jared's handsome face grim, he nodded. "He wouldn't be able to resist. It all started with Lexi Drummond. She was the most important to him."

"So her sister would be important, too?"

Jared nodded again. "So important that he's already

messing with her—with the phone threats, with the confrontation in the dressing room."

"Then that's how you catch him," the chief matter-of-factly stated.

"What?" Jared asked just as Rebecca silently uttered the word herself.

"You propose to Ms. Drummond."

"To catch a killer?" Jared asked. "You want me to use her as bait?"

Of course he wouldn't propose because he actually wanted to marry her. He didn't love her—not like Dalton Reyes loved his bride. So much so that he hadn't been able to wait to marry her. No, Jared didn't love her—not like Rebecca loved him, like she had always loved him.

"But it might be the only way," Chief Lynch suggested softly, as his hands dropped away from the wriggling little boy's ears.

"What might be the only way?" the ever-inquisitive Alex asked. He stared up at all the adults, who probably seemed way too serious to him. He also had to wonder why the chief had covered his ears.

She was glad that he had; the little boy didn't need to hear that the Butcher might have already gone after his mother. And he certainly hadn't needed to hear anything about his parents getting married. He would get the completely wrong idea. He would think that they were in love, and all of them would become one happy family.

Rebecca knew better. Jared didn't love her.

She moved forward, so that she stood beside the chief again. "They're talking about catching the bad guy," she explained to her son.

The ultimate bad guy—the man who'd killed her sister. The man who would keep killing if he wasn't stopped.

And she was the key to stopping him. Even the chief thought so.

"I'll do it," she said. "I'll help catch the bad guy."

Alex's eyes widened in shock. "But Mommy, you're not an FBI agent."

No. She wasn't an FBI agent. She was a mother who had no business putting herself in danger. She knew that, and from the disapproval on Jared's face, he was thinking the same thing she was.

If it was any other killer, she wouldn't have risked it—probably not even if she knew she could save the lives of other women. But this was Lexi's killer.

She had to do this—for Lexi. She hadn't been around when her sister had needed her. Putting herself in danger wouldn't bring Lexi back, but at least Rebecca would be able to get her what Lexi had been denied until now. Justice.

"I'm just going to help," she explained to Alex. "The FBI agents will catch him." Hopefully before he could kill her as he had all the others.

Chapter Thirteen

Jared held his temper until Alex was out of earshot. The woman who ran the wedding chapel, Penny Payne, had taken him downstairs to where the reception was being held. She'd promised him cake. Like him, his son had a sweet tooth.

But even cake couldn't tempt Jared now, as anger churned inside him—unsettling his stomach.

After the auburn-haired woman disappeared down the steps with his son, he turned to his boss and Becca. "Absolutely not," he told them. "This will not happen. You are not putting yourself in danger."

She lifted her chin, her jaw tense, and her blue eyes hard with determination. "That's not your decision to make."

"It's not yours, either," he informed her. He turned to his boss. "You can't seriously be considering using a civilian to bait a serial killer?"

"Ordinarily, I would never allow it," Chief Lynch admitted. Then he uttered a heavy sigh. "But we haven't been able to catch this man any other way."

"We won't this way, either," Jared said. Instead, he risked losing Becca—forever.

"You said yourself that he won't be able to resist trying for me," Becca said.

Jared bit off a curse. He hadn't realized she'd been listening when he'd said that. There had been so many people standing in the foyer then. Now it was only him, the chief and her. Everyone else had gone downstairs to the reception. He had to get to the reception soon, too. He had a toast to make—had a head table to sit at; he should have ignored Reyes's suggestion that he bring a date. He never should have invited Becca.

"And because you're not a trained agent, you're not equipped to deal with him," Jared pointed out.

"I got away at the boutique."

"You admitted he let you get away," he reminded her. "If he'd really wanted to abduct you, he would have. And he will if you pose as my fiancée."

She flinched. And he wasn't sure why. Because he'd told her that she wouldn't get away again? Or because he'd told her she would only be posing as his fiancée?

Did she want to be his real fiancée? Did she want to make their living situation permanent? He wanted to, but not now—not like this—when it could put her in so much danger.

"I won't be part of this," Jared continued. She was already in too much danger for his peace of mind. He couldn't use her as bait and risk losing her forever. "I will not pretend to be your fiancé."

Her face reddened—either with temper or embarrassment. And she turned to the chief. "So assign another agent to act as my fiancé," she implored him. "There has to be someone else…"

"They're all married," Jared told her. "And as easily as Kyle Smith found Alex's birth certificate, he would find their marriage licenses."

She laughed. "Every FBI agent can't be married." She gestured toward one of the men walking around. "What about Agent Rus?"

The man she'd pointed at was actually one of the bodyguards that Reyes had joked was Rus's clone. But she must have met Nicholas earlier.

"He's on assignment here—in River City," Jared said. "And the killer will know it's a trap if your groom is anyone but me. He would have seen the story Kyle Smith did on us." Unless the killer was Kyle Smith, then he had run the story himself.

She expelled a heavy sigh of resignation and said, "So it has to be you."

He shook his head. "No, I won't put you in any more danger than you already are."

He wouldn't be able to live with himself if something happened to her. She meant too much to him—more than he was willing to admit to her. He was struggling with admitting it even to himself.

"You'll ignore a direct order?" Chief Lynch asked.

Feeling as if his boss had sucker punched him, Jared drew in a quick breath. "Is this a direct order?"

Instead of answering him, the chief turned toward Becca. "Will you give us a minute, Ms. Drummond?"

She nodded. "Of course."

Jared's stomach churned with anxiety now as she walked across the foyer toward the stairwell leading down to the reception area. He hoped one of his friends was available to protect her. But it was Agent Rus who met her on the stairwell and turned around to walk back down with her. While Nick was a friend, he wasn't Jared's first choice for her fake fiancé. But he probably only felt that way out of jealousy, because Nick had been Becca's first choice.

When had he become the jealous sort? He'd never been possessive of anyone before. But he'd never cared about any other woman the way he cared about Becca. She was beautiful and smart and a loving sister and a wonderful mother and a phenomenal lover. He couldn't lose her.

"She's safe," Chief Lynch assured him.

"She won't be if you use her as bait to lure out the Butcher." Because the Butcher wouldn't stop at scaring her; he would take her, and like Lexi, Jared would never be able to find her again. "You can't do this."

"We have to catch this killer," Lynch said with all his intimidating intensity.

"I know that," Jared said. "And I'm working on it."

"For six years," Lynch said.

"I have a profile."

"White male in his thirties—single," the chief paraphrased the profile. "Charming and affable on the surface but with a sadistic streak. You have a profile but no suspects that fit it."

"Harris Mowery abused his fiancée before she disappeared," Jared said. He certainly fit the profile.

"And he has an ironclad alibi for her disappearance."

Jared silently cursed that alibi. If only he could have disproved it. But he had another suspect. "Kyle Smith."

"Is charming and affable on the surface," Lynch agreed. "But sadistic?"

Jared nodded. "He's been relentless with Becca."

"And you." The chief's dark eyes narrowed. "But with her, too. Not the other victims' families—only Ms. Drummond. She is definitely the key to catching this killer."

"The bait," Jared corrected him.

"She volunteered," Lynch pointed out.

"She isn't equipped to deal with this killer."

"Agent Campbell said she handled herself well in the dressing room at the boutique," Lynch said. "You're not giving her enough credit."

"She's smart and strong," Jared said. "But the Butcher's

other victims were smart and strong, too. I don't want her to become his next victim."

"I want her to become his last," Lynch said.

Panic gripped Jared's heart. "You're willing to sacrifice Becca to catch this killer?" That might have made sense in times of war or even in Ash Stryker's antiterrorism division. But Jared had never been a marine like so many of the other agents. He couldn't sacrifice any life for any reason. And he absolutely could not sacrifice Becca's.

"She'll be safe," Lynch said. "We'll protect her—just like we have Reyes's bride. And she'll be even safer when the killer is caught."

Jared couldn't argue with that. The best way to keep Becca safe was to catch the killer and put him behind bars for the rest of his life.

"I'll talk to Mrs. Payne about having another wedding here—yours and Ms. Drummond's." Then the chief walked away as if Jared had given his agreement to this crazy plan.

But he hadn't given Jared a choice; neither had Becca. She'd willingly put herself in danger.

He knew why—for Lexi. But from what he'd learned about Lexi, from Becca and from reading the young woman's own journals, she wouldn't want her sister risking her life. Not for any reason...

BECCA PROBABLY WOULDN'T have made it down the stairs without Agent Rus's hand on her arm to steady her. The minute she'd walked away from Jared and the chief, she'd realized what she'd just done, and she'd started shaking with fear. What the hell had she been thinking?

Like Jared had said, she was not a trained agent. She was a civilian. A mother.

Alex ran up to her the minute she stepped into the

reception hall. The room was big and bedazzled with twinkle lights and flowers and streamers. "It's pretty, isn't it, Mommy?" he asked as he clasped her hand. He gazed shyly up at Agent Rus.

"Prettier than my room," Agent Rus agreed. "I understand you've been sleeping in my bed."

Alex smiled. "It's pretty comfy. Do you want it back?"

Rus shook his head. "No. I moved all my other stuff out. I think I'll be staying here."

So Jared had spoken the truth about Agent Rus's assignment in River City. He couldn't pose as her fiancé. But like Jared had said, after Kyle Smith's report, only he could. Would he? Or would he refuse even if the chief ordered him?

"Nice meeting you both," Rus said as he stepped away.

Alex's smile widened. "Did you hear that, Mommy?"

"What?"

"We can stay with Daddy forever," he said. "Agent Rus's room can be mine now."

Her stomach pitched with regret. Moving in with Jared had been a horrible idea—because it had given her son the wrong idea. And if he heard about their *fake* engagement, he would get entirely the wrong idea.

"We can stay in Chicago," she said. She'd already decided to make the move—for his new school. Not for Jared. She knew now that Jared would never marry her—not for real. And probably not for fake, either. So she hadn't put herself in more danger than she already was—at least not for her heart, only for her life.

She leaned down and swiped a dab of white frosting from the end of Alex's little nose. "I see you checked out the cake already."

"It's so big, Mommy!" he exclaimed with excitement—his wish to live permanently with his father momentarily forgotten. "And Mrs. Payne says it's vanilla and chocolate. I can have some after the bride and groom cut it."

She wondered if he would be able to wait that long.

"Chief Lynch!" the little boy called out as his new best friend stepped into the reception area.

The chief was focused on the wedding planner, though, and he headed in her direction. Before Rebecca could stop him, Alex took off after the older FBI agent. She would have raced after him, but he was safe— probably safer here than anywhere else.

Glass tinkled as the guests tapped silverware against water goblets. "Kiss, kiss!"

Dalton Reyes needed no encouragement to kiss his bride. He stood up and drew her to her feet. Then he dipped her over his arm as he passionately kissed her.

Jared's kisses were always full of passion. But what about love?

Feeling someone's gaze on her, she glanced up and discovered Jared standing beside her. She couldn't read the emotion in his amber eyes. But she recognized the emotion in his voice when he told her, "You got your way."

He was angry with her.

"The chief agreed?"

He grimly nodded.

And her heart began to race again with panic and fear. What had she done?

He stared so intently at her that he missed nothing. He leaned closer, so close that his lips brushed her cheek, as he said, "You can change your mind."

She shivered even as heat from his closeness warmed her. She wanted to move, just enough that his lips skimmed over hers. She needed his kiss. She needed his support. His love...

He took her hands in his—like the groom had taken the bride's as they'd spoken their heartfelt vows just a short time ago. But instead of declaring his love, Jared declared his doubt. "This is too big a risk for you and for Alex."

What about for him? Was it a risk for him? How much did he care about her?

She wanted to ask him. But she was more afraid of finding out his real feelings for her than she was of baiting a serial killer.

"You don't have to do this," he told her.

As scared as she was, she had no choice. "I have to," she said. "I have to…"

She waited for him to argue some more. But he walked away instead to take his seat at the head table, next to the groom. And then, his face revealing none of his disappointment with her reply, he toasted the bride and groom.

"When I met Dalton Reyes, he was ready to pass out just from witnessing a wedding," Jared said. "He had no intention of ever marrying. Then a short while later he found his bride—in the trunk of a car. And he started making promises he'd never made before—promises we all advised him not to make." A few other men in the room laughed. "He promised that he would find who had hurt her and that he'd stop him. And he would protect her. Dalton kept all his promises and today he made some more that he will keep just as faithfully as he kept those first promises he made to Elizabeth. And theirs will be a love that lasts forever."

Tears stung Rebecca's eyes, but she blinked them away and found Jared's gaze on her as he lifted his glass. She wanted a love like the one he'd just described. But she knew that it would never be hers—even if she lived through baiting a serial killer.

Chapter Fourteen

The diamond twinkled in the sunlight shining through the window. It was probably a couple of carats—at least. Guilt gripped Jared; he hadn't even bought Becca a ring. But then their engagement wasn't real.

Was Harris Mowery's? The woman looked more fearful than in love. So fearful that she wouldn't dare contradict her fiancé's story. She stuck to his alibi.

And the sunlight illuminated more than the diamond on her hand. It shone through the layers of makeup on her face to reveal old bruises. Jared didn't need to warn the young woman about Harris Mowery; she already knew how sadistic the bastard could be.

Like Becca, Jared wanted Mowery to be the killer. He certainly fit the profile Jared had worked up of the Butcher. But Kyle Smith's grinning face stared at him from the muted television that hung over the shiny marble fireplace in Mowery's great room. Jared didn't need to hear what the man was saying to know that he was *reporting* the engagement of the FBI profiler to the sister of the Butcher's first victim. He wanted it to be Kyle Smith, too.

Maybe the two men were working together…

The front door creaked open, then closed with a loud slam. "Priscilla! Whose car is in the driveway?" Bristling with anger, Harris Mowery rushed into the great room as if ready to confront a lover. Then, seeing Jared, he drew to an abrupt halt and struggled to summon a grin. "Agent Bell…"

"Thought I would repay the visit you paid to Ms. Drummond's home," Jared said.

Harris's already beady eyes narrowed. "So that's what this is about? Payback?"

"That wasn't smart showing up at her house," Jared admitted.

Harris shrugged. "Thanks to your friend the reporter, everybody knows where she lives—probably even the real killer."

And that was why she was no longer at her home. She was in Jared's—her and Alex. They lived together like they were one happy family. But since she'd volunteered to bait the killer, she'd been sleeping in Alex's room instead of his. The past few days had seemed nearly as long as the past six years without her in his life.

His heart ached as if he'd already lost her. But he hadn't. Yet. He had a couple more weeks before his *fake* wedding date. That was why he'd stepped up his investigation, hoping to break Harris's alibi. He wanted to catch the killer before the man had a chance to go after Becca.

Harris turned back to his fiancée. "Priscilla?"

The woman cringed in fear. "Yes?"

"You didn't offer Agent Bell anything to drink," he admonished her.

"Yes, she did," Jared defended the timid young woman. "I didn't want anything."

"Well," Harris said. "I would like a drink, sweetheart. Please fix me one."

She jumped up from the couch and moved to pass Harris. But he reached out for her. And she instinctively cringed in reaction. Jared jumped up, ready to defend the woman if Harris got physical with her.

But he only kissed his fiancée's cheek. "Thank you, sweetheart."

Despite the other man's sugary tone, there was a hardness in his eyes. A coldness that chilled Jared's blood. When Priscilla passed him, he reached out, too—surreptitiously—and pressed his card into her trembling hand. On the other side of that card was contact information for a women's shelter. If she didn't call him, he hoped she would at least call the shelter.

Harris waited until his fiancée was out of the room before speaking again. "But you took care of the problem Kyle Smith caused Rebecca. She's no longer staying at her house."

Jared's blood warmed now as anger coursed through him. "You went back to her house?"

"Of course not," Harris said.

But Jared didn't believe him. Harris Mowery had lost all credibility with him.

"I know she's staying with you now."

"How do you know that?" Jared asked. Was he the one who'd attacked her at the boutique, then? Whoever had must have followed her and Blaine from his apartment to the dress shop.

"You're engaged," Harris said. "So of course she would be staying with you."

They hadn't been engaged when she'd moved in, but that was none of Harris Mowery's business.

"Congratulations, by the way," the man remarked. "I'm surprised that you'd take the risk, though—what with the Bride Butcher still on the loose."

Maybe the man was too smart to fall for a trap. Even Kyle Smith had been skeptical of their announcement.

So Jared told him what he had Smith. "I already

missed six years of my son's life. I should have been with him and Rebecca that whole time."

"Instead of chasing a killer?"

"Oh, no," Jared said. "I would have still chased him."

"You've been chasing him for six years, Agent Bell," Mowery said, his voice patronizing. "But you're not any closer to catching him."

Jared grinned. "Oh, I'm close now." He took a step toward Mowery. "Very close."

Harris uttered a nervous laugh and stepped back. "If you're close, you know that it's not me. I have an alibi."

"For Lexi's murder." Maybe he'd hired it done because he'd known he would be the prime suspect. "Not the others. Not Amy Wilcox's."

That anger gripped him again, flushing his face and bald head. "My fiancée—"

"Would say whatever you told her to," Jared assured him. "She didn't contradict you." She wouldn't dare.

Harris smirked. "Because it's the truth."

Jared shook his head.

"Because she loves me."

"Because she's afraid of you." She was obviously more afraid of Harris than she was of going to prison for being an accessory to murder. Jared had mentioned that threat to her. Maybe he was the one who'd made her so fearful. But he hadn't given her those bruises. He'd asked, but she'd denied having any.

"You're letting Rebecca and her wild accusations about me get to you," Harris said, and then he uttered a heavy sigh. "But of course you would, she's your fiancée now. So when's the big day?"

It would never happen if Jared had his way. Not that he didn't want to ever marry Becca. But he wanted a real wedding—not a fake one to trap a killer. "We're trying to keep the wedding small," he replied. "And private."

"So I shouldn't look for an invitation?" the man teased. "Well, I would at least like to send a gift. Where will it be held?"

"Again—trying to keep it private," Jared said. "For her protection."

"So if something happens to her," Mowery asked with that unsettling grin, "will you become the prime suspect, Agent Bell?"

Jared wanted to hit the guy. Hard.

"You wouldn't like that, would you?" Harris taunted him. "Of course I would believe you're innocent, though."

Of course he would because he knew who the real killer was: him.

"It's just so crazy to suspect the fiancé," Harris continued. "Like Rebecca suspecting me. Why? Why would I have killed my fiancée? I really *wanted* to marry Alexandra. I would still marry her today."

Priscilla, walking back into the room with his drink, paled, all the color draining from her face. Her hand, holding the glass, began to shake so much that the alcohol sloshed over the rim. Now she knew—she wasn't the woman Harris really wanted to marry.

He didn't even notice her reaction, or he noticed and didn't give a damn. He continued speaking to Jared as if she hadn't even entered the room. "Wouldn't it be more likely that the man she hadn't married was her killer?"

"What do you mean?" Jared asked. He'd interviewed the man before but he'd never brought up another suspect.

"Look into Lexi's ex-boyfriend," Harris suggested, "the man she dropped for me. That's the guy who probably killed her and, no doubt, all the others."

"Becca never mentioned Lexi having an ex-boyfriend," Jared said.

Harris shrugged. "Maybe she didn't know her sister

as well as she thought she did." He grinned. "Or maybe you don't know your fiancée all that well."

"I know that no one wants to find Lexi's killer more than Becca does," he said. So much so that she was willing to risk her own life to catch him.

Harris shook his head. "She only wants her killer caught if that man is me."

"Don't you want her killer caught?" Jared asked.

The other man drew himself up taller than his stocky frame. Was his lack of height another reason he picked on women? Hurting them made him feel like a bigger man?

"Of course I want Alexandra's killer caught."

"Then why didn't *you* ever mention this ex-boyfriend before?"

Harris shrugged. "George Droski was an insignificant man. I forgot all about him."

Jared doubted that, but he wondered about Harris's timing in mentioning him. He'd had an unbreakable alibi for Lexi's disappearance. But his alibi for Amy Wilcox's abduction was shaky at best. Before he turned to head for the door, he caught Priscilla Stehouwer's gaze on him. And he suspected she might call him and the shelter.

WHILE REBECCA HAD submitted her résumé and references to a few hospitals in the area, she hadn't been asked to interview yet. Which was probably a good thing because planning her fake wedding had become a full-time job.

She cradled the phone against her shoulder as she studied the images on the computer screen in front of her. Her head began to pound and all the bright colors of the collage of wedding bouquets ran together before her eyes. "They're all beautiful, Mrs. Payne—"

"Penny, please," the wedding planner corrected her. "And you have to pick one."

Why? It wasn't a real wedding. And even if it was,

Rebecca wasn't certain how interested she would be in every little detail. Lexi had tried to include her in the planning of her wedding, but Rebecca had been too busy to weigh in on any of her sister's decisions.

If only she'd given Lexi more of her attention...

"You know this isn't a real wedding," Rebecca said. The chief had assured her that the wedding planner was fully aware of the situation and the danger.

Mrs. Payne chuckled. "Yours won't be the only *not real* wedding I've had in my chapel."

"It isn't?"

"No," she replied. "But, you know, every single one of those *not real* weddings turned into *real* marriages."

"Mrs. Payne—"

"Penny," she was corrected again. "And in order for this to appear to be real, you have to pull a marriage license. So that actually makes it real, Ms. Drummond."

"Rebecca," she corrected the woman. Despite her headache, she managed a smile.

"So, Rebecca," the woman continued, "you should make all your selections based on what you'd want at your *real* wedding—because this just might wind up being exactly that."

That was damn unlikely to happen. Jared was still furious with her—so much so that he'd barely spoken to her since Dalton Reyes's wedding. Of course she hadn't given him much opportunity since she'd started sleeping in Alex's room.

She missed him. Missed lying in his arms. Missed his kisses. His caresses.

She ached for him. Not just for his lovemaking but for his companionship. If their wedding was going to be real, she would have wanted his input. He probably would have left the decisions up to her anyway, but she would have persisted until he at least offered his opinion.

She knew what his opinion was now—that she was being reckless. The pain throbbing in her head intensified. She had to squint at the pictures on her computer screen. But she made selections for the bouquet and the flowers and the cake.

"Alex will love the double chocolate," Mrs. Payne said.

The woman was sweet to have remembered her son. But then Alex—and his precocious personality—was entirely unforgettable. How well would he remember her if something happened, if the FBI agents and the bodyguards weren't able to protect her?

Now tears blurred her vision. But she blinked them back. She had to focus. She had to keep her wits about her—more so now than ever. If the agents and bodyguards didn't protect her, she would protect herself.

She wouldn't become the Butcher's next victim. And she would make certain that Amy Wilcox was his last.

"That's great," Penny said. "Your wedding will be beautiful."

If it was, it would be bittersweet: a perfect wedding with no hope of a marriage. But would she even make it to the wedding? No other bride the Butcher had targeted had made it down the aisle.

"And you'll come here to be fitted for your dress," Penny continued. Her sweet voice held no happy lilt now. It had gone flat with seriousness. She knew what Rebecca knew: that was when it would happen, when the killer would try to grab her like he had all the others. "The seamstress will come here—as well as other personnel."

FBI agents and bodyguards. They would protect her; at least Chief Lynch was convinced that they would. Jared wasn't as confident. He still thought it was too big a risk.

But Dalton's bride had been safe; nothing had happened to Elizabeth at her fitting or at the wedding. The happy couple was off on their honeymoon now.

What would Jared do if the killer didn't try to grab Rebecca at her dress fitting? Would he call off the wedding or would he see it through—to give the killer another opportunity to grab her?

Maybe she'd done all this planning for naught. "I'm sorry," she told Mrs. Payne. "I hope this all hasn't been a waste of your time."

"Not at all," the other woman assured her. "As I said, all of the not real weddings I've held have become very real marriages." She clicked off before Rebecca could tell her that was doubtful to happen in this situation.

Jared was even angrier with her for putting herself at risk than he'd been over her keeping their son from him. She'd like to think that was because he cared about her—more than he was willing to admit. But if he really cared about her, why wouldn't he admit it—especially now if he believed he could lose her?

Rebecca was still holding the phone when it rang again. Mrs. Payne probably had another question for her—another question Rebecca would have to answer alone since Jared wanted nothing to do with their wedding.

Or with Rebecca.

He hadn't asked her to move back into his bedroom. No, he definitely wasn't in love with her.

"Yes, Penny?" she asked.

But there was no reply—just that eerie silence. She should have known it wasn't Mrs. Payne. The wedding planner was too organized to have forgotten anything.

Her hand trembling, she knew she should click off the phone. But she hadn't had any threats since that one in the boutique dressing room. It wasn't that she wanted to hear any more—just that she somehow felt as if she needed to. Maybe she could figure out who was calling her—who was watching her.

But when he spoke his voice was too low and raspy to be recognizable. "You didn't listen," he admonished her. "By getting engaged, you're risking your life."

She couldn't deny that she was—willingly—risking her life. To catch a killer...

"And now you're going to die."

Chapter Fifteen

Even with guards posted outside his apartment, the killer had still gotten to her. Anger and fear warred inside Jared, making his heart pound fast and hard.

"Doesn't this prove to you how bad of an idea our engagement is?" he asked.

Becca flinched.

Had his comment hurt her? She knew the engagement wasn't real. He couldn't really propose to her because he cared too much about her to risk her life. But when the killer was caught...

Would she want to marry him? He'd never handled anything right with Becca. He'd rejected her love six years ago. So why would she offer it again?

She shrugged and said, "It was just a phone call." As if it was nothing.

"He threatened your life," Jared reminded her of what she'd told him—of what the trace on the phone had recorded.

But even though the call had been recorded, they had no clue who'd made it. "From a burner cell," he said. Which was how all the other calls had been made. "It couldn't be traced."

She rubbed her hands over her arms as if she'd gotten ten a sudden chill.

Jared was chilled, too—from the threat, from the danger she was in. "It could be anyone…"

"It's Harris," she said.

"I'll have to double-check the time the call was made," he said. "I may have still been with him."

Her face brightened. "You were interrogating him again?"

"Checking his alibi," he admitted.

"I thought you did that several times already and it can't be cracked," she said.

"For Lexi's murder," he said. "I was checking for Amy Wilcox's abduction."

"His fiancée gave him an alibi?"

He nodded. While he suspected Priscilla Stehouwer might change her story, he didn't share that with Becca. He didn't want to raise her hopes—in case he was wrong. Harris's hold on Priscilla might be stronger than Jared thought.

"He gave me another suspect, though," Jared said. And now he was angry at her again for not telling him about Lexi's ex.

"Of course he did," she said. "He wants to take suspicion off himself."

"Then why didn't he give me the name six years ago?" Jared kept his voice low—because Alex was just playing in his room, but anger sharpened his tone when he added, "Why didn't you?"

"I told you who hurt my sister, but you wouldn't believe me," she said. And now there was anger in her voice. But she glanced toward Alex's room, as if afraid that he might have heard her.

"All you would talk about was Harris," he agreed. "But I asked you about other boyfriends. Exes."

She shrugged. "There was no one else—no one she ever cared enough to talk to me about like she did Harris.

Not that she told me everything about Harris. If only she would have told me how he was treating her..."

"She was probably embarrassed," Jared said. Lexi had been the older sister. And Rebecca was so smart and so strong that it would have been hard for Lexi to admit what she'd probably considered a weakness on her part. Harris was the weak one.

"She shouldn't have been," Becca said. "It wasn't her fault."

"No, it wasn't," he agreed. Just like it wasn't Priscilla Stehouwer's fault. Hopefully, she at least called the shelter.

"So what name did Harris give you?" she asked. "Who is he throwing under the bus to protect himself?"

"Lexi's ex—George Droski."

She laughed. "George was never her boyfriend. He was like a brother to us. He grew up next door to us. He was her best friend."

"Are you sure there wasn't more between them?" he asked. "He didn't have a crush on her?"

"George loved her," Becca said. "But he loved me, too."

"Harris said George was obsessed with Lexi, and that he was devastated when they broke up." As the man had walked Jared to his vehicle, he'd made certain to add to his case against George Droski.

Becca shook her head. "No. They were just friends. George didn't like Harris, though, so that had strained their friendship to the point they'd lost touch."

"Harris says he was jealous."

"He was smart," Becca said, and there was bitterness in her voice. She didn't think she'd been smart. "He realized what a jerk Harris was before anyone else did."

The pain and guilt in her voice reached inside Jared

and squeezed his heart. He pulled her into his arms. "It's not your fault, either."

Now he understood why she was taking such a big risk to catch her sister's killer—because she blamed herself.

She trembled in his arms before sliding her arms around his neck and clinging to him.

He'd missed her. Missed her being in his arms. In his bed...

A door creaked open, and Jared tensed. But it wasn't the door to the hall. It was a bedroom door.

"Family hug," Alex declared as he wedged between them.

Jared wanted to be part of this family. He wanted to be more than Alex's father; he wanted to be Becca's husband, too. But first he had to keep her alive and stop the killer who was certain to try for her again.

REBECCA KNELT BESIDE Alex's bed as she tucked him beneath the covers. He snuggled down, his eyes already closing as he drifted off to sleep. A smile curved his lips. He was happy.

And that was all a mother wanted for her child: happiness. She leaned over and pressed a kiss to his forehead. It puckered beneath her lips. And she chuckled.

He obviously didn't want her interrupting the dreams that had already begun to play through his mind.

Still on her knees, she eased back and bumped into a hand. It covered hers and helped her to her feet. Like their son, Jared had a smile on his lips.

But she didn't believe he was happy. He was too angry with her. When she met his gaze, though, she didn't see any anger in his eyes. She saw only desire—desire that brought out her own desire for him.

"He's asleep," Jared said. He'd read him a story before

going to check with the guards in the hall. "And everything's quiet outside."

It wasn't quiet inside her. Emotions were rioting in her heart. She loved him so much.

He turned toward the door, but his hand was still around hers. He tugged her along behind him. When they cleared the threshold, he reached around her and closed their son's door. His chest bumped against hers, and he stared down at her, those amber eyes intense with desire.

"What are you doing?" she asked.

"Bringing you to bed…"

She pointed at the door he'd closed. "I've been sleeping in there."

But he headed away from that door, across the living room to the master bedroom on the other side of the apartment. "And you should have been sleeping in here."

"Why's that?" she asked as he led her into his bedroom.

"Because it's where you belong," he replied as he pushed the door closed. "With me."

Just in his bed? Or in his life?

If she were braver, she would have asked. But it seemed to be easier for her to face a killer than Jared's feelings for her. Because if he didn't feel the same…

She couldn't handle him rejecting her again.

He wasn't rejecting her now. He was quickly disrobing her with hands that shook with his urgency and his passion. Then he was kissing her with all that passion.

Her heart began a frantic beat. His tongue slid between her lips and teased hers. She gasped, and he deepened the kiss even more.

Then she was fumbling with his clothes, her hands shaking as she unbuttoned buttons and unsnapped snaps. Then she jerked down his zipper.

He groaned. Then he murmured her name. It was only a few steps, but he carried her to the bed and followed her down onto it. The rest of their clothes disappeared until there was only skin sliding over skin.

Heat burned inside her as pressure built and wound tighter and tighter. He kissed her everywhere. Her lips. Her throat. Her breasts.

He slid his lips along the curve and across her nipple. Then he drew the point between his lips and teased it with his tongue.

She wriggled beneath him as that pressure became unbearable. She needed him too much to wait. It had been too long. "Jared…"

And she touched him. She knew exactly where would drive him crazy. His chest. His lean hips. And lower…

"Becca!" His control snapped, and he was inside her—where she needed him most. Sliding deep, filling her.

She wrapped her legs around his waist and clung to him, meeting every thrust. He kissed her deeply, sliding his tongue into her mouth.

Her body shuddered as pleasure overwhelmed her. If he hadn't been kissing her, she might have screamed. Or declared her love.

Like the pleasure, love overwhelmed her.

Then he joined her in ecstasy, his body tensing as his pleasure filled her. He rolled to his side and clasped her closely in his arms. His heart beat hard and fast against hers. And he murmured her name, "Becca…"

She tipped her chin up to meet his gaze. His pale brown eyes were full of intensity. It couldn't be desire again—not so soon.

And he murmured her name again as if he was going to say more—as if he was going to express whatever intense emotion burned in his gaze.

But the doorbell rang.

Rebecca could have cursed. But he beat her to it. Then he reached for the cell phone he'd placed, along with his weapon, on the table next to the bed. He glanced at the blank screen and shook his head.

"What is it?" she asked. She shivered, maybe because he wasn't holding her anymore, maybe because she had an ominous feeling.

"The guard at the door is supposed to call me," he said, "not ring the bell." He vaulted out of the bed, pulled on his pants and reached for his weapon.

Before she could say anything—warn him to be careful—he was gone, closing the bedroom door behind him. She couldn't stay in the room. Not if he was in danger. Not if their son might be in danger, as well.

She grabbed her robe, thrust her arms through the sleeves and cinched the belt at her waist. Then she hurried into the living room.

Jared stood in the open doorway, his gun drawn. But there was no person standing in the hall. Not the guard. Not a killer. He was looking down, though, so Becca followed his gaze and saw the box.

"What is it?" she asked.

He held out his arm as if holding her back. "Don't come any closer."

Fear quickened her pulse. "What do you think it is?" She glanced across the living room to their son's bedroom doorway. "Is it ticking?"

He leaned down and listened, then shook his head. "This serial killer has never used a bomb."

She shivered. "No."

"It would be too quick for him," Jared said, almost as if he was thinking aloud. "Too impersonal."

"So what's in the box?"

"Get back," he told her as he lifted his weapon again.

Maybe the box was only a distraction, so that some-one could sneak up while they were staring at it. But she recognized the voice of the guard as he said, "Agent Bell, I'm sorry—I thought I heard something in the stairwell. It sounded like someone might have fallen. I know I should have called you before I went to investigate. But I was worried that someone was hurt…"

"It's okay," Jared assured the other man. "That was the distraction, so someone could leave this box."

Rebecca stepped closer to get a better look at the box. It was wrapped in shiny silver paper, and there was a bow on the floor beside it—like it had fallen off.

"It's a present," she said. "A wedding present."

For their fake wedding.

"It's a message," Jared said. "He knows where you are…"

"He already knew," she said. "Whatever's in the box is the message."

"Do you have gloves?" Jared asked the guard. He wouldn't want to compromise any evidence.

But Rebecca doubted there would be any inside the box. It was another threat. Another warning that she would die. But she stepped even closer as Jared donned the gloves and reached for the lid of the box.

He lifted it easily and peered inside.

"What is it?" the guard was just as curious as Rebecca. "And what's on it?"

Lace spilled from the box like lace had spilled from the trunk of Lexi's car when they'd found it. This lace wasn't stained red, though. Whatever was on it was darker and dried.

"It's a veil," Rebecca said. Just that afternoon she'd flipped through images Penny Payne had sent her of veils, like she'd sent the bouquet and cake pictures.

"A wedding veil?" the guard asked.

She nodded. Then she waited until Jared looked at her. When his gaze was on hers, she told him what she really thought. "It's Lexi's veil."

Chapter Sixteen

Other women had been murdered. The veil could have belonged to one of them. Lexi's wasn't the only veil that hadn't been found. But not all of the women had intended to wear them with their gowns.

Would Becca?

Jared didn't want their fake wedding to get that far, though—far enough that she was fitted for her gown. He needed to catch the killer first. But the next suspect he wanted to interview was proving difficult.

"I need you to come into the Chicago Bureau," Jared told the man over the phone. He was at the Bureau now—restlessly prowling his office as he waited for the lab to get back to him about that veil.

"I don't understand why you need to speak to me, Agent Bell," George Droski replied.

"It's about Lexi Drummond."

A soft sigh rattled the phone. "I haven't thought about Lexi in years…"

That didn't make him sound as obsessed as Harris Mowery had claimed he was.

"Not even when you've seen the news about other women being murdered just like she was?" Jared asked. It would only be natural to think about her then.

A heavier sigh rattled the phone. "I guess I've thought about her then."

"Another woman was just murdered."

"I saw that on the news," George admitted.

But was that the only way he'd learned about it? Or had he killed Amy like he'd killed all the others?

"Had you ever met her before?"

After a hesitation, George asked, "Who?"

"Amy Wilcox."

Another hesitation and then he said, "How would I have ever met her?"

"She was a friend of Lexi's." Or so Becca thought.

"That was a long time ago," George said. "A lot has happened since I saw Lexi last. I got married. I have two daughters. I really don't remember much about back then. I think my coming in to the Bureau would just be a waste of your time, Agent Bell."

Jared silently agreed, and he realized why Harris Mowery had mentioned George as a suspect. He'd wanted Jared to waste his time on a dead-end lead instead of pursuing a real suspect: him.

"I'd still like to talk to you," Jared persisted. He needed to meet the man in person to assess if George Droski could fit the profile he'd done of the Butcher. "If you won't come in, I'll come out to meet you."

There was another hesitation. Or maybe the man's cell phone just had poor reception. Then George replied, "I'm sure I can get to your office soon. I'll check my schedule and call you back."

Since Jared didn't have any evidence to link Droski to any of the murders, he couldn't justify having him picked up for questioning.

"I will expect a call and a meeting soon," Jared warned him. Because if the man tried to avoid meeting with him, then maybe he had something to hide. He clicked off the phone as his office door rattled with a knock.

He glanced up, hoping the lab tech had brought the results from the veil. But it wasn't a tech. He opened the door and greeted the man, "Mr. Kotlarz…"

Amy Wilcox's fiancé looked as if he hadn't slept since she'd first disappeared. A twinge of guilt struck Jared for thinking that the man had cared more about the engagement ring he'd given his fiancée than he'd actually cared about his fiancée.

"Agent Bell," the man's tone was sharp with anger and disapproval. "I'm surprised to find you here. Thought you were too busy getting engaged to work Amy's case."

He'd obviously seen Kyle Smith's news broadcasts.

"I am still very much working the case," Jared assured him.

"Do you have any new leads?"

Another person, a lower-level agent, stepped into Jared's office with an envelope. "The lab results, Agent Bell," the young woman told him. "I know you were waiting for these."

"Thank you," Jared said.

She smiled and turned to leave. And Troy Kotlarz watched her walk away. Maybe he didn't look so tired because he'd been grieving.

Jared tore open the envelope.

"Are those lab results from Amy's crime scene?" Troy asked. "Did it take all this time to get them back?"

"No," Jared said. "We got those back already."

"And you didn't call me?"

"There was nothing to report," Jared said. "Nothing to lead us to Amy's killer."

"And what about the ring?" Troy asked.

Jared should have counted how many minutes it had taken the man to ask about his family heirloom. Maybe it was all he cared about, and he'd only asked the other questions so he didn't appear callous.

Jared shook his head. "I'm sorry. It hasn't turned up yet."

Unable to wait until the man left, he pulled the lab results out of the envelope he'd already opened. The report confirmed that the stain on the veil was blood. Lexi Drummond's blood.

Becca had been right.

"Have you been checking pawnshops?" Troy asked.

"No," Jared said. "We're looking for a killer—not a thief."

"But if he pawned the ring, it could help you find him," Troy suggested.

Jared nearly laughed. Kotlarz was totally unaware of his profile of the Butcher. "He wouldn't pawn the ring."

The color drained from the brawny man's face. "What are you saying? That he's keeping it? It's some kind of sick souvenir for him?"

Jared nodded.

Serial killers often kept souvenirs, mementoes to remind them and help them relive their kills. The Bride Butcher had always kept something related to the wedding. Veils. Shoes. In Lexi's case, her veil and her body.

"So I'll never get the ring back then," Troy said, his broad shoulders slumping with dejection.

Had he already had someone else picked out to give it to?

Before Jared could ask, the man walked out. Jared didn't expect to see him again—now that he'd given up hope of finding his grandmother's ring.

The chief passed him on his way out and gave him a curious glance. "Amy Wilcox's fiancé?"

Jared nodded.

"Was he putting pressure on you to find her killer?"

"That wasn't his primary concern," Jared replied.

"Agent Munson said you had the lab results."

Jared handed them over.

The chief rubbed a hand over his chin. "This should make you feel better about your engagement."

"Better?" The bloodied veil was a message to Becca—that she would wind up like her sister if she tried to get married. "This proves how dangerous this is. We need to call off the engagement." His next call would be to Kyle Smith—to give him an exclusive on his broken engagement.

Lynch slapped the report down onto Jared's desk. "You were just given new evidence on a six-year-old case. This is the most progress you've made in a while."

"Progress?" he scoffed. "This does nothing to lead us to the killer."

"You don't have to chase the killer anymore," Lynch said. "You have him coming to you now."

Jared shook his head. "Not to me—to Becca."

"We will keep her safe," the chief vowed. "Rebecca Drummond is the key to you finally catching the killer."

He wanted to catch the killer, but not if it meant losing Becca.

REBECCA SQUINTED AGAINST the lights as she stepped out of the doors of Alex's school. Agent Campbell held tightly to her arm; whenever they were out now, he kept close to her side. He blinked against the flashing bulbs of the cameras.

The press had ambushed them—the same way they had ambushed Jared at her house that first time she'd seen him in six years. And like then, Kyle Smith led them like the alpha leading a pack of wild dogs.

He thrust a microphone into her face. "Ms. Drummond, do you really expect us to believe your engagement is real?"

Blaine tugged Rebecca away from the reporter. But Kyle followed, keeping the mike in her face. "Back off," Agent Campbell warned him.

"It's okay," Rebecca told her protector. She wanted to talk to the reporter. "I want to answer his questions."

"Of course," Kyle said. "Because you want to use me and the rest of the media in order for you and Special Agent Jared Bell to set your trap for the Butcher."

She blinked as if stunned by his accusation even as her heart pounded frantically with fear that the plan had been blown. It would never work now. She drew in a breath to steady herself and replied with a question of her own, "Do you think that the FBI would use a civilian to bait a killer?"

She had him stunned because he shot no question back at her.

"They would never risk my safety," she said.

"But Special Agent Bell would," Smith replied with his usual animosity for Jared.

"He would risk the life of the mother of his child?" she asked. "You don't know Jared at all."

"By putting a ring on your finger, he's risking your life," Smith argued.

But Rebecca wore no ring. Fortunately, she'd pulled on her gloves before she'd stepped outside, so Kyle couldn't know her hand was bare—unless he looked closely. She slid her hands into her pockets.

"I will be safe," she said and hoped like hell that she spoke the truth. "I wouldn't have accepted Jared's proposal if I didn't believe he could keep me safe."

Except that Jared had never proposed and probably never would even if she survived their fake engagement.

The reporter smirked. "Come on, Ms. Drummond. I think you would do anything to catch your sister's killer."

Maybe the man knew her better than she'd realized.

"I leave catching criminals to my fiancé," she replied. "I'm too busy planning my wedding to the man I love."

"You love him?" the reporter scoffed.

She nodded. "We've been apart for too long. You know we share a son. And we don't want to wait a minute longer to become a real family."

If only that were true...

"So you're serious—your engagement is real?" the reporter persisted.

She drew in another breath and looked directly into the camera. "I am in love with Jared Bell," she said, and realized that she spoke the truth. "I've been in love with Jared for six years."

Blaine glanced at her and nodded. Either he approved of how she was handling the obnoxious reporter or he approved of her loving his friend.

"So something good came of your sister's death then," the reporter said, as if trying to justify Lexi's murder.

Had Jared been right to suspect the reporter could be more involved than she'd thought? Had she been entirely too focused on Harris Mowery to the point that she hadn't realized there could have been another killer and Lexi was just a random victim?

"I wish Jared and I had met some other way," she said. Because then he never would have doubted her feelings the way he had six years ago. "But I'm glad that we met. And I can't wait to become his wife."

"Do you really think that the Butcher will ever allow that to happen?" Smith asked, almost as if he pitied her.

She kept her reply to herself and allowed Blaine

to escort her through the throng of reporters. But no, she didn't think that the Butcher would let her make it to the altar.

Chapter Seventeen

The way she stared into the camera as she vowed her love made Jared feel as if she was speaking directly to him. But that declaration wasn't meant for him; it was meant for her sister's killer. So that the Butcher wouldn't suspect she was setting a trap for him.

Kyle Smith had suspected it was a trap. Was he the killer?

Jared cleared his throat and gestured at the television. "You were convincing," he told her. His heart ached with longing. He wished she'd been speaking the truth, that she really loved him. But if she loved him, why had she kept their son from him?

Sure, he'd rejected her earlier declarations of love. He'd thought her feelings couldn't be real then—not with everything else she'd been going through. When she hadn't contacted him about Alex, she'd proved him right. Hadn't she?

While he sat on the couch in front of the TV, she was in the kitchen, putting away the leftovers from the dinner she'd made. Alex was reading in his room. It was like they were already married; like they were already a family. He wished that were true, too.

She shrugged. "I don't know if I was convincing enough."

"I guess we'll know soon." Her dress fitting was scheduled in a couple of days. If the Butcher followed his previous pattern, that was when he would try to abduct her.

Try. That was all he would be allowed. An attempt. He wouldn't take her as he had all those other women. Jared would make certain of that.

"I almost hope you're right," she remarked.

"About?"

"Kyle Smith," she said. "I almost hope it's him."

"Harris Mowery's wrong about you," Jared said. "He's convinced he's the only suspect you'll consider."

She snorted derisively. "I'm not going to consider George a suspect." She pointed at the television. "But Kyle Smith…" She shuddered. "It was like he was using our relationship to justify Lexi's murder."

"I caught that, too," he said. But it had been hard to focus on anything but Becca's declaration of love. "I'm still working on finding links between him and any of the victims."

"But do serial killers have to have a link to their victims?" she asked. "Or do they just randomly choose them?"

"Usually there's a link to one of the victims," he said. "The first one."

"Lexi…" She shook her head. "She didn't know Kyle Smith." She stepped away from the kitchen to join him near the couch. But she didn't sit down beside him; she didn't touch him. She didn't act like a woman in love— even though she was back to sharing his bed. "It must be Harris Mowery."

"Or it could be George Droski…"

She shook her head. "Not a chance."

"Or maybe there was a victim before Lexi…"

Her blue eyes widened with shock. "Do you think so?"

"I haven't found another death that matches the Butcher's MO," he admitted. "But there are a lot of missing persons cases."

"So, maybe, like Lexi, his first victim was never found?"

"It's something I'm looking into—if Kyle Smith knew someone who disappeared before Lexi."

She drew closer to him now and knelt before where he sat on the couch. She slid her palm over the side of his face and said, "I'm sorry."

She'd already apologized—several times—over not telling him about Alex. "Why?"

"I hope you never think I doubted how hard you've worked on this case," she said. "I hope you know how much I appreciate how hard you've worked."

He had worked hard. Maybe that was one of the reasons he'd rejected her declaration of love six years ago—because he'd wanted to focus on finding her sister's killer. He'd known she needed that more than she'd needed him.

And he'd denied how much he needed her. He leaned over so that his lips touched hers, sliding back and forth in a gentle kiss.

Her breath escaped in a wistful sigh.

He would have deepened the kiss, but the doorbell rang—like it had the other night.

She tensed. "Who would ring the bell?"

She knew that the signal was a phone call to announce an intruder or a visitor. Jared reached for his weapon, and she sprang to her feet and headed to their son's bedroom—to protect him.

Jared needed to protect them both. His weapon in his hand, he approached the door. And like the night they'd found the bloody veil, he opened the door to another ominous present. But there wasn't just one—there was a pile of them.

"WHERE DID THEY come from?" Rebecca asked as she saw the assortment of different-sized boxes wrapped in shiny paper. "Did someone sneak them up here?"

Jared shook his head. "No, they were delivered to the front desk."

"Then you'll be able to get a description of who dropped them off," she said and expelled a breath of relief. "You'll be able to find him." And stop him.

Jared sighed, too, but with resignation. "These were all deliveries. The presents were mailed here."

"From where?"

He glanced down at the boxes he'd taken from the doorman who'd brought them up from the lobby. He'd dropped them at the door when the guard had grabbed and frisked him. "Several different places."

"But we're not registered. We haven't even sent out invitations to this wedding." Because it wasn't real. "So why would anyone send us gifts?"

He shrugged but opened one of the cards attached to a present. "To Rebecca Drummond, you've been through so much with losing your sister. You truly deserve your happiness."

She took the card he held out and read the signature. "I don't know this person."

"But maybe she thinks she knows you—from the news coverage," he said. "Maybe Kyle Smith gave out your address again."

Or they'd tracked her down through him. Kyle had given out his name, too. But she looked at all the boxes and shivered. What if the gifts weren't as innocuous as the card? What if they contained other macabre gifts like the bloodied veil?

Despite her telling him to stay in his room, Alex's door creaked open, and then he bounded into the room with a shout of excitement. "Look at all the presents! It's not my birthday, though. Or Christmas…"

He looked up at his father. "It's not Mommy's birthday, either. Is it yours?"

Jared shook his head. "Nope, my birthday is in April."

"Then why are there so many presents?"

Jared looked at Rebecca now. "With the news coverage, he's bound to find out…"

"Find out what?" Alex asked.

Jared was right. They couldn't keep him reading or playing in his room all the time. He went to school. He would eventually overhear something.

She drew in a deep breath and turned toward their son. "People think your father and I are getting married."

His blue eyes brightened and a big smile creased his little face. "That's—"

"But we're not really getting married," she hastened to add. "We're only letting people think that we are."

"Why?" he asked. But she suspected it was more than his natural inquisitiveness that had him asking questions.

"Because it's going to help catch the bad guy who took away your aunt Lexi," she said. "Remember how I said I was going to help? This is how I'm helping."

"No," he said. "I meant why aren't you getting married for real?"

Pain clutched her heart. She wished the wedding would be real. She wanted it to be real. "You know that not all mommies and daddies are married."

He had friends with divorced parents.

He nodded. "But those mommies and daddies don't love each other anymore."

And he thought they did? Maybe he'd overheard the television replaying the impromptu interview she'd given Kyle Smith.

She opened her mouth but she had no words. She

couldn't deny her feelings for Jared. She did love him. And she wouldn't lie to her son.

"We have to catch this bad guy before we can do anything else," Jared spoke for her.

Alex nodded as if he completely understood.

Rebecca wished that she did. Was Jared implying that something could happen after the bad guy was caught? That he might actually propose then? Or was he only putting off Alex's inevitable disappointment?

She had a feeling that she would be even more disappointed than their son.

His eyes still bright with excitement, he moved closer to the presents Jared had piled onto the coffee table. He asked, "Are these gifts real?"

Nerves fluttered in her stomach as she remembered finding that veil stained dark brown with old blood—with Lexi's blood. What else of Lexi could be inside those boxes? Her body had never been found.

"Alex," she cautioned as she reached for him. "You really shouldn't touch them."

"So they're not real…" Alex uttered a soft little sigh of disappointment.

"We're not sure what they are," Jared said. "We need to get them checked out before anyone opens them."

"How?" Alex asked.

"I'm going to have an agent pick them up and bring them down to the Bureau," Jared said. "They'll x-ray them there."

The little boy giggled. "Like Mommy x-rays people to check for broken bones?"

Jared smiled. "Yes, like that."

"When is the agent coming?" she asked.

"He'll be here soon," Jared assured her.

Rebecca breathed a sigh of relief. She would be glad when the presents were gone.

Alex stepped a little closer to the coffee table. "That one's so pretty," he mused. And as he pointed, the small brightly wrapped present, piled on the others, toppled down onto the floor.

As it had the other night, the cover fell off the box and the contents spilled out. The box was too small for anything too gruesome or frightening.

But, like the veil, Rebecca immediately recognized the sapphire-and-pearl earrings that bounced across the hardwood. Her hands shaking, she leaned over to pick them up.

"That present was real, Mommy," Alex said. "And they're pretty."

And like Lexi, Rebecca had thought they were gone forever. That she would never see them again…

"There's a note, Mommy," Alex said as he reached down for the box.

"No," Jared told him, then softened his sharp tone and continued, "don't touch that. We might need to check it for fingerprints."

Alex nodded. "Yeah, fingerprints…but Mommy is touching the earrings. Won't she mess up the fingerprints?"

"Yeah," Jared said. "Let me talk to Mommy alone a minute while you pick out a bedtime story in your room."

Her son brushed past her on his way to his bedroom. But she couldn't take her gaze from the jewelry cradled in her palm. She was aware, though, that Jared moved, that he leaned down and picked up the note he'd told their son not to touch.

"What does it say?" she asked him.

Instead of answering her question, Jared asked one of his own, "What are they? You must recognize them or you wouldn't be staring at them like that."

She shivered. "They were Lexi's something blue..." Their grandmother had given them to her.

"I'm sorry," he murmured. "I shouldn't have brought the gifts inside the apartment. I should have had the agent pick them up from the front desk."

She curled her fingers protectively around the earrings. She wouldn't have wanted anyone else touching her family heirloom.

"What does the note say?" she asked again.

He reached out and squeezed her shoulder. "Becca..."

She wanted to lean into the warmth and strength of his hand. Or turn and burrow into his arms, seeking comfort and protection. But Jared had warned her that the fake engagement would put her in more danger, and she'd ignored his advice. She'd told him she could handle it. So she stiffened her spine and prepared to handle it.

"I already know it's another threat," she said. That was all she received lately—either through phone calls or dressing room visits or cruel *gifts*. "Just read it to me."

He sighed but he recited the words he must have memorized since he didn't even look at the note. "Something borrowed. Something blue..."

He hesitated. And she knew there was more to it than that.

"Jared..."

"Don't go through with the wedding," he continued, "or you'll be dead, too."

Chapter Eighteen

He found her in his bed. But she wasn't sleeping. She jumped when he pushed the door fully open and stepped into his bedroom. "It's just me," he said. "I didn't think you'd still be awake."

He wasn't sure if he would find her in his bed, either. He'd had to invite her every night—after they tucked their son into his bed. But Jared had left before Alex's bedtime.

"What did you find out?" she asked.

"The other boxes held just gifts," Jared assured her.

"Are you sure?" she asked. "Maybe I should have opened them because I would recognize anything that belonged to Lexi."

"If it had belonged to Lexi," he said, "there would have been some not-so-cryptic note included. There were no more notes like that one."

She expelled a shaky little breath.

"One note was more than enough," he said. It had shaken her. And it had shaken him, too. "More than enough to convince you that I'm right—that it's too dangerous to go through with this fake wedding."

She shook her head. "I was getting threats before we even got *engaged*. Someone grabbed me before we got *engaged*."

"But let you go because you weren't engaged," he pointed out. "That dress fitting is coming up in a couple of days. We need to call this off." Because he couldn't risk losing her.

"I still won't be safe," she said, her voice vibrating deep in her throat, but not with fear—with anger. "I won't be safe and neither will any engaged woman in the country until the Butcher is stopped."

He couldn't argue with her. For one, he was too damn tired. So tired that he stripped off his clothes and climbed into bed with her. And for another, she was right; nobody was safe until the Butcher was caught.

So he drew her against him and held her. He could keep her safe here—in his arms. He wished she could stay there forever, pressed tightly against his heart that filled with love for her. But he couldn't tell her of that love now; he could barely acknowledge the feelings himself. He had to focus instead on protecting her.

"We'll find another way to catch him," Jared said, "without putting your life at risk."

She settled against his chest with a soft sigh. But he knew it wasn't resignation. She wouldn't give up, which she confirmed when she said, "He's gone free too long. He's hurt too many people. This is the fastest way to catch him."

And the fastest way for Jared and Alex to lose her. He tightened his arms around her. He wouldn't let her go. "Then I'll protect you," he promised. "I'll make sure nothing happens to you."

For their son's sake but mostly for his.

Now her breath shuddered out in a sigh of relief that caressed his chest. Then her lips slid over his skin.

And he wasn't tired any longer as his pulse began to race and his heart hammer. He tipped up her chin and kissed her with all the passion burning inside him. While he didn't want to tell her how he felt about her, he set out to show her. He made love to her tenderly and slowly—kissing and caressing every inch of her silky skin.

She moaned and writhed and cried out as pleasure overwhelmed her. But it wasn't enough. He wanted to give her more. He made love to her with his fingers and his mouth and his tongue.

But she wanted more. She reached down and wrapped her hand around him, stroking him to madness. His control snapped, and he thrust inside her—into her heat and warmth. She wrapped her legs around his waist and arched into his every thrust. They moved in perfect rhythm. And together, staring deeply into each other's eyes, they came apart—their sanity and hearts lost as they found ecstasy.

The words filled his throat then—the declaration of love he wanted to give her. He had to give her...

But it would only complicate things further, and they were already complicated enough. So he swallowed his words and settled her against his chest again, against his heart, and wrapped his arms tightly and protectively around her.

And he hoped he could keep the promise he'd made her—that he could make sure nothing happened to her. He had to keep her safe.

REBECCA AWOKE ALONE the next morning. Maybe Jared was only in the kitchen or playing with Alex. But the apartment felt emptier than that. It felt like he was gone.

She felt like he was gone—because there was an emptiness in her, too. He'd promised to protect her, so there was probably a guard or two at the door. Or maybe one of his friends, a special agent, ready to follow her wherever she wanted to go. She had no doubt that Jared was trying to keep his promise to protect her—by finding the killer before she was in any danger.

But then he could be putting himself in danger. He'd interviewed so many suspects that he must have talked to the killer—more than once. If the Butcher suspected he was getting close, he might stop Jared before Jared could stop him.

Despite the warmth of the bed, she shivered. Then a phone rang, and she jumped. Maybe it was Jared, though, so she grabbed up her cell from the bedside table. "Hello?"

And her heart sank at that ominous hesitation. But after a few seconds, it wasn't the raspy voice that spoke to her. It was a familiar one. "Becca?"

"George?" She hadn't heard from her childhood friend in years. Six to be exact. He'd called and expressed his concern for her when Lexi had disappeared. How could Jared have ever suspected him? "Is everything all right?"

"Yes," he replied. "I think so…"

"What's wrong?" she asked.

"An FBI agent called me a couple of days ago," he said. "He wants me to come to the Chicago office for an interview. Do you know if I'm actually considered a suspect?"

"George, I don't know." Could Jared really consider him a suspect?

"It's the agent—the one I've heard on the news that you're engaged to," he said with an emotional crack in his voice. He was hurt.

Kyle Smith had made sure that news report had gone national—she wasn't even sure where George lived since he'd moved away from their hometown in Ohio.

"I'm sorry," she said.

"I didn't know if you were the one who mentioned my name to Agent Bell…"

"It wasn't me," she assured him. "I don't believe you

had anything to do with Lexi's murder. I know you would never hurt her."

"I would never hurt her," he agreed.

"It was Harris Mowery," she said. "He's the one who told Jared about you."

"Mowery?" He cursed. "Of course it was him."

Jared most definitely had interviewed the killer—when he'd interviewed Mowery. "I know it's him," she said. "He was the one who hurt her."

"He's the reason Lexi's gone," George said. "I'm sorry, Becca…"

She shivered again—at his strange apology. "Why, George?"

"I shouldn't have called you."

"I'm not sure why you did," she admitted. She hadn't heard from him in six years. "You don't have any reason to be concerned about Jared interviewing you."

Or did he?

"It's just strange," he said, "being questioned in her disappearance, especially after all this time."

"Jared is just being thorough," she said. "He won't arrest anyone without evidence." No matter how much she'd wanted him to put Harris Mowery behind bars for the rest of his miserable life.

Instead, the man was engaged—going to get married—probably going to have children. He was doing all the things he'd robbed Lexi of when he'd taken her life.

"I know," George said. "It's just strange. But I really called for another reason."

"What's that?" Rebecca asked.

"Aren't congratulations in order?"

She'd known George too long to lie to him. So she said nothing.

"You are getting married, right?" he asked. "That's what all the news reports are saying."

She didn't know if she would actually make it to the altar or not. Jared had promised to protect her, not marry her. But she needed to say something, so she repeated what she'd told Kyle Smith. "I love Jared Bell very much."

"You must," George said, "since you're risking your life to marry him."

She sucked in a breath of shock at his comment.

"I'm sorry, Becca," he said. "I'm just repeating what that slimy reporter's been saying—that that sick killer will probably go after you."

"I'll be safe," she assured him and herself. Chief Lynch had promised her, and now so had Jared.

"I hope so," George said. "I really wish you all the best, Becca."

"Thanks," she said. But she wasn't sure what else to say to him beyond, "Goodbye." She ended the call with an uneasy feeling twisting her stomach into knots.

George's call had been strange. She doubted he'd called to offer his congratulations. Was he really worried about Jared interviewing him?

Why?

She couldn't believe he had anything to do with Lexi's death. He'd been like a brother to them. Maybe that was why he'd called—because he was genuinely concerned for her safety.

So was Jared.

He didn't understand that she wasn't just doing this for Lexi and the Butcher's other victims and potential victims. She was doing this for him, too. He needed to catch the one killer who eluded him. The Butcher was his white whale—the one who'd hurt his otherwise spotless career, the one who caused Jared great guilt with every new victim the killer claimed.

She had to do this. For him...

That was how much she loved him.

The phone rang again, and she breathed a sigh of relief. It had to be him. "Yes?" she answered it.

But there was that ominous pause. And then that raspy voice asked, "Are you getting the message yet? Have you canceled the wedding?"

She tensed, but instead of fear, anger coursed through her. She was done playing the victim to this monster—done with the sick games. "Absolutely not."

"Then you're going to die."

The line clicked dead...like she would soon be if the caller's ominous prediction came true.

Chapter Nineteen

"You didn't have to come back early from your honeymoon for this," Jared told Dalton Reyes. But he was damn glad he had. He'd seen firsthand how fiercely Reyes had protected Elizabeth when she'd been in danger. The former gangbanger had the street smarts to help keep Becca safe.

And Jared needed all the help he could get. His stomach knotted with dread. Her dress fitting was only hours away.

Reyes smacked his shoulder. "You had my back," he reminded Jared. "Now I've got yours."

"It's not my back I'm worried about," he murmured as Becca walked into the living room after closing the door to Alex's bedroom.

With her hair caught up in a high ponytail, she looked younger than her nearly thirty years. She looked like a teenager. Too young and too vulnerable to face a killer. But as she stepped closer, he saw the resolve and determination on her beautiful but pale face. He also saw the moisture of tears in her eyes. Saying goodbye to their son had affected her. Was she worried that it might've been her last time?

Unconcerned that Reyes watched them, he pulled her into his arms. "I will protect you," he promised. He would make damn sure she saw their son again.

Fortunately their son was safe; Blaine Campbell was in his room, probably hooked up to the lie detector test with the list of questions Maggie Campbell had given the little boy to ask her husband. Blaine would protect their son with his life.

Jared had good friends. And he'd never needed them more than he did now.

Becca clung to him for just a moment before pulling back. Tilting up her chin, she said, "Let's do this."

He wanted to kiss her—wanted to bring her back to bed and make love to her. Just in case it was the last time...

Not for her, though. She would be safe. He intended to confront the killer before the man could get to her.

"You'll ride up with Reyes," he said.

"Not you?"

Because of all the tension, he tried for humor. "Isn't it bad luck for the groom to see the bride's gown before the wedding?"

But instead of smiling, her face grew even paler. His joke had fallen short. But then he'd never been funny.

"The killer will know it's a trap," Reyes said, "if Jared drives up with you."

Becca nodded. "Of course."

"I'll keep you safe," he promised again.

"And so will I," Reyes assured her.

"You can change your mind, though," Jared reminded her. "You don't have to do this." But he'd already seen the grim determination on her face. He knew she wasn't changing her mind even before she shook her head.

She swung a bag over her shoulder and spoke to Reyes. "Let's go."

"Everything's in place at the chapel," he updated Reyes. Undercover agents and bodyguards were hidden all over the place. The killer would not get to her.

Reyes nodded. "We're going to get him."

She turned back to Jared. "And it won't be George Droski."

She didn't sound as confident as she once had, though. She'd told him about the man's phone call that had unsettled her.

But the guy had come to Chicago for that interview. He'd been nervous. Nervous enough to make Jared nervous.

"It'll be Harris Mowery," she insisted.

Jared wasn't so sure. Some alibis had fallen apart but not for Harris Mowery.

He walked out with them, but when their car pulled out of the parking garage, he didn't follow. He turned toward another section of town—a higher-rent district—and found a parking spot on the street near Kyle Smith's building.

Since the guy hadn't been parked outside Jared's building the way he usually was, Jared wondered if he'd already left for the chapel. He would have found out when Becca's dress fitting was; he would have made a point of it.

Penny Payne had confirmed a break-in of the office in her wedding chapel/reception hall. And the organized woman was certain someone had gone through her date book. Jared was pretty sure that had been to find the time for Becca's fitting. He wouldn't have cared about the wedding. Nobody expected her to actually make it to the altar.

Least of all Jared. Once they caught the killer, the fake wedding would be called off. Unless he could convince her to forgive him for how he'd treated her six years ago.

Maybe she already had. But had she forgiven him enough to let herself love him?

He would find out—once the killer was caught. He stepped out of the car and swung the door shut. And as he headed into the lobby, he patted his jacket, making sure his gun was ready. Not that he would have forgotten it today.

Today was the day he needed it most. To protect the woman he loved. He flashed his badge at the doorman. "I need to see Kyle Smith."

The doorman picked up the phone. "He's not answering, sir."

"Did you see him leave?"

Had he already beat Jared to the dress fitting at the Little White Wedding Chapel?

The doorman shook his head. "No, and he didn't call for a car."

"I need to go up to his apartment," Jared said.

"Agent Bell…"

The doorman obviously recognized him—thanks to Kyle Smith. "You know he'd want to see me," Jared said. "He's usually parked outside my apartment." Or following Becca everywhere she went.

Why hadn't he called for a car?

The doorman leaned closer and whispered the reporter's apartment number. Then he winked. Apparently he wasn't any more a fan of Kyle Smith than Jared was.

"Thanks," he said as he hurried into a waiting elevator. The doorman had given him the apartment number, but Jared probably should have asked for a passkey, as well. Kyle Smith probably wouldn't be in a hurry to open the door for him—especially if he'd learned that some of his alibis had fallen apart.

Of course the reporter had struggled to remember where he'd been when each woman had disappeared, so he might have inadvertently given Jared incorrect information. Or he might have slipped up.

Finally. Six years later…

Jared paced the elevator car as it ascended. Maybe he should have taken the stairs. But finally it stopped with a sharp jerk. Long seconds passed before the doors began to slide open. Jared didn't wait for them to open all the way; he squeezed through the first crack in the doors and headed down the hall.

Hell, if Smith refused to let him in, Jared would just break down his door. Giving incorrect information in a federal investigation gave Jared the right to bring him in for further questioning.

But he didn't have to break down the door; it gaped open. Had the doorman had a change of heart and alerted Smith? Jared swallowed a curse. But then he noticed the broken doorjamb. Smith hadn't done that running out; someone had broken in. He reached for his gun and pulled it from the holster beneath his jacket.

He pushed the door fully open and stepped inside. Furniture had been overturned and pictures had been knocked off the walls. He moved slowly through the apartment, stepping over things until he came upon the body.

Kyle Smith stared up at him, but for once he didn't wear that smug grin. His mouth was open, blood trickling from the corner and over the side of his face. And his eyes were open, too, staring blindly.

He was dead. He wasn't the killer, but maybe he'd figured it out. Maybe he'd found the evidence that Jared had been looking for all these years, and that was why his apartment was torn apart. The killer had been looking for it.

Why hadn't Smith called him? Had he been saving the reveal for a special news broadcast? Probably. And trying to further his career had cost Kyle Smith his life.

Jared uttered a sigh, but the breath had barely passed his lips when he heard a creak. Maybe it was just some of the broken furniture. But before he could turn, something struck his head—hard.

Pain blinded him, and his knees folded from the force of the blow. And he fell beside Kyle Smith. But he didn't have to look into the dead man's face for long—because everything went black as oblivion claimed Jared. He only had time for one final thought: he'd broken his promise to Becca. He wasn't going to be able to keep her safe.

SPECIAL AGENT NICK RUS leaned in the open driver's side window. He wore a hard hat and looked like a road crew worker holding up traffic with a sign. "I don't think you should go on to the chapel until Jared gets here."

Dalton glanced over at Rebecca as if debating how much to reveal in front of her. Then he replied to Rus, "Jared was stopping somewhere to check out another lead before meeting us here."

"Did he bring backup with him?" Rus asked, his blue eyes darkening with concern.

Rebecca's pulse had already been racing with fear for herself—for what she might encounter in that dress fitting room. A monster. But now she worried about Jared. Was he facing the monster now?

"Where was he going?" she asked.

Dalton shrugged. "All he would say is that he was following up on an alibi that had fallen apart."

A gasp slipped through Rebecca's lips. "Harris. He had to be going to see Harris Mowery."

"Why wouldn't he say?" Dalton asked.

"He probably didn't want to get my hopes up," she suggested. Six years ago she'd been relentless in wanting him to arrest her sister's fiancé.

Dalton pulled out his cell phone and punched in a number. He muttered a curse before saying, "It went straight to voice mail."

Agent Rus glanced at the backed-up traffic, as if looking for Jared's car. "He wouldn't miss this."

"No, he wouldn't," Dalton Reyes agreed.

Her heart pounded harder and faster. "Do you think something has happened to him?"

Dalton shook his head. "No. He wouldn't have risked being late for your fitting."

"No," she said, "unless he thought he could catch the killer before…"

"The killer catches you," Dalton finished for her.

Her fear increased. "But what if the killer caught him?"

Dalton and Rus both shook their heads. "Jared's a better field agent than he even knows. He's fine."

Were they lying to her so she wouldn't worry? Or was Jared the one playing games? Maybe he thought if he didn't show, the fitting would get called off. Was that his way of protecting her—to get the whole operation cancelled?

The only way to truly protect her and countless other women was to catch the killer. If Jared had apprehended the Butcher, he would have called.

She drew in a deep breath to brace herself. "It's getting late," Rebecca said. "We need to do this."

Rus shook his head, then cursed.

"Lynch in your head?" Dalton asked.

Rus touched his earpiece and nodded. "The boss says to proceed. We have enough backup without Jared."

Chief Lynch must have come to the same conclusion Rebecca had—that Jared hadn't showed because he had never approved of setting a trap using her as bait. Anger replaced her fear for him. And that anger strengthened her resolve.

"Let's do this."

Rus stepped back from the car and waved them through to the church. Dalton parked at the curb and escorted her up the stairs. But he wasn't the only one in the area. A lawn care crew worked on the grounds around the church. One mowed while another trimmed shrubs and a third worked a weed eater.

Even if he didn't realize they were special agents and bodyguards, she doubted the killer would try to grab her with so many people around. Jared hadn't needed to worry about her. But apparently he wasn't worried or he would have showed up.

She hurried up the steps to the church as if anxious for her fitting. As if she couldn't wait to marry the man she loved.

And she did love him—despite how frustrating and stubborn he could be. But she doubted that they would ever marry. Mrs. Payne greeted her in the foyer—with a big hug.

"I remember you from Dalton's wedding," Penny Payne said. And she reached up and patted the special agent's cheek like he was a small boy. "Such a handsome groom he was. And his bride…"

"Beautiful," Dalton said with a loving smile.

"You will be a beautiful bride, too," Penny promised her. "I bet you can't wait until you see your dress…"

Rebecca couldn't wait until this was over and she could return to her son. At least Blaine Campbell was protecting him. Alex was safe. With the list of questions he'd had to ask Agent Campbell, he was also occupied and amused.

"The dressing room is right this way," Penny said as she led Rebecca to a short hallway off the foyer.

A door stood open and inside the sunny-yellow room was a tall, dark-haired woman. She had a measuring tape draped around her neck. But Rebecca recognized her from the wedding. She was one of the bodyguards.

"This is my seamstress," Penny said. "Candace…"

The other woman smiled at Rebecca. "Your dress is

in the garment bag. Please try it on, and we'll see where we need to make adjustments." With Penny Payne, she stepped out of the room and closed the door—leaving Rebecca alone inside.

But she wasn't alone. She had a mike taped onto her, so that Dalton and every other FBI agent in the area could hear her call for help—if she needed it. She suspected she wouldn't need it.

Obviously, Candace had made sure the room was empty before she'd shut her inside. So what was she supposed to do now? Try on a dress that she would never wear anyway?

She reached for the zipper of the garment bag, but just as she began to pull it down the door opened again. She drew in an unsteady breath, but it was only Candace again.

"Are you okay?" the bodyguard asked.

"Of course," Rebecca said. "Why wouldn't I be?"

"The perimeter guards caught someone trying to get in through a basement window," Candace replied.

Rebecca started forward, but Candace blocked the doorway. "Stay here," she advised her. "Until I make sure the suspect's been contained."

Goose bumps lifted on Rebecca's arms. She wasn't sure they'd contained the actual suspect. It was probably just Kyle Smith who'd been trying to break in to get exclusive coverage of her murder.

But before she could voice her concerns to the female bodyguard, Candace closed the door, once again shutting Rebecca alone in the room.

But when she turned around, Rebecca realized she wasn't alone any longer. Someone else stood inside the room with her—someone she'd never suspected.

A scream burned her throat, but she was too shocked to utter it. Too shocked to do anything to save herself…

Chapter Twenty

Jared winced when Reyes touched the back of his head. "You probably have another concussion," the agent said. "You should've gone to the hospital instead of driving up here."

But he'd promised Becca that he would protect her. He hadn't done a very damn good job of that, though— at least not personally.

"We had this," Nick told him. "You should have gone to the hospital. What the hell happened to you?"

"Kyle Smith's dead," he revealed.

Dalton whistled. "I know the guy was a pain in your ass, but I didn't think you'd actually kill him."

"I found him dead."

"So how'd you get the blow to your head?" Dalton asked. "Trip over his body?"

Jared winced as he remembered nearly falling on the dead man. "I didn't realize the killer hadn't left yet."

"You must have been out for a while," Reyes remarked, "since he beat you here."

Jared touched his head himself. While the blow had caught him by surprise, it hadn't been as damaging as the one he'd taken while protecting Elizabeth. Sure, he'd lost consciousness, but he hadn't thought he'd been out that long.

"It's probably good he was in a hurry," Reyes said as he touched Jared's wound again. "Or he might have finished you off like he had Kyle Smith. Why do you think he killed Smith? Do you think the reporter figured out who the killer was before we did?"

Jared didn't even know who the killer was. "Where is the suspect?" he asked.

Reyes chuckled. "Does it irritate you that we caught him without you?"

"I just wanted him caught," Jared said. He followed Reyes over to one of the Bureau's black SUVs. The windows were tinted, so he couldn't see inside. "Open the door."

Reyes clicked the locks and gestured at the handle. "I'll let you do the honors."

Jared pulled open the door and expelled a breath of surprise. Becca was going to be horribly disappointed that her trap had snagged the person she'd least suspected.

"It was hard to get you to come up to Chicago," he said. "Surprised to see you came all the way up here. From… Where is it you're from again, Mr. Droski?"

The man said nothing.

So Jared answered for him. "You're from St. Louis, George. Did you forget? But then you're a very busy man—busy with your wife and kids. Or busy abducting and killing brides-to-be?"

"And apparently knocking federal agents over the head," Reyes added for him.

George Droski ignored Reyes but focused his gaze on Jared. During the interview the man hadn't been able to look him in the eye. Instead, he'd stared down at the table between them. The guy had red hair—not Jared's auburn—but a fiery red. He also had freckles and pale skin. He was nobody's image of what the Butcher would look like; he looked like Howdy Doody, not a violent serial killer. "It's not what you think…"

And the nerves he'd shown during their earlier interview were gone. It was almost as if he was relieved.

Serial killers often said that they'd wanted to be caught—after they were caught. That they were hoping that someone would stop them. As a profiler, Jared knew that was bullshit and just a feeble attempt for the killer to save face. They got caught when they got cocky—when they'd gotten away with their crimes for so long that they believed they couldn't be caught.

But he didn't believe George Droski was trying to save face. The man didn't have the arrogant, narcissist personality that Jared had profiled the Butcher would have.

He shook his head. "It's not him."

Dalton laughed. "Just because you didn't catch him?"

"It's not him," Jared repeated as he turned and headed toward the church. He was vaulting up the steps when he heard Becca scream—a scream of pure terror. Other agents started forward, as well, but Jared shook his head. He wanted to assess the situation first—to make sure Becca hadn't been taken.

George Droski was talking now—drawing the attention of the agents away from Becca's scream to him. But Jared didn't care what he was saying. He cared only about Becca.

His weapon drawn, he rushed through the doors and toward the room from where the scream had emanated. Hoping he wasn't too late, he kicked open that door. Becca wasn't gone—not like all those other brides-to-be.

She was pale and shaking with her hand clasped over her mouth. There was no blood. No wounds. But she looked horrified—as shocked as if she'd seen a ghost.

"Are you okay?" he asked. "What's wrong?" Then he

turned and saw her, too. The ghost. The woman whose murder he'd spent six years trying to solve.

"No wonder I never found your body," he mused. "Hello, Lexi."

JARED SAW HER, TOO. She wasn't a ghost. Or a figment of Rebecca's imagination. She hadn't lost her mind. And apparently she hadn't lost her sister—at least not the way she'd thought she had these past six years.

And anger replaced her shock and fear. "Why?" she asked and her voice cracked. She refused to acknowledge the tears burning her eyes. Her voice had cracked because of the scream—the one she hadn't even realized had slipped out. She had stood there for so long, just staring at that apparition—because certainly it couldn't have been real. Lexi couldn't be real. But Jared saw her, too.

She cleared her throat and asked again, "Why?"

And for the first time since she'd unzipped the garment bag and stepped out, Lexi spoke. "I'm sorry…"

It wasn't enough. Rebecca shook her head. "I'm not looking for an apology. I want a reason—a reason that you put me through hell." All the pain and guilt and regret…

And the loss. That horrible ache of emptiness that Rebecca hadn't been able to fill—not with love for Jared. Not even with love for her son.

"Answer her," Jared ordered.

Tears filled Lexi's bright blue eyes. She looked the same, exactly the same as she had six years ago. That was why it had been almost easier to believe she was a ghost than to believe she was real. And that she'd chosen to leave.

"I had no choice," Lexi said. "It was the only way I could get away from Harris. Or he really would have killed me. I'm sure he's been killing those other women."

She shivered, and the tears overflowed her eyes and slid down her beautiful face.

Rebecca had missed her sister so much. All she wanted to do was pull her into a hug and hold her. And introduce her to Alex.

But there was so much she didn't know yet. "How?" she asked. "How did you do it?"

"There was so much blood," Jared added. "The coroner said you couldn't have lost that much blood and lived."

"As well as being a medical assistant, I'm also a phlebotomist," Lexi said. "I was taking small amounts of my blood for a couple of months and freezing it."

Jared nodded. He had known about Lexi's certification. But who would have believed she had used that skill to draw so much of her own blood? Not Rebecca. She was horrified. "You planned it for a while..."

And she'd never said anything to Rebecca. While she should have been thrilled her sister was alive, she still felt as if she'd lost her. Or maybe she'd never really had her at all.

"I'm sorry," Lexi said again as the tears continued to stream down her face. "But I wasn't sure you would go along with it. And I had to get away from Harris."

"You could have just dumped him," Jared suggested.

Lexi shook her head. "I tried. He nearly killed me then. And he promised me that was the only way I would get away from him—was when I died." She uttered a ragged sigh of resignation. "So I had to die."

Rebecca had seen the bruises. She knew her sister spoke the truth. That was why she'd been so convinced that Harris had killed Lexi—because he would've had Lexi given him the chance. Instead, she'd saved herself the only way she'd known how.

"Is that who the agents caught outside? Was it Harris?"

she asked Jared. "Or was it Kyle Smith?" She wouldn't have put it past the reporter to try to break into the chapel for another exclusive.

"Kyle Smith is dead," Jared said.

She noticed then the grimness on his handsome face and the streak of blood on the side of his neck. "Are you okay?" she asked. Had he fought with Smith? Had he been right that was who the killer was?

"I'm fine," he said. But the grimness didn't ease, and he still held his gun, the barrel pointed at Lexi—as if she posed some kind of threat. "And the person who was caught outside the chapel is George Droski."

"George?" Rebecca asked. "I was so sure he had nothing to do with the killings. He was so close to us growing up—like a brother."

"Maybe he was like your brother," Lexi said. "But he was never like mine."

Rebecca wondered about her sister's tone. She'd been even closer to George than Rebecca had. "But you two were so close…"

"We're closer now," Lexi said, and she smiled through her tears. "We're married."

"Married?" She'd thought Lexi had been robbed of her wedding, of her life. It was so hard to believe that she'd been living the past six years.

"He saved my life six years ago," Lexi defended the man, "when he helped me escape from Harris. George would never hurt anyone. He's only been helping me—trying to save you, too."

Rebecca's stomach churned as she had another revelation about her sister. "You were the one behind the warnings?"

"Of course it was her," Jared said. "Who else would have had the veil with her blood on it? And your grandmother's earrings?"

"Her killer," Rebecca murmured. She'd been so convinced that was who had been playing the mind games with her. But Lexi had done it. She'd never really known her sister at all.

"It must've been George calling you," Jared said. "And George who tried to grab you in the dress boutique."

"Why?" Rebecca asked her sister again. She'd always thought that Alex got his inquisitiveness from Jared. But maybe he'd gotten it from her.

"Because you are in danger," Lexi said. "Kyle Smith was making too big a deal out of you, making you too tempting a target for Harris to pass up. And I know he was going to try to kill you—especially after he killed Root Beer."

"Amy Wilcox?" Jared asked.

Lexi nodded. "That had to have been Harris. He only met her once, but he hated her."

"He has an alibi," Jared said.

Lexi snorted. "I'm sure he does. But it's not true."

"You're the expert on what's not true," Jared said. "You admit you faked your own death and terrorized your sister."

Lexi flinched as if Jared had struck her.

Rebecca loved them both. And she understood them both. Lexi had felt as if she'd had no other way out. But Jared had to be angry that he'd spent six years trying to solve a murder that had never been committed.

But then Jared pulled out his handcuffs. "Lexi Drummond-Droski, I am placing you under arrest for obstruction and harassment."

Rebecca gasped. "You can't!" Anger was one thing, but this felt vindictive. And she'd never thought Jared could be vindictive. He'd forgiven her for not telling him about his son. Hadn't he?

"I have to," he told Rebecca as he snapped the cuffs

around Lexi's thin wrists. "She's broken the law. And the ones I'm arresting her for might not be the only crimes she and George have committed."

He wasn't making any sense. Maybe the blood on his neck had come from a blow to the head—one that had addled his thinking. "What are you talking about?"

"She faked her death," Jared said, "but all those other women are *really* dead. We found their bodies. And the way they died exactly fits the way we thought she had died."

But of course they had thought that only after those other bodies had been found—with all those horrible stab wounds. Then it had made sense that they'd found so much of Lexi's blood if she'd also been stabbed.

But she'd stabbed herself—over and over again—with a needle. She'd been that desperate to get away from Harris. Lexi looked tiny standing in front of Jared—little bigger than Alex. Putting the cuffs on her was like arresting a child—someone vulnerable and innocent.

Rebecca shook her head. "Jared, you're not making any sense…"

"He thinks I killed them," Lexi said.

"You and your husband," Jared said. "It had to be you and George. He abducted the women like he tried to abduct Becca in that dress boutique."

"He wasn't trying to abduct her," Lexi argued. "He just wanted to scare her so that she wouldn't get any more involved with you and risk her life."

Jared's chin snapped up as if she'd struck him. "You think I'm a danger to Becca?"

"You broke her heart six years ago," Lexi said. "And you put her at risk today. I got in here. George nearly got in here. Harris could have, too."

"I think you're the greater danger," Jared said. "Harris doesn't know every detail about your crime scene.

You do because you staged it. And all those other crime scenes exactly match it. It has to be you and George who killed those other women."

"I didn't know those other women," Lexi said. "I only knew Amy, and I never would have hurt her."

"Like you didn't hurt your sister?" Jared asked. "You've been terrorizing her—"

More tears ran down Lexi's face. "I didn't mean to—I just wanted her to be careful. To protect herself—"

"But this wasn't the first time you hurt her," Jared said. "You nearly destroyed her six years ago."

"I'm not sure which one of you hurt me more six years ago," Rebecca said. It was as if they were having a contest, but the loser would be the one who'd hurt her most. "But you're hurting me now, Jared. I just found out Lexi is alive, and you're taking her away…" Her voice cracked with emotion. "In handcuffs."

He looked at her, his amber eyes full of regret. She noticed the dark shadows beneath his eyes and how a muscle twitched in his cheek. He was in pain. He must have been hurt earlier; that was why he hadn't shown up when he'd promised. And she'd thought he was just trying to stop her from putting herself in danger.

"I have to," Jared said. "She can't get away with what she's done."

"No, she can't," another man agreed as he stepped through the open door of the dressing room. He slammed it shut behind himself. At first Rebecca thought it was the crack of the door hitting the jamb that she heard.

But it was too loud, so loud that she winced. Then she screamed as she saw Jared crumple and drop to the floor. And she turned back toward the other man. Harris Mowery held a gun—a gun he'd just fired at the man she loved.

Chapter Twenty-One

Jared lay limply on the floor, blood trickling down his numb arm and soaking through his shirt and coat to the carpet beneath him. The bullet had missed his damn vest, hitting his shoulder instead. He'd dropped his gun. And because he'd dropped his gun, he'd dropped to the ground, too.

With a wounded arm and probably a concussion from what he suspected was now an earlier confrontation with Harris, he wouldn't be able to physically overpower him. He needed his gun. And he had to get it without Mowery noticing him reaching for it. He had to play dead and hope that Mowery didn't fire at him again.

He also had to get a message to his team so they didn't rush the room and force Mowery's hand. Because then he would definitely empty his gun—into Becca and Lexi before they'd have a chance to take him down.

Rebecca's scream had drawn Mowery's attention to her, so the man had turned away from him. But the gun had fallen too far away for Jared to reach for it quickly—without drawing Mowery's attention back to him. With his left hand, he pulled his badge from beneath him and flashed it at the stained-glass window.

He didn't flash an SOS. And because he hadn't, Rus and Reyes should know to back off and hold back the others. And let him handle it. As long as Harris didn't realize he wasn't dead...

"You shot him!" Becca yelled at Harris as she tried to move around him. But he swung that gun in her direction. "Why did you shoot him?"

"So he wouldn't try to save you," Harris said. "I needed Special Agent Bell out of my way. And you better stay where you are, Rebecca, or I'll shoot you, too. And that isn't at all what I've had planned for you."

Jared knew what he'd planned. The same gruesome death as all those other women but Lexi had suffered.

"What are you doing?" Becca asked.

The madman chuckled. "You knew I wouldn't be able to resist grabbing you, Rebecca. That was the whole purpose of your little plan. Kyle Smith was right about that..." He sighed almost regretfully. "I don't know why he resisted giving up the information about your fitting time and location. I knew he had it. And he'd always been so good about sharing his information before—until today."

"You killed him," Becca said, and her voice cracked with fear and with tears. She was probably worried that he'd killed Jared, too.

"I would've killed Special Agent Bell then, too," Harris said. "But I needed him to lead me back here. Back to you..." He swung his gun toward Lexi. "I didn't know he'd lead me to you, as well."

"You're not surprised I'm alive," Lexi said.

Clearly, Harris hadn't been as shocked as he and Becca had been.

"You're not going to be alive much longer," Harris promised her. "But first I intend to take care of your sister. She's been a pain in my ass for far too long."

He swung the gun toward Becca but Lexi lurched forward—stepping between them. She glanced down and noticed Jared staring up at her. And she shook her head in warning just before Harris turned back toward him.

So Jared closed his eyes and played dead, like Lexi had the past six years.

"How did you know I wasn't dead?" she asked, her voice, which had been so soft earlier, was loud and shrill now. She wanted to draw Harris's attention to her. And away from Jared.

She was helping him.

"I knew because I hadn't killed you," he said. "But I did—every time I killed one of those women. I killed you. I saw you—especially when I killed that insolent girl we met at the mall."

Lexi gasped. "Root Beer..."

"Whatever you called her," Harris said. "You and your childish little nicknames."

"Do you know what I called you?" Lexi asked.

"I never let you give me one of your ridiculous pet names," he said, his voice full of patronization and pride.

She smiled—a smile full of his usual smugness and arrogance. She was playing him hard, hitting all of his triggers.

For Becca...

To keep her sister safe from the man she'd brought into their lives.

"I had a nickname for you," Lexi told him. "I called you the Little Man." She laughed. "For so many reasons..."

He lashed out—just as she'd intended, striking her so hard that she dropped to her knees. "You bitch! You stupid little bitch!"

He raised his arm again to deliver another blow.

Lexi couldn't defend herself. She couldn't even lift her arm to deflect his blow because Jared had handcuffed her arms behind her back.

Jared reached for his gun, out of reflex with his right arm. But the numbness wasn't gone. It was like he was paralyzed. He couldn't move the limb that had been shot. He couldn't save Lexi from the next blow Harris dealt her.

But Becca could. With another scream, this one of anger instead of fear, she threw herself at the madman. Maybe she'd forgotten about his gun. Or maybe she was just so angry that she didn't care.

Another shot rang out, rattling the small stained-glass window in the room. Had Harris shot her?

PAIN EXPLODED IN Rebecca's head. The bullet hadn't struck her, but the barrel had when Harris swung it at her. The force of the blow made her fall to the ground next to Lexi. She'd only wanted to protect her sister—like she should have six years ago.

"And that's one of the reasons you're a little man," Lexi said. Blood oozed from the cut he'd opened on her lip. But she didn't care. She kept taunting him.

It was obvious to Rebecca that Lexi wanted him to kill her first—before he had a chance to kill Rebecca. Despite letting her believe she'd been dead the past six years, Lexi still loved her—enough to die for her. "Stop," she implored her. "Don't…"

"Don't what?" Lexi asked. "Tell the truth? I should have gone on that dead reporter's show years ago— telling what a weak, little man Harris Mowery is. That he can only pick on women."

"I killed that reporter," Harris said with pride. "I beat the dress fitting time out of him."

"I thought you said he wouldn't tell you," Rebecca reminded him. "That you had to follow Jared here."

He swung his gun back toward Jared. "I killed him, too. Or if he's not dead now, he soon will be." He pointed his barrel at Jared's head.

And Rebecca screamed. The hope that he was only unconscious was what had kept her from losing her sanity. If Jared was dead…

She would lose more than her heart. She would lose her mind and her soul, too. "No!" She vaulted to her feet and launched herself at Harris again.

But another shot rang out. She didn't know if it struck Jared or the floor near his head. She had no time to look—no time to go to him—before Harris tossed her back onto the ground like a rag doll.

She hit with a hard thud, jarring her bones and bruising her muscles. An oath slipped through her lips.

And Lexi screamed now. "Stop! Stop hurting her!"

"I'm going to do more than hurt her," Harris promised.

"I'm the one you want to hurt," Lexi said. "I'm the one you hate."

Harris cursed—calling his former fiancée every vulgar name a man could call a woman. "But you're wrong," he said. "I don't hate you. Not even now."

Lexi shivered. Maybe she would have preferred his hatred.

"I love you," he said, then cursed her again. "I love you like I've never loved anyone else…"

And Lexi had rejected him. She'd rejected life entirely over a life with him.

"You don't know what love is," Lexi said. "You have no idea."

"And you know?" he said with a snide smile. "Are you talking about your love for your sister? You put your darling *Becca* through hell when you faked your death."

Lexi shook her head. "I love," she said, "my husband. My children."

Harris's face flushed red with rage. Lexi had pushed him too far. He was certain to kill her now. "You're married?"

"Yes," she replied with a happy smile that made her swollen lip bleed even more. "And we have two beautiful children."

He lashed out again—so quickly that he struck Lexi before Rebecca could intervene. Lexi fell back on the floor. Then Harris swung the gun barrel toward her. "Don't move."

"Don't shoot her!" Rebecca yelled. She couldn't lose Lexi again—especially not if she had already lost Jared. She would need Lexi to hold her together.

"I'm not going to kill her yet," Harris said. "I want her alive to watch when I kill you." He turned back to Rebecca. But he slid the gun into the back of his belt. And instead he pulled out a knife and unsheathed it. "Of course she doesn't love you as much as her husband and children." He flicked his thumb over the shiny blade of the sharp knife. "I really should kill them instead..."

He shook his head. "But that would be breaking with my MO." He turned back to Lexi. "You know it," he said. "You gave it to me."

"How?" she asked. "How did you know exactly what happened there?"

He smiled again—that arrogant, smug smile. "Kyle Smith had a mole inside the Bureau. Some stupid female agent that fell for his slick smile—she kept him apprised of all the details of the case."

"And he told you?" Rebecca asked.

"Not intentionally," Harris said. "Probably not even consciously. He was a fool. And a braggart. It was easy to play him for everything he knew."

Except this last time. Kyle must have figured out he'd been aiding a killer, and he hadn't wanted to help anymore.

Why hadn't help arrived for Rebecca? There had been agents all around earlier. Had they left to bring George to jail? Poor innocent George who would lose the mother of his children if Harris had his way.

The agents must have left, or they would have heard this conversation through the mike she wore. They would have come to her aid and Jared's. Instead, he was bleeding to death on the floor. And as Harris swung that knife toward her, Rebecca realized that she would soon be bleeding, too.

She lifted her hands, but she didn't know how she would be able to fight off that blade. That sharp blade that had already killed so many other women.

"No!" she screamed as that knife slashed through the air on its descent toward her chest. Her heart…

Chapter Twenty-Two

Jared was right-handed, but with that arm numb and bleeding, he had to use his left hand to grab for and fire his weapon. So he squeezed the trigger and emptied the magazine, hoping that he hit the son of a bitch.

Harris's body tensed as at least one bullet struck him. But he didn't drop the knife, he clutched it harder as he lunged down on Becca.

Screaming filled the room. But it was Lexi—not Becca. She just lay still—beneath Harris's still body. Had Jared been too late to save her?

He cursed himself—furious that this killer had gotten the jump on him twice. And now he might have killed the only woman Jared had ever loved...

He lurched across the short space separating him from their tangled bodies. With one arm, he dragged Harris off her. He'd had to drop the gun. If the guy held the knife and was still alive, he could plunge that knife into Jared's heart. But if he'd already killed Becca, Jared had no heart left to hurt. And Harris had no life left to take anyone else's. His limp body slumped onto the floor, and he stared up at Jared through eyes wide with shock and fury.

He'd died knowing that he'd failed. He hadn't killed the woman he'd wanted to kill. He hadn't killed Lexi

Drummond. She scrambled to her knees, tears streaming down her face. Together they moved toward Becca.

Her eyes were open, too, and wide with shock. Her hands clasped her stomach. Jared cursed, and Lexi gasped. But then he noted that no blood oozed between her fingers. Instead of being plunged in her body, the knife was stuck in the floor next to her arm.

He had missed. Not only had he died but he'd died without taking either Becca or Lexi with him. Jared should have felt relief or even triumph. But his heart hadn't stopped pounding with fear for Becca's safety.

"Are you okay?" he asked her. He had to touch her, so he slid his fingers along her cheek. She was so beautiful but so pale and fearful. "Becca?"

Her breath shuddered out in a sigh of relief. "You're alive. I was so afraid that he'd killed you."

"I was afraid for you," he said. "And you…" He turned to Lexi. He shouldn't have cuffed her; he'd made her helpless to defend herself. But that hadn't stopped her from defending and trying to protect her younger sister.

He needed to find the key to the cuffs. But he couldn't take his good hand from Becca's beautiful face.

But then the door to the dressing room opened and he pulled his hand back to reach for his gun.

"You didn't flash SOS," Rus said as he stepped inside with his gun drawn.

"That's because I had this," Jared said.

"You just flashed once, so I knew you were alive," Rus said. "We held back because—"

"He would have shot us all if you'd tried breaking through the door," Jared said.

"We heard it all," Dalton added. "Rebecca was wearing a mike."

"So you released my husband?" Lexi asked.

"We caught him trying to break in," Dalton said. "And we heard what you and he did to your sister."

Jared pulled out the key to his cuffs and handed it to Dalton. "Let her go. She was just trying to protect her sister."

"But she faked her death," Rus added.

Jared stared down at the body of the dead man. Then his gaze went to the huge knife shoved deep into the floor. "To escape the Butcher…"

He didn't blame Lexi for what she'd done. He blamed himself. He should have listened to Becca. He'd gotten hung up on Harris having an alibi for Lexi's abduction, so he hadn't looked at him as a suspect in the other murders like he should have. If he had, he could have saved some of the other women. Harris had had no connection to them, though. He'd randomly picked brides— probably from their engagement notices in the paper— and as he'd killed them, he'd imagined Lexi. If Jared had caught Harris earlier, Lexi would have been able to come home to her sister and the rest of her family. It was more his fault than Lexi's that she'd had to stay away so long. "I'm sorry," he told her.

Dalton unhooked her, and she pulled her arms in front of her and rubbed her wrists. "I understand why you would arrest me," she said. "You must be furious over what I did."

"I understand why you had to," he said. "And that's why I'm sorry. I failed you. I should have caught him a long time ago. So you could have come home."

Tears spilled out of Lexi's eyes. "It wasn't your fault. None of it was."

She might see it that way, but he doubted that Becca did. Would she ever forgive him for not listening to her? And even if she could, he wasn't certain that he could forgive himself.

"We need to get you to the hospital," Nick said. "You should have gone after you took the blow to the head. Now you've been shot…"

Maybe it was the head wound or the loss of blood from the gunshot wound or maybe it was just hearing Rus say it aloud, but Jared suddenly got very dizzy. His vision blurred, and the pain in his head and shoulder intensified. He groaned, then dropped as oblivion claimed him again.

HER HEART POUNDING and nerves frayed raw, Rebecca paced the hospital waiting room. She'd nearly lost Jared so many times in just a few hours. He couldn't have saved her life only to leave her life. Tears blurred her vision. She loved him so much. Alex loved him so much.

Her little boy couldn't lose his father now—when he'd only just learned who he was. That was her fault. It was all her fault.

She hadn't let Jared know about his son. And then she'd committed to that crazy plan to flush out a killer. She was a physician's assistant, not an FBI agent. She hadn't been prepared for anything that had happened.

"I could help him," she murmured. "I should have helped him at the scene. I could have stopped the bleeding…"

"Harris wouldn't let you near him," Lexi reminded her. "He would have shot you, too."

She shuddered as she remembered how close she'd come to being Harris Mowery's latest and last victim. She had felt the air move from the slash of that sharp knife. If Jared hadn't shot him…

Lexi stepped into the path of her pacing. When Rebecca moved to the side, Lexi matched her movement and caught her. Then she pulled her into her arms and hugged her. Rebecca held herself stiffly. If she gave in to the tears, she probably would never stop crying.

But she felt Lexi's tears dampening her shirt and her skin as she clutched her closely. And Rebecca found her arms lifting and wrapping around her sister. She hugged her back. She was real. She was warm and soft and real. She was alive. And the tears began to fall.

"I'm sorry," Lexi murmured. "I'm so sorry…"

At first Rebecca thought she was offering the kind of apology people offered at funerals as an expression of sympathy. But Jared couldn't be dead. He couldn't…

She pulled back from her sister and looked around the waiting room. His friends were there—but for Blaine who'd stayed with Alex. Instead of pacing like her, they stood in a corner—talking and laughing. Trading stories about Jared.

They knew him better than she did. He'd been part of her life such a short time—six years ago—and a short time now. He couldn't leave her. But even if he survived his wounds, he would still probably leave her. The killer was caught now—dead now.

She trusted that he would stay part of Alex's life. But what about hers?

"He has to be okay," she murmured.

"He is," Lexi said. "He was so focused on saving you. He won't leave you."

"He did," Rebecca said, pain cracking her voice. "He left me six years ago. He didn't think I really loved him. He thought I was just using him to get over losing you." Tears threatened again, but she blinked them back. "But I never got over you."

"The news has been reporting that your son is his," Lexi said. "I have a nephew…"

"Yes, Alex," Rebecca said, and her heart warmed with love for her amazing child. "But I didn't tell Jared when I got pregnant. He just recently found out that he's a father."

"So I'm not the only Drummond who kept a secret

for years," she said. "Do you hate me for what I put you through?"

"No," Rebecca said, and she pulled her sister back into a hug. "I could never hate you. I'm so glad you're alive. Were you telling the truth—do you and George have kids, too?"

Lexi smiled again and reopened the wound on her lip. "Two girls. Becky is five, and Amanda is three." She blinked back tears. "The same years apart that we are. I think they'll be as close as we were."

"Why didn't you tell me?" Becca asked. "Why didn't you tell me what a monster Harris was?"

"He would have killed you," Lexi said. "I worried that he still would when you kept publicly accusing him. That's why George and I have kept an eye on you all these years. I've seen Alex…" Her voice cracked with emotion. "I can't wait to meet him, though. And I can't wait for you to meet my girls."

All Rebecca had wanted the past six years was to have her sister back—to share her life the way she wished they'd been doing before Lexi disappeared. But she couldn't think about her now. She couldn't think about anyone or anything but Jared.

"He has to be okay," she murmured again.

The door to the waiting room opened, and a doctor stepped inside. It was the ER doctor who'd treated Jared. She rushed forward—along with Nick Rus and Dalton Reyes, who asked, "How is he?"

"He'll be fine," the doctor assured them. "We did a CT scan. He has a slight concussion."

"What about the gunshot wound?" Rebecca asked.

"The bullet went through his shoulder," the doctor replied. "He needed a few stitches and an IV. He'll be fine. Would you like to see him?"

Rebecca stepped back as the agents stepped forward. They turned to her. "You can go first," Nick Rus offered.

She shook her head. "No, that's okay. I'm sure he'll want to talk to you about the case. He'll want to get everything finished up." She stepped back again—until she bumped into Lexi.

Lexi's hands gripped her shoulders and steadied her. The agents left—anxious to see their friend. And instead of holding her, Lexi shook her, albeit gently. "What are you doing?" she asked. "You want to see him. You've been so worried about him. Why didn't you go see him?"

Rebecca shook her head. "I don't know…"

"You know," Lexi said. "Tell me."

"Because it's over," she said. "Harris is dead. The Butcher has been stopped. It's over."

"The killing is over," Lexi agreed. "My having to play dead is over. But you and Jared—that doesn't have to be over."

"It was just an act," Rebecca said. "A trap. We never intended to get married."

Lexi uttered a soft sigh of disappointment. "So Jared was right six years ago. You didn't really love him."

Self-righteousness filled Rebecca. "No, he wasn't right. I did love him. I really loved him. It had nothing to do with filling any void you'd left. It was about him. I loved him."

"'Loved'?" Lexi asked. "Past tense? You don't love him anymore?"

"No…" If anything, she loved him more. He was such a good man. Such a good father for only just finding out that he was one. He and Alex had a bond—in their genius—that she would never share. But it was more than that. They were close already.

And Rebecca had seen what their life could be like as a family, taking care of and playing with Alex together.

And then she and Jared sleeping together every night, wrapped up in each other's arms.

"So you don't love him anymore," Lexi said.

"I didn't say that," Rebecca said. She wouldn't lie to her sister. She wouldn't lie about her feelings for Jared.

"So you do love him?"

Maybe Alex had gotten his inquisitiveness from his aunt. "Why do you keep asking? Why do you care?"

"Because I want to know," Lexi said. "You willingly used yourself as bait for a serial killer. So I thought you were brave, but you're acting like a coward now—when it comes to admitting your feelings."

"I want to know, too," a male voice added.

She turned around to find Jared standing behind her. Even though the doctor hadn't said anything about discharging him yet, Jared was dressed already—in his bloodied shirt and coat. And she was more afraid of facing him than she'd been of facing the serial killer.

What if she admitted her feelings and he didn't return them? That would hurt worse than if Harris Mowery had plunged that knife into her heart.

Chapter Twenty-Three

She wasn't going to answer him. Jared couldn't blame her. He had put her on the spot. She looked as if she wanted to be anywhere else than standing in that waiting room with him and her sister.

She probably wanted to get back to Alex. She'd been gone a long time.

"Forget it," he said. "You don't have to answer that. I'll take you back to the apartment—back to Alex." Maybe he would hook her up to Alex's lie detector test and ask her again. Then he would know if she told him the truth.

"So I can pack?" she asked. "So Alex and I can leave."

And he realized why she hadn't answered her sister's question. Because she wasn't sure how he felt. Because he'd never told her.

"I don't want you to leave," he said. "Ever…"

Then she was in his arms, clutching him closely. "Are you really okay?" she asked.

"Yes." They'd given him some painkillers that had dulled the ache in his head and his shoulder. But the narcotics had done nothing for his heart—only she could fix that.

"Are you sure you should be checking yourself out?" she asked anxiously.

"I'm fine," he replied, but it was a lie. "At least I will

be once you tell me how you feel. Do you want to pack up and leave?"

She shook her head. "No," she replied. "I don't want to leave. Ever..."

Warmth and relief flooded his heart. Her admission made him feel much better than the painkillers had. "That's good," he said as he ignored his wounded shoulder and clutched her closer. "Because I'm never going to let you go again. I love you, Becca."

He didn't care that he'd announced it in front of her sister and his fellow agents who'd joined them in the waiting room—probably when they hadn't been able to find him in the ER.

"I love you," she said. "I've always loved you."

"I know," he said. "I shouldn't have doubted you six years ago." But he'd been scared. He hadn't wanted to put his heart on the line if her feelings hadn't been real. And even if they'd been real, he'd doubted they would have lasted through her disappointment in his being unable to find her sister's killer.

"I should have told you about Alex," she said as she pulled back. "We've both made mistakes. We've both hurt each other."

He nodded. "But we have the rest of our lives to make it up to each other." He dropped to one knee right there in the waiting room. And he pulled out a jeweler's box. He'd bought the ring the day before. He hadn't had time to get it sized. It probably wouldn't fit. Maybe she wouldn't even like it. But he'd wanted to have the ring for this moment—for when the killer was caught—and it would be safe to propose. He opened the box and held it out to her. "Will you marry me, Becca? Will you become my wife?"

She said nothing; she just stood there, staring at him like she'd been staring at Lexi when he'd kicked open the door to the bride's dressing room. As if she couldn't believe her eyes. "Are you serious?" she asked.

"You can hook me up to Alex's lie detector test and ask me again," he offered with a chuckle. "But yes, I'm serious."

Her eyes widened in surprise.

"I guess I'm an old-fashioned guy," he admitted. "I don't want you to live with me forever without making this official. And as I understand it, we already have a license and a wedding all planned out."

"For a fake wedding…"

He shook his head. "Let's make it real, Becca," he urged her. "Say yes. Become my wife."

"Yes," she said. Then she shouted, "Yes! I want to marry you. I want to become your wife! I love you!"

He slid the ring on her finger, and to his surprise, it fit. Perfectly. Just like the two of them. He pulled her into his arms—where she fit perfectly. Just days ago he'd been dreading everything about their fake wedding. Now he couldn't wait to get to the altar.

PENNY PAYNE WAS RIGHT. The wedding she'd helped Rebecca plan was perfect. But it wasn't because of the beautiful flowers or the dress or the double chocolate cake that Alex and his father couldn't wait to eat. It was because of the people.

Not everybody was there, though. Rebecca's parents had not been as forgiving of Lexi as she and Jared had been. They didn't understand that she would have died had she not played dead. Rebecca couldn't be happier that her sister was alive and able to be her matron of honor. And Alex had two flower girls to walk down the aisle—one on each arm. Becky was blonde and blue-eyed like him while Amanda had her father's fiery-red hair.

And since Rebecca's father wasn't there to walk her

down the aisle, George was doing the honors. She held his arm as he walked her toward the altar—toward her groom. She had always thought of him as her brother. Now he officially was.

She smiled up at him through her veil and mouthed the words *thank you*.

And not just for walking her down the aisle. She had him to thank for Lexi being alive and happy.

Lexi had already made it down the aisle. Her girls leaned against her while Alex had gone to the men's side. He stood between Jared and his best man, Nicholas Rus. She smiled with amusement as she remembered how Dalton Reyes, Blaine Campbell and Ash Stryker had teased the other FBI agent. They'd warned him that whoever stood up as best man was the next agent to make his own trek to the altar.

Nick had laughed as if the idea was preposterous. But it had become true for all of them. She hoped it did for him, too. He intended to stay in River City, Michigan, with the family he'd only recently discovered was his.

Rebecca didn't blame him. She was thrilled with her family. She loved having her sister back and George and her nieces. But the most important part of her family stood before her. Jared and Alex. The two loves of her life.

She stopped next to Jared. He lifted her veil and pressed his lips to hers.

Alex tugged on his pants. "Daddy, you're supposed to wait until the end." He must have remembered that from Dalton's wedding. Of course the little boy forgot nothing.

"She's so beautiful I couldn't wait," Jared said.

Alex smiled. "Mommy is very pretty."

The guests laughed. The church was aglow with warmth and happiness and love. Rebecca had never felt so much love.

Jared held her hands as they repeated vows the minister fed them—about loving each other through sickness and health, good times and bad. Their love had already survived all those things, so she knew they would make it just like Jared had promised: forever.

She slid the gold band on Jared's finger, and he slid a gold band on hers, up against the diamond engagement ring he'd already given her.

"I now pronounce you man and wife," the minister said. "You may kiss your bride…again."

The guests laughed.

But Rebecca was focused on Jared as his handsome face lowered to hers again. He kissed her—reverently and then passionately. Applause burst out in the church.

Mrs. Payne had been right. It was the perfect wedding. And theirs would be the perfect marriage.

* * * * *

"You haven't slept. Do me a favor and try to close your eyes."

He pulled his hand back, gathered up used supplies and tossed them into the garbage.

"Okay." She bit back a yawn as he turned off the light.

He hadn't wanted to admit just how freaked out he'd been when he saw that she'd been shot. He'd stayed calm for her benefit.

Dylan couldn't even think about losing her, too. *Where'd that come from?*

Thankfully, Samantha would be all right.

"Will you come over here?" Her sweet, sleepy voice wasn't helping with his arousal.

The room had just enough light to see big objects without being able to tell what they were. His own adrenaline was fading, leaving him fatigued.

He walked over and sat down. She took his hand. Hers was so small in comparison, so soft.

"Will you lie next to me?" she asked in that sexy sleepy voice. "Just until I fall asleep?"

TEXAS TAKEDOWN

BY
BARB HAN

Published in Great Britain 2015
by Mills & Boon, an imprint of Harlequin (UK) Limited,
Eton House, 18-24 Paradise Road, Richmond, Surrey, TW9 1SR

© 2015 Barb Han

ISBN: 978-0-263-25321-4

46-1015

Harlequin (UK) Limited's policy is to use papers that are natural, renewable and recyclable products and made from wood grown in sustainable forests. The logging and manufacturing processes conform to the legal environmental regulations of the country of origin.

Printed and bound in Spain
by CPI, Barcelona

Barb Han lives in north Texas with her very own hero-worthy husband, three beautiful children, a spunky golden retriever/standard poodle mix and too many books in her to-read pile. In her downtime, she plays video games and spends much of her time on or around a basketball court. She loves interacting with readers and is grateful for their support. You can reach her at www.barbhan.com.

My deepest thanks go to my editor, Allison Lyons, and agent, Jill Marsal. The chance to work with both of you is truly a gift.

There are three people in this world who always inspire me, bring me joy and laughter, and teach me to be the best person I can be. I love you, Brandon (Hook'em Horns), Jacob and Tori.

To my husband, John, because you are the best part of all of it.

Chapter One

Difficult didn't begin to cover the past year for Dylan Jacobs. Not only had he discovered that he was a father, but he'd learned the mother who'd kept the baby from him was terminally ill. He'd wanted to be angry with her on both counts, but his frustration had died on the vine with every step toward the hospital where she lay losing her grip on life. And once he'd looked into his daughter's green eyes—a perfect reflection of his—he'd been wrapped around that little girl's finger.

Falling in love with Maribel had been the easy part. She had rosy cherub cheeks, dark curls for days and a laugh brighter than the Texas sun. Caring for a two-year-old who'd just lost everything known to her, everything comfortable, had been harder than his tour in Afghanistan.

What a difference a year made.

Dylan squatted at the end of the hallway just out of sight, listening intently as the sounds of Maribel's electric toothbrush hummed, then died. The pitter-patter of her bare feet on bamboo flooring in the hallway came next. She knew the drill, the same ritual they'd performed every morning since she'd come to live with him in Mason Ridge. She'd be on the lookout, ready to find Da-da.

Her giggle was like spring air, breathing life into everything around her. And he'd been on a certain path of destruction before she came into his life.

The *tap-tap-tap* of her footsteps stopped at the end of the hall. She'd expected to find him by now.

"Da-da."

He rolled and landed with his back against the floor a few feet away, arms spread open.

She jumped, squealed and clapped all at once. A second later, she launched herself on top of him. "Da-da!"

Thanks to reflexes honed by the US Army, he caught her in time.

"Airplane, Da-da," she said. Her *r* came out as a *w*.

Dylan extended his arms and made her fly. "Mrrrrrr, mrrrrrrr."

A knock at the back door interrupted their playtime. It was probably for the best. Maribel shouldn't be late to preschool again. Dylan didn't think he could stomach another disapproving look from Mrs. Applebee. He might not be the most punctual guy when it came to dropping his daughter off at school, but no one could argue his love for the child. Not even stern-faced, disapproving Applebee. She might run a tight ship, but her heart was pure gold. More important, she loved Maribel.

He set his little girl on her feet next to him. "Daddy needs a favor. Go to your room, put on your shoes and grab your backpack."

She planted her balled fist on her little hip and argued for a little more time as a plane.

The knock came louder this time. Dylan didn't like the sense of urgency it carried. "When you get home from school today, I promise. Okay, Bel?"

She pursed her lips and narrowed her gaze.

"And we can have ice cream after," he threw in to tip

the scale in his favor. "You don't want to miss your field trip to Dinosaur Park."

"Ho-kay" came out on a sigh. She turned and bolted toward her room. Toddlers had one speed. It was full tilt.

Dylan popped to his feet in one swift motion and crossed to the kitchen, his muscles still warm from his early-morning push-ups. He liked to get his workout in before Maribel opened her eyes. When she was awake, his full attention was on her, had to be on her. Three-year-olds had no sense of danger.

Only a few people used his back door. He saw his friend Rebecca Hughes through the glass and motioned for her to come inside.

"Everything okay with Shane?" Shane was the younger brother she'd recently located who had been abducted at seven years old. Dylan tried not to think about the fact that Shane had been only four years older than his Maribel when he'd been taken from Mason Ridge and the Hughes family all those years ago. Even so, a bolt of anger flashed through him quicker than a lightning rod and with the same explosive effect.

"He's fine. I'm not here about him." Didn't those words leave a creepy-crawly feeling all over Dylan?

"What is it? Something going on with Brody?" She had reunited with her high school sweetheart, who was one of Dylan's best friends, when the man responsible for kidnapping her and her brother as children had come back for her last month.

She shook her head. "It might not be anything. It's just that Samantha stopped answering her cell phone four days ago. I have a bad feeling."

"You call her father?" he asked.

"Store says he's gone fishing," she supplied. Samantha's father owned the only hardware store in town.

"So you want me to look into it?" Since opening the doors to his security consulting firm last year, he'd taken the occasional missing-person case, none of which had involved a friend's disappearance. He, Rebecca and Samantha had been part of a close-knit group of childhood friends. The group had broken up fifteen years ago when Rebecca and her brother, Shane, had been abducted.

For the past few weeks, everyone in town had been focused on the manhunt for the Mason Ridge Abductor after he'd returned to permanently quiet Rebecca. Her search for her brother had brought her too close to the truth. Thomas Kramer's grip on the community had lasted fifteen years, but luck had finally smiled on the town and they'd gotten him. He wasn't in prison, where he belonged, but he'd been killed in a car crash and that was just as good. Either way, he was no longer a threat.

Dylan thought about his word choice. *Luck?* There was a reason he didn't have a rabbit's foot tucked in his pocket. Hard work was reliable. Luck was for ladies in Vegas at the slot machines. Luck was for people who believed in things they couldn't see. Luck was for pie-in-the-sky dreamers. Dylan was far too practical to fall into that trap. People created their own luck.

With a state-of-the-art computer, a strong network of contacts and skills honed through the military, Dylan didn't have to rely on chance to help his clients.

Even so, he couldn't shake the bad feeling he had about Rebecca's visit.

Maribel bounded into the room, ran straight for Rebecca and wrapped tiny arms around her knees. "Auntie Becca!"

"Hey, baby girl." Rebecca bent down to eye level and then kissed Maribel on the forehead.

The two had become fast friends. A tug Dylan didn't

want to acknowledge stirred his heart. Rebecca was fantastic, don't get him wrong, but he suspected the bond had happened so quickly in part because Maribel missed her mother. He kept Lyndsey's picture on Maribel's nightstand. Maribel kissed the photograph every night before bed and then said good-night to her mother in heaven. It was important that Maribel knew just how much her mother had loved her. Even more important to Dylan was that Maribel knew her mother had wanted her.

On some level, he understood why Lyndsey had kept his daughter from him. He'd been partly to blame, having declared long ago that he never wanted kids or marriage. How many times had he told Lyndsey that parenthood was about the cruelest thing a person could do to a child? Too many.

His wild-child ways hadn't helped any. He had no right to hold on to anger when it came to Lyndsey's decision. She'd been trying to protect her baby.

Dylan never took for granted how very blessed he'd been from the day that little girl had come into his life. His only regret was that he hadn't known sooner, that Lyndsey hadn't realized how much being present in his child's life would mean to him. Had he been that much of a jerk?

The short answer? Yes.

He had to have been. Lyndsey would've trusted him otherwise. He couldn't blame her, either. How many times when they'd lain in bed in the mornings had he said their life was perfect the way it was? Dozens? Hundreds? He'd been so adamant that he'd almost convinced himself, too.

Down deep, he'd wanted a family of his own but he'd never have been able to admit that to himself. He'd always figured that he'd jack it up. History repeating itself and all that. Except the one thing Dylan knew above all was that he was nothing like his parents. He'd gone to great lengths to ensure it.

And yet he couldn't help but think he'd failed Lyndsey. Because of his stubborn streak, she'd gone through her pregnancy alone. Then she'd had a baby by herself. To top it off, she'd spent the first two years of Maribel's life without any help from him.

He could give himself the cop-out all day long that he'd have done better by Lyndsey if he'd known. Still didn't ease the sting of feeling as if he'd let her down in the worst possible way when she needed him. And then, before he could make any of it right, she'd died.

At least she hadn't done that alone—he'd made certain. He'd maintained a bedside vigil during her last days. She'd been in a coma and couldn't speak. The only thing she could do was squeeze his hand when he apologized for letting her down.

Dylan sighed sharply. Those memories had been packed away and stowed deep. So why were they resurfacing?

And how ridiculous did his point of view seem to him now? His life wouldn't be complete without that little rug rat. Maturity was on his side. But he never would have turned Maribel away. Lyndsey couldn't have known. She'd believed the wilder side of Dylan.

He turned to Rebecca. "I need to run Maribel to school and then I'll make a few calls. You want to stick around and wait? Coffee's fresh."

"I wish I could stay. We've got a colt that's in trouble and Brody has his hands full. I better get back and help with the other horses." She'd moved in with Brody after rekindling their romance, and they'd be announcing a wedding date any day now. Together they made a great team running his horse rehabilitation center, and the work looked to agree with her. Or maybe it was just the fact that she'd found someone who could make her happy.

Dylan had more pressing matters to think about than the complications having another female in his life would bring. His three-foot-tall angel kept him on the brink of exhaustion.

"I can take Maribel to school if you want. It's on my way home," she offered.

Dylan figured that was Rebecca's way of saying she hoped he'd get started looking for Samantha right away.

Maribel was already jumping up and down, clapping her hands.

He nodded to Rebecca, even though he'd miss being the one to take his little girl to school. His part-time nanny, Ms. Anderson, usually picked up Maribel in the afternoons. She cooked suppers and stayed as long as Dylan needed her around. Said she enjoyed keeping busy after being widowed at the young age of sixty. When he'd hired her, she'd volunteered to come in first thing in the mornings, too, but Dylan had refused. He couldn't give up being the one to wake Maribel. His daughter might've come out of nowhere a year ago, but she was here to stay, in his home and in his heart. Dylan couldn't imagine his life any other way.

Between Ms. Anderson, Mrs. Applebee and Maribel, Dylan had plenty of estrogen in his life.

Having his own business allowed him to work from home a lot of the time and set his own schedule for the most part. But there were occasions when he had to be away overnight. He appreciated Ms. Anderson's flexibility.

"I'll call the headmaster and give up my volunteer spot on the field trip."

"I'd hate for you to do that," Rebecca said.

"I have a few other things to do today anyway. And I'm pretty sure Applebee could use a break from me. There's a wait list for these trips. This'll give another parent a shot."

Maribel frowned.

"Hey, I worked the past two. It's good to share with the other parents so they can spend the day with their kids." He took a knee. "Give Daddy big hugs."

Maribel hesitated, then ran to him and he caught her as she tripped on her last step, scooping her into his arms, kissing her forehead.

With any luck, he'd be done in time to tuck his precious little girl into bed. Losing her mother had not been easy on her last year, and part of the reason he desperately wanted to make his security consulting enterprise work was so that he could be around and she could grow up surrounded by people who loved her. Dylan couldn't bring back her mother, but he'd vowed their Bel would always know she'd been wanted and loved. Unlike Dylan, whose parents had dumped him with his grandmother at six months old because the responsibility of caring for a baby had proved too much for the free-spirited hipsters. They'd split up a year later and had rarely visited. No birthday cards. No high school graduation appearance. No showing at his daughter's christening.

Dylan's child would never know that brand of rejection.

She turned toward Rebecca and launched herself again.

"Hold on there." He caught her under her arms and pulled her back toward him. He helped secure her backpack before another round of hugs came.

Maribel stopped at the door and turned, smiling, one

hand holding on to Auntie Becca's, the other waving back at him. "Bye-bye, Da-da!"

"Have a good day at school. Learn everything you can."

"So I can be smarter than you," she squealed. Those adorable *r*'s rolling out like *w*'s. The pediatrician had assured him she'd sort it out in the next year or so. He knew he should work harder on pronunciation with her but it was so darn cute the way she said her words. Because he'd missed out on the first two years of her life, a selfish part of him didn't want her growing up any faster than she had to.

"That's right." Dylan watched Rebecca buckle Maribel into the spare car seat she'd pulled from her trunk. He stood at the window until the blue sedan disappeared down the drive.

His laptop was already booted up, so he snagged another cup of coffee and seated himself at the breakfast bar. No matter how hard he tried, he couldn't shake the feeling that Maribel needed a female influence in her life even if he couldn't imagine having time to find one. Relationships were complicated. They required communication and commitment. The only thing Dylan was devoted to at the moment was finishing his cup of coffee.

When he put his full attention to the case, it took about an hour of digging to find that Samantha had withdrawn five thousand dollars in cash from her bank four days ago. The withdrawal was timed perfectly to her disappearance. His trouble radar jumped up a few notches. She might've been forced to pull out the money, murdered and then dumped somewhere. No. Forget it. He couldn't allow himself to believe she'd been killed and that he'd be looking for a body. There were other possibilities. Maybe she'd decided to pack up and take a vacation. Everyone was burned out from recent events.

A quick call to her employer shot down that prospect. Samantha hadn't been to work in a week.

The probability foul play wasn't involved shrank by the nanosecond.

Dylan scanned online news outlets for crimes with unidentified females on the date she withdrew money.

He came up short and sighed with relief.

There were dozens of hospitals in Dallas, even more counting the suburbs. He narrowed his search down to a five-mile radius of where she lived and worked. The number shrank to five. He called each one looking for a Jane Doe, relieved when he didn't find her.

Next he reached out to the city morgue, which was not a call he wanted to make.

Relief flooded him at receiving the word that no Jane Does had been received in the past week.

Having exhausted obvious answers, he had to consider other possibilities. The first one that popped into his mind said she could be on the run. But from what?

This was Samantha he was thinking about. Nothing in her background suggested she had criminal inclinations. He'd known her personally for more than half his life. Wouldn't there have been signs along the way? Lies told here and there?

Of course, the tight-knit group of twelve-year-olds had disbanded after Shane's disappearance, but they'd all gone to the same high school, traveled in loosely the same circles. Didn't he know her?

She came from a large middle-class family, the youngest of four kids. Her dad had been in sales, so she'd moved around most of her young life. He'd cashed out their life savings and rented space on the town square to open a hardware store after her mother had died. Samantha had settled in Mason Ridge in fifth grade, just a year before the tragedy. She'd been a good student. She'd played volleyball at Mason Ridge High School well enough to earn a scholarship to a small university in Arkansas. And that had been when he'd lost touch with her.

Her brothers had spread out, going to different colleges and then settling in separate cities. Last Dylan had heard, they had families of their own. The trouble came with her mom's side. Several uncles had rap sheets longer than the menu at Chili's. But Samantha never spoke about them, and Dylan figured the family had cut ties long ago.

He tried her cell. The call went straight to voice mail.

The idea one of her distant relatives could've gotten her into trouble didn't sit well. No way would she get involved with them.

Dylan made a phone call to a technical-guru friend he'd used from time to time to hack into databases and phones. If a device had a firewall, Jorge could sneak past it unseen and get out with the same ability. He was the freakin' Houdini of hackers.

Jorge picked up on the second ring. Not surprising for a man who was at his computer 24/7. "What can I do you for?"

"I got a missing person. Need to find out who she was speaking to in the days surrounding her disappearance."

"Give me the details." His voice was all business.

Dylan relayed information like her phone number slowly into the receiver.

Jorge repeated the digits.

Dylan confirmed.

"Got it. Hold on a sec." The sound of fingers tapping across a keyboard came through the line.

"I can't get a location for you, but I can see who she's

been talking to. I see your number on here. You have a relationship with this girl?" Jorge asked.

"She's a friend."

"I heard about all that mess going on in your neck of the woods. Glad they caught the dude. Gives a whole new meaning to being burned, though." His jokes were crass but Dylan got it. While women sat down with glasses of wine and talked about emotions until they felt better, men joked. Dylan wasn't arguing one style over the other. It was just a guy's way of trying to get his arms around the stuff he didn't have a good handle on. "I'll send you an email with a list of the numbers, but there's something weird. She received several calls from a burn phone in the days prior to her vanishing act."

"None after?" Why would someone call her using a pay-as-you-go phone? Dylan didn't like any of this news. It took him down the path he didn't want to be true.

"Nope."

"What's the number?" Dylan searched for a pen and paper.

"I'll send it in the report. Won't do you any good calling it, though."

"Why's that?"

"The line's been disabled."

"Which means you can't trace it?"

"Nope. Did your friend get herself into some kind of trouble?"

"Looks like it," Dylan said. Several more scenarios ran through his mind. None he liked. He thanked Jorge and closed the call.

Dylan spent the rest of the morning tracking down Samantha's landlord in Dallas, who agreed to check out her place. Her car was gone from the parking garage of her condo. A few drawers had been left open in her bedroom, and her bathroom counter was empty. Experience had taught Dylan that women didn't go anywhere without their makeup bags.

Mail sat on the counter untouched. Other than a few necessary supplies, very little was missing from her condo. When she'd decided to take off, she hadn't brought much with her. A quick escape suggested someone on the run, just as he feared she might be. But again the question came up. Running from what? Or whom?

Was she dating someone? Dylan should've asked that question first. A woman's biggest threat in life was a man close to her—a boyfriend or spouse. Dylan's fists curled and released at the thought of any man hurting a woman. The notion hit him even harder now that he had a daughter. Let any guy try to hurt his Bel…

Anger roared through him like buckshot, exploding in every direction. He didn't need to go there about his child. Samantha deserved his focus.

The next trick would be to locate her. He kept his hunt inside Texas, figuring she'd stick with what she knew. Austin was her favorite city, or at least it used to be. He'd lost touch with her after high school. Taking a chance on his hunch, he decided to start his search in the live-music capital of the world, guessing she'd go somewhere familiar.

Once he narrowed the hunt there, finding her would be easy. Apartments had managers who followed rules, so an offer of cash to pay up a few months' rent would draw too much unwanted attention. She would most likely rent a house something near campus, so she could easily get around by throwing on a hoodie and shorts to blend in with students.

A quick internet search revealed there were 387 houses for rent in the city of Austin. Twenty-three when narrowed down to places on or near campus. Dylan put his resources to work finding out which ones had been pulled from the market the day Samantha disappeared. Two. With a fifty-fifty chance of success, Dylan gambled on the house nearest campus and checked the tenant. No dice. The place had been rented by four people. He hit the jackpot on the second.

He made a quick call to Ms. Anderson to let her know he had to leave town, and then located his duffel. The hope of being home by Maribel's bedtime fizzled as he stuffed a pair of jeans in the bag. He packed a sandwich to eat on the drive—roughly four hours one way, depending on traffic on I-35—left a note for Ms. Anderson to read *Goodnight Moon* to his daughter after tucking her into bed and locked the door behind him.

DYLAN LEANED AGAINST a tree six houses down from Samantha's. He'd driven his small sedan rather than his SUV in order to better navigate Austin traffic. Based on his research, a UT shuttle should be passing by in ten minutes to pick up college kids and deliver them to campus. With others hanging around waiting on transportation, he had a better chance of going unnoticed. With his six-foot-two-inch muscular frame, he looked as if he should be in athletic housing. Camo pants and the burned-orange UT shirt he'd bought at the gas station on the way into town should help camouflage him. Duffel slung over his shoulder, he did his best to blend in.

If Samantha was in trouble or being held hostage, he didn't want to tip off her captor. He had to consider the possibility that she wasn't acting on her own free will. Dylan planned to take nothing for granted.

His pulse kicked up a notch when she came into view, walking toward the front door of her rental alone. With a long and lean body like hers, she could easily be confused for a student athlete. Her high school years spent playing volleyball had paid off, especially with those legs.

He slipped on eyeglasses specially fitted with binocular lenses. Her smoky-brown hair cut in long shiny layers with bangs that skimmed along her brows brought out a deeply erotic shade of wide-set almond-shaped blue eyes. They stood out against her oval face. Samantha had always been beautiful. At least that much had stayed the same. She'd been smart, too. Her beauty had caught his attention. Her sharp wit and sense of humor had kept it. He hoped that she hadn't gone and done something stupid. Surely someone back home would've noticed if she'd changed.

Sometimes good girls were drawn to men who were bad for them. So far, there was no sign of a boyfriend. *Good.* He told himself it would be easier to help her with fewer people involved, and he didn't like the idea she'd be on the run with a man.

She glanced around, looking more nervous than afraid. Her long fluid layers of brown hair framed an almost too beautiful face and highlighted a graceful, swan-like neck.

Ignoring the rapid increase in his heartbeat at seeing her, he bowed his head and focused on the newspaper he held, pretending to be studying it as he kept her in his peripheral.

She unlocked the door, glanced left to right once more and then slipped inside.

Paranoid?

Dylan had half a mind to stomp over and demand to know what was going on. That would be a mistake. The simple fact was that he didn't know what he'd be walking into and didn't want to tip his hand. He slipped off the glasses and then slid them inside his duffel as the shuttle arrived. The crowd around him thinned, forming a line to get on the bus. He stood back, allowing others to crowd in front of him.

At the last second, he spun around, ducked his head and made a beeline toward her place. Moving around the side of the house, he crouched below the windows, careful to avoid being cut by overgrown holly bushes lining his path. He walked the perimeter, peeking inside windows through cracks in the closed blinds. From what he could tell so far, she was alone.

The back door was locked. It took all of three seconds to change that with his bump key. He slowly opened the door, moved inside the kitchen and listened. He already knew the layout of the house. Using the Department of Defense satellite, he'd homed in on the address and taken pictures of everything inside and out, to the level of detail of her furniture arrangement. Memorizing every inch of the space, every crevice, was a habit formed during his military days. There were two bedrooms and a kitchen in back, all of which had doors that led to a dining room. The master bedroom was off the living room. The place was set up like a maze.

Telltale clicks on a keyboard said she was on her laptop. The dining room was set up as a study room with tables pushed against the walls instead of a table and chairs.

Not risking chance, Dylan palmed his Glock, using it to lead the way.

"What are you doing here, Samantha?" He lowered his weapon when he was sure the place was clear.

Samantha jumped to her feet, the shock of seeing him evident on her face. It took her a moment before she was able to answer. "Me? I could ask you the same thing, Dylan." The accusation in Samantha's voice fired at him as though he stood in front of an execution squad. A mix of panic and fear crossed her features as she sat ramrod straight. Her gaze froze on his gun.

Her fearful expression tugged at his heart.

"I'm not going to hurt you." He surveyed the area. "Is there anyone else here?"

"Not that I know of." Her gaze darted to the front door and then back.

"What does that mean?"

"Did anyone follow you?" The suspicion in her eyes hit him harder than a shot of tequila for breakfast, with a similar burn in his chest.

"No."

"Are you sure?" More accusations fired in her tone.

"Yes." This wasn't the greeting he'd expected.

"How can I trust you?"

"You don't have to, sweetheart." He had no intention of hurting her. Her panicked expression ate at his insides. What was she so afraid of? Or maybe the better question was, what had she done?

He took another step toward her so he could really examine her. With her pallor, she looked as if she'd seen a ghost. "But it's me. And you know me."

"How did you find this place?" She didn't seem ready to concede anything.

"The internet. It wasn't hard," he said casually, trying to use his voice to calm her.

"If it was easy for you, then he can find me, too. I have to get out of here." Her pulse hammered at the base of her throat.

Finally, he was getting somewhere. Someone had her seriously spooked. Dylan shot her an apologetic look.

"Who are you involved with? A boyfriend?"

Her head was already shaking.

"Then, tell me who's looking for you and I can help."

She didn't respond. He needed to take another tack. Get her in the car for four hours, gain her trust and he'd get closer to finding the truth.

"I can see that you're in some kind of trouble. What are you running from?"

Her lips clamped shut.

"Everyone's worried. Come home with me and we'll sort this out," he offered, hoping he could appeal to her on a friendship level.

"No. It's too risky. He'll find me." That same frightened-animal look was in her eyes.

"Who will?"

"Thomas Kramer." She shivered involuntarily as she said his name.

"The Mason Ridge Abductor?" *Stunned* didn't begin to describe his reaction. No way. Dylan checked her pupils for signs of drugs, even though the Samantha he knew would never do such a thing. Something had her acting cagey. He saw pure, unadulterated fear in her gaze. "He's dead, sweetheart. A pile of ash. Remember? He can't hurt you from where he is."

She stood there, trembling, looking lost. *Damn.*

Dylan made a move to step forward, to comfort her. Her body stiffened, so he froze.

"It's not safe here. He'll find me."

"What are you talking about?" Dylan held his hands up in surrender, slowly, because he half feared she would bolt otherwise. "I'm moving to the couch to sit down so we can talk about this."

He walked deliberately.

She moved to the front window, peering outside through the slats in the blinds. "He might've followed you."

The look of panic on her face couldn't be faked. Something had her completely rattled, but Thomas Kramer was dead.

"Sit down beside me and tell me what happened," he said calmly.

"I have to get out of here." Her voice shook with fear and her eyes pleaded with him. She stalked back to the desk and reached inside a drawer.

"Stop right there." The last thing he needed was for her to do something desperate. Dylan ate the real estate between them in two quick strides and covered her hand, stopping her from raising it toward him. He ignored the fizz of attraction sizzling between them.

Her left fist was closed around an object. He turned her palm toward the ceiling, noticing her white-knuckle grip. "Open your hand slowly."

She did, exposing a fistful of cash.

"What's this for, Samantha?"

"Nothing. Take it and get out of here."

"You're trying to give me money to leave?"

"Whatever you want, take it. Just go."

"Rebecca sent me." If she wouldn't talk to him based on their history, maybe he could get through to her by using her friend's name.

"She shouldn't have," Samantha shot back. "This is no one's business but mine."

That didn't work. She seemed even more agitated. Maybe he could appeal to her softer side. "How can I help if you don't tell me what's going on?"

"I can't. I don't even know myself and it's too dangerous."

Dylan took a step away from her, releasing her hand, breaking contact before he revealed his body's reaction to her. Even then he felt the tension coiling inside his body. "Why not?"

"He'll kill me and everyone I love."

Chapter Two

"No one's going to hurt you, Samantha. And especially not a man who's already dead." Dylan fished his phone from his front pocket and then paused with his thumb hovering over Brody's number. "Your friends are worried. I need to call and let them know I found you."

She shook her head fervently. "He'll know. I don't know how but he'll figure it out if you do that. And then we'll all be in danger again."

"Does this have anything to do with the phone calls you received before you took off?" Dylan wouldn't rule out the possibility someone was using her fear of the Mason Ridge Abductor to manipulate her.

A look of shock crossed her features. She quickly recovered, smoothing her open hand down her jeans.

"I already told you." Her gaze darted around the room, no doubt looking for an escape route. "You don't believe me."

Frazzled, frightened, she had the disposition of a cornered animal. And since that rarely turned out well for the person who tried to capture it, Dylan put his hands up, keeping his cell in his hand, where she could see it. "Look, sweetheart, you're safe. I'm here. Tell me exactly what's going on so I can help you."

"I don't expect you to understand. But Thomas Kramer is coming." Eyes wild, she bolted for the door.

Thomas Kramer was dead. Someone was trying to manipulate her by using her fear of the past. Dylan dropped his phone and caught her as she reached the front door. Whatever she'd gotten herself into was clearly more than she could handle. He bear-hugged her from behind and pulled her far enough away from the door that the handle was out of reach.

She kicked and screamed, and her foot connected with his groin.

Doubled over, he tightened his grip around her mid-section as he took a few deep breaths to stave off blinding pain and nausea.

He'd almost felt sorry for her when she was stumbling over her words, trying to distract him so she could bolt. But experience had taught him innocent people didn't try to run.

"BE STILL," DYLAN bit out curtly. His thick arms were like vise grips around her hips, and it was impossible not to notice the solid wall that was Dylan flush against her bottom. She couldn't blame him for his words coming out harshly after she'd kicked him in the groin.

If she could loosen his grip, she might be able to break free and run. No matter how much she wanted to confide in Dylan, she couldn't. The Mason Ridge Abductor had returned, attacked her in the parking lot of her office, and then her father had disappeared after confirming as much and telling her not to try to find him. He'd told her to hide and stay hidden until he could sort this mess out that had begun fifteen years ago. And even though Dylan didn't know it, she was saving him, too. He didn't need to get involved and she'd said too much already.

The door was so close. She stretched her fingers toward it. Too far.

Drawing from all her strength, she tensed her body and then jabbed her elbow into Dylan's midsection. If he could find her, so could Kramer, and her father had said the Mason Ridge Abductor would use her to force him out of hiding.

On some level, she knew Kramer was a pile of ashes, but someone could be using his name to hide behind.

Dylan coughed, ground out a few choice words and then spun her around to face him. His fingers gripped the flesh on her shoulders tightly.

She couldn't budge. He'd made sure of it.

"Make another move and I'll ensure you regret it." He'd bent down to her level. Penetrating clear green eyes glared at her.

This close, his face was all sharp angles and hard planes, with a severe jawline on a squared jaw, intelligent eyes. *Good-looking* didn't begin to describe his features. He wasn't a pretty boy. No, this poster child for strength and general level red-hotness had the rugged looks that came with knowing how to take care of himself. His tightly clipped sandy-brown hair reminded her he was ex-military. No way could she get away from him going toe to toe, even if she was close to his height at six foot. Growing up with three older brothers had taught her a thing or two about her own limitations.

"You're hurting me," she angled, hoping he'd slacken his grip enough for her to escape.

"I'm sorry about that. I loosen my hold and you'll run for it. I need you right here. It's me, Samantha. I've said this before but it's worth repeating. You can talk to me."

"Fine. Let me go and I promise not to do anything stupid." Even if he was determined to get himself involved, she couldn't allow it.

"And I'm supposed to believe you based on what? Your word?"

"Yes. You are." Looking into those green eyes, seeing she wasn't getting anywhere, Samantha decided to take another tack. If he was going to believe her, she'd have to tell him something concrete. And yet he wouldn't believe her if she did. She could hardly believe it. "Look, I know how crazy this sounds, but Kramer is either reaching out from the grave or someone is pretending to be him."

He shot her a look that had her wondering if he thought she was crazy. She hadn't thought about how all this might look to an outsider until then. There was a hint of curiosity in his eyes, too.

"You have my word that I won't try to run away from you, Dylan. Now let me go." She jerked her shoulders, surprised when he loosened his grip.

"Tell me something, Samantha. Because right now you look guilty of something bad, something that has you on the run, and if I didn't know you better, I'd be calling the cops." As if for emphasis, he picked up his phone.

"No cops. Promise me." She rubbed her shoulders to bring blood back to them, trying to figure out what she could say that wouldn't implicate her father. She wanted to trust Dylan, but she couldn't risk it. If he knew, he wouldn't walk away. He wasn't the type.

"Sorry if I hurt you." He motioned toward the couch. "Sit."

"I'm fine."

Sharp green eyes stared at her. He'd been wild when they were young, and there was more than a hint of that same feral tendency in his features now. "We can do this one of two ways. You sit willingly. Or I tie you up until you tell me the truth. Your choice."

She moved to the couch and plopped down. Anger boiled inside her. Everyone thought that the Mason Ridge Abductor was gone, but he wasn't. And he was coming after her. He'd surprised her, then called and threatened her if she didn't meet him after she got away.

Dylan glanced out the front window and then focused those intense greens on her. Eye contact wasn't the best idea, because when he looked at her, her stomach flipped. Dylan was easy to look at. She wouldn't deny an attraction sizzled under the surface, one that had been simmering since before high school. Even with his bad-boy reputation, she'd always known there was something good about him deep inside.

"I was careful not to leave a trail." The blood was finally returning to her shoulders. Bruising would be the least of her problems.

"Your lack of a path helped narrow the search. You were somewhere within driving distance because you used your car. I also knew you'd want an internet connection. Austin's your favorite city, so I took a chance. From there, all I had to do was figure out which house you'd rented."

She'd been that transparent? So much for thinking she could hide. Frustration burned through her. Too bad she didn't have the criminal tendencies of her mother's side of the family.

"I'm truly sorry about earlier. You know I would never hurt you on purpose," he said.

She did know. Dylan was a good guy.

"I'm going to ask you again. What's going on?" His brow arched and he was examining her face as if her head was about to start spinning.

Could she risk telling Dylan anything else? He already looked ready to strap her into the first straitjacket he could find. And what if she told Dylan what she feared? That her father was somehow involved or at least covering for someone else that night Rebecca and Shane had gone missing fifteen years ago? Or that if she shared what she feared, Dylan would be in this as deeply as she was?

The crackle of a branch breaking sent both of them to the front window.

"Don't let anyone see you." Dylan pulled her down, his strong hands firmly on her hips.

In the street, the screech of tires sent her adrenaline into overdrive. "We can't stay here."

Dylan opened the curtain in the front window and cursed. "I can't help you if I don't know what you've gotten yourself into. You haven't given me anything to work with yet."

"I don't know who I can trust anymore. All I know is this whole thing is bigger than we originally thought." Kramer was believed to have acted alone. What if he hadn't? What if others had been involved in the crime or the cover-up?

"What 'thing,' Samantha? What are you talking about?" He stared at her for a long moment.

Could she tell him? She wanted to talk to someone. The past four days had been terrifying alone. She shook her head.

"This is a college town. There are people everywhere, so the noise outside might be nothing." Dylan's voice came out in a whisper as he surveyed the area through the windows.

She had to admit, having Dylan with her steadied her fried nerves. "Do you really think I'm crazy? Or involved in something illegal?"

"No. But I've never seen you this scared." Dylan held out his hand. "Come back to Mason Ridge with me and we'll sort this out."

"I can't go home." She didn't take it.

"You can stay at my house." His expression had her thinking he believed she needed to be locked up in one of those high-priced sanctuaries by the ocean rather than his place, but to his credit, he didn't say it.

Even so, she dared to allow a small bubble of hope to expand, the first since this nightmare had begun a week ago.

Another crunch noise came from just outside the glass.

"Stay down." His gaze ping-ponged from her to the window as he tightened his grip on the handle of his gun. His movements were assured, graceful.

Even with him there, Samantha couldn't relax. Not when a man could reach out from the grave, as Kramer had. What if the guy really was dead and all logic said he was? What if someone else was involved? How big could this thing be?

The little bubble of hope burst. Despair pressed heavy on her chest.

"Several men are headed this way." The concern in his voice was enough to fry what was left of her nerves. "What aren't you telling me?"

"I told you everything."

"I asked this before and I'm going to ask it again. Are you involved in something illegal?"

"No."

"Drugs?"

"That would be illegal."

"Is someone forcing you to do something you don't want to? Are they coming?"

"It's not like that."

Dylan scooped his cell off the floor next to her. "Obviously, there's something else at work here. I don't like this one bit."

With him on her side, she might have a chance of fighting back. Grabbing money from her account and disappearing had been a knee-jerk reaction. She could see how that might make her look guilty of a crime.

"You need to get away from me before anyone sees you." Samantha hated the panic in her voice—the panic that had been beating in her chest like a drum since this ordeal had begun. The person claiming to be Kramer had been clear. Involve anyone else and he'd hurt them and everyone they loved.

"Do you trust me?"

She looked into his sharp green eyes. God help her, but she did. Of course, there weren't a lot of options at the moment. "Yes."

"Then, let's get out of here." He tucked his cell in his duffel.

"How do you plan to do that?" she asked.

The crack of a bullet split the air.

Chapter Three

Before Samantha had time to argue, Dylan had her on the floor. He needed to find cover in order to put mass between the two of them and the shotgun blasts firing toward them. He urged Samantha forward, crawling on hands and knees toward the kitchen. The feel of a body like hers underneath him, especially the way hers fit his, gave him a thrill of sexual excitement, but right now he didn't need his body reacting inappropriately. Nor did he need the distraction.

The three-foot crawl space between the fridge and the wall in the kitchen would offer some shield. Guiding her there, he followed. "Do everything I say."

Her cobalt-blue eyes were wide when she nodded.

Time to move.

Dylan shouldered his duffel and entwined Samantha's fingers in his, ignoring the pulse of electricity vibrating up his arm. His vehicle was parked two streets over. If they could make it out of the back of the house, circle around and cut across the street, they had a chance to break free.

He carefully zigzagged through the bushes along the path, hoping like hell they didn't run into whoever was shooting at them. With any luck, the shooter would be inside the house by now.

The glint of metal shone between houses directly across the street. That was what he got for wishing.

Dylan squinted against the bright sun, tucked Samantha behind him and ran like hell, darting side to side as he crossed the street.

Halfway across, a bullet struck the center of his chest, knocking the wind out of him. The impact, equivalent to being hit with a rubber mallet, knocked him back. He stumbled a few steps before falling on his backside and then scrambling behind a car so he could catch his breath. The Kevlar he wore kept the slug from piercing his chest.

Samantha's scream made the hair on his neck stand up. She obviously thought he'd been shot. And he had been. But it was okay.

She dropped down next to him.

There was no time to explain, so he gripped her hand tighter. Dylan dragged in a few breaths, and then pushed on, hoping the shooter hadn't readjusted, ready to fire another round.

Dylan guided them in between the buildings.

Forging ahead, he cleared another block and palmed his keys. His vehicle was in sight when he disarmed the alarm and unlocked the doors remotely.

If he could get the pair of them out of there, they had a chance at escape.

Dylan let go of Samantha's hand in time for her to dash around to the passenger side and get in. She sat there, stunned.

Out in the open like this, they were extremely vulnerable to attack.

Key ready, Dylan fired up the engine and peeled out of there.

"You're going to be fine."

"They shot you." The disbelief in Samantha's voice

indicated she hadn't had time to process everything that had just happened. It was a lot for a civilian to take in, and she was doing better than expected.

"I'm good. See." Dylan used his right hand to pull up his shirt enough for her to see his thin Kevlar vest. His left gripped the steering wheel as he wound through the residential area and away from the shrieking sirens. His focus had to be on the road as he assessed everyone they passed for potential threat. "I'll end up with a nasty bruise. That's all."

"Okay." That one word was spoken soft and small, almost without air. Her vulnerability pierced a different set of his armor.

He dropped his shirt and returned his hand to the steering wheel, checking the rearview to see if they had any company. So far, so good. One wrong turn and the story could change drastically. "We need to find the closest police station."

"No, please. He'll find my father if I involve the law." The desperation in her voice had him thinking twice.

"Samantha, we were just shot at. You're scared beyond belief. I believe you when you say you aren't involved in anything illegal. So let's go to the police and get protection."

"As soon as this car slows, I'll jump out. You shouldn't be part of this." She gripped the door handle. "Promise you won't go to the cops."

"Tell me why not." That was the second time she'd specifically insisted he shouldn't be involved. What the hell was that all about?

"I already did. He's going to kill my father."

"Who is?"

"Thomas Kramer, the Mason Ridge Abductor."

"He's dead, Samantha. He can't hurt you."

"You asked about the phone calls before." Her voice sounded resigned.

"And?"

"I was walking home from work last Tuesday. It was late. I stayed to finish up a project and was the last one to leave the office. Someone jumped me. I was shocked, scared, but I fought. I somehow managed to get away."

"Did you report it?"

"Of course. The police said it was most likely an attempted robbery. At first I thought the whole incident was random, too. When I told my father, he started freaking out. Made me promise not to leave my condo. Begged me not to get the police or anyone else involved. Said he'd make everything right. Told me to give him a little time and that he'd done a bad thing. I didn't know what to think or do. I panicked. Took a few vacation days and didn't leave my condo. Then the phone calls started. Someone saying he was the real Thomas Kramer said he wanted to meet. Said he had something of mine. He said if I involved the police, he'd kill me and my father. I stopped answering. When a stranger knocked on my door, I panicked again. I gathered a few of my things, waited for the guy to leave and then took off."

"Sounds as if someone is hiding behind Kramer's name. There's a cell phone in my duffel. I need you to take it out," he said.

"Please, no. Don't call the police."

"I won't. Not until we figure this out."

"Not 'we.' I need to lie low until I find a way to reach my father."

"I'm not going anywhere, Samantha."

"You can't be here."

"Why not? Whoever is doing this can't hurt you or me. We'll get to the bottom of it. I'm not leaving until we figure this out. I need to make a call to arrange a place for us to stay. Will you get me the phone?"

She blew out a sharp breath but didn't immediately move.

"I'm your only chance, Samantha. You need to decide."

"Okay. Fine. Where is it? Here?" She pointed to one of four zippers on the front of the pack.

"Inside the main compartment." He didn't take his eyes off the road. She'd find other things in there, too. Another gun. A hand grenade. Things she could use against him if she completely freaked.

"I found it." Her delicate skin had gone pale. She looked exhausted.

"Look in the contacts for Brody."

"Got him."

A helicopter flew overhead.

Dylan glanced over at Samantha in time to see her hand shaking.

She drew in a breath.

"Call Brody and put this on speaker." Dylan searched his rearview. So far, no one had followed them. He banked a U-turn.

"Where are we going?" she asked.

"Not on I-35. Whoever that was will be expecting that. And we don't know how many people are involved."

"Won't he scour the city until he finds us?"

"He'll try."

Brody answered on the first ring. "What's going on?"

"You're on speaker and I have Samantha in the car."

"Is she okay?"

"Yes."

"Rebecca will be so relieved. She's been worried sick. You guys heading home?" Brody asked.

"Can't."

"Why not?"

"Long story, but we need your help." He didn't want to repeat everything that Samantha had told him. It would only dredge up bad memories for Rebecca, especially since this couldn't be Thomas Kramer. Thomas Kramer had acted alone. And Thomas Kramer was dead. Not to mention the fact that he was part of the breakdown crew for a traveling festival. Not exactly someone who had the connections or money to hire men like the ones who'd come after Samantha. The only person in town who could financially back an operation like this would be someone like Charles Alcorn, the town's wealthiest resident. But it couldn't be him.

Alcorn had played a critical role in the investigation fifteen years ago. Everyone in town had been thoroughly investigated. Dylan was getting punchy.

It could, however, be someone tied to Kramer.

Whatever game this creep was playing was about to end.

"What do you need from me?" Brody asked.

"Get me what you can on Thomas Kramer. I want to know everything about him. Friends, family, known hangouts."

"You got it." Brody cursed under his breath.

"Why him?"

"I'll explain later." Dylan cut a hard right and then a left. "But we need a safe place to stay."

"Why not go to the police?" Having served in the military, Brody still had connections—connections that could come in handy.

"Not yet."

"I'll make a few calls and find a place for you to hide within the hour. I have a lot of friends in Austin. Until then, stay on the move. We'll figure this out," Brody said. "I'll let the others know what's going on, too."

Dylan looped around downtown four times before the phone rang again.

"I have a location for you. I found a small place behind a bar on Sixth Street." Brody relayed the address. "I would've liked to get you farther out of town but I figured you'd want internet access and you needed someplace quick. Plus, with all the foot traffic, it'll be easier to disappear in the crowd. Big Mike is working the bar and he's expecting you both. He'll have keys and can give you any passwords you need to use the internet."

"Hey, thanks, Brody."

"Keep me posted. And good luck."

Luck? He blew out a sharp breath. Since he'd left his four-leaf clover in his other pants, he'd have to rely on skills the US Army had taught him to stay alive.

SAMANTHA WAS BEGINNING to shake off the mental fog that came with the hard slap of reality that she was now on the run with Dylan. She shouldn't notice his thick, muscled arms. Nor should she get too comfortable in the sense of relief being this near him brought.

If she was going to be running for her life, she certainly wanted to be with a man who looked as if he could handle whatever was thrown at them. That was a given. But feeling as though somehow everything was magically going to be all right because Dylan had shown up was naive, no matter how capable he was. And her father was still in danger. "What's the plan now?"

"You tell me everything. We put our heads together and figure this out."

"I already said. He's going to keep coming until both my father and I are dead. Dad said as much." She rubbed her temples to stave off the headache threatening. It was a potent mix of frustration and exhaustion.

"Then, we need to write another ending." He touched her hand to reassure her but instead it sent fissures of heat swirling up her arm.

"We can't hide forever. Whoever is behind this will find us." She hated how weak and fearful her own voice sounded. But she was afraid. And there was no use hiding it.

Dylan's gaze shifted from the rearview to the road as he jerked the steering wheel in another hard right turn. "We have company."

Horns blared as Dylan made a few quick turns, navigating the crowded streets of downtown. Samantha's "fight, freeze or flight" response rocketed through the roof and she battled against the urge to jump out of the car and set out on foot.

Traffic was so thick the black sedan couldn't get close. Yet it kept pace with every turn six cars back.

Dylan muttered a curse at the same time Samantha thought it. With Dylan involved, she feared the threats against her, her family and her friends were going to be delivered on.

"I'm scared." She hated admitting it, but acknowledging her feelings had always made them less overwhelming. Especially after her mother's death.

"Think of what you'll be doing next week."

"What?" Damn weakness. Growing up in a house full of boys had taught her to fend for herself. Yet she was so out of her league here that her nerves were spiraling out of control. She needed to calm down and figure this out. Everything had happened so fast she hadn't had a chance to process it.

"You know what I'll be doing?" he said, his calm voice settling over her.

She shook her head.

"I'll be picking Maribel up from school about now."

The image of him, all muscle-and-steel man, tenderly holding his little girl, stirred her heart in ways she'd never experienced. She'd seen him at the grocery with Maribel a few times, witnessed his tenderness with his daughter.

"You need to drop me off somewhere and go to her."

"I'm not leaving you alone, Samantha. End of conversation." A mix of emotion played out across his features, determination rising to the top. "What about you? What are you going to be doing this time next week?"

"My dad invited me to go fishing with him." Her dad. Where was he? *What have you done, Daddy?*

"Good. Focus on that when you get scared. Know that you will be sitting next to him on his boat, hauling in the largest catfish either of you have ever seen."

"That's his favorite. Loves the taste of blues."

"The man has good taste."

Samantha had a clear mental picture, and it was working.

"Better?"

"Yes." Much to her surprise, it was helping a little. Then again, Dylan's confidence was addicting. She'd have to work harder to ignore the sensual shivers his touch brought.

"Hand me the duffel." His voice was level and calm, the complete opposite of the emotions still trilling through Samantha.

"Okay. What now? What do we do?" The sheer amount of foot traffic on the sidewalk and the streets made it impossible to get away. If they didn't make a move soon, the driver would edge his way closer until he could get a good shot.

Dylan told her the address of the hideout.

"On three, I want you to open that door and run into the alley. Don't look back. No matter what happens, keep going. Got it?"

"What if—?"

"One…"

The thought of splitting up and going in different directions had Samantha bracing for a full-on panic attack. She'd have to trust that Dylan knew what he was doing.

Given what she'd been through in the past few days, the idea of trusting anyone was almost laughable.

"Two…"

He glanced at her as though searching for confirmation.

She nodded and gripped the door handle.

"Three. Go!"

She pushed the door open and burst from the car, jolting toward the alley lined with parked vehicles until her thighs burned. Students were everywhere.

Dodging in and out of the human obstacle course, she ran harder as panic mounted. An icy grip around her rib cage squeezed. Where was Dylan?

She couldn't even think of anything happening to him. His little girl needed him.

The sound of shots fired made her knees wobble and the crowds scatter. She steadied herself and charged ahead, fighting the urge to look back, knowing that losing a precious second of advantage could cost her her life.

Where was he?

The absence of those intense green eyes on her was like being thrust into darkness. She'd do almost anything to see him again, to know he was okay. The only reason she missed him was because she hurt for his little girl, she tried to convince herself. Samantha knew what it was like to lose a parent. It had nothing to do with the fact that he'd become her lifeline in a matter of hours. Everything about his presence was soothing.

He'd risked his life to save her and she hadn't had a chance to thank him yet.

The thought of doing any of this without him brought on deep physical pain. She told herself it was because of his professional skills and not because of his strength or virility.

Except he had Maribel. And what if something happened to him?

Samantha would never forgive herself.

DYLAN PARKED THE car and ran. He'd given Samantha a three-minute head start. He ducked, narrowly avoiding the bullet that lodged into the brick two feet from his head. As far as good days went, barely escaping a head shot didn't rack up as one of them. With so many innocent civilians around, he wouldn't return fire and risk a stray bullet.

Zigzagging in and out of buildings, he cut left.

Samantha had no phone or GPS to guide her. She'd have to rely on the instructions he'd given her. Since she was in an understandably stressed-out state, he couldn't count on that happening.

Risking a glance behind, he caught sight of two men following him. Neither broke off in Samantha's direction. That was a win. Now all he had to do was shake them. Her theory of this being carried out by Thomas Kramer disintegrated. He'd worked alone, and whoever was behind this had resources.

Dylan pushed his legs harder, faster. The guys behind him were already showing signs of fatigue.

Good.

As long as he kept his pace, he could outrun them. Ducking in between houses, he circled back. Samantha should be long gone, but if she was in trouble, he hoped he'd get there in time.

The *whop-whop-whop* of a chopper sounded overhead; no doubt shots being fired had drawn police attention. He slid underneath a Suburban and waited.

After sixty seconds, the chopper noise faded.

Glancing around, he noted that the coast seemed clear of foot traffic, too.

As he slid out from underneath the SUV, a blow to the head came out of nowhere. Dylan stumbled forward, checking his balance by grabbing the SUV. Without turning, he dropped to a squat and, with one leg extended, swept behind him.

The contact was followed by a *clunk*, confirming a direct hit.

Pivoting, Dylan covered the guy who'd hit him with a quick jab and then ran. He needed to locate Samantha. He could only pray that his diversion tactic had worked. He'd promised to protect her. The thought of her being vulnerable was a sucker punch to his gut. He told himself it was because she was counting on him and he didn't want to let her down, and that it had nothing to do with the electricity humming inside him when she was near.

He blocked the image of her lying in the alley somewhere, hurt, out of his mind.

Focusing on their next steps, he decided his first action would be to change their appearances. The hideout would most likely have a much-needed change of clothes. He hoped she'd be there. Dylan covered the few blocks quickly.

The key was with Big Mike, just as Brody had said.

"I let in a lady several minutes ago," Big Mike said. "Said her name was Samantha. She looked scared of her own shadow."

After a heartfelt handshake and a thank-you, Dylan headed around back and climbed up the wooden staircase.

He slipped through the back door and waited.

"Samantha," he whispered. There was no sound of her. With DEFCON silence, he crept through the small apartment. The living room and kitchen were clear. He moved to the bedroom next, careful not to make a noise. If she was there, she wasn't giving away her position. Why did that make his chest swell with pride?

He pushed the thought out of his mind, reminding himself that women were good at hiding things when they wanted to be. All things done in darkness eventually came to light. What else was Samantha keeping from him?

Out of his peripheral vision, he saw movement to his left inside the closet. A curtain acted as a makeshift door.

Caution dictated that he make no assumptions. The person was most likely Samantha, but until he had a visual, he wouldn't take it for granted. There was always the possibility that someone had gotten to her.

Damn.

Dylan took a step back.

The curtain burst open and Samantha sprang toward him. She landed with her body flush with his, and he tried not to think about how long it had been since a woman had been in his arms.

"Dylan. Thank God it's you." Shock was in her eyes

and deeply written across the lines of her forehead. "I was so scared."

"Of course it is," he soothed.

She gulped in air and he could see her pulse racing wildly.

"I'm here now. Everything's okay," he said, holding her.

"They were so close and I heard the shot. Oh, God, I panicked." She gulped another breath like a fish struggling out of water. "I—I—I didn't know what to do, so I ran here as fast as I could."

Another swallow of air.

She was about to hyperventilate.

Dylan could either slap her or kiss her to snap her back to reality. Since he'd never once lifted a hand to a woman and had no plans to start now, the choice was clear. He dipped his head low and pressed his lips against hers, half expecting another knee to his groin in return.

Shock registered when her lips moved against his and her fingers tunneled into his hair, deepening the kiss.

She pulled away first, pushing him back a step and glaring at him. "We need to figure this out."

He threw his hands up in surrender. "I was just trying to calm you down. I'm here as your friend."

It was a kiss he wouldn't forget anytime soon but a line that should never have been crossed, no matter how many times he'd wanted to do that in high school. *Since high school.*

"You'd do well to remember that." Her breathing had steadied, but she was angry. "We need a different plan. I can go to one of my brothers' places. You can't be involved."

"I'm sorry for what I did just now, but I still want to help."

Her head was already shaking. "Not a good idea. He was specific. I should've just gone to my brothers in the first place and not tried to figure this out on my own. Then, you wouldn't be here."

Dylan figured he'd led this guy straight to her. What happened earlier was on him. His ringtone broke through the awkward moment. He immediately answered when he saw Brody's name, noticing that he had a missed call.

"There's no good way to put this," Brody started, and an ominous feeling rolled through Dylan.

"Just come out with it." This wasn't going to be good. Waiting never made it better.

A deep sigh came across the line. "I wanted to notify you before the Amber Alert was issued. Maribel is missing."

Chapter Four

Dylan dropped to his knees. A dozen emotions pinged through his chest, rapid-fire like an AR-15 and with the same devastating effects. Rage battled to the surface, making him want to rip apart the first thing he could get his hands on. Ten years ago—hell, three—and he would've done just that. He was a different man now, and especially since Maribel had come into his life.

The image of his little girl waving to him at the kitchen door wearing the Mickey Mouse backpack that was almost as big as she was assaulted him. His military training kicked in, and that was the only reason he didn't explode in anger. It was the only thing keeping him from putting his fist through the nearest wall.

"Tell me exactly how it happened," he said through clenched teeth.

"First of all, Mrs. Applebee tried to call. She didn't want to lose time, so she immediately phoned me when she couldn't reach you or Ms. Anderson." Ms. Anderson was first on the emergency call list. Brody and Rebecca were second.

"Maribel was on the playground at the Dinosaur Park," Brody continued, "and teachers were stationed at each corner. Mrs. Applebee blew the whistle. Kids lined up.

Teachers counted heads. They turned up one short." Brody's voice was racked with agony.

Dylan knew his friends loved Maribel, too. That wasn't the thought he intended to focus on at the moment, and yet his brain didn't want to accept the reality that she was missing.

This had to be a mistake.

"Any chance she's inside somewhere? Hiding in one of the bathrooms at the ranger station?" he asked.

"The headmaster checked each one personally. She and the staff looked in every possible nook and cranny. Mrs. Applebee called the sheriff to file a report immediately."

Dylan was four hours away in Austin while his daughter was probably scared half to death wandering around somewhere, lost. He didn't even want to go there with the possibility she could be lost in the woods overnight. What kind of father was he to let this happen?

He pushed to his feet.

"We're all searching for her. We'll get her back. Stay positive, bro," Brody said. His solemn tone belied his words. "This is not your fault."

Yes, it is. Guilt raided Dylan. He was supposed to be on that field trip. If he'd kept his schedule as planned, then Maribel would be safe right now and not out there alone, stranded, scared.

It wasn't like his daughter to wander off.

Maybe Lyndsey had had good reason to be afraid that Dylan would be a lousy parent. She'd never really told him why she'd kept their daughter from him.

Samantha took Dylan's fisted hand, opened it and, palm to palm, wrapped her fingers around his. He squeezed hers and then let go. He walked across the room, turned toward the door and spoke low into his cell. "Have you spoken to the sheriff?"

"Rebecca is trying to get through to him now. She's been getting the runaround." Brody paused a beat. "She's sick about this. Said it's all her fault for asking you for a favor."

"She couldn't have known this would happen." The hope that this could be a mistake drained out of Dylan like water out of a tub. The harsh reality set in that his baby girl was missing.

"We're going to find her," Brody reassured him. "No matter what it takes."

The air thinned as if it had been sucked out of the room. The notion that Dylan might not ever see his Bel again pressed down on his chest with the force of a drill.

"We'll find her. And we'll bring her home," Brody said.

"I'm coming."

"It's not safe for you on the highway. Whoever's after Samantha will be waiting."

"Yeah? They're about to get a surprise." Dylan searched for his duffel. He'd blow up the whole freakin' town of Austin if it meant getting to Mason Ridge faster.

Samantha sank to the floor. "He took her. He said if anyone helped me they'd regret it."

All thoughts of his daughter wandering off on her own exploded in an audible crack.

This was a coordinated attack, bringing up the question once again of who would have resources to pull something like this off.

Dylan dropped the phone, turned to face Samantha and then stalked toward her. "What else do you know?"

She gasped. Tears streaming down her cheeks did

nothing to soften the steel fury coursing through him, making his veins burn.

"I already told you everything."

"You better start talking or I'll walk you outside and dump you on the street myself. We'll see how long it takes for those men to find you." He wouldn't do it, but she didn't know that and he needed to know exactly what she knew. Rather than allow his violent side to take over, he paced.

She looked up at him. The fear in her eyes didn't sit well with him, but he didn't have it in him right now to go easy on her, not while his baby was out there somewhere, God knew where, with people who wanted to use her to get to Samantha.

Her eyes were glossy and wide, fearful. They had an almost animallike quality to them. "He must know you're involved. That's why I didn't want you here in the first place. You should've just let me deal with this on my own."

"I couldn't leave you alone, Samantha." She had tried to push him away and get him out of there from the second he'd shown up.

"Thomas Kramer or whoever is behind this didn't hurt the boys. We have to hold on to the hope that he won't change that now," she reasoned.

"We have a small army after us." Dylan didn't voice his fear that he'd led them straight to her. Someone must've been watching the movements of the group of her friends to see if anyone came to find her. But why? Who else was involved? "My daughter is missing."

The US Army–trained sniper inside him—the man who could set aside personal feelings and regard for life in order to fire at a target—wanted to force more information out of her. But the man, the father he'd become knew that would just shock her deeper into her shell. He sank down in front of her. Desperation was as unforgiving as the bare wood floor against his knees. "I've got nothing here. I need your help."

LOOKING INTO DYLAN'S intelligent and intense green eyes stripped away Samantha's defenses. She saw that same look that had been in her eyes when she'd learned about her mother's accident. That had been Samantha's fault, too. Guilt pressed down on her shoulders until her arms grew numb. Her mother had been making a school run during a snowstorm. Samantha had forgotten her math folder. Some of the roads had been icy. Trotter Road had been the fastest route to school but it had that long bridge.

Her mother's car had broken through the ice. A chill raced down Samantha's spine at the memory.

And now a little girl's life was on the line...

Telling anyone about her father might put him in more danger. And yet *not* doing everything she could to help made her feel as if she was acting right along with the bad guys—an accomplice to the kidnapping. Her father had done something. She'd known instantly when she'd heard his voice on the phone last week. He was far from a perfect man, but he was a good person deep down. And he wouldn't want an innocent little girl trapped in the middle of this horrific mess.

Forgive me, Daddy.

"I'll tell you everything I know," she said, with the caveat that it wasn't much.

She took a deep breath to fortify herself and then told him every detail she could remember about the attack, the stalker and her father's words that he'd fix this one more time.

"When was the last time you spoke to your father?" Dylan asked.

"Less than a week ago. Right before I left town. He said he needed time to sort this out and that I should be careful. I wanted to see him but he refused. Said it was too dangerous to say where he was. At first I thought maybe he would go to one of my brothers' places. I called around the next day but none of them knew where he might be. They asked if they should be worried and I told them no. They have enough on their plates already and I really didn't know what else to tell them. Plus, I just thought, what could my dad have done? He's a nice guy. Pays his taxes ahead of schedule. Tends to the shop. He gave up drinking years ago, so it couldn't be related to that."

"How's the business doing? Any chance he owes someone he shouldn't?"

"It seems to be doing well."

"Desperate people can be very good at hiding things."

She knew firsthand the truth in those words. When her father was drinking, he'd come up with all kinds of sneaky ways to cover his tracks. "I got nothing. I mean, the business is good. I'd have to take a closer look at the books to be certain. He didn't do well when Mom died but we became his life after he stopped drinking." Samantha's voice still hitched when she talked about her mother, the pain still raw after all these years.

"What are we missing?" Dylan sat back on his heels and rubbed his temples. "We need to figure out a way to get back to Mason Ridge."

"Do that and we might be playing right into this guy's hands."

"I can't sit here and do nothing." The intensity to his voice didn't ease.

"Yeah, well, go outside and we might make it worse."

"That's impossible," he ground out. "My little girl is missing and I was supposed to be the one volunteering on the field trip. Me. I should've been there instead of running off for a case. This is my fault and she's probably scared to death. She already lost her mother and now she's alone again."

"You're a good father," she said, trying to soothe him.

"Really? How so? Do most fathers allow their children to be kidnapped?" he snapped.

"You didn't know this would happen. And you wouldn't be here if you had. If anyone's to blame, it's me. This is my fault, not yours." A heavy weight pressed on her chest. It was because of Samantha that her mother was gone. And now a little girl was in danger. How could that not feel like her fault, too?

Why hadn't Dylan listened to her before?

He was right, though. This couldn't possibly be the work of one man.

She crossed her arms over her chest. "We can't change what has already happened. All we can do is find my father and find out who is really behind this. Together."

"Like hell you're coming with me. You're in enough jeopardy as it is."

"What do you plan to do alone?" Dylan was already gathering his things and searching for what she figured had to be keys.

"Find my daughter and bring her home safely."

"How do you figure you'll accomplish that?"

"By talking to your father." He located his cell and then thrust it toward her. "Get him on the phone."

"He won't pick up."

"Then, leave a message. Tell him to call you back at this number."

"And what if whoever is responsible for all this is listening?" She waved her arms. "Do you really want them to have your cell? Can't they track you or something? Watch your movements? That doesn't seem like the smartest idea."

"That why you ditched yours?"

"Yes."

"Smart." It shouldn't have mattered that there was a hint of pride in that word. Maybe a hint of forgiveness, too?

"They won't trace mine," he said.

"How is yours different?"

"I have a friend who helps me out with technology. He scrambles the number for me when necessary, and he programmed in some kind of advanced encryption to make sure no one can keep an eye on me."

She cocked an eyebrow.

"With my security consulting business, I don't take chances." He disappeared into the other room and came back holding a pen and paper in his hand. He scribbled down digits. "Give your father this number."

Samantha took the offerings. She called her father, praying he would pick up. There'd been complete silence between them since he'd told her to hide, and it raised the hairs on the back of her neck thinking about it. Had they gotten to him? A shiver ran through her.

No, please. He was old. Whatever he'd done in his past couldn't have been that bad. Sure, he'd gone through a difficult phase after her mother had died. Everyone in the Turner household had, especially Samantha. His drinking had nearly done the family in. Then came that summer when Rebecca and Shane had been kidnapped. And Samantha's father had sobered up. He'd said it was the wake-up call he'd needed. That he couldn't stand to lose anyone else. He'd checked himself into rehab while her brothers took over the hardware shop. They'd stepped in to cover at home, too, and all had pitched in with household chores.

Hold on a minute. Samantha had met up with Rebecca recently at a restaurant in town. She'd brought her father along and he'd acted strangely around Rebecca. Samantha had been confused by his actions at first, but now they made sense. Had he been uncomfortable around her friend because he'd held back information about her and her brother's abduction?

The line rang but her father didn't answer.

Where was he?

If the person responsible for this craziness had gotten to him, then they most likely wouldn't still be looking for her. Right?

Why would they be after her at all?

There was only one logical explanation. They must think she knew what had really happened.

As expected, her father's line rolled into voice mail. She bit back a curse.

"Dad, please, I'm in trouble. I need to talk to you *now*. Call me back at this number." She rattled off the digits and ended the call.

Dylan paced as she stared at the phone, willing it to ring. *Come on, Daddy. Be okay. Call me back.*

She hadn't realized her hands were shaking until then.

This whole situation sounded all her internal warning bells. She'd known this guy had meant business from the start.

Regret engulfed her.

Dylan shouldn't be there. He shouldn't be involved. His daughter shouldn't be scared and alone right now because of Samantha.

"Get up," Dylan said harshly.

"What for?"

"We can't sit around here all day."

"What exactly do you plan to do? We no longer have a car, remember?"

"Don't need one."

"But—"

"If I had my way, you would stay right here until I could send someone for you. I doubt you'd let me get away with it. So you're either in or out, and I'm leaving. You have to decide if you're coming with me. Either way, I'll walk away with a clean conscience knowing I gave you the choice. Choose wrong and that's on your head, not mine."

This was the Dylan she remembered, rough around the edges but real. He wasn't the type to go behind a person's back and exact revenge. If Dylan saw someone mistreating a puppy, a senior citizen or a kid, he'd walk straight up to them and tell them what he planned to do right before he punched them in the teeth. He'd even let them know which fist was coming. No cleaning the toilet with an offender's toothbrush while he was out of the house. Dylan would wash out the guy's mouth with soap. No apologies.

"Okay. I'm coming with you. At least tell me where we're going."

"I'm going to find the bastard who kidnapped my daughter." Dylan shouldered his duffel, turned and walked out the door.

Chapter Five

"I know what I said before but we should go to the police now." Samantha followed Dylan out the door and onto the side street. He pulled a hat from his duffel and then tossed it back to her.

"No. I won't discuss your father with them." He shook his head as if for emphasis.

His phone had been buzzing the entire time. Word must be spreading. Dylan would deal with that when he got home.

He called the sheriff and gave a statement.

"Call him back," she pleaded. "I can tell them everything I know and that might help them find her."

"Absolutely not." He kept charging forward, setting a pace she could barely keep up with.

She jogged up to him and touched his shoulder. "I think—"

He spun around on her so fast she froze.

"As long as we find them first, I have a chance to get my daughter back unharmed. We make one wrong move and she's dead. The police have done nothing but make mistakes when it comes to anything connected to the Mason Ridge Abductor. I can't risk it with Maribel."

If anything happened to Dylan's little girl…

Samantha couldn't allow herself to think about it. She had to be positive.

"Contact whoever took her. Tell them we'll trade me for your daughter. I'm the one they want. She's innocent and shouldn't be involved in any of this."

"We do that and you're dead. I won't exchange one life for another no matter how desperate this situation seems. Besides, we don't know who's behind this or where they're keeping my daughter," he said.

"There's one way we might be able to find out. You said you have a friend who can hack into any device?"

Dylan nodded. His lips were so thin they almost disappeared.

"Then, have him do whatever he needs to in order to get into my father's phone. He isn't calling me back and that's not good. There might be a clue in his log."

"I already thought of that." He dismissed her suggestion with a wave of his hand as he turned. "It won't work. My contact already tapped into your line. The caller went to great lengths to hide his identity. He's not stupid."

There had to be some way to figure out who was behind this.

Dylan stopped. He surveyed the area, eyeing a motorcycle near the kitchen entrance to a restaurant. The metal-and-mesh screen door no doubt had been left open to let out heat from the ovens.

He motioned for Samantha to stay put, slipped inside and then returned a few minutes later with a helmet in hand. She had no idea how a man of his size could go unnoticed and was pretty certain the ability had been honed in his darker days. The idea of stealing didn't sit well with her, either.

"Get on."

She slid the helmet over her head and buckled the strap. It was a little too big for her but she didn't figure this was the time to argue with Dylan about who should be the one to wear it. Besides, even she knew that her state didn't require a helmet. Texas figured if a man was dumb enough to ride a motorcycle without one, they'd like to thin the herd.

"Take a stolen motorcycle out on the road and we'll be in jail before dinner," she said, tightening the strap.

"I bought it."

"Someone sold you their motorcycle just like that?"

"I can be very convincing when I need to be."

She had no doubt.

Dylan slid onto the seat in front of her. She leaned into him and wrapped her arms around his chest, remembering how frightened she'd been when he'd been shot earlier. Fear that had been all too familiar since this whole ordeal had begun. This past week had been the longest in her life, and the last thing she wanted to do was bring someone else into her problems. And yet having Dylan there brought a sense of calm to all this insanity.

The engine roared to life.

Dylan put his head down, shades on, and then weaved into the always heavy downtown Austin traffic.

Her body finally felt the weight of everything she'd been through in the past week. She didn't want to remember the last time she'd really slept, or had a decent meal, for that matter. She'd been surviving on power bars and water. The protein was enough to keep her going, and staying hydrated just seemed to make sense, but it was all robotic.

Lack of rest settled over her like a steel blanket, pressing down over already exhausted limbs.

BY THE TIME Dylan pulled into town, it was dark. Samantha figured no one would expect them to roll in on a motorcycle. The ride had been long but, thankfully, without incident. Kramer, or whoever was behind this, would have expected them to take I-35, but Dylan had taken 190 to I-45 and come up as though from Houston instead of Austin. His plan had proved brilliant even though it had added time they both knew they didn't have.

She recognized the storage facility on the edge of town where he stashed the Honda 500 as being fairly close to his small ranch.

"We can walk it from here," Dylan said, which were the first words that had passed between them in more than five hours. If he blamed her for Maribel's kidnapping, he didn't let on. His green eyes were sharper now, determined.

Her body ached from lack of sleep and little food. Even though her stomach growled, she couldn't imagine being able to hold down food. Not with what was at stake. Knowing a little girl's life—Dylan's little girl, at that—hung in the balance pretty much ensured Samantha couldn't have eaten or slept if she'd tried.

With the dark circles cradling Dylan's eyes, that was most likely all he could think about, too. Talking about how desperate the situation felt wouldn't change anything, wouldn't help matters. In fact, he needed a distraction.

"How far is your place?"

"About thirty minutes or so from here," he said.

He knew this area like the back of his hand, so she would rely on his skills to get them there safely.

The half-hour hike wasn't bad even through burning thighs. Dylan's silence was far more unnerving. Having grown up with three brothers, she knew that a quiet man was not a good sign.

It was black as pitch outside with no sign of light.

She listened for the sound of Dylan's footsteps and stopped a little too late, running into his back.

His hand found hers for the rest of the walk.

She couldn't have seen a tree if it was right in front of her face. His phone light appeared every once in a while, guiding them through the night.

They pushed through trees and brush, eventually making their way to the edge of a clearing. This had to be his place. An outside light was on over his carport and there were two others lighting the front of the small ranch-style house.

"We'll slip in through the back," he said. "Keep the lights off so we don't give anything away."

Samantha kept close even though he'd released her hand. She missed his warmth as soon as they disconnected.

They crept in through the back door.

The outdoor light permeated the large windows in the living room. With open blinds, she could see well enough not to walk into furniture. A few children's books along with several toys were on the sofa. Most everything else had a place and the room was in order, reminding her that Dylan was ex-military.

The place was full of simple, comfortable-looking furniture. A few framed snapshots of Dylan and Maribel had been placed on the fireplace mantel. Others were on side tables.

"Make yourself at home," he said, his voice a low rumble. "Shower's down the hall. There's a night-light always on in there and that should provide enough light for you to see. Fresh linens are in the closet. You need something to wear?"

She didn't want to ask why he would have women's clothes available, but the idea of a shower was too good to pass up. "I could stand to clean up. Fresh clothes would be nice."

"Go ahead. I'll put something on the counter." He paused a beat. "I'm sorry about earlier. I got heated and I shouldn't have—"

"You don't have to apologize. Under the circumstances, I thought you were pretty restrained, actually." She knew Dylan well enough to realize he wouldn't hurt her no matter how angry he was. Just like in high school, he needed space to think. The long drive home had most likely been what he'd needed to get his bearings again after the devastating news about Maribel.

"There's where you're wrong. I do have to say I'm sorry. I'm trying to be a better man since becoming a father."

"I hear what you're saying, Dylan. But I know you. You always were a good person even when you got in trouble before. I never doubted you for a second." She walked straight up to him, pressed up on her tiptoes and kissed his cheek.

He stood there for a second looking dumbfounded.

"Don't look so surprised. It's not as if I haven't known you since we were eleven years old." With that, Samantha walked out of the room, down the hall and into the bathroom.

She slipped out of her road-weary clothes and into the warm water.

Looking around at the couple of rubber toys and the princess bubble-bath bottle, Samantha figured this had to be Maribel's bathroom. Icy tendrils closed and squeezed around Samantha's heart, and her knees buckled. She caught herself with a hand on the wall and then said a silent prayer that Maribel would return home safely, just as Shane had. Any other outcome was unthinkable.

The shower rejuvenated her stiff muscles. She toweled off and picked up the clothes on the sink, a pair of boxers and a T-shirt. Definitely not women's wear. Why did that fact spread a glimmer of light into her heavy heart?

She put on the clothes, cinching the waist of the boxer shorts with a butterfly hair clip she found in the drawer.

No matter what else happened, Samantha was determined to help get Maribel back.

By the time she emerged from the bathroom, smells from the other room said there was food working in the kitchen. Her stomach growled in spite of the fact she couldn't imagine eating under the circumstances. It was impossible to think about doing anything normal while Dylan's daughter was missing.

Samantha made her way into the kitchen.

Dylan turned as she stepped into the room, stopped and stared. Moonlight streamed in from the window, casting dark shadows across his face.

"What?" She glanced down at her outfit self-consciously.

"Feel better?" His voice was low, gravelly.

"Much. Why? Do I look okay?"

He nodded.

"Sit down." He pointed toward the eat-in dining table and chairs.

"I'm not hungry."

"Eat anyway."

Giving short answers was another bad sign. Maybe

she could get him to open up and talk a little bit. It had always helped when her brothers were angry.

One look at Dylan, at his almost savage expression, told her he'd tear apart an animal with his bare hands if it meant getting his daughter back.

"What is she like? Maribel?"

"A ball of energy. More like a three-feet-tall tornado." A brief smile crossed his lips before he seemed to catch himself. "I don't want to talk about it right now."

Okay. She'd have to try a different tack. "Have you given any thought to our next move?"

"Yes."

"And?"

He pointed to the chair. "Sit."

"Okay." She did. So much for getting him to open up.

He walked over and set down a bowl of food and a fork in front of her.

"You know how to cook pasta?"

"It's Maribel's favorite. I learned." He picked up Samantha's arm and held it out. "You're losing weight."

That much was true, so she didn't argue.

"And you could barely hang on to me during the ride. I was afraid you'd fall off half the time."

She was almost surprised he'd noticed. Her grip around his broad chest had broken a time or two, but she'd quickly recovered. "Yes."

"So make the food in that bowl disappear," came out on a grunt.

She doubted the old Dylan would've noticed any of those things. He'd been all bad boy and, in a word, self absorbed. But then, he'd had a lot of reasons to be. Life hadn't been easy or kind. The new Dylan, the one with a softer side, tugged at her heart even more. He'd always been handsome in that rugged, edgy, not-sure-what-to-

expect way. And he'd always been unbreakable. Seeing this side to him—his Achilles' heel being his little
angel—speared Samantha through the chest.

Since the reformed Dylan seemed determined to stand
over her until she got a few bites down, she did so for
the sake of show. The food tasted as good as it smelled,
so she managed a few more. And she didn't want to like
the small smile he conceded at the corners of his mouth
that didn't reach his eyes—eyes that were tormented and
angry.

That he seemed genuinely concerned about her well-
being made her unable to disappoint him. He'd been a
good friend so far. He'd put himself on the line to help
her and she'd treated him like the enemy early on.

"Since we're throwing out apologies and all, I'm not
sure if I thanked you earlier," she said, then forced down
another bite.

"That's not an apology."

"Thank you anyway," she quipped.

He turned and walked to the counter near the sink,
leaned his slender hip against the cabinet and scooped
pasta into a second bowl. He stabbed the fork inside and
then chewed the first bite. "If you're going to be strong
enough to fight back, you need to eat."

She blinked up at him. Right again. And even though
she absolutely knew that he had to be dying inside, he
was just this tower of strength on the outside. His eyes
gave away his pain, and she figured he was allowing her
to see it. If he wanted to, he could go blank so as not to
give away his advantage.

"For the record, I don't want to eat, either," he said,
anger rolling off him in palpable waves, heating the room
as he forced the fork into his dish again.

Dylan was right. She hadn't eaten a proper meal in the

past week or had a decent night of sleep. As it was, her left hand could scarcely hold the fork, let alone fight off an attacker. As much as she didn't want to eat or go to bed, a full belly would make her stronger and her head needed to hit that pillow soon.

He rinsed out his bowl and placed it in the dishwasher before returning to her side. She could feel him, even if she closed her eyes, standing next to her because Dylan was just this massive presence, a noticeable energy.

"What's the plan?" She couldn't suppress a yawn.

"Bed." He peered down at her bowl, removed the fork from her hand and swooped up the dish.

"There must be something else I can do to help."

He'd already turned his back to her. He didn't turn around. "Sleep."

"What will you do?"

"The same. I'll be no good to my daughter without grabbing a few hours of shut-eye. You need more than that." He started moving toward the sink again.

She wanted to protest, to argue that she was just as strong as he was, but it would have been pointless. And although she had every intention of pulling her own weight, she couldn't debate her need for sleep.

How on earth she'd get it, she had no idea. Being alone with Dylan was already doing all kinds of crazy things to her pulse. Adrenaline from the day had long dissipated and she was left with a beating heart in an exhausted body.

"Go brush your teeth. There's an extra toothbrush in the cabinet."

Under normal circumstances, she'd have been offended by the fact he'd resorted to using as few words as possible with her again. Except he was too much like her older brother Brent in that way. Brent would become laser focused and the little pleasantries went out the window. He'd said he didn't have time to fill his brain with nonsense when there was a serious task at hand. How many times had Brent come to the rescue in those early years after losing their mother? Too many.

She understood that, on some level, this was Dylan's way of coping.

And she couldn't find fault in that.

Before she could develop an argument for staying up, Dylan was at her side, urging her to stand.

"Lean on me," he said gruffly.

She didn't realize she needed him until she tried to stand on her own. Her knees buckled and his strong arm around her waist kept her from falling flat on her back.

Tired didn't begin to describe how she felt.

Brushing her teeth was the last thing she remembered doing.

THE HOUSE WAS still as Samantha's eyes flew open. She blinked a few times to gain her bearings. She was on the pullout sofa in a spare bedroom. He'd insisted she take his bed, but it hadn't seemed right to take that away from him. He needed sleep as much as she did, and he had a much better chance of getting it under the sheets he was used to. Besides, she barely even remembered closing her eyes before she was out.

What time was it?

She glanced around for a clock, got up and found one on a side table. Two o'clock in the morning. She'd gotten at least four hours of rest. That was more sleep than she'd had in the past week in its entirety. She'd take whatever she could get at this point. It was the little wins that mattered most right now. Celebrate all the little wins, her big brother would've told her, and that will keep you going even through the toughest of times.

It also sounded like something Dylan would say. And that was pretty much where his similarities with her older brother ended. The two were nothing alike physically. Brent was barely five feet ten inches. He had their father's small frame and their mother's brains. Thinking back, she remembered that her mother had been very bright. She'd also been artistic and had always checked the light in a room to decide where she would paint. She'd never asked for much. She'd carve out a niche in the brightest room she could find and keep a small cabinet with her art supplies there. While her mother might not have taken up much room in life, she'd occupied so much of Samantha's heart. Losing her had been a crushing blow.

She stuffed the thought down deep as she eased down the hallway toward Dylan's room. She'd have to pass his daughter's room to get there, and a coil tightened in her belly with each forward step.

The door decorated with the name Maribel was open, waiting.

As Samantha passed by, something dark and big caught her attention. Her eyes were still adjusting to the darkness, but she could see clearly enough to realize it was Dylan.

There he was, this big hulk of a man who had fallen asleep sitting on the floor of his daughter's room, leaning against the wall, holding on to a stuffed rabbit that was no doubt his daughter's favorite.

His head was slouched forward; he almost looked as if he was crying or praying. If she left him there like that, his neck would hurt in the morning. The least she could do was help him into a more comfortable position.

Samantha tiptoed inside and tried to ease the furry animal out of his hands.

In the next second, she was splayed out on her back and he was spread over top of her with a sharp object to her throat, his weight pressing her into the bamboo floor.

She'd scarcely seen the glimmer of metal before it was against her bare skin.

"Stop. It's me." She stared into dead eyes, a permanent sneer fixed on his face. Then it occurred to her. He was still asleep. One wrong move and he'd slit her throat before he woke. She kept her body very still. "Dylan. It's Samantha. Wake up. Please."

He snapped his head from side to side and then focused on her. "Dammit. That's a good way to get yourself killed."

He shifted his weight onto his right side and his groin pressed against her naked thigh. A volt of electricity trilled through her. She didn't want to feel that certain pull between them that made her remember that he smelled spicy and warm and windswept, and yet she couldn't deny its presence.

The anger and adrenaline coursed through her, igniting the sexual chemistry between them into passion and fire. He dipped his head and stopped when his lips barely touched hers.

Was he waiting for a sign that she wanted this to happen, too?

The knife hit the floor and she could hear it being pushed away, sliding across the bamboo.

"Samantha?" When he spoke, his lips brushed against hers and she could feel his breath, still minty from toothpaste.

"Yes" was all she could manage with him this close, with his body flush with hers and the material of his cargo pants against her thighs. That strong chest she'd been holding on to earlier moved up and down faster now, matching the rapid pace of her pulse.

"I've been thinking a lot about that kiss yesterday."

A dozen thoughts rushed her mind. She'd been thinking about it, too. More than she knew was good for her. She didn't want to like Dylan as more than a friend. Not now. Maybe never. This was all too complicated.

His soft lips pressed down on hers. Her hands came up and circled around his neck. He tasted so good.

He was propped up on one elbow and his free hand started roaming as he deepened the kiss. He was touching, feeling, connecting, and all she could think was *more*.

And then it dawned on her.

He was searching for comfort. It could have been any woman underneath him right then. The two of them were friends. Period.

She broke the kiss and slid out from underneath him. He didn't immediately move, as though he needed a few seconds to process her actions.

"I was out of line there."

"No. I wanted it to happen, too. But that's not good for either one of us." She started to say *right now* but stopped herself. The truth was there might never be a right time for the two of them, and she had no intention of confusing a friendship for something else again.

"You're right." Those two words stung. Had she been hoping he'd argue?

"Won't happen again." He pushed up onto his knees, then stood. "You want a glass of water?"

She shook her head, embarrassed. She'd let things between them go too far, and now it would be awkward. Dylan wasn't reaching out to her because he liked her;

it was because of the tension he was under. He needed a release. Sex with Dylan would blow her mind, she was sure. But then what?

It would get weird between them, just as it had in college when she'd been a shoulder to cry on for the crush she picked up during Freshman Lit. Jude Evers had been busy working his way through college, a single dad with two young kids. He'd caught his fiancée in bed with his best friend. He and Samantha had bonded over the really crappy espressos at the student union that were like mud in a cup. The two had become friends, then lovers, and she'd put her heart on the line with him. Hadn't that turned out to be a mistake? She'd babysat his kids so he could go to the student union to study, or so she'd thought. Boredom had gotten the best of her after she'd put his kids to bed, so she'd logged on to social media.

There he was, caught on camera kissing another girl from class, no less. He was shirtless, and the reason why was pretty obvious. They'd just made love.

Samantha had never felt so used.

When she'd confronted him that night, he'd said he thought they had an understanding—that the two of them were friends with benefits.

Embarrassment had threatened to consume her. If it hadn't been too late to drop the class, she would have been first in line. Instead, she'd had to sit through ten weeks of analyzing prose with him and the other woman.

The worst part had been saying goodbye to the kids she'd grown to love.

Samantha pushed up off the floor. At least she could try to get a few more hours of sleep. Although with Dylan's bedroom two doors down, she doubted she'd be able to completely relax.

He appeared in the doorway as she took a step toward

it, and she gasped. That man could be stealthy when he needed to be.

"Sorry about a few minutes ago," he said, and his voice was still gravelly. "I got carried away in the moment, but I'm good now. It was a boundary that shouldn't have been crossed."

This was *supposed* to be exactly what she wanted to hear…so what was up with the stinging feeling in her chest?

Chapter Six

Dylan had been resting his eyes in his daughter's room for a good half hour before Samantha had caught him off guard. Kissing her the first time had been a mistake. The second had been sloppy. Sure, he felt an attraction sizzle every time she walked into a room. The only thing that proved was that he was still a man aware of a beautiful woman.

He'd had just enough of a power nap to fuel him for the day ahead and get his head on straight. Being a fulltime father to Maribel was the greatest job he'd ever had and he wouldn't trade a minute of it. Caring for his little angel 24/7 left little time for anything else in his life. There were no regrets. Being her father was the best thing that had ever happened to him. But there was no time for detours, or *anyone* else in his life.

Besides, Samantha was a friend. Sure, she gave him signals. And they had chemistry. Again, it was down to man and woman, primal urges and all that. He'd been seeking proof of life and so had she. They'd been through hell together, so hormones had gotten out of control.

They most likely wouldn't go away anytime soon, either. So he'd have to work a little harder to keep them under wraps.

Besides, Dylan Jacobs didn't "do" relationships. He

also didn't engage in flings, not since he'd screwed his head on straight a few years back, and especially not since Maribel had shown up.

His feelings for Samantha were nothing more than a snag he could deal with. The last thing he needed right now was another complication in his life. His hands were full with the serious situation he found himself in. And it would take all his energy to remain focused on the jerk who'd taken his baby girl. Once he got her back, his days would be filled with work and play and preschool.

Besides, there were about three females he trusted, and one of them was three feet tall. The other two had been carefully screened during the interviewing process: his housekeeper and the preschool headmaster.

Dylan shook off his emotions as he moved to the bathroom for a cold shower.

Fifteen minutes later, he walked into the kitchen. As soon as it was daylight, he needed to swing by the sheriff's office and see what kind of leads they were following through on. More than anything else, he needed to come up with his own plan to find Maribel.

At the moment, all he had to go on was the name Thomas Kramer. A dead man couldn't kidnap a child. Whoever it was had to have enough money and connections to fund the recent attacks. That led Dylan to believe there could be some sort of crime ring involved. Seemed as though there was a story in the national news at least once a week about child abduction rings, and it would take serious money to pull off having a crew in Austin and in Mason Ridge to pursue them. Kramer might've been involved in a bigger organization.

On a related topic, there was the matter of finding Samantha's father. Involving her more than Dylan needed to was a bad idea for more reasons than just his growing feelings toward her. His best chance to find her father rested on her, though, so there was no choice but to keep her close and in the loop. For now.

If the man behind all this had gotten to her father, he wouldn't have taken Maribel. His daughter wouldn't be harmed as long as Mr. Turner was on the run.

Other than that, he had precious little to go on and no way to find his baby. Dylan refused to think about how scared she must be right now. Or that this was the first night she'd spent away from home since she'd come to live with him a year ago. His hands fisted as he checked the clock. Nearly two hours had passed since the incident with Samantha. Time was not his friend.

He ignored how empty the house felt without Maribel in it. Instead of focusing on the negative, he booted up his laptop, located a pen and paper in the kitchen and then wrote the name Thomas Kramer in the center.

The next name he wrote was Samantha's father's, Henry Turner. He circled both names and drew a line connecting them. What did her father know? He put Samantha's name on top and then his own across from hers. From his, he drew a dotted line downward and then scribbled his daughter's name.

The sheriff's office didn't know about the link to Mr. Turner, at least not yet.

So far, they thought they were looking for a lost girl, not a kidnapping case. No matter how desperate he was to get his daughter back, he couldn't risk involving the law yet.

There had to be another way, a connection he was missing.

Talking to Samantha's father was a top priority. Finding him would be the challenging part. His house would most likely be a dead end. He'd know better than to stay there. Where else did he like to go?

How about the hardware store that he owned? Mr. Turner wouldn't likely be there, because it was too obvious, but Dylan wanted to know what the hours were so he could drop by and ask a few questions to Mr. Turner's employees. Dylan located his cell and called the number.

The recording said the place didn't open for another five hours.

Dylan ended the call and then jotted down the time. Surely Mr. Turner wouldn't be stupid enough to walk in the front door of his shop. He'd have to get someone to open for him, though, or people would get suspicious.

Where else had Samantha said her father liked to go?

He was a fisherman, so he would know all the area lakes. There were dozens of good spots in North Texas alone, depending on what he liked to fish. She'd already mentioned catfish. Dylan wrote down the words *fishing cabin* with a question mark. Mr. Turner might have a few secret hiding spots that only his daughter would know about. Dylan would ask Samantha as soon as she stirred.

In the meantime, he could send a few emails to his buddies with an update. His inbox was already loaded with concerned friends reaching out to him. Samantha had given out his number to her father, whom the kidnappers might already have found. Again, Dylan guessed they hadn't.

There were twenty messages in his spam folder. Every once in a while there was something useful in there, so he opened the folder. He scanned the usual scam emails.

Midway down the list, his eye stopped on one. It was an invitation of some sort.

Knowing he might regret his actions when a new virus blacked out his screen or some other irreversible nonsense occurred to his laptop, he took a chance and opened it anyway. It had arrived in his inbox within an hour of Maribel's kidnapping.

The heading read Want to Trade?

Red-hot fury licked through his veins, burning his skin from the inside out.

Dylan clicked on the message.

There was a meet-up spot. 1212 Whistle Bend Road, Mason Ridge, Texas. And a request to bring the *Brave* Barbie doll from the second shelf in his daughter's room. He pushed off the counter and made a beeline to Maribel's room.

Had that bastard been inside Dylan's house? In his daughter's room?

Anger roared through him as he stalked to her bookshelf. She never played with her *Brave* doll. Maribel kept it on her bookshelf as a reminder to be strong.

Had they taken more of Maribel's things? Dylan hadn't thought of that before. He began checking her drawers. Whoever had been in the house had been careful not to leave a trace. There wouldn't likely be fingerprints, either. This guy was good at covering his tracks. Should this situation go south, he'd make sure the son of a bitch paid dearly.

Her favorite pajamas were missing, along with a couple outfits. Someone had gone to great lengths to make sure she had supplies.

When he really looked around, he saw that a few other things were gone, too. Several of her toys had disappeared. Dylan scooped her favorite bunny, Rofurt, off the floor.

He held the stuffed animal as he moved to the laptop. Someone who went to the pains to take the child's personal items couldn't intend to harm her. Could they?

His first real sense of hope bloomed. He was cautious not to be too optimistic, understanding he wanted her back so badly that his mind would look for any positive sign to latch on to, real or imagined. He didn't want to kid himself.

He immediately pulled up the address on Google Maps and switched to Earth mode. There was a semiwooded lot with nothing on the front of the property but a mailbox. Anyone could stay hidden in the nearby tree line, watching.

Dylan's next call was to Jorge. He was the only person Dylan figured he wouldn't be disturbing in the middle of the night.

Jorge picked up on the second ring. "What can I do for you, my man?"

"I need you to track down an IP address. I got an email."

"On it." The sound of Jorge's fingers tapping on the keyboard came through the line. He already had been given access to Dylan's accounts when they'd first started working together.

"Also, I need information on the location."

"Name it." The staccato sound stopped.

"I want to know who owns that piece of property. Can you expedite that for me?"

"You know I'd do anything. Does this have to do with…?"

Dylan was relieved Jorge didn't finish the question. Jorge would've seen the Amber Alert and known Maribel was missing. He didn't need to hear those words from anyone. "Yeah."

"I'm on it right now. Call you back in a minute?"

"I'll keep the phone in my hand."

The call ended and Dylan stared at the piece of paper

with the names. What was he missing? What possible connection could any of these people have to each other?

SAMANTHA TOSSED AND TURNED. Again. Sleep was about as close as New York to Texas, and neither had a fast track to the other. She peeled off the sheet and tiptoed to her door.

If Dylan was awake, he was quiet.

She pushed thoughts of his body pressed to hers out of her head as she opened the door and walked into the hallway. She heard typing noises coming from the kitchen area. He had to be up.

The promise of freshly brewed coffee kept her feet moving toward the scent. She didn't want to surprise him, so she relaxed into a normal pace and cleared her throat.

Turning the corner, she immediately noticed his tense posture. He was leaned over his laptop, intensely studying the screen. She wasn't sure he'd heard her walk into the room.

"That coffee I smell?" she asked softly. The only light came from the glow of his screen.

His gaze didn't waver. "Help yourself."

What could have possibly happened in the middle of the night?

Samantha easily located a mug and then poured a cup. She took a sip, enjoying the burn on her throat, the taste of the dark roast.

Tension sat thickly in the air, and she hoped it wasn't because of what had happened between them earlier. She wouldn't get through any of this without Dylan.

"Can I pour you another cup while I'm in here?" she asked as a peace offering.

He grunted something that sounded like an affirmation.

As she returned with a full mug, his head snapped up

and his gaze focused on her. He spun the laptop around so that she could read the screen.

Fear exploded through her as she read the email.

Next, Dylan produced a list of everyone they knew. She recognized all the names of their friends and the half dozen or so older boys.

"You think one of our friends could be involved?"

He steepled his fingers. "It's possible, or they might have seen something that could help us figure out who else is."

"At least we have a direction now," she said. She nodded toward the laptop, knowing he was grasping at straws. "When do they want to make the exchange?"

"Midnight tomorrow."

"I wonder why they're giving us so much time."

"My guess is that they're hoping to find your father first. Maybe they think they're close."

"This doesn't give us enough time to prepare." She took another sip of fresh coffee.

Samantha planned to personally see to it that Maribel returned home safe. The question was whether or not she should split up from Dylan to make it happen. The thought of doing any of this without him made her shoulders tense.

"Hungry?" She moved to the kitchen, needing something to do with her hands or she'd go crazy.

He made a move to get up. She held her hand up to stop him.

"No. I got this." She opened the fridge. "Let's see what we have to work with in here."

DYLAN WANTED TO talk to Samantha about more than just food. He wanted to tell her that everything would work out and that they'd be fine. The words fell dead on his tongue. Putting much thought into doing anything besides getting Maribel back was near impossible.

They also needed to find her dad before the other guys did. The sun would be up in an hour or so. He figured they could leave before first light.

If Dylan was a betting man, he'd put his money on the fact that the property would be near one of the sheds where Rebecca and her brother had been held when they'd been kidnapped fifteen years ago. Everyone knew Brody had torn one of them down. Hell, Dylan had been right there alongside his buddy, shredding the cursed building.

"Where should we start looking for my father?" Samantha pulled out what looked like the fixin's to make a country-style omelet.

"At the beginning," he said, trying to analyze how they'd get through the woods and to the shed area unseen to scope out the place.

"What are we missing? We know Kramer's name is being thrown out there to distract us. Right?" she asked.

"Whoever's doing this is twisted. Maybe Kramer wasn't even the bloody fool who'd taken Rebecca and Shane in the first place. We might have it all wrong."

"Whoever is behind this must have some money or connections."

"I thought about that, too. The men in Austin were most likely hired guns."

"Where's a knife?" She laid out an onion and bell peppers on the counter.

"The top drawer to your left. There's a safety lock on it," he said.

She fumbled with trying to open it.

He moved beside her. She smelled like Maribel's favorite flowers, lilies. It was the shampoo he kept in her bathroom, which was also shared with guests. Maribel had picked it out for when Ms. Anderson stayed overnight. He'd also seen it as a sign his daughter wished there were a woman in the house on a more permanent basis.

As much as he wanted to be Maribel's world, he acknowledged that he was limited on what he could teach her due to a severe lack of estrogen. He filled in the gaps with Ms. Anderson and Mrs. Applebee, knowing full well there would come a day when Maribel needed more than he could provide.

He'd cross that bridge when he came to it. In order to have a relationship with a woman, he'd have to trust her. And thanks to his mother's disappearing act, that wasn't likely. He always disconnected with a relationship when it came down to it. Even though Lyndsey had had her reasons for lying, Dylan had loved her. He'd been devastated when she'd suddenly accepted a new job and moved to New Mexico without leaving an address. She'd gone to great lengths to keep him out of her life.

His stubborn streak had kicked in, saying he didn't go where he wasn't wanted. He'd taken the hint and walked away.

How many times had he regretted that action since then? How many times had he wished he could go back and get those precious few years with Lyndsey back? He would've tracked her down and sat on her stoop until she'd been forced to listen to his side.

A big part of him wished Lyndsey was still around, and not just for Maribel's sake. He and Lyndsey had enjoyed each other's company and had great sex, and everything else could have been built from there. Lots of relationships had weaker foundations than fantastic sex, easy conversation and a great kid.

Then again, if Lyndsey had still been alive, he might

not even have known he had a daughter. This was the kind of mixed blessing that defined his life.

And he couldn't ignore reality. What kind of relationship could they have had if they didn't talk about anything important? Conversation must not have been her forte, because she hadn't even had one with him to let him know he was a father.

Dylan wished she'd known him well enough, trusted him enough to attempt to coparent together. Had he really been such a jerk that she'd never considered letting him in on her secret? She'd known about his background. While he hadn't wanted kids, she had to have known he wouldn't have turned his back on his child, either. If Lyndsey had known anything about him, she should've known that.

He shook off his reverie as he stood next to Samantha.

Trips down memory lane didn't change a thing. He should know. After losing Lyndsey, he'd taken a bunch of them.

"Here. You open the drawer just a little, then press this plastic piece down." His arm grazed Samantha's, causing electric impulses to fire through him. He didn't want to think about how soft her skin was, or those slender, long legs being right next to him. How much she trembled when he stood close.

Or how well she'd fit him earlier when she was underneath him.

He was pretty sure any of those things would wreck a friendship faster than a mosquito bite itched.

Samantha hesitated for just a second before gripping the wooden knife handle.

Dylan took a step back, then took his seat at the breakfast bar as she went to work chopping the green bell peppers. She seemed to know her way around the kitchen, and he caught himself staring at her fluid movements.

What the hell?

He chalked up his being sentimental to watching too many Disney movies with Maribel. They were making him soft.

Dylan Jacobs needed another person in his life like dry grass needed a lit match.

Chapter Seven

The second Dylan's ringtone sounded, Samantha's heart raced. It was bad enough that every time he was near, her pulse quickened. And that every time he touched her, awareness skittered across her skin.

And now every sound had her on edge.

She'd been jumping at shadows for a solid week. Every time she thought she saw something move, her stomach lurched. She exhaled slowly and refocused on the pan in front of her, turning the omelet.

"Yes, sir. She's right here," Dylan said. His voice carried a sense of foreboding. She turned off the heat on the stove and set the pan aside.

"It's for you." Her heart dropped to her toes when he turned and caught her gaze. One look in his eyes said there was trouble. "It's your father."

She studied Dylan's expression carefully as they met in the middle of the kitchen.

"Daddy?" she said into the receiver.

"Don't say anything to anyone. You hear? Don't let them get to you. I'm going to fix this," her father said. Rustling noises came through the line.

"To who? Fix what? What are you talking about?" She listened closely, trying to identify a noise that might give away his location.

A crack sounded, followed by a grunt, and she couldn't breathe.

Fear roared through her, causing her hands to shake.

"That's not what you're supposed to say to her. I thought we had an understanding," a male voice said.

"Daddy? What's going on? Where are you?" Questions fired out frantically. Her heart pounded in her chest as she looked straight at Dylan.

"Try to keep him on the line for as long as you can," Dylan whispered. He'd already picked up his landline and was making a call. Dylan was the picture of focus.

She figured he was calling his technical contact to see if they could get a trace.

"Hello? Who's there? Talk to me, Daddy. I can't help you if you won't tell me what's going on," she said quietly. The silence on the other end was deafening. "Tell me who is doing this to you."

"I tried to run but they found me" came through on a raspy, winded breath. "I know what's really going on and it's big, he's big. It's—" More shuffling noises came through the phone and her father screamed.

Her entire body began to shake.

"Please don't hurt him. Who is it, Daddy? Who's hurting you?" Desperation sat like an anchor in her stomach.

This was so not good. Her father was getting older, and no way would he be able to protect himself against younger, stronger men.

"Daddy. Are you there?" She said a quick prayer that her father would be all right. She couldn't imagine life if anything happened to him. The two of them had been the closest. And he hadn't been perfect but she'd always known that he'd been the best father he could be, especially when he'd had to step in to be a mother, too. And even though it was Samantha's fault her mother was dead, her dad had never once made her feel that way. He wasn't that kind of person. How on earth could he have gotten himself into this kind of serious trouble?

"They already know I confessed everything to you," he said loudly, through labored breathing. Then he whispered, "They won't hurt me as long as they can't find you."

A thousand fears raced through her all at once, and at least a dozen scenarios of ways they might torture him.

"Daddy?" What could she do? Call Brent? If she could get ahold of her brothers, would they know what to do? She needed her father too much for anything to happen to him.

More sounds of struggle came over the line before it went dead.

"Oh, no. No!" A heavy weight pushed down on her as she looked toward Dylan. "This isn't real. This can't be happening. They're going to kill him."

Dylan ended his call. "I have someone all over this. Maybe we'll get lucky this time and get a location. We'll know something in a few minutes."

"And then what? Go to him? They found him. They're going to kill him. He'll be dead by the time we start the car." Panic was getting the best of her and she knew it. She needed to take a few deep breaths and calm down. Except that was her father out there. Alone. And he didn't deserve to die by the hands of some jerk, no matter what her father had seen or did fifteen years ago.

She relayed what her father had told her.

"Now we know for certain why they've been looking for you," Dylan said quickly.

"But I have no idea what my father knows," she said quickly.

"They don't know that. He said that for leverage."

She paced back and forth in the kitchen. "But they will kill him. He might be dead already."

"If they wanted to kill him right away, then why not shoot him and stuff him in the back of the car? Why subdue him? They're using him to get to you. Once they tie up that loose end, they have no need to keep anyone alive."

His words, as direct as they were, did their job well. He was right and she couldn't come up with an argument to his point.

Samantha thought about Dylan's words as she stalked back and forth in the kitchen. "He said this whole thing is bigger, that he's bigger."

"Meaning Thomas Kramer was only a small part of it, like we suspected."

"Daddy was clear." She stopped for a second. "This nightmare just won't end."

"There's only one thing we can do."

"And that is?"

"Scout out the meet-up location and then wait."

WHEN DYLAN'S PHONE RANG, he snatched it off the table, in part to stop himself from walking straight over to Samantha and pulling her into his arms. The last thing he needed was for this situation to get stickier than it already was, and he shouldn't get any closer to her than he felt. Being there for each other during a difficult time was one thing. Friends did that without question. There was something else going on between them and that was sending him into a tailspin. One he didn't have time or energy for.

"What do you have for me?" he asked Jorge after checking the screen.

"Good news. I figured out who owns the plot of land for the address you gave me. Sort of."

"What does that mean?"

"Whoever owns it is smart enough not to use a traceable company."

"Are you saying there's a dummy corporation in place?"

"The one listed is offshore," Jorge confirmed, "making it that much more difficult to pinpoint."

"Any chance you can figure out who owns it?"

"Can a retriever bring back a ball? Of course I can. It'll take time, though. These things are like peeling an onion once you dig into them. The best are smart enough to put up a lot of layers."

"What about the call that came in on my cell a few minutes ago? Did you pick up anything on that?"

"That's easy. That came from a pay phone at a gas station near Eagle Lake," Jorge supplied.

Dylan repeated the information to Samantha.

"Daddy likes to fish there sometimes. It's not his favorite spot, but he's been there once or twice." Her mind looked to be clicking through the possibilities.

"Which is smart. He'd know the area fairly well but most people wouldn't associate him with that place when they thought of him leaving town."

"True. You'd have to be really close to him in order to figure that out."

"Who might know about this other than you and your brothers?"

"My brothers wouldn't know. Only me. I'm the one who fishes with him. My brothers haven't gone since we were kids. It was sort of mine and Dad's thing. I think he did it to make me feel special after my mom…" Her tone changed when she spoke about her mother. He'd noticed it before. There was a subtle shift. He doubted she would tell him what it meant even if he asked outright.

He turned toward the cell in his hand. "What about the IP address? Get anything there?"

"Sorry, man. It's a dead end," Jorge said.

Dylan thanked his friend and ended the call.

"Eagle Lake is not that far—less than a half hour's drive from here." Dylan grabbed his keys from the counter. "We'll head out as soon as you're dressed."

It took Samantha only three minutes to throw on the clothes he'd had Rebecca drop off for her, pull her hair up in a ponytail and walk into the living room with an expression that said she was ready.

Even wearing running shorts and an athletic shirt, she was stunning.

"Think he'll still be anywhere near there?" she said as she followed him into the kitchen and toward the back door.

"I doubt it, but there's no way to know for sure unless we chance it. I want to ask around. See if anyone saw anything. Maybe we can get a description of the person or persons who took him." Dylan grabbed Rofurt. For reasons he didn't want to examine, he laced his and Samantha's fingers and led her out the door. His sport-utility was parked out back. He surveyed the area as they stepped outside.

The first light would break the horizon in an hour, which gave them just enough time to slip out of town in the dark.

"Think we should split up? Would that make things easier?" Samantha asked.

The question caught him off guard as he opened the door for her. He glanced at the empty car seat in the back and a coil tightened in his stomach. He clenched his teeth.

"We need to stick together. It's our best hope of finding either of them." Since Maribel's kidnapping was connected to Mr. Turner, Dylan planned to be glued to Samantha. Besides, she was the missing piece. They got her and it was game over.

He moved to the driver's side, took his seat and fired up the engine.

Neither spoke on the half-hour-long drive to the gas station where her father made the call.

"Do you have a picture of him in your purse?" Dylan parked near the pay phone.

"No. I ditched my phone a long time ago. That's the only place I have… Wait a minute. My phone automatically updates to storage in a cloud. I can give you the password and you can get in."

"Good." Dylan handed his phone to her.

"We were fishing two weeks ago and I snapped something… There." She held up the screen. Her father had a decent-size fish on the line.

"Show that around inside."

"Think they'll ask questions about his disappearance? I don't want to make it worse for him if someone gets the bright idea to call the police."

"Tell him he's been forgetful lately and that he might've wandered off. Say you're heading to the police station next."

Samantha agreed and then disappeared inside the store.

Dylan searched the grounds for anything that might help, any clue that might assist him in finding her father and, dare he hope, his Maribel. He didn't want to think about how scared she might be right then.

Anger tightened the coil.

He fisted his hands and focused on the ground as Samantha stalked toward him.

"Any luck?" he asked, instantly regretting his word choice. Luck was for slot machines.

"No one has seen him."

He'd feared as much. It would've been dark and this area was known for fishing. No one would've thought much about a man in a truck. "Hey. Wait a minute. If your dad was out here, where's his truck?"

"That's a good point. Wouldn't they have taken it?" she asked.

"If they did, there had to be at least two of them. Maybe they didn't want to cause a stir when the truck was left overnight." Dylan searched the ground for tracks, heel marks, anything that might indicate they were in the right spot.

Stepping lightly, he noticed a thick line in the gravel. "Come over here."

Samantha did. "What is it?"

"What does that look like to you?"

"It's the size of the heel of a boot." She gasped. "Daddy?"

"Could be. Looks like the person might have been dragged over here." He pointed to a boot imprint. "Might've gained his footing here."

The trail stopped.

Glancing a few feet away, he saw tire tracks. "This looks suspicious, doesn't it?"

"They went in this direction." Samantha's line of sight traveled away from the boot imprint.

"Took him in his own truck," Dylan said. "They must've had another vehicle here."

"He said he knows what really happened all those years ago, and all I keep thinking is how can that be if he wasn't involved? If he wasn't out there that night? It would make sense. He was drinking back then. Cleaned up his act after... Maybe he was so shaken up by what he'd done he started walking the straight and narrow?"

"Doesn't mean he was part of it." Dylan didn't say that his reassurance meant very little, and the look she gave him said she appreciated him for it.

"He wasn't home a lot during that time. He'd stay out after the shop closed and drink. I thought he was going to disappear like my mom, so I'd wait up for him. I could tell something was wrong with him but I didn't know what. I thought he was sick or something, so I asked Trevor."

Dylan was so caught off guard that she was opening up to him. "That's how you found out he'd been drinking? From your brother?"

"Trevor sat me down and explained to me how much Daddy loved our mother. That her dying had been difficult for him and that we should cut him some slack. I felt so betrayed and so stupid. How did Trevor know all this but I didn't?"

"He was older, for one."

"True, but he had his own life. I was closer to Daddy than the boys were. Or so I thought."

"Your father was trying to protect you."

"That's exactly what Trevor said. How did you know that?"

"I have a daughter. And it's the easiest way to get to me, which was most likely the reason they tried to take you in the first place. Everyone knows you and your father have always been close."

"I saw you with her at the grocery last week."

"Why didn't you say anything?"

"You looked as though you had your hands full."

He cracked a smile. "She keeps me busy, that's for

sure. But I don't bite and neither does she, no matter what her teacher says. False accusations."

"Did you teach her to do that to keep boys away?"

"Not yet. I figure I have a few years before I have to start worrying about them. And then I'm not too concerned. I have weapons." He chuckled, and it felt good to release some of the tension knotting inside him. "You could've said something in the store."

"What? It's not as if we've kept in touch since high school."

"We knew each other."

"I remember you getting into a lot of trouble. What happened to change that?"

"The US Army. They gave me a brotherhood. Taught me life was about more than myself and my problems."

"You ever hear from your folks?"

"No."

"Well, they're missing out. Maribel is a doll. I could seriously pinch those cheeks for days. And that curly hair. Who could miss out on such an adorable thing?"

"I did. For a while," he said.

"I wondered what had happened."

Dylan wasn't prepared to talk about Lyndsey to anyone. Not yet anyway. If he was going to talk about her, then Samantha would be exactly the kind of person he could see himself opening up to. He just wasn't the type, or maybe this wasn't the time. "It's long over. I didn't even know about Maribel until last year."

"I'd heard you bought your ranch a little more than a year ago. Dad's a bit of a gossip in his old age. He's lonely, I think. I wish he'd found someone to spend time with. He just withered away after Mom. Honestly, I was surprised to find out you had a daughter."

"You and me both," he said a little more curtly than

he'd planned. Talking about the past was opening old wounds—wounds he didn't want to think about right then.

She seemed to take the hint, and kept quiet as they walked the perimeter of the parking lot.

He saw something out of the corner of his eye. Might be nothing, so he didn't want to raise the alarm just yet and get Samantha's hopes up unnecessarily.

On closer look, there was a phone on the ground. He picked it up and examined it. There was a picture of a bass on the protective cover. "What kind of phone does your father have?"

"An iPhone. Why?"

"Any special markings on it?"

"Yeah. What do you have?" Her eyes grew wider as she moved closer. "He has that picture on his phone. That has to be his."

The battery had been pulled out. Dylan fished his own phone out of his pocket. Since it was the same model, the battery should work in both. He popped it in.

Several text messages had gone unanswered from the boys and Samantha. "Have you been helping out at the store lately?"

"Sometimes."

"Has anyone been in that you didn't recognize? Anyone talking to your father on the side?"

"No. Not that I can think of off the top of my head."

Dylan searched through pictures, stopping on the last few. "Your dad may have just told us who was after him."

"Those guys are wearing security uniforms. Wait. I recognize the outfits. Do they work for Charles Alcorn?" His name had a habit of showing up in connection with the crime, usually in a positive way. "That's the security uniform for his company. They might be posing as employees, trying to fly under the radar. People wouldn't bat an eyelash at someone who works for Alcorn. Does your father have any dealings with him? Get any supplies from one of his companies?"

"None that I know of. That's so weird. You know, I have seen that guy in the store." She pointed at the guy on the left, who had a big build, light hair and a beard. "He was there a couple Saturdays ago asking for my dad. I overheard from the stockroom. Dad said he was going fishing. Who knows what he was doing now?" A look flashed behind her eyes that Dylan told himself to ask about later. He couldn't pinpoint the emotion and he didn't think it had anything to do with her father's disappearance.

Dylan forwarded the pictures to his secure phone line in case someone was watching Mr. Turner's line. "We figure out who these guys are and we might get lucky with a connection."

Chapter Eight

Samantha rubbed her temples to stave off a splitting headache as Dylan pulled out of the parking lot. Her brain felt as if it might explode. "How do you intend to find out who those guys are?"

"Jorge can help figure it out. If they really do have security jobs, then they've been through some kind of screening process. That'll make his job a lot easier. He can hack into almost any system except law enforcement."

"Can't or won't?"

Good call. "Won't. And I'd never ask. I find that I get a lot more information playing nice than breaking the law. That I only do when I have no other choice. I don't think we're going to find anything else here."

"Where to next?" The way he'd talked about his daughter a few minutes ago had nearly cracked her heart in two pieces. There'd been a softness to his voice she'd never heard before, and his entire disposition had changed. And there'd been something that looked a lot like love in his expression.

Samantha knew firsthand how important a dad's love was to a girl. It would define every future relationship she had with a man.

"Can I ask you something?" Dylan secured his seat belt at the same time she did.

"Sure."

"You don't have to answer. It's really none of my business."

"Go ahead. What's the worst that can happen?" she asked, still massaging her temples.

He pulled the sport-utility onto the stretch of highway. "Your father lied to you when you were a kid. That had to make you angry."

"Yeah. Of course."

"But you forgave him?" he asked.

"Yes."

"Why?"

She shrugged. "Because deep down he's a good person."

"You think liars are good people?"

"Life's not black-and-white to me. No one's perfect. Surely you understand that after what you went through when you were younger. You made mistakes, but that doesn't make you a bad person." The sincerity in her words impressed him.

"The only good thing about me is Maribel."

"That's not true. She might bring out the best in you but the good was always there," she said matter-of-factly.

"I'm not so sure about that." Was it true, though? Mostly Dylan remembered being angry when he was younger. He'd been so furious with the world when he was a kid that he'd thought he might literally burst into flames from the inside out. The military had seemed a better place to take out his anger, and he'd known on some level that he needed the discipline. He'd been paddling in a sea of anger and self-hate before finding his true brotherhood in the military. As a kid, he'd blamed his parents' rejection on himself. He'd figured he had to be one pretty messed-up kid if his own parents didn't like him. Gram had reacted with an iron fist, and that had gone over like battery acid in a punch bowl. Dylan had rebelled even more, and then she'd died while he was in Afghanistan, before he'd had the chance to tell her he was sorry. If he could go back…

"You don't have to be. I saw it before in you and I see it now."

"And what is *it*, exactly?"

"I was in trouble and you refused to turn your back on me. Even when I tried to push you away. What does that say about you?"

"You kicked me in the groin," he said flatly.

"I'm still sorry about that, by the way." She smiled weakly.

"That's okay. But I still haven't forgiven you," he joked, trying to loosen the knot tightened in his gut.

"Great. Now I've gone and reminded you of the whole thing."

"We've had better moments since then." He was thinking about her soft skin. Dylan had a weakness for great legs, and hers were perfect, long, silky and sexy. He'd like to start at the ankles and kiss his way up to the insides of her thighs. There were other things about her that he found increasingly difficult to push out of his mind. The curve at the small of her back where his hand had rested earlier gave way to a taut waist that blended into soft hips. Dylan wouldn't mind spending a little time touching her, exploring her long curves, kissing her. He couldn't remember the last time a kiss had rocketed his pulse like the two they'd already shared. And that was just the icing on the cake. Appreciation of her real beauty came from looking into her eyes and seeing a whole different world he wanted to get lost in. Samantha was sharp, intelligent and *dangerous*, he reminded himself.

"Can I ask you something else?"

"Go ahead."

"How'd you take it when you lost your mom? You were older than Maribel. I honestly don't know how to explain any of this to her. I tell her that her mother is in heaven, whatever that is, and I'm not even sure if she realizes that means she'll never see her again. To her thinking, heaven might be some place, like Florida, where moms go on vacation and don't come home from."

"Be honest with her. You don't have to explain it to her like you're talking to me but she deserves to know the truth, that her mother isn't coming back."

"I know. Damn. For the first six months of the year all she said was 'Mama?' every time someone came to the door. She'd run, expectant, as if she'd been at the babysitter's all day and it was finally time to come home. There were tears, too. She cried herself to sleep for weeks calling out for her mother in the night." He stopped to gain control of his emotions.

"What did you do?"

"I'd settle in next to her and tell her that her mother was in heaven."

"Like I said, tell her the truth. Mom's not coming back, but that doesn't mean she doesn't still love you or want to be with you. Use whatever language is age appropriate but be honest. The worst feeling in the world would be thinking that a mother would come back once she was gone. Tell her that her mother would come back if she could. That she didn't want to leave her. And most of all, tell her that none of this is her fault." Samantha's hands started trembling. "It's not her fault," she repeated.

Dylan turned on his signal, changed lanes and then

pulled over to the side of the road to park. He turned off the engine. He reached across the seat for her. The pain in her eyes was a knife to his chest. "Losing your mother wasn't your fault, either. Accidents happen and take away people we love and there isn't a damn thing anyone can do about it except enjoy the time we have together, make it mean something."

She scooted over and burrowed into his chest.

"It's okay. I'm here," he soothed. He said other things softly into her hair.

He held on to her as the tears fell, staining her shirt.

She lifted her head, tears dripping. "You're doing everything right with her. Don't be too hard on yourself."

He thumbed away her tears.

"I've been so afraid of saying something wrong that I've been avoiding the topic. She stopped asking when her mother was coming back, stopped running to the door yelling, 'Mama!' every time UPS dropped off a package. And I just let it go."

"Sometimes people only come into our life for a moment and we'd like them to stay longer. And we want the world to know what a beautiful person they were, to know them like we do. But all we can do is honor their memory, their legacy. And be brave enough to live without them because I know in my heart that they wouldn't want us to be sad. Maribel's mother would want her to be happy. And you, too."

Dylan let those words sink in. Had he been punishing himself the past year because of his guilt over not being there for Lyndsey sooner?

He stared out the windshield for a while, thinking about everything Samantha had said.

Then his mind wound back to the present situation. "I just want you to know that I've heard everything you said. I have a lot of thinking to do." He paused. "First, we have a situation to take care of."

She nodded.

"My first instinct is to go to Alcorn directly, straight to the source."

"Roads keep leading to him, but he's the richest man in town. He has a lot of influence and it seems out of place that he'd do something like this."

"I'm not taking anything for granted when it comes to our families."

Sun was bright in the midmorning sky. Dylan noticed a glint from in between two houses across the street. "We need to—"

A crack sounded as a bullet whizzed past.

"GET DOWN," DYLAN commanded; his voice took a second to break through in her head.

Samantha dropped to the floorboard.

"Stay right there. You'll be safer."

Disbelief shrouded her. No way could any of this be real. Could it?

For all her panic, Dylan seemed amazingly calm.

"How'd they find us?"

"Someone might've been camping out at the gas station, waiting," he said, cutting a hard right.

One hand against the dash and the other against the seat, she crouched low and balanced herself.

Another round fired, from behind this time. The shooter was following them.

"Stay as low as you can while I lose them. Got it?"

"We can't be out in the open anymore. They'll kill us and then the people we love."

"If we keep you alive and out of sight, your father and Maribel will be safe."

Frustration peeled away her tough exterior.

Dylan made a few sharp turns, mixing lefts and rights. Suddenly, he stopped. "Get out."

Samantha pushed up. Her legs wobbled. Dammit. This was no time to let fear get the best of her. Toughness and strength defined the Turners. She commanded her legs to hold her. Surprisingly, they cooperated this time, and she sprung from the SUV.

"This way," Dylan said, his weapon drawn and ready.

Samantha ran in and out among the houses in the residential neighborhood until her thighs burned and her lungs clawed for oxygen.

Dylan finally stopped, barely breathing heavy. "We need alternate transportation."

"Where can we go? Neither of our houses is safe."

"I have an idea." He walked, surveying the area, until his gaze fell on a garage. "Wait here."

Samantha tried to hide behind the tree where Dylan had told her to stay put, praying the men wouldn't find her before he came back.

An electric car pulled up near the tree. She caught and held her breath, afraid to look to see who it was.

"Get in." Dylan's voice was a welcome relief.

With the way her body was beginning to burn, she didn't think she could make it any farther. She glanced down and saw blood on her shirt as she moved to the car. Panic stopped her. The blood was hers.

"Get in the back and stay down. Now," Dylan said firmly.

She did as he said, curling up across the backseat. She caught enough of a glimpse of him to see that he was wearing a ball cap.

A ripple of heat started in her stomach and was quickly

followed by a full-on wave of nausea. Light-headedness engulfed her like a flame. "I was shot."

"I know. You're going to be fine." Dylan's words came out strong and confident. There was an edge of anger there, too. "Can you see where you were hit?"

The numbness and the shock were wearing off; her left shoulder burned. "Yes."

"Stop the bleeding with this." Dylan passed back a shirt. "It's clean."

"Okay."

"We need to get to Brody and Rebecca's place."

"Won't they be watching our friends?" Samantha knew one thing was certain. If the guys got to her, then her father was as good as dead. Keeping herself out of sight was his only chance.

"Which is why we can't walk through the front door. I need to call Brody to let him know that we're coming."

"I've been thinking about something you said earlier. About my father's business."

Dylan nodded, eyes focused on the road ahead.

"I remember him being stressed a lot the first couple of years we came here. There were late-night discussions with Brent and Trevor as to whether Daddy had made the right choice in coming to Mason Ridge. Stevie was too young to weigh in. I blamed it on the changes in our lives, losing Mom..."

"But then Rebecca and Shane were kidnapped. Suddenly, Daddy was home every night. His drinking slowed down and then he quit altogether. His business turned around, too. He seemed sad but not as stressed, if that makes sense."

"It does."

"On the phone, Daddy said he knows what really happened that night. What if someone had bribed him to be quiet?"

"That was fifteen years ago. It would be impossible to trace the money now."

"Not with computers. Daddy keeps everything."

"So if we get into your dad's system, you think we'll figure out who's behind this?"

She was already nodding. "Except that every time we're out in the open, we seem to get shot at."

Dylan didn't argue that. He made a few more turns and then parked on the side of the road. Then he called Brody and asked for permission to come onto his land. Brody said he'd make arrangements for one of the guys to pick up Dylan's SUV. He turned to Samantha after ending the call. "We'll have to walk it from here."

Dylan opened her door and extended his hand.

She took it, noticing how strong and capable it felt. His hand was surprisingly soft, and she already knew how adept it was from the few times he'd touched her.

They hiked what felt like ten miles before Brody's barn came into view. Dylan led her into the back, and she could see all the way through to light at the other end. Both doors must have been open.

The barn was one big, impressively long hallway with light streaming in from both ends. The floors were made of concrete and there was hay strewn around everywhere. A dozen or so horse stalls with red metal gates flanked the left-hand side and there were a quarter as many doors to the right. She assumed they were supply rooms and offices.

Dylan opened the first, held on to her hand tightly and ushered her inside. "The horses must have been turned out in the paddock."

This room had to be Brody's office. Centering the

space was a large oak desk with a leather chair behind it. There was a matching sofa to her left. It was a rich dark tone and massive in size. Dylan guided her there and helped her ease down onto it.

There were no windows. It would be dark inside without the light on.

"Lie still." He placed a throw pillow behind her head.

On top of the desk was a white case with a red cross on it. A medical kit. Dylan retrieved it and instructed her to roll up the sleeve of her shirt.

She did.

The sofa dipped where he sat.

"No good. I can't see. Take it off." His words came out harshly. He clenched his jaw. "I can turn around if you want, but I'm going to need to see to fix you up anyway."

"It's okay. I have on a bra, which is a lot like wearing a swimsuit anyway, right?" She tried to sound convincing. Mostly, she needed to reassure herself that it was no big deal. Heat flushed her cheeks anyway as she eased out of her shirt with his help. Her left shoulder had been hit and it hurt when she moved. The wound itself was too bloody for her to really tell how bad it was, but the bleeding had stemmed.

Dylan grunted a few words under his breath when he saw it and she assumed they were the same words she was thinking. He pulled out the antiseptic wipes first, opened them and lined up a few on the sofa.

"This is going to sting. Let me know if it gets to be too much." He went to work cleaning her gunshot wound. His hands were assured and surprisingly gentle. She didn't want to know how he'd become so good at it, figuring he'd picked up the skill during his time in Afghanistan.

"How bad is it?" she said, not wanting to look anymore, wincing with pain.

"I'm sorry if I'm hurting you." His voice sounded pained.

"It could be a lot worse," she offered.

"The bleeding has stopped, so now we want to clean it up well to keep out infection," he said, tenderly blotting her wound with antibacterial pads before bandaging them.

When he was finished, his gaze drifted across her chest.

"Thank you for taking such good care of me," she said, ignoring the rapid rise of her pulse.

"That should do it." The words came out clipped.

She wondered if it had to do with the fact that she was lying there topless.

Chapter Nine

"All done," Dylan said as he forced his gaze away from her creamy skin. Her lacy bra didn't help matters. It had taken considerable discipline to avert his eyes from the soft curve of her full breasts peeking out over the top.

He told himself that it had been too long since he'd had sex, and that part was true. He didn't want to acknowledge how much it might not matter when it came to Samantha. Even so, when had there been time this past year to do anything but potty train Maribel? No wonder his body reacted every time he touched Samantha. She was a beautiful woman. He was a man with needs. If it had been that simple, he was pretty sure they'd have been in bed already, recent events aside. There was so much more to it than that. They had history. He knew that she secretly liked being silly and she prided herself on not being too much of a girlie girl. He figured that was a gift from growing up with three brothers. Her laugh filled him like spring air. She had a single dimple on her left cheek that came out only when she smiled real wide.

She'd asked to hold his hand earlier, to help deal with the pain, and he just now realized that his thumb was moving in small circles against her palm.

One look into her cobalt-blue eyes—eyes that had

darkened with the look he hadn't allowed himself to see in far too long—and his heart clutched.

If she hadn't been injured, he might have done something they'd both regret.

"You haven't slept. Do me a favor and try to close your eyes." He pulled his hand back, gathered up used supplies and tossed them into the garbage.

"I feel as though I should be doing something."

"We can't. Not until we know what their next move is," he said.

She seemed to carefully consider his words.

"You're right." She bit back a yawn as he turned off the light.

He hadn't wanted to admit just how freaked out he'd been when he saw that she'd been shot. He'd stayed calm for her benefit.

Dylan wouldn't survive losing her, too. *Where'd that come from?*

Thankfully, Samantha would be all right.

"Will you come over here?" Her sweet, sleepy voice wasn't helping with his arousal.

The room had just enough light for him to see big objects without being able to tell what they were. His own adrenaline was fading, leaving him fatigued.

He walked over and sat down. She took his hand. Hers was so small in comparison, so soft.

"Will you lie next to me?" she asked in that sexy, sleepy voice. "Just until I fall asleep?"

He settled onto his side, being sure to keep a safe distance between them, and realized she was trembling. A lightning bolt of anger sizzled down his spine.

"I'm right here," he whispered into her thick dark hair.

She wiggled until her back was flush with his chest, and she made a mewling sound as she snuggled against him. Her hips readjusted, causing her sweet round bottom to press against his swollen erection. His jeans were uncomfortably tight, so he shifted his position and she pressed into him farther. Blood pulsed thickly through his veins, and all he could think about this close was the lilac scent of her shampoo.

"Samantha."

"Yeah."

"You might not want to get so close to me."

"Sorry. I didn't mean to trap you." She made a pained noise as she moved.

"That's not the problem."

"No?"

"If those hips of yours press into me one more time, I can't be held responsible for my actions."

"Oh." It was dark in the room, but he could sense that she was smiling.

She shouldn't want anything to do with him. His life had been beyond messed up before the military. She swiveled her hips until she surely felt his straining erection.

"Samantha, I'm warning you not to do that."

"Now you're starting to sound like one of my brothers."

"I have nothing brotherly in mind to do to you right now. And if you weren't injured, we'd both be in serious trouble, because I don't make a habit of forcing myself on anyone."

"What makes you think I'd say no?"

That was the last thing he needed to hear.

"Are you intent on causing me more pain?"

"Sorry. No. Of course not." She wiggled again, this time to inch away from him. Big mistake.

He stopped her with a hand on her hip. He curled his fingers around her waist, which felt tiny in comparison to his hand, into her taut skin, and he knew he was falling down the rabbit hole. She was so close he could feel her breathing against his chest, her breath hitching with his touch, her body trembling underneath his fingers.

Neither said a word, but the moment felt insanely intimate.

After a few seconds passed, she finally said, "Is it wrong that I like how your body feels against mine?"

"No. But if we let this go any further, it would kill our friendship." Her shirt was still off and there was enough light for him to see her sexy silhouette. If trouble had a name, it would be Samantha.

His life had been ticking along fine before she waltzed in. Everything had finally made sense. He was meant to be Maribel's father. To this day, he figured he'd go to his grave wondering why Lyndsey had truly ditched him. Maybe she'd been smart enough to realize he wasn't good for her, for anyone.

And he'd surely kill his friendship with Samantha if he didn't maintain control, which was beyond difficult watching her breasts move up and down as she breathed.

Plus, he'd thought about those couple of kisses they'd shared way more than any man should.

Good grief, would he be calling his friends together for a glass of wine and to share feelings next?

How far did this out-of-control-emotions thing plan to go?

"You're probably right, but I can't help wondering what it would feel like if you ran your finger along here." She picked up his hand and ran his index finger along the waistline of her shorts.

She rolled onto her back, looked into his eyes and traced the lace on her bra next.

All he could do in that moment was dip his head and

claim her pink lips. He cupped her breast with his palm, and a jolt of need burst through him as her nipple beaded. His need for her, to be inside her, was so powerful it was a physical pain. And that scared him because he'd never felt that deep-seated need for anyone, not even Lyndsey. He'd never wanted to be inside anyone so much.

Her mouth moved under his, inviting him to explore. He slid his tongue between her lips and she opened her mouth to give him better access.

With her hands tunneling in his hair, roaming his chest, his skin burned with sexual energy.

All that was between his hand and her breast was a thin piece of lace. He traced down her stomach, lowering his hand until he was on her sex.

She moaned and bit his bottom lip, drawing it out between her teeth.

His desire for her was almost a savage force inside him now.

"Samantha." He pulled back long enough to look into her eyes, needing to know she wanted this as much as he did, because much more and he'd be over the tipping point, no turning back. Her eyes were dark and glittery, her face flushed, her lips pink and swollen from kissing. She was the most incredibly sexy woman...

And it was clear she wanted exactly the same thing he did—mind-numbing, mind-blowing sex.

Dylan took in a sharp breath.

There was one more thing he wanted. And that darn thing would stop him from getting the others.

He'd promised himself that the next time he had sex, it would be with someone he had strong feelings for. He didn't want to say love, because, frankly, love was complicated as hell.

"I let this go too far," he said, pushing off the sofa and

into a sitting position. His punishment pulsed painfully against his zipper.

"Oh. You don't like me enough?" He hated the sound of embarrassment in her voice.

"I like you just fine. You're freakin' beautiful. And that body." He took in another sharp breath.

"Then, I'm confused. You want me, right?"

"Yeah."

"And I want this to happen, too."

"It would seem so."

"Then, what's the problem?"

He didn't want to tell her that he didn't have strong enough feelings for her. His were strong. And confusing as all hell. But mostly a complication he couldn't afford right now. Introducing another change in Maribel's life when he'd just given her some stability was out of the question. "It's Bel."

She gave him a confused look.

"If things were different, then maybe we could take our time, date and see where this goes. But that's not a priority for me right now and, frankly, I don't have time for it to be."

His words had the effect of a slap in the face. He didn't enjoy being harsh, but he'd said all of that more for him than her.

She covered herself with her shirt, turned on her side and then did what every woman he'd ever known had done to him when he'd said the wrong thing. Gave him the silent treatment.

HUMILIATION WAS A PYTHON wrapped around Samantha, squeezing. Not only had she basically just thrown herself at one of her oldest friends, but she'd been rejected by him. Painfully. And if her shoulder didn't hurt so much, she'd have tossed and turned on this sofa or gotten up and stormed out. But it did. And she couldn't move any more than she could allow herself to cry. *Mortified* didn't begin to cover her embarrassment. If there'd been a crack big enough in the wall, she'd have slipped through it. While she was at it, why not ask for a tiny bottle or a looking glass? Her life made about as much sense. Then again, if she was really having her wishes granted, she should definitely aim for something higher, like forgetting any of this had ever happened. Or getting her father out of trouble. Or, better yet, saving her father and Dylan's little girl.

Frustration burned through her like chunks of a comet spiraling toward Earth.

They had no idea who they were really chasing and time was running out.

She strained to listen to Dylan, who was talking quietly into his cell phone on the other side of the room. Her eyes had adjusted to the dark. He was bent forward, his arms resting on his knees, being too quiet for her to be able to hear what he was saying. Most likely because he didn't want to interrupt her while she was supposed to be sleeping.

Slowly, she eased onto her back. The pain in her shoulder had already started thumping, and she could feel it worsen with every beat of her heart.

He ended the call and crossed the room, setting himself up to pace. He glanced down, looking as if his anger was barely contained, and his gaze stopped on her. She could've sworn his tongue slicked across his lips.

At his full height, he was imposing, to say the least, especially with his arms folded across his broad chest. And, as much as she didn't want to think about it, he was incredibly sexy.

"Who were you talking to?"

"Jorge. He sent me photos of Alcorn's security team and I didn't see our guys."

"Which means they don't work for him."

"They might be off the books, but we can't link them." He stalked to one end of the room and back.

"Have you figured out what they want us to do next?"

"You're injured and need to rest." Surely he wasn't saying what she thought.

"Oh, no. You're not leaving me here while you go out there." She motioned toward outside.

His face was carved in stone. "They have my daughter. And I'm running out of time."

"We are. Or don't you do 'we'?" She shouldn't have gone there but she did anyway. His earlier rejection still stung.

She geared up, expecting a fight. Instead, he softened his stance and there was a quirky little smirk settled into the corners of his mouth. *Damn.* Even when she wanted to throttle him, he was being sexy.

"You got me there. But that doesn't change the fact that you've been shot. You lost blood today and you have to take that seriously. You're safe here for the time being, and that's the best gift you can give to your father and Maribel. They don't want me. They want *you*. Even if they catch me, I'm not the target. *You are.*"

Didn't those words send a chill up Samantha's spine?

"I see your point but I have a question. Where does that leave me? You're all I have right now. Anything happens to you and I might as well walk into the center of Main Street and take a seat. They'll get to me. You're the only thing keeping me safe." As much as it scared and angered her to admit it, she needed him. And a traitorous piece of her heart actually didn't mind depending on someone else. And that was just ridiculous, because she'd fought for her independence from her three older brothers for how long?

What was so different about Dylan that depending on him didn't make her feel as if she was being less than in some way?

His hands came up, palms out, in the universal sign of surrender. "I want you with me. Believe me. That's the only way I can be guaranteed of your safety. Your injury is making bringing you with me that much more difficult. We might end up in a situation where we have to be able to run and get away quickly. I don't know what I'll be facing but I have to investigate those woods."

She appreciated that he didn't point out that she'd be slowing him down, even if that was the writing on the wall. He would be right. She would hold him back. The men she and Dylan were up against seemed to anticipate her movements. They had resources. And they seemed to be right there, waiting, no matter which way she and Dylan turned.

And that was definitely not good.

"I'll have Brody check in on you. He doesn't normally spend much time in his office, so he's trying not to change his behavior in front of his staff. It's best if we can fly under the radar as much as possible right now. Rebecca said she'd figure out a way to send food in. She wishes we'd stay in the house but she understands that it's too risky."

"I don't want to put anyone else in harm's way. There's already enough on the line here as it is." She didn't want to think about what those men might be doing to her father.

"They won't kill him. Not as long as you're out here and they believe you know the truth." Dylan didn't say that they wouldn't torture her father, beat him trying to get information out of him. The thought left acid churning in her stomach. Bile rose to her throat, burning her esophagus.

"Whatever he might've done or been involved in, he's not a bad person."

"I know."

She looked up at him, grateful. An emotion she couldn't quite put her finger on crossed behind his eyes.

"Speaking of which, we need to get your father's computer information to my contact. He might be able to access it remotely and quite possibly give us a name to work with." Dylan held up his phone.

"Right. Let's see what he can dig up."

Jorge, true to form, picked up on the second ring.

"I need you to take a peek into a computer for me," Dylan said into the line. "And there's someone I'd like you to talk to."

After relaying her name, Dylan passed the cell toward her.

Samantha took the offering and said, "Hello."

"Nice to meet you. Well, sort of. What do you have for me?" Jorge asked.

"I can give you file names and passwords. How you'll get into the system, I have no idea."

"Don't figure you have an IP address for me?"

"That would be a no."

"You have a website or social media page?"

"Yeah. Both."

"Give me the company name and I'll work from there." That was all he needed to access data files? That was scary, she thought as she rattled off the information.

"Cool. Tell Snap-trap to stay put. Let him know that I'll call back in a few minutes."

"Snap-trap?" She glanced at Dylan, who was shaking his lowered head.

"Oh, yeah. Crud. I'm pretty sure that'll get me in trouble. I mean that big ugly guy standing next to you."

She thanked Jorge and ended the call with an eyebrow cocked toward Dylan. "You plan on explaining that one?"

"You don't want to know what it means."

"I think I do, actually. How on earth did you pick up the name Snap-trap?"

Had his cheeks just flushed red-hot? It was about time he was embarrassed instead of her.

"I'd tell you but I took an oath never to discuss it. And he wasn't supposed to, either."

She stood so she could look him in the eyes. Thankfully, only her shoulder hurt and not her legs. "I have one word for you."

"Really?" He crossed his arms over his chest. "Do you care to impart your...wisdom?"

"I sure do."

"Today?"

"Fine. Here goes. My word for you is...*chicken*."

Chapter Ten

Chicken? Dylan had half a mind to show her what was really on his. If he did, there'd be no going back, because it involved the two of them being naked on that couch. And he couldn't go there right now, no matter how much his body battled him.

"I have a word for you, too," he said.

"I'm not so sure I want to hear this." Her tongue darted across her lips, and he thought about how good she tasted, how he liked the way they fit when their bodies were molded together.

Against his better judgment, he wrapped his arm around her waist and pulled her toward him until her body was flush with his. He was tempting his self-control with the move but there were times when he just had to say to hell with it.

"Beautiful. Sexy. Intelligent."

"That's three words," she said against his mouth.

"I never was good at following rules." He stood his ground. For the moment, logical thought ruled. If he stayed much longer, he couldn't be certain he wouldn't change his mind. And that was another reason he wanted to break off on his own. He needed to clear his thoughts. Being this close to her was doing crazy things to his normally practical head.

"You lose." With that, she delved her tongue inside his mouth. His body tensed, all his muscles locking up at the same time, and he decided not to fight it. Instead, he placed his hand on the back of her neck, curling his fingers around the base, and tilted her head.

Dylan had had wild sex in the past but nothing that compared to the heat in this kiss.

When he gathered enough willpower to pull back, he pressed his forehead to hers. "*Damn*. Keep that up and you're going to destroy me."

He'd never believed in kisses that made a person go weak at the knees until right then.

His cell buzzed.

Dylan took a sharp breath. He needed to put a little space between him and Samantha. He liked how she fit him a little too much for either his or her own good.

A glance at the screen said it was Jorge. He showed it to her and then answered.

"I got interesting information for you, bro."

"Hit me with it." Dylan held the phone so that Samantha could hear.

"The corporation that owns the property for your drop is the same one that sent considerable funds to her father's company about fifteen years ago. They've been making deposits ever since."

Samantha sank down to her knees and folded forward. Dylan guided her to the couch.

"You got any idea who's behind that company?"

"Not yet. I'm still digging, though."

"Thanks, man. I appreciate it."

"You might not be thanking me when I send you my invoice this month." Jorge laughed.

Dylan ended the call. Samantha sat there looking lost and alone, in fierce contrast to the woman who'd been in his arms moments ago. A little piece of the armor guarding his heart cracked.

"We'll get to the bottom of this."

"You know what this says, right?"

"It doesn't necessarily mean—"

"What? That my dad is blackmailing someone? I think we're both pretty clear on what's happening."

It certainly explained why he had the money to send four kids to college after cashing out their life savings to move to Mason Ridge. Dylan hadn't really thought about it before, but her father had sure pulled off a miracle. Bringing up kids was expensive. He knew that firsthand.

There weren't exactly long lines out the door of the hardware store. Purchases were small. Her dad would've had to sell a lot of nails to pull off raising four kids. Not that they were rich by any means. But sending four kids to four-year colleges was no small feat these days.

Then again, Samantha had gone on athletic scholarship.

"Did you or your brothers take out college loans?"

"Nope. None of us. Most of mine was paid for by my scholarship, but he paid for the boys."

"I know how this looks, but we don't want to convict him without hearing his side of the story."

"You're being awfully generous to a man who is most likely a criminal."

"Nope." He leaned back on his heels. "I'm covering all the bases. Your father blackmailing someone is just one angle out of a possible half dozen scenarios."

"You have other ideas?"

"Someone could have been paying him to stay quiet, threatening him. We keep circling back to Alcorn, and he has the money to silence pretty much anyone. Your dad might've decided to break the deal, and so Alcorn came after him. And when he couldn't get to him, he tried to snatch you."

"That explains a lot. You might be right and I want to believe it. Even so, that's still breaking the law."

"Maybe he didn't feel as if he had a choice. A desperate parent would go to any lengths for their children." Dylan had no doubt he'd kill for Maribel if push came to shove. Other than that, he couldn't see himself breaking the law, but then, he hadn't been in a position where he'd needed to. He didn't rule anything out.

She stared at him for a long moment. "I can see that you'd do anything for your daughter."

"Without a doubt. A parent's love is a powerful thing."

Her chest deflated and she winced at the motion, glancing toward her sore shoulder.

"I can give you something for the pain. You don't have to be a hero." He made a move toward the first-aid kit.

She nodded.

Good. Watching her suffer when he knew he could help was worse than him being the one to take a bullet. There was already so much pain he couldn't take from her. At least he could give her a pair of ibuprofen and help her shoulder. Dylan located a bottle of water and brought the pain relievers to her.

She dry swallowed them, squeezed off the plastic cap and then took a good drink.

He had to fight the urge to take her into his arms again. He'd just be playing with fire. Dylan needed space. His fingers curled and released a few times, and that was better than letting them do what they wanted. If they had their way, they'd be tunneled into her dark mane while he kissed her again.

And that would be a mistake.

"Think you can rest?" he asked.

"Probably not but it never hurts to try."

"Good. Close your eyes and by the time you open them again, I should be back." Dylan had no plans to be a liar. He pressed a kiss to her forehead.

Dylan packed his duffel with a protein bar and water and then listened at the door for a solid twenty minutes before making a move. He slipped out of the office and the barn and into the nearby woods without drawing attention to himself.

Hiking to the abandoned car took half an hour on his own. He made much better time that way. Too bad he couldn't use the small sedan. There'd be a stolen-vehicle report by now. Last thing he needed was to be picked up and detained.

Normally, he liked being on his own, but his thoughts bounced back and forth between Maribel and Samantha, and worry was a wildfire unleashed inside him, engulfing him. He told himself that this was exactly what it would be like to have a woman in his life permanently. His attention would be divided. He'd always be battling between needing to protect Maribel and be both mother and father to her and trying to spend enough time with someone new to develop a relationship.

Maribel deserved better. She was his priority, *had* to be his main concern. Always. She'd already lost so much.

Otherwise, Samantha would have been exactly the type of woman he could see himself asking out, spending some time getting to know better.

He almost laughed out loud. He'd known Samantha since fifth grade. He'd kissed her more times than he'd intended to in the past twenty-four hours, and his body already had her imprint. How much better did he need to *know* someone in order to go on a date?

Luckily, Brody's place wasn't too far from Mason

Ridge Lake. Dylan slipped through the woods rather than taking a main road. He could hike there in an hour at this pace. This time, he fully intended to surprise the bastard who'd taken his Maribel instead of being on the receiving end of the surprise again. His plan was to come from behind the lake, gain a perspective and then secure the target.

He figured the item was near the shed that Rebecca and Shane had been taken to when they'd been kidnapped, a sick reminder that this guy was still in control.

Not for long.

Dylan held on to those three words as he pushed through the underbrush, thankful he was wearing jeans. At least he had something to cover his ankles. His arms were getting torn up by the branches thanks to short sleeves.

For the past hour, he'd been able to think about only two things: Maribel and Samantha.

It would be dark in a few hours and he hated the thought that his baby would sleep away from her bed another night. Fury tore through him.

No. Maribel would sleep at home in her own room, wearing her own pajamas by the time the sun rose on a new day. He repeated the mantra over and over in his head.

He pulled his binoculars out of his pack and crouched low. Patience won fights. Fights won battles. Battles won wars.

And he had a deep freakin' well.

Dylan hadn't counted how many hours had passed since he'd taken his position. Three guys, together, came and went at different points during his stay. They were checking back regularly, trying to be stealthy but making a ton of noise to his trained ear. There was always something with civilians that made it easy to track them. He'd followed them to their vehicle once, his heart pounding by the time he reached the Ford F-150, thinking they might have brought her with them. Maribel had not been inside.

The guys left again and Dylan decided to make his move. At a minimum, he had half an hour to find the doll. None of the guys hung back, so it was now or never.

SAMANTHA HAD BEEN pacing for hours when a soft knock at the door came. Her nerves were already set to burning embers, so she jumped at the noise. No way would Dylan knock, and she didn't want to give away the fact they were staying in the barn should this be a worker looking for Brody. She scooted around the side of the desk, out of view, and searched for a weapon just in case. Samantha had no intention of being caught off guard ever again. She might startle at noises for the rest of her life but she would never be jumped again.

The door slowly opened as she gripped a fire extinguisher and crouched low. Anyone who got close was about to be clobbered.

"Samantha?" Rebecca whispered. The door closed softly.

"Right here." Samantha let out the breath she'd been holding on a small sigh and stood. She glanced at the fire extinguisher in her hand at the same time Rebecca did. "Sorry. It's been a rough few days."

"Believe me. I know." Rebecca, white-knuckling a food container, lightened her grip as she walked over to Samantha and hugged her.

"I'm so sorry for everything you've gone through." And Samantha meant every word. Guilt washed over her as she embraced her friend. If her father really had known what had happened that night all those years ago, as he claimed, then he could've helped find Shane. Losing him had destroyed the Hughes family, the town. Samantha didn't want to admit to her friend what she suspected about her father. And yet not telling Rebecca felt like a whole different kind of betrayal.

"We found him. He's alive. That's all that really matters," Rebecca said.

"But your family…"

"My parents would've split up eventually. I've come to realize that now. Probably better to have figured it out years ago so they could get on with their lives," Rebecca said thoughtfully. "I don't know if I can ever truly forgive Thomas Kramer for what he did—don't get me wrong. Losing Shane was the hardest thing I've ever been through, and I never want to go through that again. I still can't even think of having children of my own yet. But I also don't want to walk around with a chip on my shoulder."

"Makes it feel as though they've won in a weird way, doesn't it?" Samantha hated that feeling. She wanted to tell Rebecca the person truly responsible might be Charles Alcorn. She couldn't. Not yet. Not until they had evidence.

"Exactly. Nobody has time for that." Rebecca smiled.

Maybe Samantha could forgive her father. She'd done it before when he was drinking. Not that being a drunk was a good excuse or gave him a free pass, but she knew he never would've made the decision to cover up a kidnapping if he'd been sober. If that was in fact what he'd done.

He'd been part of the search team. Had all that been for show?

Chapter Eleven

Dylan stretched his sore legs to work out a cramp. He'd learned to slip through worse terrain unnoticed during his tour, and the few scrapes he'd collected on his arms weren't anything more than a small nuisance. Nothing a little antibiotic ointment couldn't fix.

The shed where Rebecca had been taken when she'd been kidnapped had long since been destroyed. Dylan stood on the same ground now. A cold chill tickled his spine.

Even in summer there were dead leaves scattered on the ground.

These activities being tied to a corporation gave him the impression this might be one helluva sophisticated child-selling operation. That was the only thing that made sense. Had more kids been taken in other counties across Texas? Across the country?

A dummy corporation with lots of money was in the game. People hid behind overseas accounts because they were committing crimes. Child slavery. Sex trade. Those were two realistic options. Shane was older. He hadn't been sold or hurt. Kramer had raised him as his own son. After he left for the military, Kramer had taken another boy, Jason, who'd been returned to his family after a year.

There was clearly a bigger story. Otherwise, everything would've died with Kramer in the car crash that had taken his life.

Mr. Turner was the only one who knew what that story was, and quite possibly the only one who could prove Charles Alcorn was involved.

There was nothing at the site, no clues.

A thought hit him. Those jerks patrolling the area might know something. And Dylan had ways of making people talk.

He retraced his steps, moving stealthily through the trees.

One of the guys was leaning against the tailgate of the pickup. Another was talking—he was nearby, but Dylan couldn't get a visual from his vantage point to the left of the Ford. He'd need to get closer.

There were three men—he already knew that—and Dylan could be certain he knew the location of two.

He had two choices. He could attack and then force one of them to talk. Three against one wasn't bad odds against civilians. He'd sized them up earlier. Two were a little smaller than him. One was similar in size. That guy might present a problem. All three together, considering each one carried a weapon, might be difficult to take down. If he could isolate them, he'd have a better chance at walking out of this alive and, better yet, with the information he was looking for.

His other choice?

He could wait it out until they left. Make himself a passenger in the bed of the truck and let them lead him to whoever was behind this. What if they made contact only via the phone?

Dylan couldn't be certain they would go to the person in charge. In fact, that would be a stupid move, when he really thought about it. The most likely scenario was that they were low in the pecking order. They wouldn't have direct contact with the boss.

Recognition dawned. These were the same guys from the pics on Mr. Turner's phone.

The third guy, the big bearded one, came into view. Unfortunately, he stepped out from behind a tree five feet away from Dylan, and the guy's eyes were locked onto his target—Dylan.

Fighting had just made top priority.

Dylan rolled back onto his shoulders and then popped to his feet. Using momentum, he brought his elbow down on Bearded's face. The crack was so loud it echoed. Bearded, blood shooting out of his nose, already had Dylan in a bear hug.

There'd be no wiggling out of the guy's viselike grip.

"Hey, guys. We have company," Bearded yelled toward the truck.

Dylan couldn't reach the gun tucked into his waistband, either. Well, hell's bells, this wasn't how he'd planned for this little exchange to go. He needed to even the score.

He reared back and then head-butted Bearded.

More blood splattered on his T-shirt. Wouldn't be salvageable once this was over. No amount of bleach could get it out.

At least his maneuver loosened Bearded's grip enough for Dylan to drop down and roll away. He came up with his Glock pointed at Bearded.

The other two jerks were already rushing over.

"Stop or I'll shoot your friend here," Dylan said.

"Hold on there, country boy. We didn't ask for trouble," one of the guys said, hands up in surrender.

"Then, you won't mind if I leave." Dylan took a step back. If he could gain a few steps of advantage, he had no doubt he could outrun these guys. Once safely in the trees, it'd be hard for them to get a clean shot. He could get away and get back to Samantha.

He took another step backward as he evaluated his options. At this distance, he could spin and dart through the trees with certainty the men wouldn't be able to catch him.

Or there was another idea worth considering…

"I'm going to put my hands up and step toward you guys," Dylan said as he did what he said—took a step toward the men.

Bearded's slack-jawed expression outlined his shock. He was right, though. No one in his right mind would give up when he had the advantage.

Dylan placed his gun on the ground, kicked it away from him and then rose to an athletic stance, feet wide with arms crossed. "So, fellas, where are we headed next?"

"I'm just glad you're all right," Rebecca said as she thrust the Tupperware toward Samantha.

Even though whatever it was smelled amazing, she didn't think she could take a bite until Dylan came back.

"Thank you for helping us." Samantha opened the container and found chicken and mushroom risotto. She grabbed the fork.

"He's pretty special. Dylan. And his daughter is the most adorable thing I've ever seen," Rebecca said, sitting next to Samantha on the couch.

She moved a piece of chicken around in her bowl.

"You can eat that later if you want. It won't hurt my feelings," Rebecca said, smiling. "There's a small fridge behind the desk. I totally understand if you want to wait for Dylan."

"It looks amazing. I don't know what's wrong with me," Samantha said.

"You're worried. Like I said, Dylan is a remarkable person." Rebecca smiled and something lit up behind her eyes.

Samantha chose to ignore the comment. Her friend was absolutely right. But Dylan had no intention of allowing anyone else into his life, and she understood that on some level. Her father had closed up to relationships after her mother had died. Once he'd sobered up, he'd thrown all his energy into being a good dad. If he couldn't be at one of her volleyball games, he'd made sure one of her brothers could. He'd never raised his voice or given her pointers while he was watching from the stands. All he'd ever given was a few words of encouragement, lots of smiles and support.

Had he done all that because of a guilty conscience? Tried to make up for his greatest sin by being the perfect father to her? If so, that would make him almost as bad as the criminals who'd committed the crime all those years ago.

No. He's a good man.

There had to have been extenuating circumstances for him to hide the truth about what happened that night. He was a father and knew what it was like to lose someone, and he wouldn't want to put another family through the sorrow his family had endured in losing Samantha's mother.

She wanted her father home more than anything. And not just to figure out what the heck was going on, although she wanted to know that, too. He was getting older, and he'd seemed frail to her lately. She feared his heart wouldn't be able to take whatever these guys did to him.

Maybe his memories haunted him? And that was why he wanted to come clean now?

"How is Shane?" Samantha asked.

"Good. He's overseas, so we haven't had a chance to speak to him that much. He's so grown now." Rebecca had a wistful look in her eyes.

"Do you talk about what happened?"

"Not really. His calls are limited while he's deployed. We're just happy to know he's healthy. We've promised to catch up when he has a little time to spend with us."

"And your mom? How's she doing?"

"Better, actually. She finally agreed to take the medicine the doctor's been trying to get her to take for months and it seems to be helping. She's still weak but improving. I know she won't be around forever, but it feels good to be able to give her son back to her before she…" Rebecca focused her gaze on her shoelaces and twisted her hands.

"I'm so grateful that everything worked out." Samantha hated lying to her friend, especially since Rebecca had been through so much already. And to think her dad had been somehow involved…

"We've spent so much time in the past." Rebecca stretched her legs out in front of her. "Time to switch gears, you know? Besides, what can be gained by going back now? We have the rest of our lives to get reacquainted and it feels good to have my family back. Brody and I are starting to plan the wedding, and you have to be there."

"I can't wait." Samantha managed a smile. It faded almost immediately. "Dylan should have returned already. I have a bad feeling about this."

Rebecca put her arm around Samantha's shoulder, careful not to touch the gauze. "He's strong and he knows what's at stake. He'll walk through that door any minute."

"I hope you're right." She closed the Tupperware lid.

"You don't have to talk about it if you don't want to, but are you okay?" Rebecca asked.

How did Samantha answer that truthfully?

"When this ordeal is over, I will be." She didn't add *if I'm still alive*. Then there was her father to think about…

Or the fact that she'd never be able to forgive herself if anything happened to Maribel or Dylan.

"Can I ask a question?" Samantha needed to know more about Dylan.

"Anything."

"How did Maribel's mother fit into the picture?"

"She kept her pregnancy a secret, which tells me she didn't really know Dylan very well."

"For as much as he used to talk about never having kids, he would never walk away from his child," Samantha agreed. "How did he find out about her sickness?"

"Dylan hasn't said much to me. I don't think he talks about it to anyone, not even Brody, and you know how close the guys are."

Samantha nodded.

"Brody and Dylan lost touch during Dylan's tour. One day, Brody gets this call out of the blue asking him to come to New Mexico. He took off that day not knowing what he was going to find, only that it wasn't good based on the sound of Dylan's voice.

"Dylan was holed up in a motel room, a mess. Brody asked what was wrong but Dylan was too inside himself to speak. He just held up a bottle of tequila, so Brody took it and drank with him. The next morning, Dylan was up by dawn. Brody was hungover and fuzzy but he hopped out of bed, showered. Next thing he knew, he dressed, followed Dylan to the car and then the two of them rode in silence to a funeral."

It wasn't the same thing, but she remembered the silent car ride to her own mother's funeral. Everyone had been too overwrought with emotion, too spent, to speak. Samantha hurt from the inside out for Dylan.

"When my mother passed away, it was tough. I can't imagine losing a spouse."

"If anything happened to Brody, I'd be lost," Rebecca said wistfully. "We could never be sure if Dylan and Lyndsey were married. In fact, I don't think they were. He never talks about it, though."

"Brody never mentioned anything about going to a wedding?" Samantha asked.

"No. You know Dylan, though. He's always been private. He doesn't let anyone in."

"True." Samantha could attest to that. She'd been close a few times, but each time it was as if a door had been slammed in her face. When she really thought about it, he'd always been like that. He was the first person to jump in if a friend was in need but she couldn't remember a time when he'd asked for help. And he could be trusted with secrets. "Remember that time when we all decided it would be a good idea to go swimming in the lake after school?"

"What was that? Fifth grade?" Rebecca asked thoughtfully.

"Yeah, it was. I'd just moved here and someone, I can't even remember who now, thought it would be a good idea to welcome me by taking me to the lake."

"Which was strictly forbidden without an adult present, but what did we know?"

"We came running back, laughing, soaking wet, the whole lot of us, and Ryan's dad stopped us in the street."

"He had such a bad home life. We knew it wasn't good

to see his father." Rebecca's eyes grew wide as if they were reliving the episode.

"His dad was so angry we all froze. Not Dylan. He stepped up and said we were walking home cutting across the McGills' yard when the sprinklers came on."

"I do remember that. We all smelled like lake water, so Dylan stayed in between Ryan and his father." Rebecca smiled. "He most likely saved Ryan from another beating."

"Then he hosed us all down to get the lake-water smell out of our clothes. He thought of just about everything." She didn't say why he'd learned to be so diligent. His grandmother had been kind enough to take him in, but she had been a spare-the-rod-spoil-the-child type. And that was probably half the reason her daughter, Dylan's mother, had taken off and not returned. Growing up in a house with an iron fist tended to create rebellion.

"This group has been through a lot together," Rebecca said. "You guys were a lifesaver for me, which is why I'd like to be there for you. Are you sure you don't want to talk about whatever's going on? I know you, and there's something you're not telling me. There's nothing you could've done that can't be fixed."

Didn't that make shards of guilt pelt Samantha's skin like a needle shower? What if her father could've saved Rebecca all that heartache but didn't? Everything inside Samantha wanted to come clean with her friend and tell her everything. The right words didn't come, so she said, "No one's perfect, including me, but I didn't do anything illegal. My situation is…complicated. It involves more than me and I hope you can understand that I need to protect the other person right now even if that means keeping secrets from my friends."

"Just know that we're here for you, no matter what."

Rebecca nodded her understanding, but her eyebrow lifted so slightly that Samantha thought she might've imagined it.

She'd told the truth. Even though she felt like the biggest liar, she had to protect her father. He owed them an explanation. A piece of her couldn't think that he'd knowingly done anything illegal.

Samantha hated secrets.

If her father hadn't kept his, none of this would have been happening right now.

Oh, Daddy, what have you gotten us into?

"I better get back to the house," Rebecca said, looking Samantha in the eye. "You gonna be okay?"

"Yeah. Thank you for dinner. And everything else." Samantha hugged her friend.

For now, all that mattered was bringing her father home alive. Dylan and his daughter, too, for that matter. Samantha glanced at the clock. It was nine thirty. He'd been gone four hours and twenty-seven minutes.

Where was he?

"No problem. If you need anything, use the phone in here to call the house. It's just me and Brody, so one of us will answer." Rebecca rose and started toward the door. She stopped short. "And be careful."

"Of course I will."

"Not just with what's going on. I'm talking about with Dylan."

Had Rebecca picked up on the fact that Samantha had feelings for Dylan? Had she been *that* transparent?

"Don't worry. We're good. It's nice to have a friend who has your back," she managed to get out, hoping the emphasis on friendship would throw Rebecca off the trail. Samantha wasn't sure why she wanted to keep her feelings for Dylan private, but she knew that telling everyone wouldn't change the fact that a relationship between them wasn't going to happen.

Samantha sat quietly for a long while after the door closed. She tried to get food down, remembering what Dylan had said about how important it was to keep nourished. It was no use. She couldn't manage more than a couple of bites.

She'd been pacing for a solid hour when she decided to venture outside, knowing full well she'd face his wrath if he caught her.

It didn't matter. The thought of him lying in a ditch somewhere, bleeding out, spurred her to make the decision. She'd deal with the consequences of her actions when she had to.

Chapter Twelve

Dylan was sure he'd been hit by a semi. That was the only logical explanation for the degree to which his head pounded, other than Bearded, of course, who'd gone to town with the butt of his gun on Dylan's face. *That's gonna leave a mark.*

He had to be amused. He'd had no plans to fight back. All he'd done was protect his head and vital organs as best he could.

The toe of Bearded's boot could have done a lot of damage to Dylan's spleen or any number of other essential organs. And after Dylan had split the guy's nose, revenge was fresh on Bearded's mind.

Dylan wanted the guys to take him with them, hazarding it was his best chance to get answers or get closer to Maribel. He'd made a promise to himself that she'd sleep in her own bed before first light, and he had every intention of following through on that commitment. He didn't care how determined these guys seemed to be that this would go down another way.

There'd most likely be more beatings tonight. They'd want to try to scare him to find out if he knew where Samantha was hiding. And he'd act the part.

And then when he was ready to walk out the front

door with his Maribel, he had every intention of doing just that, too.

Timing and discipline were two of Dylan's best virtues.

For now, he needed information, so he'd let the bad guys think they'd won. He'd played the role of the broken victim, needing to know more. His fear was that this operation was bigger than anyone had imagined. Texas was the perfect place to move "product." And that meant innocent kids. His hands involuntarily fisted and he realized his nails were digging into his flesh. Not good to let them get at him emotionally.

Dylan needed to remain calm and cool, ready to play his part when they came back to teach him another "lesson." And they would come back. But first he needed to survey his surroundings. They most likely wouldn't take him straight to the boss, whom he fully expected to be Charles Alcorn.

That would be a stupid move.

However, they might take him to a warehouse on the outskirts of town. He blinked his eyes open, squinting through the burn. He tried to move his arms, but they were bound behind his back at the wrists. Had they subdued him enough to throw him into something… A locked room? Maybe an office?

This was not the time to be thinking about the feel of Samantha's body against his, her silky skin or the lilac smell of her hair. He especially shouldn't be thinking about those intelligent dark eyes staring into his. Or the sexy way her lips parted for his.

Distractions had no business on a mission.

Footsteps echoed from down the hall.

Dylan wiggled around on his side. He blinked to try to get his eyes adjusted to the darkness.

His legs were loosely bound and he was on top of some kind of wooden table. He rolled onto his back, ignoring the piercing pain screaming between his shoulder blades, and looked up. A single bulb hung from a socket. There were plastic-looking panels on the ceiling. When it was light outside, sun would stream through the half wall of windows. How many hours had he been knocked out?

There was one thing this place would be good for. *Torture.*

Dylan thought about all the scenarios that could possibly go down. He visualized his movements in each, prepping for the very real possibility he'd be fighting all three men or more.

He wanted time to investigate the building, figure out if this was a holding cell for their product. He hadn't heard a noise in the few minutes he'd been conscious, and that led him to believe he might be the only one there.

As he tried to finagle his arms free, something stirred down the hall. He stopped and listened carefully.

The sound moving toward him was boot on concrete. It would be Bearded or one of the other guys. Maybe all three.

Dylan's senses were dulled by the ache splitting his head into two pieces. Damn. If only he had time, he'd be more than happy to return the favor to Bearded. A few punches in the gut should do the trick. It wasn't as though the guys were in shape. Dylan was almost embarrassed about letting the guys get the drop on him. Their skills weren't exactly what he was used to coming up against in the military. But then, that had played to his advantage, so he'd swallowed his pride and let them think they had him.

Getting Maribel back was the goal.

That was the only thing that mattered.

He imagined gently placing his sleepy girl into her bed, tucking her under the covers and retreating to the corner to watch her sleep. When he got her back, he had no plans to let her out of his sight again.

The metal door creaked and groaned as it opened. No doubt whoever was there intended to torture Dylan. He could only wonder what they would use. Waterboarding? Nah. That was probably too sophisticated for these small-time criminals.

The ceiling was high, but they could still manage to throw a rope around the exposed beam and tie him up, beat him with a pipe or other metal object, use pliers to pull his fingernails or use wire cutters on him. They could shoot his feet so he couldn't try to run, blindfold him and perform the ever-popular mock execution. That generally got the blood pumping.

Either way, they wouldn't be able to get him to tell them where Samantha was hiding.

"Sit up." The deep-boom voice belonged to Bearded.

"I'm a little tied up at the moment." Dylan quirked a smile as he raised his head.

His smart-alecky retort was rewarded with a punch to his face. His head popped back but he kept on smirking.

"That all you got?" Dylan turned his head to the side and spit blood. All he needed to do was keep them off balance just a little. Have them thinking about how much they hated him rather than wondering why he'd give up so easily in the first place. He moved his jaw from side to side, his hands still bound behind his back as he tried to work the bindings. He wasn't getting anywhere on freeing himself. Rolling to the side earlier, he'd realized that they'd taken his cell. That was a bugger.

Bearded reared his balled fist back to take another

swing, but one of the other guys grabbed him at the elbow.

"Save it for later. He's just being a jerk. We've been told what to do with him."

That sounded ominous.

The other guy who had been silently standing near Bearded had moved behind Dylan.

What the heck was he up to?

Dylan coiled into a tight ball to protect his organs. There wasn't much he could do about his head being exposed. But he could salvage other important things. He hadn't been able to work the binding—what he figured was duct tape—around his wrists enough to free himself. With his knees at his chin, he could buck and take out at least one of them, maybe two.

As he waited for the right moment to strike, he was suddenly hauled up to a sitting position from behind. Something was shoved over his head, plunging him into complete blackness again. A canvas bag? The next thing he knew, there was pressure against his larynx. He could feel anxiety tightening inside his chest. *Count backward from ten...nine...eight...seven...* The object pressed harder against his throat... *Six...five...four...* A few more seconds and he'd be fine... *Three...two... one.* There—his pulse returned to normal. The military had taught Dylan to adjust his body's response to stress. He took in a deep breath. The pressure around his neck eased. Whatever they'd used was too soft and too thick to be a cord. He was most likely dealing with a rope of some sort. And that was about the best news he'd gotten so far. He continued working his hands against the tape, trying to break free.

Still no luck there.

The next thing he knew, he was being pushed off the

table and onto his feet. His knees buckled. Hands on his elbows righted him and kept him upright. With a bag over his head and his arms bound behind his back, he immediately thought that he was being prepared for execution. Nothing Dylan hadn't been exposed to before. Dylan walked through the scenario in his mind to prep himself for it. They'd most likely take him out to the field and then force him onto his knees. There'd be bright lights in his face once the bag came off again, loud cursing and threats.

His adrenaline spiked thinking about it. Good. He'd rather have that happen now while he was being forced to walk than once the bag was off. They'd probably get in a few more jabs, especially if Bearded had anything to say about it.

He pictured himself being calm, watching for an opportunity to fight back. If any one of them got too close with a gun, Dylan could disarm the guy in two seconds flat. If there were still only three of them, the odds were decent that he'd be able to take them down.

Without the free use of his arms and hands, that would be tricky but not impossible. He tried to move his hands again. Nothing. His wrists were wrapped up too tightly.

Most likely, this was all a big bluff. Dylan had to consider every possibility. He had to prepare for the scenario that they were actually going to execute him, as well. He thought about why they'd shoot, and his muscles coiled as anger burned through him. They would have to have Samantha. That would be the only reason they no longer needed him. Plus, since he'd seen their faces, they'd have no choice but to do away with him. He'd committed all three to memory. Bearded was the tallest and scruffiest. The other two looked as though they could be brothers. There was only an inch of height difference between them. Both had bright red hair and blue eyes. Bright Guy One had tattoo arm sleeves and his theme seemed musical. There were staffs filled with notes running up his right forearm. On his left were instruments linked together. The other Bright Guy had a snake eating a bird while wrapped around a tree.

Dylan could identify all three men and testify against each one. If a smart prosecutor did enough digging, it couldn't be that difficult to tie them to their boss.

So, basically, whatever was about to happen wasn't looking good for Dylan. He needed to think his way out of this situation. Based on the grip they had on his arms and the fact that no one had said anything yet, he didn't figure these guys would be much on conversation.

With one on either side of him, flanking him, he guessed the third was walking behind and had his gun pointed at Dylan's head. If that man happened to be Bearded, then he wouldn't need much encouragement to pull the trigger.

But they'd said they had orders. *Great.*

He'd given up on the chance that he'd be taken to the guy in charge.

A door opened and then shut behind them.

The ground underneath his shoes was forgiving, which told him that he was no longer walking on concrete. So they'd taken him outside and not into another room. Okay, this was bad, but Dylan had been in precarious situations before and managed to get out alive.

"On your knees," one of the guys shouted. "Where is she?"

Yeah, this was about to be a picnic for four.

Dylan shrugged.

"Boss just wants to have a conversation with her."

"He ever hear of a cell phone?" Dylan shot back.

Any second now they'd be jerking off his head covering and then he'd be blinking his eyes to adjust to the bright light. Guns would be pointed at him, so he needed to ready himself for that.

Since they hadn't shot him already, he held on to the hope that Samantha was still at the barn and didn't answer.

He didn't want to think about how much he missed her. Or the fact that he couldn't get her out of his thoughts. Maribel was already his kryptonite, so he didn't want to have to worry about another human being. Bel was enough to think about.

Dylan tensed and relaxed, trying to get his muscles to stop from knotting up on him. His arms were already cramping. Even if he could get the bindings off, he doubted it would do any good. Then again, adrenaline did funny things to the body. And just thinking about Samantha's and Maribel's safety had his pumping.

"You think you're funny?" The toe of a boot nailed Dylan in the ribs.

"I'm a freakin' comedian."

"I bet she's gone. He doesn't know anything," one of the men said.

Ready for the bag to be pulled off, he tensed when hands gripped his biceps and he was hauled up and then tossed onto hard metal. A latch clicked, like a gate.

The sound of doors opening and then closing came next. Car? Truck?

He couldn't be sure until the engine roared to life. Then he was certain that he was in the back of a Bright Guy's truck.

Excitement trilled through Dylan's body. There were

two scenarios possible here. Either he was being taken out of town for a body drop or he was going to meet the guy in charge. He kept working the bindings against his wrists, trying to get a little wiggle room.

Nothing was happening there.

Dang. Whatever material they'd used was unyielding. It was wide, covering at least three inches of his wrists. It was sticky, so his earlier assumption that it was duct tape was probably spot-on.

So far, the roads were bumpy. The truck had kicked up dust, so the warehouse he'd been taken to had to be on the outskirts of town.

Dylan made mental notes about everything he remembered. Didn't help that his head was still splitting from one helluva headache. Everything might be riding on what he thought, heard or felt.

So he shoved his pain to the back burner and listened. They were traveling fast down the rutty road. Air cooled his skin. Even though it was the hot part of summer— eighty degrees when he went to bed, eighty degrees when he woke the next morning—the draft was nice.

He counted in order to track how long they'd been driving.

By the time they stopped, they'd been on the road at least thirty-five minutes. The roads had smoothed and then gotten bumpy again.

They could've been anywhere. He hadn't heard anything to distinguish the area they were taking him to. No noises typical of a city at night either, so they must've stuck with the country.

His shoulder hurt from being bounced around. It battled with his head for the body-part-in-the-most-pain award.

The gate opened and he was suddenly being dragged out by his ankles. *Damn.*

A set of hands gripped his body, pulling him by his shirt, but he bounced on the hard dirt anyway.

Someone stepped over him.

"Boss says you have twenty-four hours to find and bring the lady to the drop spot and then he'll give your daughter back. Time's ticking."

"He hurts my child and it'll be the last thing he does," Dylan ground out.

"There are other ways to take care of your daughter without putting a hand on her."

The noose loosened around Dylan's neck and the canvas bag was jerked off. Dylan blinked, trying to gain his bearings as he lay on his side in the dirt. Not exactly the best vantage point. The pickup truck was behind him. It'd be all too easy for one of the guys to put the gearshift in Reverse and back right over him.

A cell phone was shoved in his face.

There was a picture of Maribel standing in the corner, arms folded, with a copy of the day's newspaper. Her stubborn streak could get her in trouble with these bastards. Rage boiled through Dylan. He reminded himself to stay calm. She was healthy, alive and it didn't look as if anyone had laid a hand on her. As long as they kept it that way, they were cool. None of those men wanted to see the hell Dylan would bring forth if anything happened to Maribel.

"You want her back in one piece. Do as the boss says," Bearded said.

Dylan surveyed the guys. Two were to his right. Bearded was to the left. He was the only one looking away. The big man didn't seem to like the idea of a little girl getting hurt. Did he have kids of his own?

"Let me tell you something and, please, do me a favor and take this back to whoever's in charge. If anything happens to my daughter, if she so much as snags a fingernail while in your boss's care, then every last one of you had better sleep with your eyes open for the rest of your lives, because there is no length to which I will not go to personally destroy you and everything you love. And if anything happens to me, I have half a dozen friends who will see the job through on my behalf. That you can count on," Dylan ground out.

Something flashed behind Bearded's eyes. Since it didn't faze him to beat the heck out of Dylan, the man had to have a family.

The other two didn't flinch.

"Forgive me if I'm not scared," one said, making his body tremble in order to mock Dylan. "You're not exactly in a position to dish out threats."

"My name is Dylan Jacobs. Remember it. Because if this goes down wrong, I'm the man who will put you in your grave."

One of the men reared his foot, ready to kick, but Bearded stepped in between the guy and Dylan, putting his hand against the guy's chest. "Let's go. Like you said before, this dude is all talk. He's not worth it. We did what we were supposed to. Now let's grab some food."

"Whatever." The guy blew out a sharp breath, turned and moved to the passenger side of the truck. The other one took the driver's side.

"Where are you keeping the old man?" Dylan shouted toward them. He couldn't go back without news about Samantha's father.

Bearded turned his back to Dylan and started toward the truck. The big guy paused, and then a small shiny metal object landed near Dylan's head.

Out of the side of his mouth, Bearded said, "The old guy is with your daughter."

Dylan was already scooting toward the ditch. He managed to palm the object as he rolled out of the way. Giving those guys an easy target wasn't in the plan today. Besides, the driver would've been all too happy to put some tire treads on Dylan's chest.

Feeling the oblong object with grooves down the side, Dylan realized he'd been given a pocketknife.

He had no idea why Bearded was being so generous. The other two seemed intent on making things as difficult as possible. As it was, Dylan was stranded on the side of the road with no idea where he was or how to get back to Samantha. He had no phone and no way to get word to Samantha that he was safe. She had to be worried sick by now, and his biggest fear was that she'd go out looking for him. Based on the position of the moon and the time of the year, he figured it was before midnight. He opened the knife and cut his hands free. Then he sat up, rubbing his sore wrists to get the blood going again.

If it was close to midnight, he'd been knocked out in that warehouse for a couple of hours.

There were two things saving his sanity right now. Maribel's picture, for one. She might not be happy, but she was fine. They seemed to be taking good care of her. *They'd better be.*

And he knew Samantha was safe as long as she stayed put. They still wanted her and they were willing to do pretty much anything to get her, including set him free.

Dylan hoped like the dickens that she'd stayed inside the barn, where she was safe. It would be just like Samantha to take off looking for him, and he'd been gone too long already.

SAMANTHA WOKE TO the sound of the door opening. She bolted upright. "Dylan?"

It was late and she'd almost gone looking for him. A foreboding feeling had returned her to the office. No way did she want to jeopardize the innocent lives tangled in this web.

"I'm here." His voice was gruff.

All she could see was his silhouette with the light streaming in from behind him. He was limping.

She pushed off the sofa and was at his side in a second. "You're hurt. What happened to you?"

"Get me to the couch." He put a little of his weight on her for the rest of the walk. There was so much blood on his shirt.

In the soft light, she could see bruises on his face. There was a cut over his right eye.

"What did they do to you?" She pushed back the tears threatening, grabbed the first-aid kit and bent down in front of him. She immediately went to work on his injuries.

First she cleaned the cut with fresh water and a wipe. He flinched at her touch.

"I ran into a few of his guys." He sat with his elbows on his knees, looking down.

"What did they put you through?" She blotted antibiotic ointment on the cut, fighting the panic that he was truly hurt.

He pulled back and caught her wrist in his hand. It was then that she saw how red his were.

"I let them take me, thinking I'd end up wherever Maribel was." He loosened his grip on her wrist and pulled it to his lips, placing a kiss on the soft skin. "Sorry. Keep going."

Then he released her hand altogether.

She ignored the sensations pinging through her body and instead focused on the degree of his injuries. He was back, safe. She could only imagine what had happened to him.

"Does this hurt?" She gently blotted his cut again.

He sucked in a burst of air but shook his head.

"You're a terrible liar," she said, placing gauze over the wound, then taping it to hold it in place. She wiped his face with a clean cloth, being extracareful on the spots where bruises were beginning to form.

His hands closed on the sides of her waist, and he bent forward until his head rested on her stomach.

"They're going to hurt her if I don't figure out a way to find them in the next twenty-four hours."

"What did they say, exactly?" She ran her hands through his dark hair.

He lifted his gaze to hers. "First of all, she's with your dad."

Relief washed through her. "They're both safe?"

"As far as I know." He caught her eye and she knew he was being completely honest. Besides, it wasn't like Dylan to sugarcoat things. She could trust what he said. "They want a trade."

"That could work. Same meet-up location?"

"No way. I'm not having it. They kill you and she's dead. So is your father."

"And what will they do if I don't show?"

"You don't come and they'll kill one of them, or both, which might just be a threat. We can't be sure they'll follow through."

"You really want to take that chance?"

"No. Of course not. But we're not exactly dealing in ideal circumstances right now." He bowed his head for a second. "The other choice is that we get evidence against

Charles Alcorn and force his hand. We have to bring the fight to his doorstep."

"It sounds too risky. What if it's not Alcorn? Then we have nothing."

He slanted a look at her.

"Did they give you any way to contact them?" she asked.

He shook his head.

"Would you tell me if they had?" she asked, guessing she already knew the answer to that question.

He just stared at her, didn't speak, didn't make a move to speak.

"I thought as much."

"They didn't, though. I'm being honest about that, which reminds me—I have to call Jorge."

She watched as Dylan moved to the desk and called his friend, explaining that they'd gotten his cell phone and he'd had to pick up a pay-as-you-go phone from the convenience store. She couldn't hear what was being said on the other end of the line, but Dylan nodded his head and thanked his contact before returning to his spot on the couch.

"Dylan, listen to me. I would do anything to get your little girl back. If they want me, let them take me. I'll go alone. I'll tell them that I told you everything and that you're going to the police if I don't walk out of there with your daughter."

He didn't immediately respond. Instead, he seemed to carefully consider it. "No."

"Not so fast. This could work."

"I won't trade one life for another." There was so much torment in his gaze that it momentarily robbed her breath. "Besides, we don't know if it will work. I've thought through every scenario, and every single one carries too much risk. I won't allow anything to happen to you."

He might not be able to choose between her and his daughter, but she certainly could. Nothing was worth that little girl's life. Samantha would figure out a way to make the trade on her own if she had to.

"I know where they'll be in twenty-four hours. That's more than we've managed to figure out so far."

"How do you know Maribel is okay?" She didn't want to ask but she had to be sure.

"They gave proof of life."

When she responded by lifting her eyebrow, he added, "Her picture with today's paper."

"Why would someone know to do that?"

"This isn't their first rodeo. They also had access to an out-of-town warehouse and I'm guessing they move 'product' through there." The way he emphasized the word made her think he couldn't say what they really moved—children.

More children.

"Did they say anything about my father's health?"

"No."

"What about a picture of him?"

Dylan took in a sharp breath. "We're going to get them both home safely. We'll figure this out. You have my word."

She wanted more from him than that and he seemed to sense it. He pulled her closer until her body was pressed against his and she could feel warmth radiating from him. She leaned into it, into him, and let him guide her mouth to his.

There were about a thousand reasons why she shouldn't allow this to happen, not the least of which was that her feelings seemed to run deeper than his. It had been all too easy for him to push her away every time they got close. Even though logic said the pull between them was strong enough for him to keep coming back, it also said that past behavior was the best predictor of the future. Or, as she liked to think of it, when someone showed her who they truly were underneath it all, she believed them.

Was there a strong attraction between her and Dylan? Sure. They both had to feel that same electric jolt every time they were near each other or their skin touched. Did she want him to kiss her? Yes.

She parted her lips to give him better access, because all she wanted in this moment was to feel the comfort of his arms around her, as they were, and the safety she felt with him this close. No one had ever had her back like Dylan. It was a feeling she could get used to, *wanted* to learn to depend on.

And even though everything inside her said he wanted more than friendship, she'd be stupid to let this attraction get out of hand. Precisely what was happening.

She pulled back and then stood.

"I think we should figure out our next move."

"Right." A hurt look crossed his intense green eyes, and she couldn't say that she blamed him for feeling that way.

But she'd already touched that stove how many times? And it was always the same result. They got close and he pulled back. At least Dylan was more honest than Jude from college. He'd betrayed her in the worst way, taking what he wanted from her and then making sure he was getting it everywhere else he wanted, too. All the while, she'd happily played into his sob story about how hard it was to be a student and a single father.

Dylan never complained about parenthood, or anything else, for that matter, but that still didn't change the fact that he would never seriously entertain his feelings for her. He was one of the good guys—she knew that.

And that would make walking away from him hurt like hell.

Chapter Thirteen

"Rebecca brought food earlier," Samantha said as she sauntered across the room toward the minifridge. Nervous energy had her needing to move around.

Dylan sat there for a long moment, thinking about what had just happened. The pull he felt toward Samantha was incredibly strong. He chalked it up to their history, their friendship and the craziness going on around them that only the two of them could understand. But was it something else? Something deeper than circumstances?

And maybe a better question was…could it be more?

Another time, another place, and they might have had a shot. His existence was a wonderful chaos by the name of Maribel. With that little girl in his life, he didn't have time for anyone else. Period.

As long as he was playing "what if"—*if* the circumstances had been different, then Samantha would be exactly the kind of woman he'd be interested in pursuing a relationship with.

This back-and-forth without going anywhere needed to go, and she was clearly just as tired of it. Good thing one of them had the presence of mind to keep them honest.

Samantha stood in front of him not two feet away, staring with a bowl in her hand. "Hungry?"

"Nah. I'll grab a power bar. You go ahead and eat."

"What were you thinking about just now?" She eased onto the couch next to him.

"How crazy life can be."

"One minute you think you know where you're going, what you're doing, and then wham! A curveball," she agreed. She took a bite and chewed.

"I'm proud of you, Samantha. You've been through hell and back but you're still standing. That takes guts," he said. "No matter what happens, I hope you know you can always count me as a friend."

"And what about you? It couldn't have been easy to wake up a father one day. I've seen you with your daughter. You're a great dad."

"Thank you," he said and meant it. "I had no idea that parenting was mostly about second-guessing yourself all the time."

"I can only imagine," she said. "Think about all the stuff we used to do to our parents and your grandmother when we were kids."

"Yeah, she might've been too strict, and that presented a whole different set of problems, but I'm pretty much thinking she was a saint for taking me in when she did. She was still working her way toward retirement when I showed up. I'm sure she hadn't planned on that financially." Had the strain been too much for her? Was that why she'd pulled back on the leash harder? The two of them had clashed like soap and vinegar.

"I had four fathers after my mother died."

"Must not have been easy being the baby."

"You remember that I had to sneak out to do anything. I was way too overprotected, and that wasn't good, either.

I didn't get a chance to make my own mistakes, because there was always somebody there to guide me in a different direction before things went haywire." She paused. "Either extreme isn't good for a kid."

"I try to walk the middle ground with Maribel."

She shot him a look.

"What?"

"I've seen you. You're not middle ground, Dylan."

"Okay, fine. You got me there." He held up his hands in surrender. "More than anything, I just want her to know how much I love her and want her. Everything else seems so much less important." Dylan paused, his emotions getting the best of him. Truth be known, all he really wanted was her to be there with him.

"We're going to get her back. They won't hurt her as long as I'm out here, just like you said. I won't let them get to me." She leaned into him, shoulder to shoulder, and those thousand little fires lit inside him again.

"That's why I've been thinking we have to find them first."

"Okay, what do we have to go on? Anything that we haven't already thought of?" She set the bowl on the side table next to her.

"I've been racking my brain. All I keep thinking about is Maribel's face in that picture. She looked confused but brave. I can't let her sleep another night away from home, Samantha."

"What else was there in the background? Where was it taken?"

"Good questions. She was standing in the corner of a room. I have no idea where but it didn't look like a house. It wasn't a warehouse, either. The lights were bright and there was a wooden rocking horse to her left."

Samantha's jaw went slack. "What did the horse look like?"

"It was black with white spots and a white saddle. Looked as though they'd pushed it over toward her to get her to—"

"Hold on a second. That's my horse. We have to go to the store."

Dylan was already on his feet. "Maybe I should go alone."

"Not a chance. You need me with you, and I have a key. Just get me to my dad's house so I can get it."

"I doubt this is a trap. However, we need to be careful." Taking Samantha anywhere out in the open was a huge risk. All anyone needed was a clear shot and it would be over. They already had two of the three puzzle pieces in check. They didn't see Dylan as a threat, which was why they'd let him go. Then again, they didn't know him.

Dylan called Brody to get permission to borrow his truck.

"Brody said there's an extra set of keys in the top desk drawer," Dylan said to Samantha.

She retrieved them and followed Dylan to the door.

They listened as they leaned against the door, quietly, so that the only sound that could be heard was their breathing and the occasional neigh, snort or whinny of a horse or shuffle of hooves.

After turning off the tiny light in the office, Dylan took Samantha's hand and led her outside. Keeping their backs against the barn, they moved in perfect unison to the truck.

Once they got on the road, with any luck, people would confuse them for Brody and Rebecca.

Dylan moved into the driver's seat, put the key in the

ignition and started the truck. A few minutes later, they were on the road headed toward town.

The Turner house was a few blocks from the hardware store. Dylan had never been inside Samantha's childhood home. Her brothers never would have allowed it.

"What was it like growing up with all those men in your life?"

"I couldn't get away with much."

"Is that a good or bad thing?" Sounded pretty darn good to him about now.

"Both. I rebelled from being smothered, so you don't want to go that route. That's why I sneaked out, and looking back, I realize that was such a stupid thing for any of us to do."

"Getting out, being with you guys, kept me sane. Or at least somewhat," Dylan said, half smiling.

"Don't get me wrong—I loved it. Spending time with you guys made me happier than I'd ever been. If everything hadn't backfired, it would've been a great thing. But we left ourselves vulnerable because no one knew what we were doing."

"Except people playing the game," he said.

"Why does everything have to circle back to that horrible summer?" she asked, her tone heavy.

"I wish it didn't."

She just sat there and stared out the window for a long time. "To answer your question, I think you're a terrific dad. You don't have to worry. Maribel will be loved, and that's the best you can really do for a kid."

"I failed her mother and I'm scared I'll do the same with her."

"YOU BELIEVE THAT, don't you?" Samantha looked at Dylan, at the anguish on his features, and her heart did a free fall. From what she'd been told, none of this had been his fault. Did he always carry the weight of the world on his shoulders? Was that why he'd been so tough all those years ago? He'd had to be? She'd been the complete opposite. Everything had been done for her, handled for her. Trevor had walked her to school and Brent had picked her up.

Looking at Dylan now, she could see how absolutely alone he must feel in bringing up his daughter by himself.

"I should've known that Lyndsey needed me. I was a selfish bastard. All I could think about was how great it was to see her when I was on leave. I had no idea what she was going through on the inside. She must've felt rejected and abandoned by me to do what she did. Then to suffer her sickness alone with a toddler..." His voice trailed off. "The news about her leaving town was like lightning striking on a clear blue day. I had no warning, and it feels as though if we were really that close, shouldn't I have realized something was up?"

"No one can know how someone else is feeling unless that person is willing to share. You're not a mind reader, Dylan." A little piece of her heart opened up at the thought that he was confiding in her. Dylan didn't talk to anyone about what he was feeling.

"You're mad at me. I keep frustrating you. I know that because I can read you, Samantha. With her, I had nothing to work with."

"We've known each other forever, Dylan. I'm not someone you met six months ago. We have a long history together. But let me ask you this. How did you really know I was angry?"

"Your lips thin just a little when you're mad. Not much. And you frown when no one's talking. You get quiet and go inside your head. You're a thinker and you've always been that way," he said.

Samantha wasn't sure if she liked how well he seemed able to read her.

"Okay. My turn. You're confused. You have feelings for me but you'd never let them surface. You put everything else above those feelings because they scare the hell out of you."

Dylan grunted. "I don't do afraid."

"If that's true, then you're just a jerk, and I know better than that."

He sat silent for what felt like an eternity as they slipped into town, heading toward Main Street.

"You asked about my nickname before. I'm not proud of it. That's why I didn't want to tell you."

"Aren't nicknames supposed to be embarrassing?"

"Yeah, well, this one has to do with some of the more immature activities we participated in while on leave."

"And?"

"Mine has to do with how fast a woman's bra tended to unsnap when she was alone with me."

"Oh." Snap-trap. It made sense now.

He seemed to be waiting for more of a response from her but it took her a minute to process. He added, "I was young and stupid."

"And good-looking," she said. It was no surprise women would throw themselves at Dylan. He was the very definition of *strong, hot male*. Although she didn't like hearing how many— Jealousy coursed through her. But he was opening up a little more to her. He was trusting her with information that obviously embarrassed him. She couldn't fault him too much for his past mistakes.

Maybe that explained why he was so cautious with her now.

"Your dad's place is a few blocks away. To be safe, I'll park behind the restaurant. We can walk from there. Take alleys."

"It'll be better to take Oak instead of Maple. No dogs," she said.

They got out and he fell in step beside her.

At the end of Oak, he stopped. "I just want you to know that I heard what you said in the truck and I apologize. I have some serious thinking to do."

With that, he urged her to keep moving.

What was she supposed to do with that information?

Chapter Fourteen

Tension corded Dylan's muscles with each step closer to the hardware store. They'd retrieved her store key in silence. Samantha deserved an explanation. She was right. He'd been hot and cold with her and it had nothing to do with his feelings. They were always hot. Too much like an out-of-control forest fire for him to be comfortable.

There was a connection between the two of them that he hadn't experienced with anyone else, not even Lyndsey.

Was it because of shared history? Possibly. And something else, too. Something more primal. Something that he didn't have to work at. He just understood Samantha, and it seemed to go both ways.

But he couldn't think about that right now. All he could focus on was getting Maribel back home safe and sound.

His fists curled and adrenaline pumped through him as he thought about the possibility of facing down the jerks who'd taken his daughter. She'd been photographed in the back room of the hardware store, so they needed to enter through the front.

"What about an alarm?" he asked.

"I know the code."

"The noise will give us away if someone's inside, and we don't want that."

"Good point." She stopped and he took her hand in his. Her fingers went still, then wound through his.

Dylan led her around toward the back of the building. A single light fixture stood sentinel over the metal door. The back parking lot was completely empty.

Gravel crunched underneath their shoes as they moved to the side of the building. Downtown, stores were linked together by a common wall. The hardware store sat at the mouth of the alley and anchored the strip.

He leaned his head at the crack of the door, listening for any sounds coming from inside the stockroom.

All was eerily quiet—the kind of quiet where even the air felt stale.

After ten minutes, Dylan was certain that if anyone was in the building, they weren't awake.

He took Samantha's hand again and moved down the side of the building toward Main Street and then turned right. The windows were dark. There was no sign of movement inside.

Samantha squeezed his fingers and then angled her head toward a blinking red dot on the wall.

"The alarm isn't armed," she said.

There were no signs of forced entry, either, in back or in front.

"I want to go in first." He didn't admit his worst fear that her father and his Maribel might be inside, dead. Anger burned in his gut. Dylan blocked out the possibility. *They're safe. They'll be home tonight.* Those were the only two thoughts he could allow in his head. He couldn't afford to think any other way.

Samantha unlocked the wooden door that was half-glass. The hours of business were posted on the top half.

Other than that, the hardware store had two bay windows with *Turner Hardware* etched in white letters on one side.

A bell tinkled as Samantha opened the door. She winced. "Shoot. I forgot about that."

If there was someone inside, he'd know they were coming now. So much for stealth.

Samantha stepped aside so Dylan could go first.

"Wait here," he said, and then stopped. He pulled out his Glock and let the weapon lead the way. Anyone who jumped out or tried to surprise him would get a bullet between the eyes.

First he checked the aisles. Behind the counter came next. The front of the shop was clear.

He turned and waved Samantha inside.

She closed the door behind her.

The damn bell tinkled again.

There was no metallic smell in the air, and that was a relief. If anyone had been killed and brought to the stockroom, it would've had to have been recent. Bodies wasted no time starting to decay. Clean air was a good thing. In fact, it smelled like the inside of any hardware store. And it was neat. Everything seemed to have a place.

He moved toward the stockroom. Samantha was right behind him. He started to argue, to tell her to wait, but she deserved to know just as much as he did. His protective instincts had him wanting to shield her. Samantha was strong. No matter what happened, she could handle herself and then some. She'd proved it time and time again. He respected her for it.

The door to the stockroom had no lock. It was the kind that swung loosely on its hinges for an easy pass-through.

Samantha squeezed his shoulder, so he stopped.

She disappeared down an aisle and returned with a hammer in her left hand.

He smiled at her and hoped she could see him in the dim light.

As he turned, the door smacked him in the face. His body acted as a doorstop but he held his footing. The person on the other side was weaker, so Dylan braced himself and pushed back.

The battle between them held until Dylan counted to five. Then, picturing his little girl, he grunted and gave a shove so hard the other side buckled. The door swung open and Dylan used the opportunity to rush the guy.

Out of nowhere, Dylan's right knee buckled and he landed flat on his back. By the time he popped to his feet again—which took all of two seconds—the guy had pushed past Dylan and knocked Samantha down. She recovered a second behind Dylan.

Both ran after the mystery guy, who bolted through the front of the store and outside, Samantha a half step behind. Those powerful legs of hers kept her within spitting distance, even though she had to be in considerable pain, but the guy in front had a couple of seconds' advantage and could keep pace with both of them.

Dylan kept running, pushing through burning legs until his lungs felt as if they would explode. He had no doubt that if he'd been 100 percent, the guy in front of him with a medium build wearing jeans and sneakers would have been knocked out flat by now. Even a burst of adrenaline couldn't overcome the gap, because the runner had a rush of his own slamming through him.

He hopped a fence and Dylan was right there on his heels.

For a solid ten minutes, they ran.

After a good five more, Samantha dropped off.

"Keep going," she said breathlessly.

If Dylan hadn't been so close, he'd have given up.

The guy was just out of reach, and Dylan wanted more than anything to close his fingers around his neck and choke the bastard. He'd talk first, though. This guy would sing as soon as Dylan applied the right…motivation. And Dylan would have an address. Maribel would be home.

He felt torn between catching this guy, the only viable link to Maribel, and stopping to hang back in order to protect Samantha. That momentary hesitation cost him another two seconds between him and his target. *Well, hell on a roller coaster.*

The runner darted between trash cans, knocking them over. Dylan jumped in time to avoid them. It cost him another second. At this pace, no way could he make up five seconds of delay.

After the guy cut right at the next house, Dylan followed.

The first dog barked, and if Dylan was lucky, that would be the extent of it. He'd lost visual with the runner and that wasn't good. A couple more dogs sounded off, seeing which one could yap the loudest.

If he woke up the neighborhood, someone would end up calling the police. This whole situation would get even stickier.

More dogs weighed in. Was he on Maple? Wasn't that where Samantha had said the dogs were?

He kept running for at least another ten minutes, well aware that he was moving farther from Samantha and no closer to his target. She was there at the hardware store, alone.

When Dylan rounded the next house and the guy was nowhere to be seen, Dylan released a string of curse words under his breath that would've made his grandmother wash his mouth out with that deodorant soap she'd bought for him as a teenager.

Dylan stopped in the alley and listened.

He'd completely lost the runner, so he circled back and jogged toward the hardware store with a bad feeling. What if there had been another person waiting in there?

That person would have complete access to Samantha and then it would be game over. The guttural cry begging for release inside Dylan was more than just frustration that he'd never find his daughter. It was also for Samantha. And he didn't want to feel that way about anyone.

Why?

Being a parent made him feel exposed enough already. He didn't want people to have any additional ways to hurt him, and especially not in the way he'd been hurt when Lyndsey had died. It was immature to feel that she'd abandoned him because she'd died, and yet that was exactly how he'd felt. Abandoned.

Frustrated and defeated, Dylan picked up the pace. If anything had happened to Samantha—and he'd never forgive himself if it had—he needed to know, like, now.

With every forward step, his heart grew heavier in his chest and it was harder to breathe. Ignoring the pain in his calves from bursts of running, he pushed ahead, harder, faster. Getting to Samantha, knowing she was all right, was suddenly more important than air.

The hardware store was two blocks up on the right. It felt like the longest stretch of his entire run even though he ate up the ground in record time. No way could the guy have circled back and beaten Dylan to the store. And yet every possibility started roaring through Dylan's brain.

Samantha wasn't out front. Dylan wasn't sure where he'd expected her to be but maybe he'd hoped that she'd be standing on the sidewalk, waiting, so he could see her first thing.

That would be stupid, though. She'd become pretty

darn good at keeping herself alive. Only an idiot would stand out in the open, exposed. Samantha was much smarter than that. It was her intelligence that had first attracted him.

Sweat dripped down his face, his eyelids, his nose by the time his hand closed around the door handle. He turned the knob but it clicked instead. It was locked.

A few light taps on the glass and he caught sight of her silhouette moving toward him in the darkness.

Instantly, his heart filled with warmth and light. His need to hold her hit as swiftly and as piercingly as a lightning bolt straight through him.

The door swung open and she launched into his arms.

"You're back. I was so worried." She burrowed her face into the crook of his neck.

"I wouldn't go anywhere without you." He didn't want to admit just how absolutely freaked out he'd been. Not to her. Not to himself. Because needing her opened up a whole new can of worms he wasn't sure he was ready to deal with. And what he'd felt running toward the hardware store felt a whole helluva lot like need.

He walked her backward into the store and closed the door behind them.

The smell of her lilac shampoo filled his senses as her body pressed hard against him, giving him other ideas he needed to control.

For now, he'd give in to weakness and hold her.

"Did you catch him?" she finally asked, still nestled against him.

His pulse raced. His breathing was ragged. And he noticed the instant he went from heaving air to breathing in her scent. The air in the room thickened and tension coiled low in his gut. This time he needed a different kind of release. Dylan's feelings for Samantha were getting more difficult to maintain. He had to remind himself they were friends. And he didn't want to do anything to jeopardize that bond. More than anything, he wanted to be with her. And he appreciated whatever kind of connection was growing between them.

"No. He got away. I couldn't get to him in time. He was too far ahead." Dylan took a step back, frustration eating at his stomach lining.

"It's okay. We can figure out who he is anyway." Samantha held her left palm out flat, a cell phone sitting on top. "I found it here on the floor when I came back. I stepped on it, actually, and that completely freaked me out because once I realized what it was, I thought I broke it."

She pushed it toward Dylan. "It's password protected. I tried but couldn't get anything. I bet your friend can."

THE LOOK OF relief that washed over Dylan created a seismic shift on his hard features. Hard lines softened. His lips, which had been permanently formed into a frown, relaxed. His intense eyes lightened. Giving him the break he so desperately needed sent ripples of warmth and happiness through Samantha.

"We need to get this to Jorge for analysis," he said. "He'll be able to give us the name and address of the owner."

"And hopefully more than that," she agreed, starting toward the front door. She stopped when Dylan didn't follow. "I checked the back room. I didn't find anything. The computer's been tampered with, though."

Dylan nodded and they moved to the front door together. "Covering their tracks."

"I assume so."

"Where does your friend live?"

"In Garland."

"That's almost an hour away."

"I know." Dylan walked, glancing up occasionally from the phone. He pressed combinations of numbers. "It'll lock me out soon. Might have already taken our pictures."

"Cell phones can do that?" she asked, stopping at the truck.

"Some are set up to snap a shot the first time the password fails." Dylan opened the door for her.

"Maybe we'll get lucky and find pictures of who's behind all this on that phone." She climbed into the cab.

"Not with my luck, we won't," Dylan said under his breath.

Chapter Fifteen

Dylan knocked softly on the door of the small ranch-style house in the suburban Garland neighborhood. It was dark as pitch outside, but a glow came from inside and the porch light was on.

The door opened quickly.

"Thanks for remembering not to ring the bell. The kids are sleeping." Jorge wasn't at all what Samantha had expected based on his voice. He was taller and his skin was too pale for someone who lived in Texas. He had sunken dark eyes. Then she remembered what he did for a living and realized his appearance must be from staying inside so much to work on computers.

"Thanks for seeing us so late," she said, and introduced herself.

"I'd do just about anything for this guy. What happened to your face?" he asked Dylan.

"Walked into a wall."

"That was some wall," Jorge said. He turned to Samantha and stuck his hand out. "Nice to meet you. Come on in."

He stepped back and opened the door wider for them but then bear-hugged Dylan as he entered.

She followed Dylan inside.

"We need to know who owns this phone." Dylan handed the device over.

The front room had two sofas facing each other, a fireplace to the right of them. Kids' toys were scattered around, but everything else had a place. A quilt was folded over the back of one of the couches. Small frames with pictures of little kids lined the mantel.

The place had a warm feeling to it.

"Step into my office and we'll get to work." Jorge led them down a hall, practically tiptoeing past rooms with crayon drawings taped to the doors.

He didn't speak again until they'd gone into the last room on the right and he'd closed the door behind them.

"Welcome to my humble abode." He spread his arms out. The office, which was really a back bedroom converted, had a desk on which she couldn't see the top. Papers were stacked a foot high at a minimum, and where there wasn't paper, there was a manual of some type.

A cream-colored futon was positioned across from the desk.

"Take a seat," Jorge instructed. "Where'd you get this?" He hesitated, then held up a hand. "No. Don't answer that. Never mind. What I don't know, I can't testify to in court."

"I appreciate what you're doing."

"You know I'd do anything for you, bro." Jorge popped out the SIM card and stuck it into another device. He plugged that into his computer and then turned the screen around so they could see.

"He most likely had security set up on his phone if he went to the trouble of locking it," Dylan said.

"Most people do."

Not Samantha. She'd only scratched the surface of her iPhone's capabilities.

"Bingo." Jorge popped back in his chair and looked at Samantha. "That's a nice pic of you."

Samantha's face was right there, as obvious as the nose on his face, staring straight into the camera. Dylan filled the screen next. Jorge put both up side by side on a split screen.

"You two sure make a nice-looking couple." His gaze immediately bounced between them.

Neither spoke, but Samantha was pretty sure Jorge picked up on the red flush in her cheeks.

Jorge pulled up another pic, loading it onto the screen. He continued, "Does this guy look familiar?"

Dylan shook his head before turning to Samantha. "You know him?"

"Afraid not."

There were half a dozen other faces, none they recognized.

"No luck there." Samantha shrugged.

"Yeah, well, luck has never been my thing," Dylan said quietly. She tried not to notice the hurt in his voice when he spoke. She wondered if he was talking about Maribel's mother. He seemed to blame himself for everything that had gone wrong in their relationship. Samantha wondered whether, if Lyndsey had given him a chance and told him the truth—if she'd asked him point-blank what he'd intended to do—things would have worked out differently.

Knowing Dylan, he would've figured out a way to get his head around the surprise and done his level best to be there for her every step of the way. Being robbed of that chance had taken away so much from him. He'd mentally placed himself in the same boat as the parents who'd abandoned him.

When this was all over, she had every intention of telling him just that. And not because she expected anything to turn out differently between them. She realized he couldn't give her what she needed. His daughter was his focus, and that was the way it should be anyway.

"I got something here," Jorge said. "I got a number, which led me to a name. Wait a minute. Here it is. This phone belongs to…Troy Michaels." He looked up at them expectantly.

Samantha shrugged at the same time as Dylan. She figured they were repeating the same swear word in their heads, too. Neither said it, but they'd both most likely believed this guy would somehow be connected to the game. See his face and everything might finally make sense.

"Okay, we have another route. If you don't recognize the name of the guy who owns the phone, I can tell you it's a 214 number."

"That's a Dallas area code. That much I know," Samantha said.

"Okay. And he doesn't seem familiar to you at all?"

"No. But he messed with my father's computer equipment in the hardware store that he owns. This guy wanted something in the files."

"That the same system I've been running?"

"Yes," Dylan said. "You get anything?"

"Just the money connection. Deposits started being made fifteen years ago and they haven't stopped."

"They started in the summer, right?" Dylan asked.

Jorge confirmed with a nod. "I heard about that crazy stuff that happened in Mason Ridge. This is connected?"

"It would seem so," Samantha confirmed.

"Okay. Okay." Jorge rubbed the day-old scruff on his chin. He looked as though he hadn't had a good night of sleep in weeks. "Let's see who this guy's been calling, then."

He punched keys on the keyboard, then sat back.

A string of numbers showed up on-screen.

One repeated quite often recently.

"Let's just do a reverse number lookup here on Google." More keystrokes. "Private number." He laughed at the screen. "You want to play hardball, then. Okay. Let's try this."

His fingers danced across the keyboard again.

"Looks as if this guy has been calling Charles Alcorn."

Samantha looked from Jorge to Dylan. "We have proof the two are connected. People have to believe us."

Tension radiated from Dylan. "Beckett played the game with the older boys fifteen year ago, remember? Alcorn must've known his son was involved and used it to his advantage. Plus, we already know he's the only one with enough resources to pull off what he did to us in Austin."

"That's right. I didn't have much contact with Beckett, so I didn't even think about him being involved."

"Can I see that phone?" Dylan asked, his back teeth grinding.

Jorge put the SIM card back in and handed it over.

There was a missed call.

The number was Charles Alcorn's—the end to which all roads led.

"Let's see what he has to say." Dylan placed the call.

"He's probably wondering where his contact is. Maybe our guy from earlier was supposed to take the computer drive to Alcorn or check in," Samantha said.

Dylan put the phone on speaker and held it out as the line rang. "Guess he's about to get a surprise, isn't he?"

"I've been expecting your call," Charles Alcorn said.

"Or maybe not," Dylan said through clenched teeth.

"If you want your daughter back alive, you'll agree to an exchange. You know who I really want." Alcorn should sound shocked. He seemed to be expecting the call from Dylan on this line.

The runner must've let his boss know that he'd lost his phone when they'd given chase.

"Fine. Tell us where," she interrupted, knowing full well Dylan would never make that trade.

The look he gave her could've shot daggers right through her. His lips thinned.

She gave him a pleading look in return even though she knew no one would get out of this alive if Alcorn had his way.

"Tomorrow. Noon. At the fork in the road between Benton County Road and Oxford on the way into Dallas. People will be watching, and if you bring in anyone else, the girl dies," Alcorn said.

"Fine. Bring my father, too, or there's no deal."

The line went dead.

Dylan was already shaking his head. "This is a no-win situation, Samantha. I can't allow you to do this."

"How else do you plan to take him down and get your daughter back?" She sat there boldly waiting for an answer. "That girl needs to be home in her own bed. Not spending another night with those creeps."

"You can't go. They get to you and it's over." Dylan was already on his feet, gripping either side of his head with his hands. He looked at his watch. "We only have ten hours to figure this out."

"For now, we know your daughter's safe. That's all that matters." She put a hand on his arm.

"You're important, too. Can't you see that?" Standing at his full height of six foot two with muscles for days, he was a strong physical presence in the room. The man took up a lot of space and she could see how that might be intimidating to anyone who didn't know him. To her, he was Dylan. Bold and brave. Honest. Forthright. All the characteristics she respected in a man.

Jorge slipped out of the room as if aware the energy had taken on a new form, something more intimate.

"If they get to me, it's all over. I know that," she responded quietly, suddenly aware of being alone with Dylan.

"That's all you think this is about?" His face looked thunderstruck. "We've been friends a long time, and you mean more to me than just a…a…pawn to get my daughter back."

What was she supposed to do with that? Of course they were friends, but she felt so much more for Dylan than that. If that was how he classified their relationship, there wasn't much she could do about it except try not to embarrass herself again.

The way his eyes darkened when he stalked toward her and stopped not more than a foot away almost had her believing there was so much more there than friendship.

And that was just wishful thinking on her part. Dylan didn't know what to feel. He kept emotions like that under lock and key. It didn't matter how hard her heart beat with him this close or that she knew his beat hard, too. He was stubborn. He'd never allow himself to indulge in his weakness for her or anyone else. She tried not to take it personally.

"Dylan, we have to do something. You said yourself that they'll get desperate if we don't. That could lead to bad things."

"We could march over to Alcorn's front door and kick his—"

"You know he's not stupid enough to be home."

"Then, we'll get the law involved," he said.

"That won't work, either. He won't keep them where they can be connected to him. He's not that stupid. He has too many places to hide people."

"Fine. Then I'll put that bastard under surveillance." Dylan's anger was a third physical presence in the room and it obliterated all other emotions on his face.

She needed to let him talk this out before he'd be able to see reason. She could see his wheels spinning behind his eyes.

"Good idea. Call Brody. He and Dawson can do that. Or Ryan," she said. "Have people watching him that he's not expecting."

"I'll think about it." Dark circles cradled his eyes and she'd never seen him look more tired.

She walked over and stood toe to toe with him. "Even if Alcorn was keeping Maribel and my father at his house, he won't be now. He knows we're onto him and the stakes have been raised."

"Are you saying it's not worth the time to watch him?"

"No. Not exactly. I think it would be good to have someone track his movements," she clarified. "But let's not walk into a trap here."

He seemed to really consider her ideas. The pulse at the base of his throat had returned to a reasonable beat. "You're probably right."

"We should go back to your place or mine. Actually, now that I think about it, my place is better. I have security in the building. At the very least we'd be safe while we figure out our plan. We'll be twenty minutes from the meet-up spot. I have food there. All we've been eating so far to keep us going is power bars, other than the little bit of pasta I ate in the barn. We need something more substantial." She didn't feel like eating but was pulling out all the stops to coax Dylan to go to her place. Going home was something she hadn't believed possible before. Not when she'd taken off days ago with her car and a little cash. It seemed almost a lifetime ago now.

"Now that I have proof Alcorn is involved and this operation has to be bigger than just a couple of local kidnappings spaced years apart, I don't trust the sheriff, either," Dylan said, rubbing the scruff on his chin.

"I've seen them around each other quite a bit, too, when I visit Dad. It does make me suspicious of our law enforcement."

"What if they're all on Alcorn's payroll? What then?" Dylan asked.

"I don't think that's true. I could see the sheriff not wanting to rock the boat any more than he had to, maybe even looking the other way from time to time, but the FBI would've figured out if those two were in league years ago. Don't you think?" Samantha didn't want to believe that Brine could be covering for Alcorn.

"You're right. Sheriff Brine isn't smart enough to fool the FBI. So we can be relatively certain that he didn't know who was really involved fifteen years ago. Do you think he suspected his golfing buddy?" Dylan asked bitterly.

"I doubt it. If you remember, Alcorn was out there volunteering to search for Rebecca and Shane just like everyone. I think he even donated a hundred thousand dollars to the search. I know he hired private planes to watch from the skies."

"I never really thought about it before, but it would be easier to keep an eye on things if he was involved in the search party. Isn't that the reason criminals return to crime scenes? That and the high they get from reliving it and outsmarting everyone," Dylan ground out.

"True. Call me naive but I never believed it could be someone who lived in our community. How can a person look people in the eye every day knowing they did something so heinous? It gives me the creeps to think we all cried together, searched together and mourned together. And there he was, right there under our noses."

"If I had to guess, he didn't authorize Kramer to take Shane. Even dumb criminals aren't stupid enough to mess around in their own backyards," Dylan said after thinking about it for a few seconds. "And that's the reason Shane wasn't sold."

"Mind if I come back in?" Jorge peeked inside the door. His voice was low, an indication his kids were still sleeping and he'd like to keep it that way.

"Come on in," Dylan said, and then turned to Samantha. "At the very least, Alcorn's a big donor to the mayor's campaign fund. They'll protect him no matter what he's gotten himself involved in."

"True."

Dylan really looked at her. "Because you know what I'm thinking? We've known this was bigger than what we realized. It's not one kid taken here and there. Shane was the first from our town and he was the oldest until that other boy, but my guess is that they like to take younger kids. There's a huge market for them. One thing I do know is that your dad saw something he wasn't supposed to fifteen years ago and he's been paid to keep quiet ever since."

"You might be onto something there. The fact that the money keeps coming in also leads me to believe there's more going on than just what happened before." Samantha stood, hoping Dylan would take the hint that she was ready to leave.

"Kramer was part of the operation," Dylan said. "Alcorn is the brains."

"They found that kid at Kramer's house recently," she pointed out.

"True, and everyone chalked it up to him losing his own son. He was working for Alcorn all along. They were snatching kids and this guy decides he wants one for himself. Maybe he even thinks he deserves one since his son was taken from him. In the process, he brings all kinds of heat on Alcorn's operation. They're forced to stop for a while but then they get things going again."

"Eventually everything calms down until Kramer takes another little boy for himself last year, plus the fact that Rebecca refused to stop digging into the case," Samantha said.

"Right." Dylan turned to Jorge. "We're taking off."

"Okay, my friend. Just so you know, I'm heading to the meet-up location while it's still dark outside to plant a few cameras in the trees. I checked out the site and it should be easy enough to hide my equipment. I can go wireless, too. It's close enough to the city that I should be able to get a decent connection. I'll dig into Charles Alcorn's finances, too. Anything happens to you guys… I'll go straight to the feds."

"Good. Local law enforcement might be tainted," Dylan said. He paused for a beat, taking in the change in situation. "I can't thank you enough, man. You know I don't want you taking any unnecessary risks. You got a family to take care of, too, and they need you."

Everything about Dylan's demeanor—his rounded shoulders, earnest eyes—said he meant those words.

"I'm doing it for my family as much as yours. I can't let those bastards get away with taking Maribel. Besides, the two of you are my family!"

Samantha bit back the emotion building in her chest, climbing up the back of her throat, threatening to spill out of her eyes.

"You have no idea what it means to me to know you're watching my back." A look of friendship, kinship, passed between the two men.

Dylan turned to Samantha, his gaze softer now but still determined. "We can head out. I may not be able to sleep but you might."

"I'll keep working on everything you sent me. Now that I know more of what I'm looking for, I might get lucky and piece it all together. If I can link this jerk, we can turn the information over to the feds. They don't take lightly to hidden offshore bank accounts." Jorge stuck out his hand.

Dylan took it and shook, followed by Samantha.

"Thank you for everything, Jorge. It was nice meeting you," Samantha said, noticing the moisture gathering underneath Jorge's eyes. His and Dylan's relationship clearly was stronger than friendship. It was more like a brotherhood. She'd seen it all too many times with her own brothers. Mess with one and they all came running in defense. Plus, Jorge was a father. She imagined his children playing with Maribel in the past year since she'd come to live with her father. Jorge seemed almost as affected by her disappearance as Dylan. And what was happening to Dylan was unthinkable for any parent.

"Same here. When this all blows over, we should throw some steaks on the grill. We got a swimming pool in the back. Kids love it. Bring Maribel." An emotion flickered behind his eyes… Anxiety? Sadness? Pity? He seemed to quickly recover. "We'll figure this out. That

jerk won't get away with this. We'll hang that SOB for
what he's doing. That I promise you, bro."

"We'll get him and we'll bring her home," Dylan
repeated like a mantra, a promise.

Chapter Sixteen

To say Dylan had a lot to think about was like saying bombs exploded. And that analogy wasn't too far off from what his head felt as though it might do. The drive to Samantha's place, a route he'd taken only a couple days ago, was almost too quiet. He'd switched out the truck for his SUV on the way and texted Brody to let him know where to find his pickup.

Dylan had urged Samantha to sit close to him, needing to feel her warmth, and she'd fallen asleep with her head on his shoulder.

His heart ached because he could get used to this. It felt right to have someone like Samantha in his life, on his shoulder, curled up against him. But his life was no longer about what he wanted.

Besides, it was good that Samantha was resting. She needed sleep and he needed time to come up with a plan. No way could he allow her anywhere near the meet-up site.

It wasn't until he was pulling into her parking garage that he felt her stir. "I can't believe I fell asleep for a solid hour. It felt like five minutes." She yawned and stretched. "Doesn't help much that I feel like a zombie. You know how it is when your eyes open but you don't really feel as if you woke up? It's as though you're dreaming that you're awake."

"Yeah. It's the worst. Feels like walking in quicksand."

"That's exactly how I feel right now. The only thing I know is real is how tight my shoulders are." She rolled them a couple of times as though trying to work out the kinks.

"Let's get you upstairs and into your own bed for a change." He parked in a visitor space, cut the engine and surveyed the garage. "I made sure no one followed us."

He moved quickly around the back side of the truck to open the door for her. She took his hand and he ignored the jolt of electricity running through his as soon as they made contact. This would all be over soon and he warned himself against getting used to the feeling of having Samantha next to him or the constant sexual current running between them.

Space would normally be a good thing in a situation like theirs, except the time they'd spent apart had left a cavern in his chest. He filed away his thoughts as he walked with Samantha to her condo, his hand resting on the small of her back.

Inside, after the door was secured, she turned to him. "I bought a multipack of toothbrushes two weeks ago at the grocery. They're under the bathroom sink. Feel free to use one. Shower's that way. I'll put on a pot of coffee and see if I can wake up. I'll be no good to anyone like this." She moved into the open-concept kitchen.

"I have a few calls to make first. Go ahead and shower while the coffee brews. I'll bring you a cup as soon as it's ready. Mind if I check out the balcony?"

"Not at all. Make yourself at home."

Dylan blocked out how much he liked her place and

how homey it felt, figuring he could be in a cardboard box with her and it would somehow feel just as nice. Thoughts like those were about as brilliant as waterboarding himself. There was only one thing missing in order to make his life complete at the moment and it was Maribel.

As soon as he was sure Samantha couldn't hear and no one was watching her place, he fished his burn phone out of his pocket.

Brody answered on the first ring. "What's going on?"

"How are you still awake? It's the middle of the night. I was afraid I'd wake you."

"I can't sleep, not while they have... Not until we get Maribel back," Brody said wearily. "Neither can Rebecca. We were just talking about ways we can help."

"Are you sitting down?" Dylan appreciated the support of his friends more than he could say. After basically being on his own his entire childhood, he especially respected the friends who'd become his surrogate family. And it made him even more proud that Maribel would never face the kind of loneliness he'd experienced as a young child. She would always have half a dozen surrogate aunts and uncles around. She'd be surrounded by people who loved and protected her, made her feel safe. And maybe that would provide the support she needed after losing her mother at such a young age. Maribel not having memories of him and her mother together was on him. If he hadn't been so selfish, so vocal, he and Lyndsey might've gotten married and provided a real home for Maribel.

He could beat himself up all day over that, and yet he knew the outcome wouldn't change. Lyndsey would still be dead. Dylan gripped the phone tighter.

"Yeah, why?" Brody asked.

"We caught a trail tonight and it led us straight to Charles Alcorn," Dylan said matter-of-factly.

"Seriously?" Shock was laced all throughout Brody's tone.

"I wouldn't joke about a serious accusation like this."

"No. Of course you wouldn't." When Brody repeated Alcorn's name, it sounded as if he moved the phone away from his mouth. He was most likely telling Rebecca. She would be just as stunned as the rest of them after all that Alcorn had done to find her younger brother fifteen years ago. Or, at least, all he'd pretended to do to help.

"I talked to him on the phone myself. He set a meet-up for tomorrow at noon. He wants to trade Maribel for Samantha." Dylan waited, keeping an eye out for Samantha, who'd disappeared into a back room, presumably the bathroom. The warm breeze blew on his face as he studied the blue and green etchings around buildings of the Dallas skyline.

"Rebecca just texted Ryan and Dawson. They're both up now. What can we do to help?" Brody asked. "I put you on speaker so Rebecca can hear."

"I don't want Samantha anywhere near the meet-up. It's going to take some doing to keep her away. She's convinced that she's responsible for Maribel being involved and she wants to help," Dylan said.

"I'll take her place," Rebecca offered.

"It's too dangerous. I was trying to figure out a way for one of the guys to step in," Dylan said. "Besides, you're a good six inches shorter than her."

"One of us would fit the height requirement better, but our shoulders are too broad. Alcorn's not stupid. If we have someone stand in for Samantha, they have to be believable," Brody said.

"You're right," Dylan agreed. "This will be trickier than that. I'm grasping at straws here."

"We'll put our heads together with the others and see what we can come up with," Brody said.

"Thank you. Also, I need to keep eyes on Alcorn. Can you help with that?" Dylan asked.

"Done. The guys and I will figure it out. Everyone wants to play a part in this, man," Brody said.

"You know how much it means to me to hear you say it," Dylan said, choking back the emotion clotting his throat.

"We'll get someone on Alcorn and I'll call you back with more ideas," Brody said before ending the call.

Dylan took in a deep breath and then once more called the image of him tucking Maribel into bed to his mind. *If not this night, then soon, my Bel.*

A different cavern opened in his chest, despite his best attempts to contain it. He needed a distraction. He'd been overthinking the situation and his brain was fried.

Coffee.

He'd promised Samantha a cup.

Dylan moved to the kitchen and located two mugs. He filled both with fresh brew and walked to the bathroom. The shower was running, so he knocked on the door.

"Come on in."

He did. The room was spacious. All top-of-the-line fixtures, he noted. Overall, the place was modern but warm, and he wondered if it was the color choices or if it had to do with the fact that the place was Samantha's.

The water stopped in the shower.

"I'll set the coffee on the counter." He figured he needed to get out of there, because being a half wall away from her, knowing she was completely nude, had his pulse hammering. He'd noticed right away that his body had reacted to her nearness, to the fact that she was completely naked on the other side of those block tiles.

"Okay."

He started to turn around and leave but hesitated.

She stepped around the block wall, her dark hair soaked and off her face. She looked as if she'd just risen out of a swimming pool, water beading and rolling down her face and neck.

A towel was tied loosely around her chest, and it was barely long enough to hit midthigh.

"Coffee's fresh but I'd rather you get some rest." The words came out huskier than he'd intended. He cleared his throat.

She seemed unaware of the effect she had on him, and he thought that was probably a good thing. They had a good couple of hours before they needed to kick it into gear and he hoped she'd rest while he tried to figure out his next move. His head was already pounding from hunger and exhaustion. He could live in the field for days on power bars and water. This was different. Having Maribel involved was far more emotionally draining.

"Are you sure you're okay?" Samantha slid in between him and the counter he was facing and then hopped up to sit. She took coffee from him in her right hand and used her left to trace the worry lines in his face.

He closed his eyes and took in a deep breath, keenly aware that the air in the room had become charged. Her flowery scent flooded his senses. He looked at her as he sipped his coffee. She was stunning.

"I will be."

Her finger ran along his jawline, sending awareness jolting through him. Then the tip moved over his lips, her touch lighting up all his senses. His pulse raced.

"But you do that much longer and I can't be held responsible for my actions."

She froze for a second, smiled and then traced around his ears, down his neckline. "Maybe you should let go of all that control for once."

"And ruin our friendship?"

"Let me be the judge of that, Dylan."

He shouldn't let this go any further while he still had a hint of restraint inside him. She set down her mug and then her hands came up, sliding into his hair, and she pulled him toward her until their mouths moved together. She tasted like a mix of mint toothpaste, the coffee she'd just sipped and something sweet that was uniquely Samantha.

Dylan reminded himself that it wasn't too late to stop this. He didn't do casual relationships or sex anymore. Being a gentleman, he should stop this. Now. Before there was no turning back.

He pulled away and rested his forehead against hers. They were both breathing rapidly, and he could hear her heartbeat pounding as quickly as his own.

"Dylan, I want to have sex with you."

"It's never been a matter of what I want, Samantha. We'd have been in bed by now if it was."

"I hear what you're saying and I understand the consequences."

"Good. Now you're making sense. You are so damn sexy. Believe me, you have no idea how much restraint it has taken for me to hold back."

"Then, don't." She looked him square in the eyes.

"I don't want you to regret anything you do with me."

"Is that true? Because I couldn't. I want you, Dylan. Do you want me the same way?"

Better judgment flew out the window the second she

opened her towel. He pushed in between her thighs, curled his hands around her sweet bottom and pulled her toward him until her heat pressed against his denim— denim that needed to go.

Her hands were already to his zipper before he could readjust his position and do it himself. He stood there, still, long enough for her to unzip him and free his straining length. His shirt joined his jeans on the floor.

He helped her shove his jeans down along with his boxers, and he stepped out of them and kicked them both aside.

With a groan, he pressed their bodies flush, leaving only enough space to palm her breast.

She wrapped those long legs around him and he nearly blew it right then. He wanted this to last, to be good for her, too. He had no doubt it would be amazing for him.

"It's been a long time for me. We need to slow down, take it easy."

"Or we could just do it twice." She smiled. Damn, her pink lips were sexy. Then again, everything about Samantha was smokin' hot. Her intelligence and quick wit were the foundation on which her physical beauty flourished. There wasn't much sexier than a smart and beautiful woman.

Dylan ravaged her mouth with his tongue, his need so intense he could hardly contain it.

Her hands were all over him, his face, his neck, his chest, before settling onto his shoulders, digging in with her nails.

She tasted so sweet. She pulled back long enough to bite his bottom lip, and electricity shot through him.

"You're going to destroy me."

"That's the plan," she said with a mischievous hint of a smile.

He ran his tongue across her lower lip, then down the cleft of her chin, then lower.

Her nipples were already beads in his hands and she moaned when his tongue flicked the crest of one, then the other. He took her full breast in his mouth and her entire body tensed.

Then he ran his tongue down her belly and into the warm dark curls of her mound. She leaned back against the glass and drove her fingers into his hair as his tongue slid down even farther.

Her silky thighs were still damp from her shower as he planted a hand on the inside of each and opened her legs.

As he delved his tongue inside her, she made low, sexy noises and whispered his name. Her body quivered as he worked her bud with his thumb and slid his tongue in and out of her sweet heat.

He could feel her thighs quiver as tension corded her body and her breathing quickened.

Faster, deeper, he inserted three fingers inside her again and again until she came unbanded all around him.

Satisfaction roared through him as he felt himself being tugged up. She opened the drawer next to him and pointed.

He located a condom, tore it apart with shaky fingers and slid it over his straining erection.

Her long legs wrapped around his midsection as her fingers curled around his erection, and then she brought him toward home. With one thrust, he was deep inside her. She was so wet and ready for him, stretching to take in his full length, that he had to stop and tense his body to maintain control or he'd detonate right there.

It had been a long time since he'd had sex, but no one had ever had that effect on him.

Dylan was all about control and yet he was constantly

on the edge of losing it with Samantha. She drove her tongue in his mouth and he started a slow pump, not wanting to rush, even though his body already begged for release.

Her fingers dug into his back and he thrust harder, faster.

She tightened around him and the tsunami started building. Her hips moved against his, matching his stride. Urgency roared through him.

Faster.

Harder.

Deeper.

This woman, her body, drove him to the brink. He held on for as long as he could, making sure she was satisfied first.

The second he felt her muscles clamp around him, he knew. He pumped inside her sweet heat.

He gave a guttural groan, and his release shattered inside her. And so did he.

"I love you," he whispered quietly into her neck as a thousand tiny bombs exploded inside his body all at once.

SAMANTHA LEANED AGAINST the mirror, heaving, her body still tingling. She could've sworn she'd heard Dylan tell her he loved her, but that couldn't be right and she didn't want to ruin this moment of absolute bliss a second before she had to by overanalyzing things.

In a minute, they'd need to untangle their bodies and sort out their next move.

But for now, just for this second, she needed to feel him inside her, skin to skin, his warm breath surrounding her.

They both stayed perfectly still in that flawless moment for longer than she could count.

"Are you hungry?" She moved first, and it was most likely out of self-preservation.

"I am now," he said, nuzzling into her hair, his arms tightening around her waist.

His voice did all kinds of crazy things to her insides.

"Good. I can whip up something to eat while you shower." She started to peel his arms off her.

"Do you really have to go?" He almost sounded hurt. Now she really was hearing things. Or making things up. Because not only was that the best sex of her life but she'd fallen deeper into the hole of loving him, needing him.

And that was going to hurt like hell once this ordeal was behind them and they returned to their normal lives.

It didn't help that he was already kissing her neck and her body was melting under his touch.

Way to be strong, Samantha.

And the truth was she didn't want to be resilient with Dylan. She wanted to be vulnerable with him and just feel.

"No. But stay here much longer and I can't be held responsible for my actions," she shot back playfully, echoing his earlier sentiment.

"Me, either." He leaned his head back enough to look at her, his sharp green eyes taking her in. And there was a promise in those words he didn't quite look ready to deliver on.

He pressed a kiss to her temples, her nose, her lips. "This changes things. You know that, right?"

"What does that mean, exactly?"

"I'm not sure yet." He kissed her again, tenderly this time, and her heart filled with love.

And none of that meant anything until they got her father and Dylan's daughter back alive.

"I'm going to rinse off. Want to join me?"

There was an adorable twinkle to his normally intense eyes.

She should make an excuse and retreat to the kitchen, but looking at him naked and sexy…how could she?

Samantha nodded.

He took her hand and led her into the shower.

Chapter Seventeen

Samantha hadn't been home in days. Having Dylan there made it feel complete, which was dangerous thinking. She pulled bread from the freezer and warmed a few pieces in the microwave. There wasn't much around except fixings for BLTs and tomato soup. It would have to do.

The water turned off in the bathroom.

"I put out clean boxers and jeans for you," she said from the kitchen.

Dylan walked into the room holding out the items.

"Whose are these?" He didn't look impressed.

"Trevor's. Why? You look about the same size."

"Oh. Okay." He disappeared down the hall.

What was that about? Then it dawned on her. Dylan must've thought that they belonged to a boyfriend who'd left them over.

Was that jealousy she'd seen in his eyes? More important, why did that make her feel so happy?

Dylan returned a few moments later wearing the items. The Metallica T-shirt fit snugly.

"I can't say that I agree with your brother's taste in music, but at least the shirt fits well enough." Dylan walked up behind her until his chest was flush with her back and wrapped his arms around her. He kissed her at the base of her neck, and it sent warmth running down her body, pooling between her thighs. "Mmm. You smell nice."

"So do you." She closed her eyes.

"How are you feeling? Are you tired?" His erection pressed against her, sending want spreading through her.

"Not too tired."

"Good. I wanted to test out your bed."

"I've never had four orgasms in an hour before."

"Well, you've never had sex with me," he said, grazing her ear with his teeth. He caught the lobe and bit ever so slightly.

Damn, this man did crazy things to her body.

"So there's even more? I really am impressed now." She set down the tomato she held before turning around to face him. She looped her arms around his neck.

He picked her up and took her to bed, where they made love slowly, sweetly.

"WE SHOULD EAT and check in with the others," Dylan said.

"I'll get dressed." She made a move to get up.

"Not so fast." He caught her and tugged her back into his arms, where he was all warmth and strength.

She kissed him and she honestly couldn't remember the last time she'd felt so happy. Nothing about their current situation should have made her feel safe, and yet she felt just that. Her warning bells sounded and she needed to put a little space between them. "We probably shouldn't get too comfortable."

He looked a little hurt by the barb but he didn't immediately say anything. He just loosened his grip so she could get up.

When he strolled into the kitchen five minutes later,

she had everything heated and ready to go. Thank heaven for microwaves.

They ate in silence but Dylan had returned to his heavier thoughts. She could see it in the worry lines in his face, in the heaviness in his eyes.

After finishing up the snack and doing dishes, Dylan motioned for her to sit by him on the couch. She snuggled up against him and closed her eyes. She had never felt so close to another person, so comforted as when Dylan's arms were wrapped around her.

That was the thing she remembered thinking before waking with a jolt.

The sun was already up, peeking through the crack in the closed curtains.

"Dylan?" She glanced around. No sign of him. She listened, hoping to hear water running in the bathroom.

The place was quiet.

She scrambled to her feet and checked every room.

Had he just left without her?

Her heart pounded in her chest at the thought of not knowing what was happening. It was eight o'clock in the morning, so the meet-up wasn't for another four hours.

The door handle jiggled and Samantha's back tensed, fear coursing through her. She dropped down behind the couch and grabbed the metal candlestick on the side table. If she needed to defend herself, she would fight to the end.

It was as if the air had stilled from the tension racking her body.

Footsteps fell closer and she tightened her fingers around the makeshift weapon.

"Samantha?" Dylan's voice was like a rain shower in a drought, bringing nourishment to parched land.

"Right here." She popped to her feet.

"I went out for breakfast and to survey the area." He was in an athletic stance, his weapon drawn. He lowered it the second his eyes made contact with hers.

"When I woke and you weren't there, I was afraid you'd gone without me." She set the candlestick down and rushed into his arms.

He tucked his gun into his waistband and set the bag of food down in time to hold her.

"I wouldn't just disappear on you. Believe me, I thought about it, but how could you ever trust me if I did that?" Dylan asked, then kissed her forehead.

Despite all the craziness going on, his reassurance brought a sense of calm over her.

"You don't want me anywhere near the meet-up and I get that. I do." She looked straight into his eyes. "Here's the thing. I have to be there. Maybe not with you, exactly, but I need to be near."

"Absolutely not." Dylan shook his head for emphasis.

"Hear me out."

He nodded but one look in those green eyes said he was reluctant to agree. She searched for the right words to convince him.

"I'd like nothing more than to be able to put this whole ordeal behind us. And believe me when I say I want to be alive to see it. I know what's at risk here and I take that very seriously. My fear is that if I'm not nearby and this whole thing goes south, the two people we love most will suffer the consequences."

"I can't allow anything to happen to you," he said, his eyes pleading. "You don't understand how deeply I mean those words."

"But I'll be safe."

"I can't guarantee that. If they get a clean shot, they'll kill you. Once you're taken care of, they'll do the same thing to your father. The entire trail leading back to Alcorn would be erased and my daughter will be killed in the process."

"There is no other choice. If I'm not there, Maribel and my father will be killed anyway." She stood her ground. "I'll take whatever risk is necessary if it means getting my father and Maribel back. I don't see any other way around it."

"What if I can't agree to this? Would you do it anyway?"

"This won't be over until the man behind these crimes is locked behind bars forever. You need me. They have to see me." She paused, waiting for a response. When none came, she added, "Do you have a better plan?"

"Send in someone for you. Make them believe it's you. Lure Alcorn to the drop and then take our families back."

"Fine. I'll stay with Brody and Rebecca. But you have to let me be there. I'm just as vulnerable here alone as I would be with you guys."

He didn't voice an argument but she could see the battle going on inside his head. She could also tell that she was getting to him.

She pressed up on tiptoe and kissed him. "We can finish this, figure out what *this* is when my father and Maribel are safe again."

He blew out a breath and held her tighter, his arms looped around her waist. He pressed his forehead to hers. "I meant it when I said nothing can happen to you or my daughter, Samantha. I couldn't survive losing either one of you."

DYLAN WENT OVER the mission in his head for the fiftieth time in the past half hour. There were three roads that merged at the fork, the meet-up spot, so they formed three teams aside from Dylan's. Each team would stake out a road. If they had an opportunity to intercept the "packages," they would.

If the package made it to the drop, then their friend Lisa would stand in for Samantha. Lisa would ride with Dylan. If Alcorn and his men got too close, they'd easily see that they were being tricked.

Samantha would be in another car with Brody and his team, and Rebecca would ride with Dawson. Ryan was on his own but all teams would be in constant contact.

Minutes ticked by like hours until it was time to trade Samantha for Lisa.

Dylan and his companion waited at the place where all roads merged.

The only comfort was that Dylan knew everything was being recorded on video, so even if the situation went to hell, Alcorn wouldn't get away with it. His operation would be shut down and he'd spend the rest of his life in jail.

Of course, Dylan preferred to have Maribel home, Samantha and her father safe and Alcorn in prison.

At the site, noon came and went and Dylan had a sinking feeling in his chest that Alcorn had outsmarted them. He and Lisa stayed put and waited anyway.

Twenty minutes later, word arrived from Ryan that he could confirm a car with a car seat and young child in the back had just passed him.

A few minutes and Maribel would be close enough to grab.

After what felt like an eternity had passed, Dylan's phone rang. He could see by the number that it was Brody.

"They got her," Brody said breathlessly.

"Who?" But Dylan already knew the answer to that

question. His entire world caved in all at once and his knees buckled.

"Samantha. They got her. I'm so sorry, man. We headed over to assist Ryan and they came up like a swarm around us. There had to be at least a half dozen of them."

Dylan couldn't breathe. His entire world crumbled around him. Lisa was beside him, trying to comfort him, but there were no words that could take away this pain. He'd lost the two people he loved most in the world.

"They came from every direction. I shot at least one of them but they snatched her. I couldn't shoot again without possibly hitting her. There was nothing I could do, man. I'm so sorry." Brody's voice relayed his anguish better than his words.

"Where are you?" Dylan popped to his feet.

"I'm on Benton Road."

"Which way did they go?" he asked, but he already knew, because if they went north, they'd cross paths with him. No way would Alcorn allow it.

"South. Away from town." Brody paused, heaving into the phone. "They shot out my tires so I couldn't follow."

Dylan had been so close to Maribel, so close to bringing her home. He glanced in the backseat at her stuffed animal, Rofurt. Agony bore down on him, cutting him to the core. His phone beeped. He had another call. "I gotta go. I'll pick you up."

He was already in his SUV, barreling toward Brody's drop spot.

Dylan one-handed the phone while watching the road and answered the next call with Bluetooth.

"I've got eyes on a vehicle heading toward County Road 83." Jorge's voice was rife with fresh adrenaline. "I saw Maribel in the car. She's okay."

For now. Dylan knew they'd use her to get away. As

soon as they were clear, they'd dispose of her and Samantha's father. Samantha didn't have long, either.

"That's toward Alcorn's private airstrip. We can't let him leave with them," Dylan said.

"Let me call the feds, bro. Tell them what's going on."

"Okay. I'm heading there myself, though." Dylan ended the call before Jorge tried to talk him out of it. His friend would only be wasting his breath anyway.

Dylan spotted Brody running on the side of the road. Dylan roared toward his friend and stopped quickly.

Brody hopped into the backseat. Lisa, who had been quiet up to now, filled Brody in. He pulled his weapon and replaced the clip. "Let's get those sons of bitches."

With the exchange a total disaster, Dylan prayed they'd get there in time. He had to be a good ten minutes behind Alcorn but if he made it to his plane, it would be all over. He could illegally hop over the border in hours and disappear until he bought the judge or influenced a congressman to give him pardon.

Samantha would be dead. Maribel would be...

Just as Dylan feared all hope was lost, he saw an older man running toward the road while holding a little girl. In fact...that was not just any child...it was Maribel. Dylan's heart could have exploded for how much joy he felt.

He angled the SUV toward the pair and pulled close to them. The old man held Maribel protectively as he turned toward the woods.

Dylan put the SUV in Park and hopped out.

"Mr. Turner. It's Dylan," he shouted, running toward the man holding his little angel.

Maribel turned at the sound of his voice.

"Da-da!" She smiled and cried at the same time.

Dylan held out his arms and she practically flew into

them. There were no words to describe how good it felt to hold his daughter again.

Keenly aware Samantha was still missing, Dylan turned to Mr. Turner. "We need to go. I have a tip on where they're taking Samantha."

The old man looked as though he'd aged ten years since Dylan had last seen him. Worry for a child, no matter how old, would do that to any parent.

"Thank you." Mr. Turner limped toward the SUV.

"Here. Lean on me." Dylan offered his shoulder.

At the vehicle, he climbed into the backseat with Brody's help.

"You drive," Dylan said to Brody, unable to let go of Maribel. He placed her in her safety seat and buckled her in, holding on to her the whole time. Her grip around him was viselike. He gave her Rofurt and her *Brave* doll and she immediately hugged them both to her chest.

Dylan was all too conscious of the danger of taking this group toward Alcorn. He had Mr. Turner and Maribel. It was a calculated risk he had to take in order to save Samantha.

"How did you get away from them?" Dylan asked Mr. Turner as Lisa phoned Ryan and filled him in.

"I wouldn't have without Samantha. They were trying to put us into one car when she got hold of someone's gun. She shot two of Alcorn's men before they subdued her. One had a beard and the other one was a redhead. The second one had a brother there, as well."

Bearded and the brothers. Dylan knew exactly who they were.

"She told me to grab Maribel and run." Anguish turned down the corners of Mr. Turner's lips. His eyes were burdened. "The one with the beard didn't stop me."

"We'll get her back. And when we do, I need to have

a conversation with you," Dylan said, keenly aware of the sacrifice Samantha had made to save his daughter.

Maribel was crying softly, fighting sleep.

"Hey, Bel," Dylan soothed. "Da-da is here. You're okay."

He noticed that she'd placed her *Brave* Barbie doll over her heart. He was thankful the last gift from her mother was safely in her arms.

Dylan said a silent prayer of thanks and hoped that her mother was an angel watching out for Maribel.

He thought about Samantha's unselfish act of trading herself for Maribel and her father. He was beginning to realize just how brave and devoted she was. Samantha was nothing like his own mother. All women didn't bolt when times were tough.

Damn, he also realized just how much he'd fallen for Samantha. He wouldn't rest until his family was complete—which meant Samantha being home with him, where she belonged.

"This is all my fault. I saw him that night near where the children were kidnapped. I could put him at the scene moments before it happened. Then I went to talk to him about what he might've seen and I overheard someone ask him about the kids. He told them to 'find Kramer and take care of those brats.' They discovered I was listening but not before talking about how Kramer might jeopardize their entire operation," Samantha's father said. "I should've told on him before when I had the chance. I'd been drinking too much and was scared of him."

"You aren't responsible for a criminal's actions."

"He saw me and then threatened me, my family. The only reason he didn't kill me right then and there was because of all the heat on the town. I never wanted the money but I was afraid if I didn't take it, he would hurt

Samantha. He knew how much I loved her, all of my kids. He held their safety over my head for years. Doesn't excuse what I did."

That explained why he'd been so overprotective of her, made sure one of her brothers was with her at all times.

"I wanted to make it right all those years ago and failed. When Shane showed up, I figured it was only a matter of time before the truth came out. I was ready to face the consequences of what I'd done and tell the law what I knew. But Alcorn has eyes everywhere and figured me out. You can't trust anyone. The sheriff is too friendly with Alcorn," he said. "And now that he has my baby, he'll kill her."

"Your daughter is strong. I will bring her home. You have my word." Dylan couldn't ignore the ache in his chest at the thought of losing Samantha. His heart didn't feel divided between her and Maribel. Instead, it had grown to make room for both.

He could only hope that he would get there in time.

"Do you know the shortcut through the Hatters' land that's coming up?" Dylan asked Brody.

"Yeah. I sure do." Brody cut the wheel right and the SUV bounced as he took it off road.

"If we stop before the clearing, then you guys can stay here while I hit the hangar."

"You're not going by yourself."

Dylan texted Ryan the plan as Brody parked the SUV near the tree line. The clearing was twenty-five yards ahead of them.

"I need at least one person who knows how to handle a weapon to stay back." Dylan motioned toward Maribel.

Lisa seemed to take the cue and moved to the backseat as Dylan, heartbroken at Maribel's tear-soaked face, slipped out. Luckily, his daughter felt at home with Brody and Lisa. Otherwise, no way would he have been able to leave.

They were engaging her in a game of peekaboo when he cleared the back of the SUV and moved toward the trees.

Dylan, staying low, spotted his buddy Ryan on the east side of the hangar as he came up on the west.

Dust was still kicked up from the cars that were already parked in the lot. Four men surrounded Samantha, who was fighting every step of the way. Alcorn led the pack toward the hangar.

Dylan's chest filled with pride. *Keep fighting, sweetheart. I'm almost there.*

Five against three, counting Samantha, wasn't bad odds. The men closed rank. If Dylan fired, he risked hitting Samantha.

Damn.

No way could he take that chance. *Come on, sweetheart. Give me something to work with.*

Another twenty seconds and they'd have her inside the building. If Dylan ran full force, he still wouldn't make it in time.

Samantha reared back and kicked the guy in front of her, then dropped down.

Dylan charged toward them. Ryan fired, creating a distraction.

The men's heads turned in the opposite direction of Dylan, searching the east side.

Dylan launched forward as the second group disappeared into the building. He was closer than Ryan and, therefore, had the best chance of getting there first. It went without saying that Ryan would have his back.

By the time Dylan reached the hangar, Samantha was

being forced inside an airplane. There was a pilot in place and ready to go.

Dylan couldn't allow that plane to get off the ground. He took aim and shot the wheels. The pilot ducked, and then disappeared into the back of the aircraft, closing the door to the cockpit.

"You think you got us? You think you've figured this all out?" a male voice shouted from behind the aircraft. "You don't know anything."

Alcorn.

He forced Samantha in front of him as a shield. "You're going to let us walk out of here or she dies."

Dylan held up his hands in surrender. Where was Ryan?

"Okay. I'm setting my weapon down on the floor. See." Dylan did.

"Step back!"

Dylan complied.

Alcorn stepped into view, a struggling Samantha still held in front of him, a gun pressed to her temple.

"It's okay," Dylan soothed, taking another step back to allow Alcorn passage. "I'm nowhere near my gun."

Alcorn forced Samantha to the door and then pushed her toward Dylan and ran.

Dylan dived, rolled and plowed into Alcorn's legs. Where were the other men? He already knew Bearded had been shot and at least one of his companions. Dylan couldn't worry about that now.

Alcorn tried to get up, but Dylan was sitting on his chest. Alcorn managed to point his weapon. Dylan grabbed the guy's hand and spun just as a shot fired.

Alcorn spun, fighting his way next to Dylan. A kick landed in his groin and he bit back blinding nausea in order to keep fighting. His hesitation gave Alcorn the space he needed to break free, push up to his feet and run. He kept going, unaware of the red dot flowering on his right shoulder. A few steps before reaching the vehicle, he crumpled to the ground.

Ryan entered the hangar slowly, his weapon drawn. "I got three of them outside, trying to get out the back."

"Come out of the plane. Leave your hands where I can see them," Dylan shouted to the pilot.

He complied. Dylan found rope and Ryan tied him to a chair.

Samantha was already in Dylan's arms.

"Everyone okay in here?" Ryan asked through heavy breaths as he finished his work with the pilot and called the police.

"We're good," Dylan replied, pulling Samantha into his chest, kissing her forehead. "We're more than good. Let's check on the SUV."

"I'll sit on Alcorn until the cops arrive," Ryan said.

All three moved to check on him.

"He'll live," Dylan said. "If that shot had been a little to the left, he'd be going to the morgue. I hope you enjoy prison."

Alcorn didn't respond.

The sound of sirens moved closer.

"You two get out of here so you can be with Maribel when you give your statements. I'll make sure this guy sticks around," Ryan said, digging his knee into Alcorn's back.

It took every bit of Dylan's self-control not to walk over to Alcorn and beat the man until he took his last breath.

But his daughter waited, and she'd made Dylan a better man than that.

He and Samantha made it back to the vehicle, where

everyone waited. Brody let Maribel down and she launched herself toward Dylan.

He scooped her up just in time to stop her from tripping and held on to her.

With Samantha, the missing piece of his heart, there, he felt whole for the first time in his life.

Samantha hugged them both and his heart lurched when Maribel leaned over and rewarded Samantha with a kiss.

Mr. Turner made his way toward Samantha. Maribel hugged him, too.

Dylan's cell phone vibrated, breaking into the moment.

"Hey, bro. You okay?" Jorge asked, worry in his voice.

"We're all good." Dylan paused to kiss the two most important people in his life again. "We're safe."

"I made sure the feds have the footage from today and Alcorn's account information."

"I can't thank you enough," Dylan said. "It's over."

Dylan repeated those two words.

He thanked Jorge again before hanging up.

After statements were given to the feds who showed up, Dylan loaded up the SUV and asked Brody to drive them home.

Dylan kept one arm around Maribel and the other around Samantha as he filled her in on his earlier conversation with her father. "I'd like you and your father to stay over tonight, if that's okay."

"What do you think, Dad?"

Mr. Turner nodded and smiled before leaning his head back against the headrest and closing his eyes. "It's finally over. With the other evidence and my testimony, it's done."

That night, Dylan had a lot on his mind as he placed

a sleeping Maribel under the covers. He kissed his baby, placing her *Brave* doll under the covers next to her.

Samantha was in the kitchen, cleaning up dishes.

Her father was in the guest room, resting.

And in a rare moment, the world felt right.

Dylan knocked on the door of the guest room.

"Come in," Mr. Turner said.

"I don't want to disturb you."

"I'm awake. Been in and out of sleep. It's nice to be in a bed."

"You get enough to eat?"

Mr. Turner nodded. "Best steak I've ever had."

Dylan sat next to Mr. Turner on the edge of the bed. "I'd like to have your blessing to ask your daughter to marry me if she'll have me."

Mr. Turner smiled and reached over for a hug. "You do. I'd tell you to take good care of my daughter, but based on your love for your child, I figure that's a given."

"If Samantha does me the honor of being my wife, I'll need something else from you."

Mr. Turner's eyebrow arched.

"I want you to come live with us."

"I'd like that very much," Mr. Turner said, embracing Dylan in a hug.

"Wish me luck."

"You don't need it. She's crazy about you. A father knows these things." Mr. Turner paused. "Thanks for giving me the chance earlier to explain everything I've done to protect my daughter. I made a lot of mistakes."

"Every father does." Dylan smiled as he left the room. He walked into the kitchen, unsure of himself. If he asked now, would it be too much too soon? Would she say no?

"Hey, there," he said, admiring her as she stood looking out the window. He walked over to her and took her hand, surprised at just how nervous he'd become. This time, he wasn't leaving anything to chance. He needed to put his cards on the table. "Samantha, I love you."

She smiled. "I can't imagine loving someone more."

"I know this is going to sound crazy and you might think it's too soon, but I know what I want." He bent down on one knee. "Will you do me the honor of becoming my wife?"

Samantha wrapped her arms around Dylan's neck. "I can't imagine living another day without you. Dylan Jacobs, you are my home. I belong with you. So yes. Yes. I will marry you."

"Damn. I'm the luckiest man on earth right now." He rose to his feet and kissed her. "I've always believed in family, but it was this vague ideal to me. Having Maribel show up in my life taught me what it's like to put my heart in someone else's hands. Now that you're here, I'm whole."

"I love you, Dylan Jacobs. And I want to spend the rest of my life showing you what that means."

* * * * *

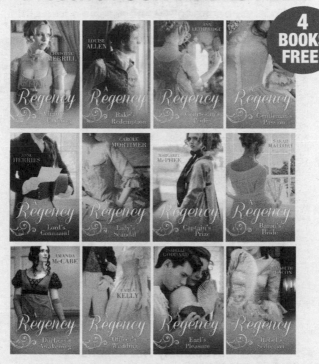

MILLS & BOON®

Why shop at millsandboon.co.uk?

Each year, thousands of romance readers find their perfect read at millsandboon.co.uk. That's because we're passionate about bringing you the very best romantic fiction. Here are some of the advantages of shopping at www.millsandboon.co.uk:

* **Get new books first**—you'll be able to buy your favourite books one month before they hit the shops

* **Get exclusive discounts**—you'll also be able to buy our specially created monthly collections, with up to 50% off the RRP

* **Find your favourite authors**—latest news, interviews and new releases for all your favourite authors and series on our website, plus ideas for what to try next

* **Join in**—once you've bought your favourite books, don't forget to register with us to rate, review and join in the discussions

Visit **www.millsandboon.co.uk**
for all this and more today!

MILLS_WEB

MILLS & BOON®

INTRIGUE
Romantic Suspense

A SEDUCTIVE COMBINATION OF DANGER AND DESIRE